RULING
PASSIONS

By the same author

Behind the Image (under the name Susan Barnes)
Tony Crosland
Looking Out, Looking In

RULING
PASSIONS

SUSAN CROSLAND

HENRY HOLT and COMPANY
New York

Library of Congress Cataloging-in-Publication Data
Crosland, Susan.
Ruling passions/Susan Crosland
p. cm.
ISBN 0-8050-1220-6
I. Title.
PR6053.R597R85   1989
823′.914—dc20   89-35289
                                                      CIP

Henry Holt books are available at special discounts
for bulk purchases for sales promotions, premiums,
fund-raising, or educational use. Special editions
or book excerpts can also be created to specification.

For details contact:
Special Sales Director
Henry Holt and Company, Inc.
115 West 18th Street
New York, New York 10011

First American Edition

Printed in the United States of America
1   3   5   7   9   10   8   6   4   2

RULING
PASSIONS

I

Daisy In London

1

Daisy burst into tears – which made her angrier, for he just lay there, smiling, tolerant, as if he was a demi-god and she a schoolgirl whose tantrum would pass. What made the thing so maddening was that she agreed with Carl Myer's estimation of himself: he was the most fascinating person she had ever met in her twenty-three years.

'Come back to bed for a moment, Daisy.'

'I don't *want* to come back to bed.' She managed not to stamp the foot which she had just reshod. 'You think that any time I have a grievance, all that's required is for you to exercise your skills in bed.'

The row had started when she had nearly finished dressing.

She picked up her belt from the floor, turned her back on Carl and faced her reflection in the mirror over his bureau. Because she gave such a furious tug at the belt, she notched it one hole too tight for comfort. In the mirror she could see behind her the naked man lying comfortably on his bed, watching her with that amused expression. The belt would have to stay too tight: if she started adjusting it, he would look more amused because he would know her bad temper had caused her to misjudge her stupid belt. He always knew the cause and effect of everything, damn him.

She turned to face him.

'The thing about you, Carl, is your arrogance. *You* know you're the brilliant intellectual of the new right. *You* know you're going to get one of the key posts in Washington. *You* know you're the great artist in the sack. You don't need anyone else to tell you so. Sometimes it makes me feel I'm simply a doll.'

She glanced out of his bedroom window: all at once the late afternoon had darkened. It was going to rain. Well, that was all right: she enjoyed driving in the rain. She could be back in Manhattan in an hour and a quarter. She went to the window and looked over the quadrangle to the opposite neo-Gothic building: already lights were on, making the lancet windows into bright pointed patches in the ivy-covered stone. Despite her present mood, she liked Princeton. She turned again towards the bed.

Carl had propped himself on one elbow as he reached over to the bedside table and took a cigarette from the open pack. Daisy could see the black curls that grew low on the back of his neck. She loved the way his hair grew, the contrast with the pale skin. She loved the beginning of the tonsure among the thick curls: one bit of him, at least, was vulnerable.

He lit the cigarette, then shifted his weight off his elbow and made himself comfortable again, the pillows propped against the varnished wooden bedhead. The top sheet and blankets were still shoved down at the foot of the bed. Carl liked to keep November's biting cold outside where it belonged; his bedroom was seldom less than 70 degrees. He lay with his knees up, his right hand with the cigarette dangling over the edge of the bed. He was totally at ease with the nakedness of his pale, wiry body. Suddenly Daisy found she had to remind herself she was angry.

'It's a free country,' he said, the molten brown eyes twinkling, 'you can stay angry as long as you like. But when you're ready to discuss the thing, perhaps you would be so kind as to explain why you think I regard you as a doll. For that matter, I'd be interested in knowing why you think I should want to marry a doll.'

Daisy didn't say anything. She stood with her back to the window.

Carl went on smoking.

'Perhaps doll is the wrong word,' she said. 'Perhaps teacher's pet would be better.'

She had met him when she was a junior at Radcliffe. At thirty-four, he was already well-known as the brash professor of international studies at Princeton. Anyone interested in politics who visited Princeton from abroad wanted to hear at least one of Carl Myer's lectures, renowned for the caustic charm with which he presented his hardline strategies.

'I loved the way you confronted people – me – challenging and teasing at the same time. You always seemed to be deliberately alternating – teaching my body how to feel things it'd never felt before, opening my mind to concepts, ways of thinking I'd never known before. I adored being teacher's pet. But I'm not sure I want to marry you – yet. I've only just finished at Columbia. I want to try actually being a sculptor.'

She sat down on the buttoned leather armchair by the window, ignoring Carl's clothes half on, half off the chair where he'd dropped them forty minutes earlier.

'I've told you, Daisy, you could go on with your sculpture. I think it would make more sense if while I'm at Princeton you had your studio here rather than New York. But that's a detail. At the moment your father gives you an allowance. If you married me, I'd be the one backing your career until you're able to earn good money from your work. I'm not proposing that you turn into the little housewife and mother.'

She looked down at the chair button she was delicately twisting between her thumb and third finger. One of the shoulder-length auburn curls fell forward onto her cheek. She lifted a hand to push it back. Carl enjoyed watching any movement by Daisy: she was graceful. She looked up at him, her grey eyes serious. Her bad temper had passed.

'Look, Daisy,' he said. 'There's going to be an election in two years. If Ford is re-elected, Kissinger will continue to run the international show. Everyone knows he's influenced by my stuff on defence in *Commentary*. True, for that very reason he could see me as a personal threat in Washington. But my bet is that anyone as confident as Kissinger would take that risk and use me on the arms control side of foreign policy. If that happened, I'd take an indefinite sabbatical from Princeton to go to Washington. Who knows where it would end? American cabinet secretaries don't have to be elected. Kissinger has never been elected to anything. And intellect is in short supply in Washington.'

He kept his eyes fixed on her face.

'You'd like Washington, Daisy. There's a lot going on there. At the same time as being married to me, you could advance your sculpture career. Think of all those politicians just waiting to have their portraits by Daisy Brewster cast in bronze. It would all be at your fingertips. You'd be in your element in Washington. Your parents would have to accept the situation.'

Daisy looked down again. She could never quite decide whether her parents' hostility to Carl actually made him more attractive to her. Anyway, this wasn't the moment to think about her parents' objection: it wasn't relevant to her present concern. She looked up again.

'You know so much more than I do,' she said. 'You always will. And actually I like that. But I think if I married you now, I'd feel sort of bulldozed by you. I've never really been anywhere on my own. Radcliffe doesn't count as being on my own. And I share the flat in New York. And I'm always going back to Philadelphia to stay with my family.'

Still lying with his knees up, Carl lit another cigarette. He lifted his right leg and rested the ankle atop his left knee, watching Daisy. She smiled to herself: here she sat in her cream-coloured silk blouse and soft tweed suit and he lay naked and at ease while they discussed the future.

'When I was home last weekend, Daddy and Mummy asked if I'd ever thought of going to London and studying sculpture at the Royal College of Art for a few terms. They'd foot the bill.'

A flush spread slowly over Carl's face.

'In their genteel Wasp way, Daddy and Mummy are pretty goddamn determined, aren't they?' he said.

Under Daisy's light freckles her face coloured. It was one thing for her to criticize her parents' attitude; it was another thing for Carl to jab at them.

'Actually, I'm tired of being taught by others all the time,' she said abruptly. 'I don't want to be taught by you. I want to go to

London for maybe a year and get a job and support myself.'

'How can you support yourself as an unknown young sculptor in London? You're being childish, Daisy.'

She stood up.

'That's what you always say when I want to do something that you don't want me to do,' she said. 'So I can't yet earn a living as a sculptor. Okay. Lots of people seem to manage by working at Woolworth. There must be a Woolworth in London.'

'I'm sure there are many Woolworths in London, Daisy, though I doubt that many of the shop assistants have their wages buttressed by an allowance from Daddy.'

Carl's deep voice had taken on a hard edge.

Daisy picked up her handbag from the bureau. Without glancing again at the naked man who fascinated her, she walked to the bedroom door, opened it and closed it behind her.

2

1976 had barely begun when she arrived in London. Three weeks later she emerged from Blackfriars tube station into the crisp clear air of late January. The reputation for fog and smog, she'd soon discovered, was long out of date. At Ludgate Circus, lorries careened past as she waited for the light to turn green. Supposing she was late? She didn't wear a watch, and for some reason she'd not yet fathomed, there weren't any clocks on the front of buildings in this country. In downtown Philadelphia you couldn't walk fifty yards without seeing a clock. This must be the longest red light in history.

The cold magnified the clattering of her high heels as she crossed to where Fleet Street began. Her tongue flicked out to moisten her lower lip, and immediately she reminded herself that above all she must not *seem* nervous. The English girl with whom she was staying had drawn a little diagram, so Daisy knew the *Rampart* was just a few buildings along. Here it was, looming over her, the name in vast letters over the entire front of the building. People say if you can manage not to look anxious, it affects you as well as others: you actually feel more confident. Hope they're right, she thought as she paused on the wide front step, checking her hair in her pocket mirror as a platoon of number eleven buses lumbered past in the direction of St Paul's. She glanced back at the cathedral's dome against the cobalt sky beyond Ludgate Circus. Then she stepped through the cavernous portals of the famous Sunday newspaper which was required reading for nearly all of the British Establishment.

Behind the reception desk the uniformed commissionaire was deadpan as he watched her approach. He could tell she'd never been there before by the way she looked up at the two-storey-high ceiling. She might be an upmarket messenger, she might be a director's daughter. These days you never knew.

'My name is Daisy Brewster. I have an appointment at eleven with the editor.' Thank God there was a clock on the wall behind the commissionaire. She saw it was still one minute before eleven. Then the long hand jerked to the hour.

He dawdled over his big looseleaf book of numbers.

'As that clock behind you says it's already past eleven, do you think you could get through to Mr Franwell's office so at least they know I'm here?' Daisy said politely. This idiot must know the editor's number without laboriously turning all those pages, but better to appeal than demand or he'd simply take longer.

'What'cha say your name is?'

'Brewster. Daisy Brewster. My appointment's at eleven.'

The commissionaire relayed this information into his telephone, then pointed to the double row of lifts with their gleaming brass doors. 'Top floor. Someone will meetcha.'

Even though a dough-faced youth shared the lift and watched her, Daisy concentrated on the mirror fixed to the back wall, rapidly adjusting two curls so they fell at a different angle onto her cheek. The youth got off at the third floor. If he was a reporter, he certainly didn't look like much.

At the top floor she stepped out into a vestibule between two sets of swinging doors. As she wondered which way to turn, through the doors on the right came an immaculately groomed young woman. She was somewhat older than Daisy, and her immense self-possession was slightly overbearing.

'Daisy Brewster? I'm Rachel Fisher, Personal Assistant To The Editor.' Rachel's voice was precise and mellifluous at the same time. She always managed to convey her title in capital letters. 'You can wait in my office until the editor is ready to see you.'

Daisy saw that the corridor ahead opened into a large area where she glimpsed desks and people, but before they got that far, Rachel opened a frosted glass door on the right, marked 'Private' in black letters.

They were now in an outer office and Daisy saw a closed door that looked like ebony, with 'Private' printed in gold letters this time.

'Please sit down. Would you care to take off your coat?' Polite and imperious at once, Rachel gestured towards the beige leather sofa. She herself took the beige leather swivel chair at the beige oak desk and turned her attention to a document beside her typewriter.

Three large palms of different varieties stood in baskets in one corner. The lack of clutter emphasized the dominance of the woman at the desk. Daisy put her houndstooth coat beside her on the sofa. She didn't like the way Rachel Fisher meant her to feel daunted. She wished her heart would wallop less loudly.

A buzzer went on Rachel's desk. Unhurriedly she picked up one of the telephones. 'Yes? ... I'll let the editor know you want to see him. Will you be at your desk after lunch?' She said nothing further before replacing the receiver.

A different buzzer sounded. She picked up a red telephone. 'Yes, she's here.' Replacing the receiver, she rose from her chair and gestured graciously towards the ebony door.

'The editor can see you now.'

Daisy took her coat over one arm: it matched her skirt. Rachel opened the ebony door, led Daisy in, then withdrew and shut it.

Across a large room was an enormous desk. Fixed to the wall behind it was an eight-foot-square sheet of steel. On it, engraved in what looked like gold (in fact, brass), was a blown-up map of Britain; around Britain, on a much smaller scale, the rest of the world was engraved in copper. The floor was covered in thick black Wilton. The furniture was black – except the desk which was mahogany. The man sitting at it looked up. He grinned.

He got to his feet and came around his desk to shake hands with Daisy. He was of medium height, only a few inches taller than she was, and burly. He had brown hair and a fleshy face. Immediately Daisy was struck by the intense blue of his eyes. His jacket was hanging on the back of the chair he'd just left. His camel's-hair waistcoat was unbuttoned, his shirt sleeves rolled up, tie loosened. At thirty-three he was the youngest editor in Fleet Street. Daisy felt a mixture of intimidation and attraction. Lots of people felt that way when they met Ben Franwell.

'Sit down, Miss Brewster,' he said, pointing to the outsize black leather chesterfield against a wall of plate glass. He took one of the black leather chairs that flanked the sofa. In 1976, Charles Eames's classic chair with its ottoman was to be found in a number of top executives' offices. Daisy's father had one at his bank. But this was the first time she'd seen two Eames chairs in the same room. She saw that Ben Franwell was holding the letter she had written him. She knew it word for word: at the house in Chelsea where she was staying with hospitable English friends of her family, she had typed the letter five times before she'd got it right.

'Why did you say you met me at a BBC party?'

Ben Franwell didn't go in for social preliminaries. Had Daisy been able to tell one English accent from another, she'd have recognized the vowels as Yorkshire.

'Because the girl I'm staying with works for the BBC and took me there. And when I told her I wanted to apply for a job on the *Rampart*, she said I ought to write directly to you as you were one of the people I'd met at the party.'

'Haven't been to a BBC party in years,' said Ben Franwell. 'Can't stand those puffed up know-alls.'

Daisy flushed. No wonder she couldn't remember having seen this man before. Christ.

'As soon as I walked in your office, I realized my friend had made a mistake,' she said.

'At least you were right in believing that when you want something, always go to the top to ask for it. So here you are. What do you want?'

'I've moved to London. I admire your newspaper. I wanted to ask whether you might have a writing job that I could do.'

She knew how to be courteous and assured at the same time, though with Franwell's blue eyes fixed on her while he continued to grin, the assurance was strictly a pose.

'How much experience have you, Miss Brewster?'

'When I was still at Radcliffe College I began contributing to *Ladies' Home Journal*. Since then I've freelanced for American *Vogue* and the *Philadelphia Enquirer*. I've been doing that for a couple of years,' she added.

The trouble with Daisy when she lied was that because she didn't like lying, she tended to add details that were unnecessary and which more often than not gave the show away.

'You don't look like a young woman half way through her twenties.'

'That's because I've led such a pure life,' said Daisy.

Franwell laughed. He liked the auburn curls that bobbed on her shoulders, the clear grey eyes, even the freckles. She was a very pretty girl.

'Where's your home?'

'It *was* in Philadelphia. I'm looking for my own flat here.'

'Why?'

'I want to work in London. And I think an American could write about things from a slightly different angle. I hoped you might think that could be of use to your paper.'

'Are you a member of the union?'

'No. There's not yet been time to do anything about that.'

'Are you married?'

'No.'

'Do you want to be?'

'I'm in no rush.'

She wondered why he was grinning. It was disconcerting.

'You know that these days most papers in Fleet Street are so tyrannized by the unions that they don't dare employ reporters who haven't already done a stint in the provinces. I'm one of the very few to run my own show. Is that why you came to me?'

'Well, I was told you make all decisions at the *Rampart*.' Until this moment, she hadn't really taken in what her BBC friend had meant about there being no closed shop at the *Rampart*.

'In a month I expect to have an opening on the features pages. Give Rachel Fisher the telephone number where you can be reached. I'll have the features editor ring you tomorrow. He'll commission you to write a piece. If we like it, he'll be in touch with you again. Until then there's no point in discussing the method by which we might get around your not yet belonging to a union. You know that if you write for the *Rampart*, you can't write for any other publication.'

'No, I didn't know,' said Daisy. 'I'll have to think about that.' Instinctively she went for the reckless bluff: 'I'd be reluctant to give up all my other work unless the *Rampart* could pay me a decent salary. But I suppose the first thing is for you to decide if you like my writing.'

Franwell was on his feet, his hand out to shake Daisy's. 'I'll expect you to post me cuttings tomorrow of your pieces in – what did you tell me? oh yes – *Ladies' Home Journal* and *Vogue* and the *Philadelphia Enquirer*. Don't send a lot – just one or two from each.'

'Oh Mr Franwell,' said Daisy. Her face felt so hot she was sure it was crimson. 'I can't.'

'Why not?' he said, grinning.

Confess or try to brazen it out? She opted for the second course.

'I didn't bring them with me. They're in my desk at home. In Philadelphia,' she added, trying to make the Birthplace of Independence sound as inaccessible as the steppes of Siberia.

'Then you'd better ask someone to post them to you, hadn't you?' he said, enjoying himself.

He turned and walked back to his desk.

She made her own way to the door and went out.

For a moment Rachel Fisher didn't look up. Daisy had to stand there.

Then Rachel said: 'May I do something?'

'Mr Franwell asked me to give you my telephone number.'

Rachel handed a small lined pad to Daisy. 'Please write it here with your name,' she said.

Daisy did so.

Rachel got up. 'Let me show you out,' she said, contriving to make ordinary good manners sound superior.

As they stepped into the corridor, Daisy glanced towards the far end where it opened into the big room with the desks and the people. She was relieved that Rachel didn't accompany her beyond the lift doors.

Downstairs in the lofty foyer, she saw that the clock behind the commissionaire said 11:30. Only when she was outside the building did her heart leap. She'd got through it. Ben Franwell seemed to like her. But what on earth was she to do about her nonexistent newspaper cuttings? How much would it matter that they could never materialize? She looked up and down Fleet Street at the big-facaded office empires standing cheek by jowl with pubs and dinky cafés. Just suppose she got the job. Would Carl be proud of her?

Her high heels clattered gaily as she strode towards Ludgate Circus. Instead of returning to Blackfriars tube station and Chelsea, she made for St Paul's Cathedral. Every American wants to see St Paul's.

After Ben Franwell had turned his back on her, he spent less than a minute thinking about Daisy Brewster. He didn't doubt the Philadelphia and Radcliffe bit: she was classy enough. But he was 90 per cent sure she'd never written for a newspaper in her life – he could feel it in his bones. He liked her aplomb: it could be useful in getting past people's front doors. He had no real interest in checking her credentials: if she could do the job, that's all that mattered to him.

And he could get around the fact she didn't belong to the union. He detested trade unions and their highwayman attempts to tell him how to run the country's most successful Sunday paper. They and their bloody closed shops might lead the fancy-pants softies by the nose. *He* would employ anyone he liked, when he liked, as long as he liked. Sod them.

3

'It's for you, Daisy. Will you take it in the drawing room?'

She hadn't moved from the Cadogan Square house all day in case the *Rampart* rang. She seized the drawing room telephone which for some reason stood on the grand piano beside a silver-framed signed photograph of the Queen with her corgis.

'It's James Allen here. I'm the *Rampart*'s features editor. I believe you saw the editor yesterday. You'll have noticed there's a lot of interest just now in prostitutes. We're thinking of running a piece on the subject a week this Sunday. Would you be interested in submitting 1500 words? I'd want to see your copy before the end of the week.'

Daisy averted her eyes from the Queen, lest she be distracted. 'What sort of angle have you in mind?'

'That's for you to decide, so long as it's lighthearted with a hard centre. And not too far out: whatever your private view on the matter, marital fidelity must win the day. When I speak of prostitutes, by the way, I am referring to streetwalkers and such. Should you hold the view that the golddigger wife is hershelf a prostitute, try not to stress it. And take it easy if you find a proshtitute who is happy in her work. Thish is a family newshpaper.'

Daisy glanced at the carriage clock ticking sedately on the mantelpiece. It was only 3.30 in the afternoon. It must be her imagination that the features editor slurred his words. Maybe he had a speech impediment.

'Do you want me to interview a prostitute?'

'I should if I were you. Actually, how elsh would you proceed? I suppose you could ask someone who's been to a prostitute. Lucky man: no complications. We can offer you £150 if we accept it, £80 if we have to turn it down.'

'The end of the week doesn't give me a lot of time. Today is Wednesday.'

'First thing next week would be all right, just. 1500 words. On my desk when I come in Tuesday morning.'

'Did you say Tuesday?'

'We're a Sunday paper. We don't work on Mondays.'

'Of course,' said Daisy. 'I'm so sorry, but could you tell me, please, how to spell your name?'

'James. J-A-M-E-S. Allen. A-L-L-E-N.' This was followed by what sounded to Daisy like a giggle. It was unfortunate that his name was not more complicated. But how else could she have discovered what it was? All she'd taken in at the beginning was 'features editor'.

'Anything else you want to know?'

'No, I don't think so. The copy will be on your desk on Tuesday morning.'

'Good. Goodbye.'

'Goodbye.'

'Make it up,' her BBC friend said that evening. 'You couldn't do that at the BBC, but everyone knows that some of the *Rampart*'s features are half fantasy, even though they're pretty careful about news coverage. You're not writing an earnest analysis of moral turpitude for the *Guardian* Women's Page. Any feminist who reads the *Rampart* does so only to pour scorn on it. Why not do what that features editor suggested and ask some man to describe his experience with prostitutes? You might get a kernel of truth, I suppose.'

'But who can I ask? If I were in Philadelphia, there'd be plenty of people – I suppose,' Daisy added, not at all certain which

Philadelphians frequented brothels. She bet that Carl would know someone who did. 'But I hardly know anyone in London except your family.'

'Then I suppose you'll have to ask Daddy. But wait till Mummy's not around.'

The Sloane Square platform shared by the District and Circle lines was packed. On the train Daisy stood among bodies destined mostly for the City, though a fair mass of them got off with her at Blackfriars.

Just past nine she handed her envelope to the commissionaire, different from the one on duty exactly a week before.

'They don't come in until ten o'clock, Miss.'

'Will he be absolutely sure to get it? I promised I'd have it here this morning.'

'I'll see that his secretary gets it first thing.'

Daisy turned up her coat collar as she left the *Rampart*. The sky was overcast with long grey clouds scuttling before the wind, and office workers scurried close to the walls of the buildings, hoping for shelter from the bonechilling gusts. When Daisy turned the corner at Ludgate Circus, the wind's bite made her catch her breath.

At least the piece was delivered on time. Now she'd go back to Cadogan Square and wait. Probably it would be rejected. She'd devised a wry little tale about a conventional middle-class young lady who thinks the short way to fortune is to dance in Raymond's Revue. (Her English host had kindly offered to take her to Raymond's, so Daisy now had firsthand knowledge of London's most artistic erotic show.) Dressed in blue ostrich feathers, the young lady is handed a note from a middle-aged gentleman in a pinstriped suit who (ignoring the club's rules) invites her to dine with him at the Caprice. Unfortunately, half way through the *foie gras*, the young lady takes such an acute dislike to the manicured hand on her thigh that she comes out in a rash. The middle-aged gent snatches away his hand, certain she has some disease, at which moment another gent approaches their table because both men are members of the Garrick Club. The young lady, now truly deformed by her burgeoning rash, takes offence at being introduced as a niece, and decides to consider a nunnery instead.

Daisy was the one who answered the telephone when it rang half way through Wednesday morning.

'It's James Allen at the *Rampart*. Good piece. We're running it on Sunday. We can offer you a six-months' contract which can be worded to get around the union problem and is renewable if acceptable on both sides. £120 a week. Starting the second week of February.' Daisy noticed that his speech impediment had disappeared. His voice was crisp.

'But didn't you say you're paying me £150 for this single piece?'

'That's a one-off. If you come on the paper with a contract, you have the security of regular work.'

'But I can't manage on £120 if I'm to give up my freelance work for American publications,' said Daisy. She didn't want to sound desperate for the job lest she start off in a weak position.

'I'm afraid that's the rate.'

'Well, I'd like to write for the *Rampart*, but I don't think it's possible for that money if I really can't write for any other publication.'

'Let me think about it. Perhaps I can manage something.'

Daisy spent an uneasy twenty-four hours before he rang back.

'I can offer you £140 a week,' he said. 'That's the absolute outside limit.'

'I suppose I'll say yes then,' said Daisy. Thank God he hadn't asked if her nonexistent cuttings had been posted yet from Philadelphia.

'Can you come in early next week so we can finalize details?'

'Yes.'

When she put the telephone down, she improvised a Red Indian war dance in the middle of the Persian carpet.

Then she went to her bedroom where, sitting by the window overlooking Cadogan Square, its plane trees stripped for winter, she wrote to her parents telling them she hoped she soon wouldn't need their monthly cheque.

After that she called on three local estate agents to ask about one-room flats with kitchen and bathroom.

Everybody else being out that evening, she ate in the kitchen and then went upstairs and got ready for bed, pillows propped up, lampshade tilted, wishing the English used brighter lightbulbs. From her bedside-table drawer she took out a lined notepad and a pen.

Dearest Carl,

They're going to PRINT my piece this Sunday. And they've given me a job as a feature writer, starting in a fortnight. (Note my showing off – though I still haven't the faintest idea why the British decline to say two weeks like anyone else.) I've already got a list of bedsitters to start looking at tomorrow.

I've been thinking about your last letter – not just because I like looking at it, feeling it, savouring it before I reread it for the hundredth time – but because of what you said half way through. As I'm not a psychoanalyst, how can I know whether you're right in thinking my decision to 'put an ocean between us and strike out on my own for a year' was influenced by my parents' ridiculous attitude to you?

But I think the sole reason was what I told you. You say you're proud of me, and yet your presence is so dominating that I am actually *reduced* in your company. If I can be self-sufficient for a while, I think I could then be with you without this sense of being overwhelmed by the sheer force of your personality.

Not that I feel very self-sufficient. I miss you even more than I thought I would when I was shedding those buckets of tears onto your pillow that last night at Princeton. And only a month has gone by. Everyone in the Cadogan Square house continues to be charming to me, but at the same time there's no suggestion that we might talk about anything personal. They gave a little party for me last Friday, yet I'm terribly lonely. 'I'm so lonely I could die.' I never really knew what that song meant before. I've had two dates with people I met at the party. But they were so *limp* compared with you. I am not referring to their private parts about which I am ignorant. But their conversation was nonstop supercilious without any reason I could discover for their superiority. I gathered they are what the English call Something in the City.

Getting my 'Woolworth' job (okay, that *was* a bit childish) has obviously been a preoccupation. Even so, there's still been time since I wrote last week to go twice to the British Museum. So far I like the Assyrian horses best. They must stand nearly twenty feet tall, and something about their formality of design makes them amazingly sexy. But then I always find when I'm moved by a work of art that I'm moved sexually as well. Do you suppose all the senses are connected? Standing there looking at the Assyrian horses, I suddenly felt that thing inside me go click, and immediately I was thinking of you.

Just writing about it has started it all over again. There is a small problem, however. The man who taught me how to open myself to that exquisite ecstasy is on the other side of the ocean. I suppose I might lean out the front window and call down to the first guy who walks past: 'Hey . . . I'm lonely.' But somehow I don't think that would do the trick. It's only your hand I want to touch me.

Good night Carl Myer. I love you more than anything in the world.

Daisy

4

At ten o'clock on the second Tuesday of February she knocked on the door marked 'Features Editor'.

James Allen beamed at her. 'We have a desk waiting for you. You'll find you meet people pretty rapidly. They'll show you the ropes. You'll be sitting in rather a no man's land – feature writers, a few columnists, occasionally someone who just happens to have a desk there. I'll take you around now and introduce you to your nearest neighbour.'

To Daisy the room they entered seemed absolutely enormous, and indeed it was almost the entire top floor of the building, containing sixty men and women – three-quarters of the *Rampart*'s journalists. The other quarter were in glass cubicles along two sides. Grey steel filing cabinets in front of the windows blocked out most of the view across to rival newspaper offices on the other side of Fleet Street. The room was strictly utilitarian, big, nondescript, airless.

James Allen stopped at an abandoned desk which stood back to back with another whose occupant looked up from his typewriter.

'This is Giles Alexander. Giles, this is Daisy Brewster. You saw her piece on why she doesn't want to be a prostitute. She's going to write features for us. I'll see you later, Daisy. Drop in if you have any problems.'

Giles Alexander had a narrow face that made Daisy think of a hungry wolf, but he looked quite humorous when he smiled with his lips closed and got up to shake hands. He was quite tall, thin, and appeared loose-jointed. His hair shot aggressively out of his head and was exactly the colour of a carrot.

'I'm the biggest prostitute you're going to encounter on this rag,' he said.

'Why do you say that?' asked Daisy.

'Because I despise everything that the *Rampart* represents – all that drumbeating Britain-can-rule-the-waves-again if only we throw out the Labour government and cleanse the Tory party of their pathetic bleeding hearts.'

'Is that what you write?'

'Clearly you haven't perused the *Rampart* too closely yet. Nor do I blame you for that. I write an "independent" column. One of Benjamin Franwell's whims is to have a couple of tame left-wingers on his staff to show his paper is not entirely fascist. Thus you see me. I hope you enjoy it here, Tulip. Let me know if I can help you find your way around.'

He resumed his seat and returned to his typewriter, at once totally reabsorbed in what he was writing; Daisy might have been on another planet instead of six feet away.

A wave of excitement rushed over her as she opened and closed her desk drawers, even though they contained little besides paper clips, envelopes, half a ream of typing paper. A small pile of paper headed '*Rampart*' produced a frisson of self-importance.

Feeling slightly less self-conscious, she looked around the room and saw several people standing in front of a long raised shelf, flicking through newspapers clamped in open files. Having nothing else to do, she decided to flick through a few herself, though her self-consciousness returned in force as she made her way through the assemblage of desks, some of whose occupants eyed her curiously, a few with hostility.

But when she reached the shelf of clamped newspapers – every national morning, evening, Sunday paper going back for a month – she felt something like rapture at her sense of embarking on an entirely new life. Her delight caused her no sense of disloyalty to Carl, rather pleasure at being self-supporting for the first time in her twenty-three years.

On returning to her own desk, she found a young woman sitting on it, slim trousered legs crossed.

'Welcome to our happy home. I'm called Angela. Angela Brent. I live over in that corner with all those telephones and the bottle of champagne. The handsome youths just beyond the bottle assist me in writing the gossip column. That's why we have so many phones. The bottle hasn't had champagne in it for a long time, and I dread to think what liquid has been currently substituted.'

Daisy liked the way no one required her to say much in return.

Angela was almost five feet ten, slightly taller and even slimmer than Daisy and probably a few years older. Her nearly black hair was half an inch long, and she wore large pearls in her ears, her face made up to look like painted porcelain. She was dressed in an elegant parody of a City gent's double-breasted navy blue pinstriped suit. Daisy thought she'd never seen anyone look as sexy as Angela.

'As Benjamin Franwell has semi-seduced the soul of this man of conscience who faces you,' Angela said, 'I'm working on his other component. Would you happen to be free for lunch, Giles?'

'Why not? Perhaps Tulip would join us.'

'Will you, Daisy?'

'Are you sure?'

'Good. I'll wander back at one.'

Angela strolled off in the direction of the desk with the champagne bottle.

'I like her,' Daisy said across their desks to Giles.

'You're not alone. She comes from the most conventional of county families, but she's entirely indifferent to their idea of who – or what – is suitable. All that interests Angela is whether she likes you. And she has very catholic tastes.'

'I hate that word,' said Daisy.

'What word?'

'Suitable.'

'To be continued over lunch.' Giles re-focused on his typewriter.

*　　*　　*

They walked together towards the top of Fleet Street, Giles frequently dropping behind to make way for those hurrying through the cold in the opposite direction.

'Does everyone pour out onto the sidewalk at precisely one o'clock?' asked Daisy.

'Not quite,' said Giles. 'The editor's car will have departed for Soho twenty minutes ago. And anyone lunching with a "source", as they say, might leave the office at 12:30: "Can't keep a Cabinet minister waiting, old boy" — nor a girlfriend whose lavish lunch you're going to put down as "hospitality for a Cabinet minister (receipt enclosed)". Political writers get away with murder: Cabinet ministers are one of the few categories you don't have to name on your expenses claim. If accountants of the different papers in Fleet Street ever got together, they'd discover that on the same day thirty-six unnamed Cabinet ministers were lunching with thirty-six hacks.'

'How many Cabinet ministers are there?' asked Daisy.

'Twenty-four.'

Three-quarters of the way up Fleet Street, they turned right into Chancery Lane. The small Italian restaurant was already nearly full, but Angela had reserved a table.

When they'd placed their order, Daisy asked: 'Does anyone ever tell feature writers what to do – give me an assignment? Or is it up to me to think of something to write?'

'An excellent question,' said Giles. 'Poor old James Allen's main function is to think of ideas for feature writers, no easy task if you consider there are fifty-two weeks in the year. If he can't come up with anything, and God can think of nothing for you to do, then you're expected to make a suggestion.'

'God being Ben Franwell?' asked Daisy.

'Who else? Features are meant to be topical, and there's always a danger for a Sunday paper that if you busy yourself writing a story early in the week, the same subject is covered in Friday's *Times* or *Mail*. Your piece, which you handed in so proudly, is then spiked.'

'But supposing my piece is better than theirs?' said Daisy.

'No matter. Yours is dead as a dodo, rammed onto the steel spike until the spike is so full of corpses that they all have to be pulled off and formally discarded to make way for the next unlucky batch. Editors – certainly Franwell – are stupendously vain about having *their* paper's story the first on a subject.'

'Try being a gossip column editor one day,' Angela said. 'I must be the only one in Fleet Street who is not an alcoholic. All those male diarists who pretend to be nonchalant are desperate when a rival beats them on the draw, so they charge over to El Vino and put away half a bottle of whisky and get maudlin with the news reporter whose precious work has just been spiked because it was scooped by the *Evening Standard*.' Angela wrinkled her nose in disdain at such mawkish behaviour.

'The gentle sex takes these setbacks more philosophically,' she said.

Gentleness not being the foremost quality that Angela's appearance and manner brought to mind, Daisy began to laugh.

'The great thing on a Sunday paper, Tulip, is not to start writing until Thursday. Treat Tuesdays and Wednesdays as days for "background work", i.e., bugger all.'

'But you're typing away furiously today.'

'Ah. I'm making notes for future work – "clearing my mind".'

'I.e., he's writing something that has nothing whatever to do with the *Rampart* – probably his tome on the innate anti-socialism of the E E C.'

'But doesn't the editor object?'

'You'll find out quickly, Tulip, that Ben Franwell is only interested in results. If you haven't produced a good story for a couple of weeks, he'll appear behind your shoulder on a Tuesday to make plain that you'd better start earning your keep and fast. But if he gets the copy he wants, he doesn't give a toss what you're writing on Tuesday. But he wants you in the office: it reminds him and you that he's the master. What sort of journalism were you doing before?'

Daisy flushed.

'I'll tell you some time,' she said, awkwardly.

She didn't want to deceive Angela and Giles, nor did she want to risk the truth getting back to Ben. So she galloped in another direction. 'I only arrived in England last month. I was born and bred in Philadelphia of all places. My parents don't like the man

I'm in love with. They see him as a great spider enmeshing their darling daughter. They say he's not suitable. But that's not why I came to London. I came because I wanted to be independent of *everyone* for a year. At least, I think that's the reason.'

'Do you mind a lot that your parents don't think your beloved is suitable? I can see why you don't like the word,' said Giles.

'I don't want to hurt them,' said Daisy. 'Maybe in the back of my mind was the thought that if I went away from Carl for a year, when at the end I still loved him, my parents would accept the thing.'

'Are you the only child?' asked Angela.

'I have an older brother. He's married. We're fairly close, though he can be a bit pompous. He's a lawyer, you see. Although my father has a bank and is a pillar of the community and all that, he's not one of those ghastly Republicans who think Medicare means the country is on the verge of communism. He'd be seen as a *liberal* sort of Republican.'

'A Nelson Rockefeller?' said Giles.

'But not rich like that. Though we're certainly not poor. But it turns out that my father is no liberal when a Jew seeks his darling daughter's hand in marriage. It's funny. At the beginning I never discussed it with my parents, although they must have guessed that Carl and I were having an affair. They never made a big stink about it – though no one could say they were exactly warm in their manner when Carl would sometimes call on me when I was home in Philadelphia. I suppose they hoped it was a passing fling. I met Carl when I was still at Radcliffe – at a Princeton weekend. He teaches there. He's ten years older than me. After I graduated I didn't live at home: I shared a flat in New York with a girlfriend while I was studying sculpture at Columbia.'

She realized they were certain now to know she'd never before been a journalist. Giles glanced sharply at her but said nothing. Angela's porcelain face was expressionless.

Daisy rattled on as her companions made their way through their tortellini. It was the first really personal conversation she had held since she came to London nearly six weeks before.

'I majored in English at Radcliffe, but I also studied sculpture. Then I took a two-year course at Columbia studying under this sculptor who was a really fantastic teacher. The fact that my parents have always encouraged me made it worse when I started thinking about a marriage that they are absolutely certain I'll regret. And the fact that Carl is brilliant doesn't make any difference. He's still a Jew.'

Giles picked up the decanter of red chianti and topped up his and Angela's glasses. 'Aren't you going to eat something, Tulip?'

'In the end I decided to come abroad on my own for a year.' She took two enormous swallows of chianti.

Giles topped up her glass.

Then she tucked into her fettuccine with cream and gorgonzola.

'Well,' said Angela, lighting a cigarette, 'my parents would faint dead away if they got any consideration from me on that sort of thing. Their secret terror is that one day I'll present them with a Hottentot for a son-in-law. Actually, so far I've not gone in for dark meat, but you never know. I don't think they'd care particularly if I married a Jew. There's not much of that Wasp mentality in this scepter'd isle, do you think, Giles?'

'Depends on the Jew. Every aspiring mum would be delighted if her daughter married a Rothschild: but then they don't count as Jews. If you haven't yet noticed, Tulip, the English have the most materialistic of all cultures.'

'Though we're usually a bit ratty when anyone else points out that in Britain it's money that maketh the man – or woman – suitable,' said Angela. 'Does Carl have money, Daisy?'

'Only what he earns from teaching and writing – which is sufficient but not enormous.'

'Oh,' said Angela.

After lunch Daisy looked at her typewriter. She could write a letter yet look as if she was earning her pay. She began: 'Dearest Carl'. Then she rolled the sheet of paper out, screwed it in a ball and threw it at her wastebasket. She'd observed that no one around her actually put discarded paper *in* their wastebasket.

She started on a fresh sheet. If she skipped the first two words, anyone passing her desk and glancing down would see nothing but a lot of paragraphs that could be a feature story for all they knew.

Yes, you're right: starting a new life *is* a distraction from missing you hour in, hour out. Even so, on my way to the tube station this morning, I found myself staring at the back of a man walking ahead. I felt that thing inside me go 'click'.

Daisy paused. Carl had written that while he was gratified by reading her descriptions of how she felt about him, he also liked learning of her life in London. She'd tell him about her first day at the *Rampart* later in her letter. For the moment she was absorbed in her love. Daisy wasn't used to drinking at lunchtime.

She went on:

It was the way his hair grew – the beginning of the tonsure and then the short thick dark curls that finish against that lovely unmarked part of the neck just before the armour begins. Do you suppose it's unhealthy to be fixated on the contrast of dark hair and pale skin? Last night I yearned for you so achingly that I decided to pretend with myself I was you. Lately I saw a book about women's fantasies, but I got bored. I suppose other people's fantasies are always boring. Anyhow, mine have nothing in common with the ones in the book which involved donkeys, ducks, even a vacuum cleaner if you please. I still don't know why the English call a vacuum cleaner a Hoover – even when it's manufactured by someone else. Very strange language in this country.

My fantasies are fixed on you. You lying on the middle of your back in your armchair. You standing at the drinks table. You loosening your tie and undoing the top button of your shirt. You lying in the bath with your left hand on its edge and the cigarette half smoked. You lying on your bed watching me undress.

Daisy sat with her elbows on her desk and her chin in her hands, staring at the page, remembering.

'I wonder if anybody has told you that everyone here has long sight and can read everyone else's copy at several paces. Is that a short story you're writing?'

Daisy, scarlet, wheeled about in her chair.

Behind her stood a shortish young woman with dark glasses pushed up onto silver-blonde hair which was bone straight and hung to her shoulders. Her eyes were so pale that except for the pupils they seemed almost colourless. With her slightly simian features she looked exceptionally intelligent and, like Giles when he was relaxed, humorous. Daisy was immediately attracted.

'I'm called Frances. When I'm not standing behind you reading what you think you're writing privately, I write the book review page. For some reason, that entitles me to my own cubicle. Not only that. It's alongside Rachel Fisher's office. If I ever write a novel, it may feature Ben Franwell and Rachel Fisher. Sometimes when that modulated Fisher voice grows suddenly strident and I sit with the back of my head pressed tight against the wall dividing me from her, I overhear such extraordinary things that I cannot imagine *what* goes on when she and our editor are within his inner sanctum. By the way, our editor takes particular delight in suddenly materializing behind one's desk – and he can read even faster than I do.'

Daisy turned back to her typewriter and rolled the page out and put it in a drawer.

'Have you time for a drink after work?' said Frances. 'You may have noticed one doesn't have to walk more than ten feet of Fleet Street before coming to a pub. Some of them aren't too bad.'

Just past six they stepped out of the *Rampart*'s big front door and crossed Fleet Street.

An hour later they emerged from The Bell and went their separate ways, Frances towards her two-room flat in the Barbican, Daisy towards Blackfriars tube station.

After a few steps, something made Daisy look back.

Frances was standing still, watching her, the light from a streetlamp making the platinum hair eerie.

Daisy waved and then resumed her path.

Frances continued to stand there, watching the receding figure. After a minute or two, she turned to resume her own path.

5

Benjamin Franwell was a rough diamond. Nor did he wish to be otherwise. He had the aggressive Yorkshire self-assurance that tips into cocky conceit. His father, a Sheffield newsagent, called up for army service, had returned on home leave just before being shipped out to North Africa in 1942. Ben was born the following year. Like millions of other British children during the Second War, he was without a father during his first years, and he had become close to his mother. They lived in a council flat. She was deeply ambitious for him.

When he became active in student politics at Hull University, he joined the Conservative party. His father, a lifetime member of the Labour party, was hurt, but Mrs Franwell was glad. She saw her son's membership in the Conservative party as a step up in the world.

His first job had been as a reporter on the *Sheffield Post*. Within three years he was news editor. When the self-made millionaire who owned the *Rampart* came to Sheffield to receive an honorary doctorate, he was impressed by the combative, coarse-featured young journalist seated across the lunch table, his blue eyes always intent, sometimes merrily mocking.

Two days later Ben Franwell received a telephone call inviting him to join the *Rampart* as deputy news editor. That was in 1970, just after the Conservatives had toppled Harold Wilson's second Labour government. Three years later Ben Franwell was editor of one of the most influential right-wing Sunday papers in Fleet Street.

Some editors go in for the option of superiority. This means they appoint a tier of deputies who stand between the editor and his staff. A writer goes to the relevant deputy and complains that her copy is being mishandled and if it isn't put right she may have to quit. The deputy says he'll try to get a word with the editor. But he knows the editor has other things on his mind and doesn't want to be involved. So the deputy tells the writer that unfortunately the editor is tied up, and will she therefore be tolerant and put up with the situation this time? If she does, good. If she quits, the editor still has the option of superiority: he can now step in and say it was all a misunderstanding, he hopes she'll change her mind and stay, and he'll make sure she's not messed about next time.

That wasn't how Ben ran his paper. He put his nose into everything. Every single week, one thing alone mattered to the writers: did Ben Franwell like their copy? Feature writers delivered their copy – in duplicate – to James Allen, but everyone knew the top copy invariably was sent on to Ben Franwell's office. Whether it was used depended solely on him. When he liked it, he was generous in his praise. But they never forgot his eye was on them: if their expenses claim was over the unstated limit, it was Ben who told them so. He was absolute boss.

By the same token, if any member of the staff wanted to complain about *anything*, they went to Ben. Consistent with his interfering toughness was the paternalism with which he treated his staff, especially the women. He was resentful of the feminist movement. He didn't need a bunch of middle-class busybodies to tell him, for Christ's sake, that women have more housekeeping and family responsibilities than men. That's why, unless they were news reporters, he didn't make women writers come in on Saturday, even though it would be two o'clock Sunday morning before he – on the stone, with the hard core of his staff – would finish the final edition and put the paper to bed.

Ben had been utterly contemptuous of the last Tory prime minister's inability to deal with the trade unions. Anyone with balls could see the unions needed to be ground underfoot, was Ben Franwell's view. But Ted Heath let the miners run rings about him and then, to prove how virile he was – 'Who runs the country?' – he called an election and Labour won. God. What a cockup.

In the Tory leadership contest in 1975, Ben Franwell gave the *Rampart*'s support to the first woman who'd ever had the guts to throw her hat in the ring. He admired that. He liked the fact that Margaret Thatcher's father had been a grocer. Ben was always ready to recognize women as equals when they had earned their credentials.

At a VIP drinks party given by the Party treasurer at that autumn's conference, he met Rachel Fisher. She'd stood as a Conservative candidate in the last two general elections – in constituencies she had no chance of winning. But they blooded her. Ordinarily Ben reacted against traditional Tory hunting phrases, yet he took to that one. And he took to Rachel Fisher.

She was then twenty-nine, three years younger than Ben and, like him, unmarried. She stood no more than five and a half feet, but her manner made her seem taller. Dark-haired, dark-eyed, with handsome features, she conveyed a curiously strong impression that she knew what was right – what was right for national self-reliance and international respect, what was right for families ambitious for themselves and their children, what was right for its own sake.

She'd started off with more advantages than Ben. Her father was a solicitor in Bedford and was active in the local Tory party. Like many of the middle classes, he sent his daughter to a private day school simply because it was private. The local comprehensive was one of the best state schools in the country, better academically than the private school which was good at teaching deportment but mediocre when it came to academic achievement. But what mattered to Mr Fisher was that his daughter attended a *private* school. And in fact, she managed to win a scholarship to St Hugh's

College, Oxford, where she got a First in Philosophy, Politics and Economics.

When Robin Day introduced Rachel Fisher to Ben Franwell at the Party treasurer's drinks bash in Blackpool, Ben was instantly attracted: she was a woman who was going far in politics: he knew it the second he clapped eyes on her.

One month after that 1975 conference, he replaced his personal assistant at the *Rampart*: he'd never felt entirely at ease with her, even though she'd been good at organizing the redecoration of their adjacent offices. In her place came Rachel Fisher. For the present it suited them both.

The telephone on Daisy's desk was ringing when she returned from reading newspapers at the file. Rachel's voice said: 'The editor would like a word with you. Will you come in now?'

Daisy was nervous as she approached the outer door marked 'Private'. Was he going to ask her if she'd received the nonexistent cuttings? She didn't yet know him well enough to have discovered he had long since lost interest in them.

The inner door was already open to Ben's office. Rachel motioned her in.

'Close the door behind you,' said Ben.

He stayed seated at his desk.

'Sit down.' He gestured towards the straight chair on her side of the desk. 'How're things going?'

Daisy looked bright and cheerful, but she remained distinctly uneasy. The immense square of steel engraved with the blown-up map of Britain loomed even larger than usual. Though it was fixed to the wall behind Ben's chair, it seemed today to be part of him – as if he were an enormous steel giant.

'I'm getting the hang of things,' she said.

'I liked your piece last week on the English attitude to American accents – as if the English didn't have some pretty rum accents of their own. But it had to go on the stockpile because it had nothing to do with anything in the news.'

'If it became topical, might you then use it?' asked Daisy.

'We might do,' said Ben. The girl had only been there a fortnight. She'd learn soon enough that when he wrote at the top of her copy: 'James Allen: A good piece. For stockpile. BF', it wouldn't surface again unless half the paper suddenly became unusable on a Saturday.

'What are you writing this week, Daisy?'

'I'm not sure. Have you something in mind?'

'Part of your job is to come up with ideas for features.' His voice was curt, the blue eyes hard. 'Anybody can *write* a feature.'

Daisy felt her face go hot. She bit her lip. She couldn't have told you – because she wouldn't have known – whether the second response was born from instinct as well as distress.

For she had been raised in a family where her mother ran the household and yet her father *seemed* the head of the household: Mrs Brewster treated her husband as the pivot around which most things revolved, yet more often than not, Daisy had noticed, things were done her mother's way. In fact, Daisy had long realized, her parents were equals and regarded themselves as such. Yet her mother's example had suggested that getting your own way was easier if you went about it with some subtlety. This approach was one of several in which Daisy differed from the more dogmatic feminists who'd been with her at Radcliffe.

When she momentarily caught her lower lip with her teeth, Ben read it as distress: the blush had appealed to his protective side.

'I don't mean literally that anyone can write, Daisy. Otherwise I wouldn't have bothered to take you on the staff after reading that first good piece you sent us. But you can't expect to be spoonfed with ideas. Think for yourself: what do people want to read about this week? Is Jeremy Thorpe going to be able to hang on as leader of the Liberal party? How does his wife feel about her creep of a husband being forced to come out of the closet? Why don't you go and ask her?'

'Why would Jeremy Thorpe's wife choose at this stage in her life to talk to a journalist she's never heard of? *Probably* never heard of,' Daisy corrected herself. Angela had said never undersell yourself with Ben.

'*You* choose to set it up. The Thorpes' house is only two minutes from Notting Hill Gate. Hang around Boots and the most expensive butcher. She's bound to turn up at one of them. Then present yourself. You're very personable. You're concerned that her husband's side of the story be given fair treatment. She might then and there take you back to tea. It's always a gamble. But what have you to lose? If you succeed, your story will be on every news-vendor's placard in Britain.'

He made it sound so easy.

'I don't think I'd be good at that approach,' Daisy said. 'If I could make an appointment in advance with her, it would be different. Then I could do the interview very well.'

'So could many others,' said Ben. The blue eyes had hardened again. 'You bloody well better had come up with something if you intend to earn your living on the *Rampart*,' he said.

He didn't tell her to leave, but it was implicit, and she did.

In the outer office, Rachel did not look up from her typewriter.

Returning to the main room, Daisy saw that Frances was in her cubicle marking a book she was reading.

'May I come in for a minute?'

'Of course. Move the books off that chair onto the floor.'

'They make you feel you're fucking five years old,' said Daisy. To her fury, tears came into her eyes.

'Let me guess: you've just paid a visit next door. We've all had the experience. The whole idea is to *make* you feel like this,' Frances said. 'It's part of the power mania. The next time you see Ben, he'll probably say something flattering. He does that with women – though not much with me, because he's learned I'm not his idea of a woman.'

Too preoccupied with her humiliation to follow up Frances's allusion to herself, Daisy said: 'But why does Rachel Fisher have to treat you like a stupid infant?'

'I've decided that Rachel genuinely regards herself as morally superior to the rest of us – though I'm not sure on what she bases this assumption. What did Ben say?'

'He said I should go to Notting Hill Gate and stand around buying Alka-Seltzer or chicken livers until Jeremy Thorpe's wife comes in to do the same. Then I should buttonhole her and ask if the rumours about her gruesome husband are true.'

Frances laughed.

Daisy's tears began to go back where they'd come from before one of them, she was glad to find, could trickle down her face.

'Ben's just trying it on, Daisy. That's a reporter's job he's asking you to do. The reason why there are forty reporters on the *Rampart* is their job is so awful they have to spend half their lives getting sloshed. Or they have breakdowns. Feature writers aren't expected to go through all that foot-in-the-door crap, which is why there are only seven or eight of you. What did you say to Ben?'

'I said it wasn't my scene. So he told me to come up with some way of earning my living on the *Rampart*. Then I was dismissed from his presence. And Queen Rachel didn't deign to see me as I passed her desk. How on earth does anyone think of a subject for a feature?'

'Supposing the Savoy Hotel burns down. You could telephone various well-known people who are used to lunching at the Savoy restaurant and who will now be desolate, unable to look out over the Embankment as they stuff their faces and make their deals. You could ask them how they will survive their frightful loss.'

'But how do you discover which well-known people lunch habitually at the Savoy?'

'Angela and her henchmen know that kind of thing. Giles takes politicians there for lunch. He's always going on about the top civil servants he observes – all those permanent secretaries nearing sixty – lunching at the Savoy with the captains of industry, lining up their cosy business directorships for when they retire from the civil service with their knighthoods – peerages if they've been really good boys.'

Daisy smiled wanly.

'Go and talk to James Allen,' Frances said. 'That's one reason he is features editor. Even though today neither of you can come up with more than a so-so idea, do it to show willing. Then Ben or somebody will have an inspiration next week, they'll assign it to you, you'll do it well, and after that you can relax for a couple of weeks – so long as you're in evidence in the office. They don't actually expect you to produce forty-eight publishable pieces a year.'

Daisy blew her nose.

'And don't forget,' said Frances, 'once you've established your-self as good at your job, Ben Franwell will respect you for not selling your soul to get a story. Not because he has the slightest interest in your soul. But very soon after you sell it, the word gets around, and people won't give you an interview. That's what happened to Davey Jones, the feature writer you replaced. Davey is a decent bloke. But Ben put the heavy treatment on him, and Davey thought if he was to go on paying his mortgage, he'd better come up with a scoop fast. So he used a private conversation with a literary agent to write sexual innuendos about one of her authors – who happens to be a minister at the Department of Trade. Most Labour MPs took smug delight in their randy colleague's public discomfiture. At the same time they realized Davey might now do the same thing to them. So immediately after his story had been the best scoop the *Rampart* has had this year – Giles says you should have seen Ben's face that Saturday evening, swollen, reddened with glee as he heaped praise on Davey – lo, no politician would talk indiscreetly again with Davey. And those were the very contacts where he'd made himself useful to the paper. So Ben sacked him.'

'Gosh,' said Daisy.

'Yeah. The moral of the story is that when you knuckle under and write something that offends your own sense of decency because you're trying to please your boss, you may find a week later that you've lost out all around.'

'Do you suppose that's true of most relationships?'

Frances was silent for a moment, the pale eyes expressionless, before she replied: 'I often ask myself that question. I don't know the answer. Perhaps you'll tell me one day.'

6

Few things excite the British as much as a sex scandal and political scandal combined. In mid-March, in an Exeter courtroom, a male model's charges against Jeremy Thorpe became public knowledge. That Thorpe would weather the storm and remain leader of the Liberal party became increasingly unlikely.

Angela had chosen a Tuesday evening for her drinks party because the first half of the week was a good bet for most of her guests. By Thursday evening journalists on the Sundays are getting jumpy and working late. And while MPs can get stuck at the House with a three-line whip at any time from Monday to Thursday, with luck it would be only a one- or two-line whip on a Tuesday, in which case they could pair with an opponent and both of them be absent from the vote. Anyway, Pimlico was so close to Westminster that if the whips' office rang an MP at Angela's house to alert him, he could make it back in time to vote: there were ten minutes between when the division was called and when the doors to the vote-tellers closed.

Angela tried to get members of both parties at her parties, but she knew many more Tories. Too bad they were in opposition. She used the presence of influential journalists among her guests as bait to get a few Labour ministers there. Though the Liberals bored her – typical, she thought, that their chief whip, that son of the manse David Steel, still refused to believe the allegations against Thorpe – even they were interesting now that the charges against Jeremy were coming to the boil.

Her house was typical of those two-up-two-down Pimlico terraces fashionable among childless members of London's intelligentsia. Islington and even Kentish Town were the in-place for young marrieds with families. But Pimlico, five minutes from Westminster and the West End, ten minutes at night from Chelsea and South Kensington, was what Angela wanted. She had it on a short lease paid for out of a trust fund set up by one of her grandparents to avoid tax.

The party – drinks only, not counting a taramasalata dip and smoked salmon on bread triangles – began at seven and was in the ground floor rooms, both of which she used as small drawing rooms. It would never have occurred to her to have one furnished as a dining room: she always ate out.

Coming in from the raw March wind, her guests had to go upstairs to leave their coats piled on the elegant Louis XIV three-quarter bed. All were in a hurry to get back downstairs to discuss the day's extraordinary events.

For not only was there the lurid testimony in the Exeter courtroom: Buckingham Palace had just admitted that a separation between Princess Margaret and the Earl of Snowdon 'has been discussed within the Royal Family'. An announcement was 'imminent'.

Most dazzling of all was the day's announcement from No. 10 Downing Street: Harold Wilson had resigned as Prime Minister.

'The first his colleagues knew about it was when Cabinet met this morning. Without preamble, Harold told them he's going. The entire Cabinet was transfixed,' the *Times* political editor said to the Tory Shadow Foreign Secretary.

'Who do you think will be the next PM?' a *Daily Mail* columnist asked a backbench Labour MP – even though every politically sophisticated person present knew this backbench chap had no role in the leadership contest to follow. For by late Tuesday afternoon the key Labour parliamentarians were devising ways to

induce their colleagues to vote for their man – and none of them
had time to come to Angela's party.

In the other room, Giles was taking a respite from the subject.
He'd suddenly wearied of discussing it, as no one here had the
foggiest idea why the Prime Minister had resigned let alone which
Cabinet minister would succeed him.

Daisy joined Giles. She was not surprised to see he was helping
with the drinks: she knew from Angela that Giles was now familiar
with the Louis XIV bed.

'There's a settee in the corner, Tulip. Let's sit down. Never
understood why people want to stand round while holding a
conversation.'

'Look who's with Ben Franwell,' Daisy said.

Giles glanced across to the door.

'From time to time our editor and Rachel Fisher appear in
public together,' he said. 'One of these days I may make up my
mind which one is the tougher. Probably Rachel Fisher. Like a
lot of bullies, Ben has a strong streak of sentimentality. Rachel has
none that has yet been detected.'

'Is she a bully? I thought it was bossiness,' Daisy said.

'Perhaps you're right. Her greatest desire is to tell others what
to do. That's why she's going into politics.'

'Rachel?'

'Didn't you know? This Right Hand Of The Great Editor thing
is a stopgap. Others might call it a launching pad, but I don't
agree: even without Ben Franwell's help, Rachel Fisher would
become an MP. Once there, of course, she'll find his support
useful.'

'Is she qualified to be an MP?'

Giles gave his short laugh that sounded like a bark. 'Dear
darling Tulip. What on earth has led you to think the House of
Commons requires any qualification in its members other than
overweening self-importance and an insatiable desire to tell others
how to lead their lives?'

'Well, all I can say is that most people I've met here are more
polite about British politicians than Americans are about theirs.
Where is she planning to become an MP?'

'With luck in a Conservative stronghold in Bedfordshire. That's where she comes from. As she's already stood for two hopeless seats, she reckons she's earned the right to be selected for this safe Conservative constituency as soon as the aging buffoon now there can be persuaded to retire.'

'How old is Rachel Fisher? She seems kind of ageless,' said Daisy.

'Thirty. I knew her slightly at Oxford. We had the same economics tutor. Then she became a speechwriter at Central Office.'

'What's Central Office?'

'You do ask sensible questions. The Conservative party's headquarters. Then, last autumn, she suddenly became Benjamin Franwell's PA. It's all useful for an aspiring Conservative MP.'

'Does she go out with other men?'

'Oh yes. Gluttons for punishment they are. But I suspect it is Ben Franwell who is able to touch whatever approximates to her heart.'

'Has Ben ever been married?'

'No. Hasn't had time, I imagine. Has he made a pass at you?'

'No.'

'He will. What do you think of Frances's current love?'

Daisy looked around. Entering the room was Frances, and alongside her was a girl whose hair was as red as Giles's and cropped as short as Angela's.

'Where?' asked Daisy.

'There. Beside Frances,' Giles said. There was a curious note in his voice.

'You mean that girl with the red crewcut? Oh.'

Daisy was silent for a few moments, watching, thinking about the thing. 'She's awfully pretty. Do you know, in the month that I've known Frances, she's never mentioned her private life.' As she said it, Daisy remembered what she hadn't taken in at the time – Frances saying she wasn't Ben's 'idea of a woman'.

'One of the things that intrigue me about Frances is the way she doesn't conceal her bisexuality and yet she doesn't go around boring everyone else about her proclivities,' said Giles. 'Actually, when I speak of her bisexuality, that's hearsay from when she was at Oxford. I've never seen evidence of her friendships with men being erotic. Has *she* made a pass at you?'

'No. It hadn't occurred to me that she might.'

'Would you like it if she did?'

'I don't think so. I've never gone in for that.'

'I don't know whether or not Frances gets a kick from turning another woman on. In fact, I'd be very interested to know,' Giles said.

Again there was the curious note in his voice; Daisy wondered if it was excitement.

'I have a friend at home who says that is his greatest pleasure – but he's talking about turning someone on intellectually,' she said. 'Though while he's about it, I expect he often turns them on sexually as well. Heterosexually, I mean.'

It occurred to her that she'd had too much to drink. When she got squiffy, she found she could not resist referring in some way or other to Carl. It made him seem nearer.

Giles gave his wry smile with the lips closed. 'I do hope you're not referring to your friend Carl. We can't have *all* our university teachers making a practice of turning their students on sexually.'

Daisy began to laugh uncontrollably before getting a grip on herself. 'I wasn't suggesting that Professor Myer goes around turning on each and every woman he meets,' she said.

'Carl *Myer*? The company you keep,' said Giles. 'You've never mentioned his last name before. Still, I suppose that as neither of you is English, none of us thought to ask. I heard Carl Myer lecture when I was on a visiting scholarship at Princeton two years ago. He may be brilliant, but my God he scares me. If he had his way, the President of the United States would actually press the button once just to prove he was prepared to do it. True, he'd wait until the wind was blowing the right way, and he'd release only a teensy weensy missile, and it would be pointed at an island with only brown people living on it. So really, the rest of us needn't feel too bad about it or worry about retaliation. Tulip, if this is your bloke, I'll have to reconsider the proposal I intended making to you one day.'

He looked up.

'Here comes a Tory who bears some resemblance to a human being,' he said, 'though remembering your remark about your brother being a pompous lawyer, you may be sorry to learn this man's a lawyer too.'

Giles stood up.

'Hullo, Andrew. This is Daisy Brewster. She has just joined our august company at the *Rampart*. Tulip, this is Andrew Harwood. I think the lady is suspicious of lawyers.'

The settee was only big enough for two. Daisy stood up.

'Why them more than anyone else?' Andrew Harwood asked.

Daisy wrinkled her nose.

'I don't like the way they go in for injustice,' she said. She made it sound challenging, even flirtatious, rather than offensive.

Andrew Harwood was amused. 'You must lead a very protected life if you think only lawyers are capable of injustice.'

'I'm unjust all the time, but it's usually by accident,' Daisy said, 'whereas lawyers seem to make a career out of it.'

Had she been hard-eyed and complacent, Andrew would have turned away. As things were, he stayed where he was, looking at her. In her high heels she was within a few inches of his six-foot height.

Daisy took in his sandy hair and hazel eyes and the way his skin was lightly freckled like her own. So far as she could tell, his London stripy clothes apart, he was pretty much the same colour all over. He was good-looking but not too good-looking. Whenever she met a really beautiful man, he always turned out to be so narcissistic he was incapable of any relationship other than with himself.

Giles said: 'I should tell you, Tulip, since the last election this lawyer is also an MP. One day we may see him riding his charger at the front of all those vile Tories. That's assuming, Andrew, that you are not overtaken by our own Rachel Fisher once she has swung herself into the saddle.'

'What do you think of Harold's going, Giles?' said Andrew.

'Extraordinary. You'd almost think he had a debt of some sort to pay off to Jim Callaghan.'

'Why do you say that?'

'Well, if Harold had stayed on through the government's likely term of office, Callaghan would have been too old to succeed him. By going now, Harold makes Jim his likely successor. Hullo,

Bron. You know everybody. Except Daisy Brewster. Tulip, this is
Auberon Waugh. What he writes about politicians makes my
column seem as sweet as a marshmallow. Why do you think
Harold did it, Bron?'

'Andrew. *Darling.*'

A tall heavily made-up woman in a tight white fine wool dress
had appeared out of the growing crowd. She put an arm through
Andrew Harwood's in a proprietary way as she gave a brilliant
smile to each of the well-known faces and ignored Daisy.

'I *promised* the Shadow Chancellor that I'd find you. He's in the
other room. He's *dying* to ask you about something *very* important.
Angela said you were here. I've been looking for you *everywhere.*'

'How exhausting for you. Two whole rooms to search,' Andrew
said. 'You know everybody else. This is Daisy.' He hadn't registered her last name.

'*So* glad to meet you. Andrew, darling, I *promised* to take you to
Geoffrey.' She had kept her arm entwined in his.

'Okay. Let's go. Hope to see you later, Giles, Bron. And you,
Daisy. We ought to talk.' Andrew moved off with the woman in
white.

'Who is she?'

'An actress,' said Giles. 'Currently on Andrew's arm, as you
may have noted. It looked to me as if she's having to hold pretty
tight to it. If she's lucky, she might hang on for another week or
so.'

Andrew Harwood didn't get together again with Daisy for their
talk. Nor did she feel like going on to dinner with either of two
men she met later. Instead, when the party was thinning out at
9:30, she pushed off alone and caught a taxi back to the tiny flat
she'd found in a Victorian terrace house in Lower Sloane Street.

The flat was on the first floor, at the front. A steady stream of
cars and lorries from Chelsea Bridge revved their engines below
her window, waiting for the traffic ahead to get past the pedestrian
crossing at Sloane Square. She had definitely had too much to
drink, and she definitely did not want to bother with food. She
wanted to go to bed.

Once there, she found herself wide awake and restless. Reaching
over to the drawer in the wobbly bedside table, she took out the

large lined pad and a pen. She sat up against the pillows.

Dearest Carl,

She sucked one thumbnail as she considered what to say next.

Tonight I was told by someone who once heard a Myer lecture that
you are a bad thing. True, this was said by the same Giles of whom
you have already complained just because I told you his dim view of
American airbases. (In answer to your question, no he does not 'preach
that garbage' in the *Rampart*. The editor gives Giles his head on
dissecting politicians' characters, but only oblique attacks are permitted on policies the editor supports. That's why Giles is going to
depart fairly soon.) And you'll be gratified to know that at least he
concedes your brilliance.

No, I haven't noticed anti-Semitism here. You say it's probably
more discreet here, in which case that may be why I haven't noticed
it. When I told Angela and Giles about my parents' attitude, Angela
said she'd never understood the Wasp mentality. Said that English
parents don't regard Jews as unsuitable so long as they're rich. But
then I said you weren't rich, and she said 'Oh.'

I haven't yet told her that you are already celebrated among the
Big Brains as The Intellectual Hawk, but I'm not sure she'd be as
impressed by that as Giles is. Nor was I, at first. It was the physical
side of you that first overwhelmed me. In that respect, my parents are
right. But where they're wrong is in thinking that is the basis for the
whole attraction and therefore I'll 'get over it'. When my mother
would ask plaintively why I couldn't fall in love with some other
academic, she was always annoyed when I said that academics are
boring – though I certainly liked the head of Radcliffe's sculpture
department, but that may have been the combination of his being
macho and all those naked models and so on putting non-spiritual
thoughts in my head.

Macho. Naked. You will guess my stream of thought. I wish there
was a telephone in my room so I could make your phone bill bigger
even though you say you like letters better.

The thing about making love in daylight or with the lights on is
that at the same time as I am responding to what you are doing to
me, I am watching you as you do it. Lately I've been brooding about
which I prefer: watching your hands or watching your face with that
concentrated look.

A sharp crash of metal and the sound of breaking glass interrupted her thoughts.

Daisy got out of bed and drew back one of the curtains, her face close to the window pane so she could see down. A man was getting out of a car that clearly he had rammed into the back of one already parked at the kerb. He surveyed the damage. From above Daisy could see the broken glass of the other car's rear light. As the driver stood with his hands on his hips, surveying the matter, a street lamp shone on his sandy-coloured hair.

Immediately the thought came into her mind: supposing it was Andrew Harwood, and he'd learned where she lived, and he'd had had too much to drink and had decided to come and ring her bell.

The sandy-haired man walked to the step of the next door house, rang its bell, and half a minute later disappeared inside. Daisy felt a pang of disappointment.

Turning away from the window, she taxed herself: this was ridiculous. It was just because she was lonely.

She put her unfinished letter to Carl in the drawer, turned out the light and climbed back into bed. She lay on her side, looking at the street lamp's light which filtered palely through the closed curtains.

That same night the Conservative backbencher who Giles had referred to earlier in the evening as 'the aging buffoon', the MP for Bedford Forge, fell over with a heart attack.

7

The following afternoon, Giles pushed the *Evening Standard* across their desks to Daisy.

'That's politics,' he said.

The front page devoted two short paragraphs to the sudden death of the Bedfordshire MP. The small photograph of him must have been twenty years out of date. Most of the story was speculation about who would be selected to succeed him.

'If you turn to page two,' said Giles, 'you'll see rather larger mugshots that are up-to-date.'

Daisy turned the page.

The larger mugshots were of half a dozen possible Conservative candidates for Bedfordshire. The most striking of the photographs was a full-face picture of Rachel Fisher.

The next morning Daisy was frowning at her typewriter as, absently, she picked up the ringing telephone.

'It's Andrew Harwood. I hope you recall meeting me two nights ago. Giles says your desk faces his. Is he sitting at it now?'

Daisy looked up. 'No.'

'As it's Thursday and he'll be thinking about his column, I

expect he's gone to the chemist to buy caustic soda. Is everyone in your office placing an early bet on who'll be the next prime minister?'

'That's all they talk about,' said Daisy. 'I wish I knew more about the Labour party.'

'You have a good tutor in Giles. I wondered if you'd care to have dinner with me one night and explain in a bit more detail why you dislike lawyers.'

'All right.'

She sounded pert, casually pleased, but when she replaced the receiver, Daisy was astonished at the wave of delight that moved through her. Shouldn't she feel guilty at being quite so happy at the thought of an evening with someone other than Carl? Not being a person who enjoyed guilt feelings, she banished them. Probably her excitement was all part of this new adventure of living in a foreign land, she said to herself.

Monday evening they met at Langan's Brasserie off Piccadilly. She had not been there before. She liked the 1920s ceiling fans that slowly revolved, the mirrored pillars and *belle époque* ambience.

The head waiter led her to the far end of the room where Andrew was at a window table looking out on Stratton Street. He got up to greet her.

She wondered why she'd thought he was all the same colour when she first met him at Angela's party. The hazel of his eyes was definitely different from the sandy colour of his hair. And his skin – it was nice skin, she'd noticed that before – had a light flush under the casual freckles. Funny that she should find his looks so attractive, given that she was hooked on the contrast between pale skin and dark hair.

'As you're an American, would you like a dry martini cocktail? They know how to make them here. Straight up,' he said to the waiter looking spruce in his self-consciously French waistcoat, 'with two olives *and* a twist of lemon.'

Turning back to Daisy, Andrew asked, 'What's it like working for Benjamin Franwell?'

'It's too soon to say. He seems to be a bully who can also be protective.'

'Does he try to make you take his line in what you write?'

'No. But perhaps I've not yet written about anything that titillates his prejudices.'

'There's nothing in the world that can't excite Benjamin Franwell's prejudices.'

'What do you think of his column? I hear that all politicians read it.'

'It would make one's hair stand on end were he not also a master entertainer. He says such frightful things about people that he makes me laugh. So far,' Andrew added.

He gestured to the *Evening Standard* he'd put on the floor beside them. He'd been reading it while waiting for Daisy. Its front page was filled with pictures of the five men who so far had entered the race for the Labour leadership and Number Ten. 'Are you interested in all this?'

'Naturally. But I haven't been here long enough to know very much about these people whose names I read every day. And I haven't begun to understand the Labour party's passion for civil war.'

'We too wage a bit of our own – but not in public. You should hear some of the vitriolic judgments that Tories pass on Margaret Thatcher behind closed doors. Still, she's only been our leader for a year. It's early days. Did you take part in politics in the United States?'

'No. I have vague feelings for the underdog. I liked sticking pins in my conservative "admirers". But unlike a lot of people at Radcliffe, I didn't get involved in politics.'

'Is that where you were educated?'

'Yes – though I spent the last two years studying sculpture at Columbia. What I actually want to do is carve statues.'

She was pleased her martini was straight up: it made the tastebuds on her tongue tingle; she disliked martini-on-the-rocks, all that ice diluting the thing so that not only was it less exciting but also you forgot how strong it still was.

'What sort of sculpture do you want to make?'

'Portraits: heads. And birds, horses. If I was doing them now, I'd want them to be the way one imagines a bird feels, or a horse feels, rather than the way they appear to us.'

Andrew gave a small smile as much to himself as to her. 'What sort of material would you use?'

'Clay. Though one day I'd like to chisel away at a piece of marble – when I can afford it.'

'Why aren't you going on with your sculpture in London instead of working for the *Rampart*? Or are you making preliminary studies for a portrait bust of Benjamin Franwell?'

The thought made Daisy laugh.

'I can't support myself as a sculptor. At least, I certainly couldn't as a total novice. The *Rampart* pays you a decent wage, even when you haven't had a lot of experience. Also it's fun. Terrific way to make friends in a foreign city.'

'Why'd you want to come here? Half the people I know are on the lookout for grants to take them to America for a year.'

Daisy didn't want to lie to him. On the other hand, there was no law requiring her to unfold her life story to everyone she met. Occasionally, though, she suspected a natural flirtatiousness might also have something to do with a disinclination to tell one man about her love for another. In silence she examined what remained of her martini.

Andrew laughed. 'It's none of my business, I admit. Shall we order?'

Over the *croustade d'oeufs de caille* she asked some questions of her own. She learned that Andrew Harwood was thirty years old. He supposed he had been conceived almost as soon as his father returned after the Second War. He'd been educated at Marlborough; that's where he'd met Giles. Then Oxford – at Balliol. His parents actually liked each other. ('So do mine. A lot. They're lovely together,' Daisy said.) The Harwoods had quite a bit of land in Shropshire. His father called himself a farmer, though others might call him a landowner. He was a baronet.

'I still don't know what a baronet is,' said Daisy.

Andrew laughed. 'Why should you? No one outside this country understands any of our quaint titles.'

'But is it the same as a knight?' Daisy persisted. 'They are both called "Sir Somebody Jones", aren't they?'

'Absolutely right. The difference is that a knighthood dies with you. A baronet's title is inherited. My father is the 17th. One day

probably I'll be the 18th – though you never know: I might go
under a bus before then.'

'Does that make you feel grand – being a baronet?'

'Not particularly. I should tell you, Daisy, it's the lowest of all
hereditary titles. The good thing about it is it's the only hereditary
one that you can have and still sit in the House of Commons. So
if you want to be Prime Minister, you don't have to go through
a great song and dance to renounce your title as Tony Benn and
Lord Hailsham had to do.'

'Do you have brothers and sisters?' asked Daisy.

She was surprised when he hesitated.

'I have a brother.'

'You sound as if you're not certain,' she said, laughing.

He frowned slightly.

'Don't you get on?' she said.

'Very much so.'

Daisy had seen the frown. She wished she hadn't gone on asking
him questions about something he clearly didn't want to talk
about.

She looked at the paintings that crowded the wall opposite. She
liked the way David Hockney's paintings were hung between
1920s French posters.

When next she glanced at the face across from her, Andrew's
expression was friendly and reserved at once.

'Why did you want to be a lawyer?' she asked. After all, they
had to talk about something. And she was curious.

'You may well ask. But first tell me why you said what you did
when we met at Angela's – though I think I could guess. Lawyers
make a career, you said, pursuing injustice.'

'I'd always thought of my brother as fair. When he won his first
case as a defense lawyer and came home so proud of it, it turned
out he had defended and got off a villain – and the innocent party
who had brought the case was the one punished.'

'What sort of case was it?'

'It wasn't rape or anything like that. It involved money. On
some legal technicality that my brother unearthed, he got his
client off scot free, and the widow who sought justice was left
impoverished. I think it's revolting.'

'So do I. In fact, it's now difficult for me to remember what led me to read law.' Again there was the slight hesitation.

Then he went on as if he was talking about someone else. 'From Oxford Union days I thought of going into politics – yet for a long time I didn't. Perhaps the reason was simply that I wanted to earn some money.'

She wondered why his laugh was strained. She also felt a little disappointed. An upper-class Philadelphia upbringing had conditioned her to be contemptuous of those whose first priority was making money.

Her slightly fallen expression made Andrew smile.

'You may find such things vulgar,' he said, 'but the fact is that in this country a politician's wages are dramatically lower than what you pay your legislators in the States. And I saw no reason why a lawyer should not occasionally pursue justice. What I hadn't taken into account was the boredom of having to join an inn of court and eat some set number of dinners a year. Lunatic English ritual. Perhaps you'd like to come and have a look at the Courts of Justice one day.' He smiled, again at ease. 'Under a lot of expensive secondhand wigs you'll find my colleagues strolling about, enjoying some private joke incomprehensible to anyone else.'

'How do you have time to practise law *and* politics?'

'I wouldn't if I was a minister. But it's possible if one's in opposition, as we are. The House of Commons doesn't meet until half past two in the afternoon.'

'What sort of cases do you go in for?'

'They vary. Tomorrow I'm defending two chaps who can't afford a lawyer, so they're given legal aid. Work for legal aid isn't brilliantly paid, but I like it. I'm not 100 per cent avaricious.'

An absolutely horrendous crash occurred at the front of the long room. Andrew turned around in his seat. Daisy craned around him. Neither had noticed three people who had arrived at the bar ten minutes earlier.

Two bar stools now stood empty. A third was on its side. A carrot-coloured head and a silver-blonde one could be made out leaning over someone. Giles Alexander and Frances were helping their fallen companion to his feet, while a waiter righted the tall stool.

'Ah well,' Andrew said ruefully, though as he got to his feet he began to laugh. 'You stay here. I'll be right back.'

Daisy watched him approach the trio at the bar, still the centre of general attention. She saw that the young man dusting down his trouser legs had sandy hair like Andrew's, and Andrew now had his arm lightly across this person's shoulders. All four then walked away from the bar towards the front door, Frances linking arms on one side of her unsteady comrade, Andrew linking arms on the other side, Giles drawing up the rear.

A few minutes later Andrew resumed his seat across from Daisy. 'That was Nelly,' he said.

'Who's Nelly?'

'Nelson Harwood. He's my brother. He doesn't realize that at twenty-eight he might give some thought to growing up.'

Shortly before midnight Andrew drew his Scimitar SE6 to the kerb in front of the converted terrace house in Lower Sloane Street.

Where women were concerned, he was rather spoiled in the way that eligible bachelors often are. He wondered if one reason he found Daisy appealing was that she showed no sign of falling in love with him. They'd lingered over dinner, enjoying their conversation about their varied outlooks, each following up indications of how the other thought, but they'd revealed little about their personal lives. She had never told him why she'd come to London in the first place. It would be a mistake, he decided, to push things tonight.

He walked with her to the outer door of the house where he leant over and kissed her lightly on one cheek: it could have seemed a mere courtesy. 'I'll give you a ring next week.'

At the first floor, turning the key in her latch, she felt relief that he hadn't asked if he could come in for a nightcap. The flat was so small – an L-shaped bedsitter with the kitchen and bath just off – that two people sitting in the two armchairs were compelled to feel intimate, whatever their relationship, as she'd become uncomfortably aware when another man she'd dined with had come up for a nightcap. And it could be awkward getting the person out again. So she was glad Andrew had said goodnight outside.

At the same time, she felt a small tug of anxiety. Perhaps he didn't find her attractive. Well, why should that matter to her when she was wholly involved with Carl? The only thing that made her care what Andrew Harwood thought of her, she said jauntily to herself, was her vanity. She nearly persuaded herself it was so.

8

When someone was with Ben Franwell in the back seat of the Jaguar, his driver always closed the partition glass. To avoid claustrophobia, Angela pressed the button to lower her side window a few inches. The March air tonight was more fresh than cold. As the car rounded the western side of Parliament Square she smiled. 'Do you realize that at this very moment the entire Cabinet is trooping into Number Ten for the Prime Minister's farewell dinner? What on earth do you suppose they'll talk about?'

Ben grinned. 'The six candidates will pretend they're entirely unaware that just over the road their sidekicks are applying neckholds to any wavering Labour MP.'

Angela turned away from the window. 'Have you thought of marrying Rachel?'

Ben said: 'Yes. I find her very attractive. I like her guts. But she's not what I want in a wife. I want someone who puts me – and that means my career – first. Rachel requires a husband who will put her – and that means her career – first. We admire that in each other. It's a bond between us. But it rules out marriage between us.'

His hand was on Angela's left knee. He was glad she was

wearing a skirt. He remembered feeling uneasy when driving to lunch one day he put his hand on her knee when she was wearing her City gent trousers.

He began to stroke her knee. He had never felt entirely comfortable with women. One of the things he liked about Rachel was the way she approached sex almost as if she were your buddy. She never went in for what he thought of as female tricks, like Angela making herself look half girl, half boy. He had to admit, however, that he found Angela extremely sexy. And he liked being seen with a variety of women. These days if you were over thirty and a bachelor, you had to make it plain that it wasn't because you were a fucking pansy.

The driver stopped the Jaguar outside Annabel's. The doorman tipped his hat. 'Good evening, Mr Franwell.'

The lackey who swung wide the brass studded door said: 'Welcome back, Mr Franwell. May I take the lady's coat for her?'

The head waiter came forward. 'Your usual table, sir?'

A waiter pulled the table forward so Angela could slip around it to sit on the banquette against the wall, Ben beside her. She liked being able to see other diners at the same time as being psychologically separated from them by the mirrored chunky columns that supported the vaulted ceiling. But she always took a minute or two to adjust to the subterranean gloom of Annabel's.

'If I'd known we were coming here, I'd have eaten a handful of carrots first. Can't see a bloody thing,' she said. 'When you were growing up in Hull, did you imagine that one day all these minions would be saying, "Is there anything you require, Mr Franwell? Would you like me to clean the shit off your shoes, Mr Franwell? Would you care to kick me in the teeth, Mr Franwell?"'

'I imagined that. And I also imagined having on my arm a beautiful young woman who had been raised with privileges denied me. What do you want to drink?'

Over her vodka Angela reverted to Rachel Fisher. 'It's not that she is exactly rude to the rest of us. She simply doesn't see us – unless we have asked to see you.'

'That's what makes her such a good PA for me. Actually, she sees more than you know. When she goes, I'll miss her.'

'Why can't she go on working for you until she actually gets into the Commons?'

'I intend to support her political career. Better if she cuts her formal ties with the *Rampart* as soon as she's selected as a candidate.'

'What makes you so sure she'll be selected by those Bedfordshire Tories? They've never had a woman MP before.'

'Nothing's sure in politics. But she's got them by the short hairs. She's written speeches for their former hero. She's done her stint standing for hopeless seats. Her half year on the *Rampart* hasn't hurt, and at the same time she's been making speeches around Bedfordshire and the Home Counties. Rachel stands for the decent, hardworking values that a lot of Conservatives in their hearts prefer to the la-dee-da of those upper class twits with all their garbage about compassion. Anybody can afford to preach sodding compassion if he's never had to go out to work. So if she's turned down, it will be because she's a woman – and with Margaret Thatcher the party's leader, even the most blimpish Tory selection committee hesitates to say publicly that a woman isn't up to the job. I think Rachel can sell herself to them. And once they've chosen her as their candidate, she's home and dry. Bedfordshire is one constituency that will never elect an MP who isn't Conservative.'

Seconds after Angela put out her cigarette in the onyx ashtray, a waiter appeared and bore it away, another waiter immediately returning with a clean onyx ashtray. Angela lit another cigarette.

Then she turned towards Ben. 'Not long after I joined the *Rampart* you said to me: "People claim that power corrupts, money corrupts. I'll tell you what corrupts: Friendship."'

Ben laughed with pleasure. 'How shrewd of me. Imagine that a theatre critic has to review a bad play written by his best friend. Do you think when the critic sits down to write his review he can be truthful? One reason I don't want a lot of friendships is because they'd make me go soft: I couldn't do my job as it should be done.'

Angela went on smoking.

'I know what you're thinking,' Ben said. 'But Rachel is already my friend. She'll never be attacked by the *Rampart*. What's the point in having power, for Christ's sake, if you can't exert it as you like? Only boring twerps expect you to be consistent all the time.'

Angela's face remained expressionless. 'Do you think Giles is going to stay much longer?' she asked.

'You know what these left-wingers are like, shedding their tears for the underprivileged. So long as Giles Alexander has a handsome salary and the limelight, he'll manage to reassure his conscience. I'll tell you exactly how he sees it: since no literate left-wing paper can provide such a big audience for his anti-Tory venom, it's in the interest of the Labour party for him to write for the *Rampart*.' Ben grinned. 'His interest and my interest coincide nicely: I enjoy keeping a pet left-wing cobra.'

'Frances says you told her last week to remove an anti-Tory jibe she had in her book review.'

'That's because it was totally irrelevant to the book. Most of the time I let Frances get away with murder because her column is so good. Anyhow, it's not her left-wing thing that sticks in my gullet. It's the pervert stuff. She never displays it, Rachel tells me, around the office. She'd better not. The first time she tries any of her disgusting antics with my girls, she's out.'

Most of their conversation over dinner was gossip. The *Rampart*'s lawyers were so fussed about libel that Angela's column often had to be altered. Ben always wanted to hear the non-publishable dirt. Angela was a mine of information about who were lovers, which marriages were in name only, what prominent figures preferred sleeping three to a bed. Ben had the prurience of someone whose own sexual life is less than satisfactory. Angela was less gripped by all these salacious details, but she was happy enough to entertain him.

Over coffee he said: 'You see quite a lot of Daisy Brewster. What's she like?'

'She's an amusing, nice, clever girl who's in love with an American academic whom her parents regard as unsuitable. Interesting to see if she stays in love with him. The other night Frances saw Daisy dining at Langan's with Andrew Harwood. Frances couldn't watch how things were developing because someone fell off a bar stool and required her ministrations.'

'One of her revolting young ladies?'

'As a matter of fact, Frances was with two men you know. Nelly Harwood and Giles.'

'I can see that Nelly Harwood and Frances have something in common. Where does Giles fit into that picture?'

'Honestly, Ben. Not everyone treats homosexuals as lepers. Giles and Nelly have been friends since Marlborough. And it wouldn't surprise me if Giles is more than platonically interested in Frances.'

'He must be fucking crazy.'

'Assuming you're speaking figuratively, why do you say that? Frances has various men friends. At Oxford she was supposed to have had several love affairs with men.'

'And women. It makes you sick.'

Angela shrugged and lit a cigarette.

'Which one fell off the bar stool at Langan's? Nelly Harwood or Giles?'

'Nelly. He does drink a fair bit.'

'All queers do. It's their way of avoiding thinking about themselves. What happened after that?'

'Frances says that Andrew joined them long enough to assist gracefully in getting Nelly out of the place.'

'I'll lay you a bet, Angela. One day when Andrew Harwood's political ambitions are hanging in the balance, that pervert brother of his will cause a public scandal that will ditch Master Harwood's career once and for all.'

'Why have you got it in for Andrew?'

Ben wasn't much given to reflection, yet this time he hadn't a ready answer. The intense blue eyes looked around the darkened room, fixing for a moment on the well-fed, well-known faces just visible at several other tables.

Then he said: 'He gives me a pain in the arse with that compassion crap. I can't stand those fucking aristocrats with their *noblesse oblige* – patronizing the rest of us just because they can afford to be magnanimous and "caring".' He pronounced the word contemptuously in quotes. 'Give me the guts of a Rachel Fisher who's had to make her own way. Do you want to stay here any longer?'

'Not particularly,' said Angela.

When the Jaguar stopped outside her house in Pimlico, Ben's

hand was on her knee. 'Shall I come in for a drink?' he said, grinning.

'Not tonight,' said Angela. 'I've got my period. And I want to get a fairly early night. No doubt tomorrow my editor will be demanding that my mind is clear and bright.'

As soon as she mentioned her period, he withdrew his hand. But she had been careful not to hurt his feelings. She had a shrewd idea he was pretty buttoned up sexually. Certainly he was unconfident in personal relations with women.

Actually, she did have her period. But even if she hadn't, she said to herself as she undressed in front of the long mirror on her bedroom door, she wasn't sure how involved she wanted to be with her boss. Perhaps the simplest thing was to let his hand stray no higher than her knee.

At her Barbican flat where review copies of books were piled helter skelter on most flat surfaces, Frances kept her pale eyes on Giles's face as his hand moved up her thigh.

'I see you don't go in for preliminaries,' she said.

A minute earlier he'd been sitting across the room, sipping a scotch and soda, talking about the contest to succeed Harold Wilson as Prime Minister. Giles had explained why four of the candidates hadn't a hope. 'So that leaves Michael Foot and Jim Callaghan. Labour MPs have a perfectly natural interest in someone who will give jobs to his supporters. Jim has been operating for thirty years. Jim delivers the goods.'

Whereupon Giles had put down his scotch and soda, crossed over to where Frances sat on the settee, sat down beside her and pushed her skirt above her knees.

'The preliminaries have gone on for weeks,' he said. 'Whether we are talking about Iris Murdoch or Harold Wilson, I'm always trying to tell you that I'm interested in knowing about your body as well as your mind.'

'I'd begun to get the message.'

'Do you like it?'

'The message? Or the way you're feeling what my mother would call my private parts?'

'Oh Frances, let's go into your bedroom.'

When they were there, Giles undressed her. To start with he kept his own clothes on, unfastening only his fly. Lying beside her, still not having kissed her, he touched each of her nipples. They were erect on the plump round breasts. Then he moved his hand down where it had been before, but this time he held it still, cupping the hair which was the same silver colour as the fine straight hair that fell onto her shoulders.

'Tell me what it's like when you go to bed with a woman,' he said. 'Do you do to her what I'm doing to you, or does she do that to you?'

'It varies,' Frances said, her eyes on his, only her nipples giving any outward sign of her physical response to him. 'Usually we take turns.'

'Who starts it?'

'I like to.'

'Do you like to seduce women who've not been with another woman before?'

'Yes.' She answered his questions gravely and simply. Giles loved her for that.

'What do you do first?'

'Sometimes I do what you did in the other room. Sometimes I start here – with or without clothes.' She moved his hand up to rest on one of her breasts. 'If she's dressed, which tends to be the case at the beginning, I might unbutton her shirt and put my hand inside. If she's wearing a bra, I might slip my fingers inside it. I love it when the nipple suddenly stiffens.'

'You mean hers?' said Giles.

'Yes.' Giles felt the nipple under his hand get harder. He began to circle it with his finger.

'What is so extraordinary about another woman is the sameness of us,' she said, 'feeling another woman's breasts against mine. Sometimes I wonder if it's a form of narcissism – the thing most like me is another woman. Other times I think it's the sympathy we have for each other, the understanding of each other's bodies, how to make each other respond. Men, I'm told, like to imagine that lesbians are rough with each other, ramming great dildos in one another, doing the violent things that men do to each other. It's not like that with us – at least not with me. The eroticism is more tender – and skilful, because you know exactly what it feels like to the other person. With another woman I can draw it out longer than a man can possibly imagine.'

'You'd better stop describing it for a moment,' Giles said, 'or you'll make me come here and now, even though I don't want to yet. I'd better take my clothes off.'

'Don't,' she said. 'I wonder what would happen if I pretend you're a woman dressed as a man?'

'You'll have a slight problem about this,' Giles said, taking one of her hands and putting it on his penis. 'Let's see if we can think of something we can do tenderly and skilfully that you can't do with any of your women friends, even that one with the short red hair.'

9

In the first week of April, Labour MPs elected Jim Callaghan, the Foreign Secretary, as their new leader. Within the hour he left the Foreign Secretary's official home in Carlton Gardens and stepped into the back of his government car. At St James's Palace, sentries in red tunics and black bearskins presented arms as the black Rover sped by, police outriders clearing the way. At Buckingham Palace one of the elaborately wrought iron gates already stood open as the Foreign Secretary's car approached. More sentries presented arms.

Half an hour later when James Callaghan departed from Buckingham Palace, he was the Prime Minister. Instead of heading back down the Mall the way they had come, his driver went further round the Victoria Memorial and turned into Birdcage Walk: it was the most direct route to Number Ten.

That same evening the Conservative party in Bedford Forge was sitting in judgement. Prime ministers could resign without warning, governments could come and go, but this Tory stronghold in rural Bedfordshire was unaffected by political gales that might sweep over other parts of the nation.

The local party headquarters were in the Conservative Club, a brick mansion built at the turn of the century in a street that ran through the most prosperous part of this busy town. Lime trees met above the wide road while behind them the carefully sedate houses stood in rectitude amid their carefully tended gardens. Local bigwigs – timber merchant, department store chairman, solicitor, stockbroker – lived in these substantial houses, as had similar citizens before them.

The business side of the Conservative Club was conducted on the ground floor. The wide hall with its Regency-striped wallpaper, polished parquet and an enormous brass bowl bristling with dried flowers opened into a small waiting room, and tonight the large room beyond it had been prepared – with fifteen rows of metal chairs – for a public meeting.

In the preceding weeks a selection committee had narrowed the choice of candidates to three. The party members who now sat in the rows of metal chairs felt wonderfully puffed up: on them would depend the final choice of the candidate who would be the next Member for Bedford Forge.

Facing them, the chairman sat at a table, and on either side of him was an empty chair – one for the candidate who was to be examined, one for his wife. (The Conservative party was very particular about who would open their garden fêtes: on a famous occasion when a candidate's wife stood to answer the little social questions being put to her, she was asked to turn around.)

The late MP had been an affable enough chap who was competent at his constituency work, yet the local party had taken no great pride in him. For constituents have dual feelings: they want the Member to have their local interests as his first priority, and they also like the Member to be a figure on the national stage. No television camera ever homed in on poor old Archie. This time round, those sitting on the metal chairs said to one another, perhaps they should go for someone with a bolder future.

The door into the room was closed.

Outside in the little waiting room the three candidates made desultory conversation, each trying to seem nonchalant as from time to time all glanced at the closed panelled door looming ahead. Two candidates were accompanied by nervous wives.

Suddenly the door opened. A solemn man in his portly middle years called the name that came first in the alphabet.

One couple got up and disappeared beyond the panelled door. Half an hour later they emerged again, the candidate's manner imparting no information about his feelings, though his wife's face was white with strain.

Fisher was the next name alphabetically. Rachel was summoned.

Standing very erect she nodded to the rows of metal chairs before taking the seat on the chairman's right.

'We already know,' he said, 'of your services elsewhere to the party, Miss Fisher. Could you tell us how you think you could serve us?'

Rachel stood up.

'Mr Chairman, ladies and gentlemen.' She looked proud as she addressed her judges. 'I am willing to do my utmost to serve the interests of Bedford Forge and to help any *deserving constituent*. From my personal experience of this part of Bedfordshire – I grew up in this area – I know that most men and women in this constituency *are* decent and industrious and deserving.' She looked directly from one face scrutinizing her to another.

'I cannot pretend that I would do all that much to help those totally unprepared to help themselves.' Her tone implied she was referring to contemptible layabouts receiving supplementary benefit, not anyone present who might be sufficiently prosperous to avoid working. 'The rest of the community should not be expected to *pay indefinitely* for those who simply want a *free ride*.'

She paused in a manner that made plain she wanted her judges to reflect on the importance of her words.

'More than that, I think it is *unhealthy* for people to be assumed to be unable to look after themselves. We should not be so *patronizing* to others. Hard work, frugality, foresight – these are values that can be held by the less privileged as well as by the rest of us. If instead of being expected to be *incapable*, the poorer members of our society were encouraged to practise these mundane virtues, they would soon discover *they too* could put down a mortgage on their own house, *they too* could have some choice in how their children are educated – as well as enjoying other fruits of their endeavour.'

She'd had to be careful not to sound as if she was sniping at the paternalist philosophy of the One-Nation Tories: some of her judges probably shared their views. She chose her words so that they would be interpreted as an attack on the Labour government's welfare policies.

'I find it *deeply offensive* to suggest that the people of this country – the *British* – are *incapable* of holding the *simple values* that would enable them to *look after themselves*, and thereby *liberate* themselves.'

She sat down.

What was a skilful performance was reinforced with an inimitable quality – Rachel's genuine belief in the virtues she advocated.

A woman in the second row cleared her throat.

'Miss Fisher. I'm sure I do not speak for myself alone when I say how much I agree with the statement you have made so forcibly. Therefore it grieves me to say this as well: it is a fact that women in general have less political clout than men.' She was pleased with the word 'clout'. She'd only lately picked it up from Robin Day's television interview with the Chancellor. 'Can you tell us why you feel we should select someone who because she has less clout may therefore represent our interests less effectively than...'

Hesitating in her question to Rachel, the woman's face turned a dull crimson. She knew, and everyone else knew, she had meant to say 'less effectively than a man could'. It was true, but these days it was embarrassing to acknowledge it. She settled for: 'less effectively than someone else could'.

Rachel stood to reply.

'I hope,' she said, 'that you will be influenced by the same reasons that influenced our Members in the House of Commons when they decided that Margaret Thatcher's resolution would overcome any difficulties which sometimes confront a woman more than a man. I have your interests at heart, and if you give me your trust, I will never let you down.'

'Miss Fisher,' said a man in the front row. He allowed a portentous pause as if he had already completed a sentence of immense significance. 'If we select you as our candidate, you will, of course, be elected to Parliament. Would you think of this constituency as your overriding priority? Or do you want to play a major role on the national stage?'

'I would combine the two. By influencing national policy at the Cabinet table, I shall be affecting the quality of life in this constituency.' Rachel had unconsciously stopped using the conditional.

A man in one of the back rows put the next question. 'Miss Fisher, your curriculum vitae states that you have a flat in London for your working week, and that your parents live just outside our constituency. Would you be willing to have a home of your own within the constituency of Bedford Forge?'

'Of course. I'd intended buying something small in the town. Obviously I'd also need my London flat because of the late-night sittings at the Commons.'

The man cleared his throat before going on. 'Ordinarily the Member's wife takes part in a number of civic functions.' Unable to sort out grammatically how to proceed with his question, he decided to leave it as implicit. He looked at Rachel intently.

'I hope one day to make a suitable marriage. It would, of course, be to someone who appreciated the priorities of my constituents. You will forgive me if I cannot at this time throw more light on that part of my future.' She had adopted a manner that assumed their good will.

The chairman said: 'Has anyone else something to ask Miss Fisher?' He looked around him magisterially. 'No? Thank you, Miss Fisher.'

From her throne beside him Rachel rose and gave a slow slight bow along with a cordial smile. Then she turned and left the room.

As she resumed her place in the waiting room, the second couple disappeared through the door. Outwardly Rachel was composed, but her heart was beating so loudly that she had to assure herself it couldn't be heard by the candidate sitting nearby.

Half an hour after the third candidate and his pale wife had reappeared, the panelled door opened once more. The chairman stood self-importantly, his eyes on only one candidate.

'Miss Fisher, will you please return with me?'

She stood on his right as he intoned to the rows of metal chairs: 'As chairman of the Bedford Forge Conservative Party, I have the honour to ask Miss Rachel Fisher to be our candidate for the House of Commons.'

A half moon shone as she drove the six miles to the pokey 1930s hamlet. Like most such houses of that period, her parents' neat brick 'villa' was solidly built. Lately, to her father's great satisfaction, it had been embellished with a classical-style front porch and a Georgian bow window. Shortly before midnight Rachel turned the key in the new front door.

Her parents were waiting for her in the rather cramped room, overfurnished with bottle-green leatherette armchairs, which her father liked to call his 'lair'.

'I've got it,' she said.

Her mother's rumpled face was suddenly alive with joy. Then she began to cry.

Mr Fisher got up from his armchair and shook his daughter's hand, pumping it up and down, beaming with pleasure and pride.

'Well, well, well,' he eventually said, relinquishing her hand. Then he took it again, pumping it up and down afresh. Both of them laughed. 'Well, well, well. Shall we have a glass of port to celebrate?'

'Actually, Dad, I wouldn't mind a whisky.'

He went over to the mock Tudor cabinet and fussed over the bottles.

'I almost forgot,' he said, leaving his bartending to go over to the telephone table where he picked up the note he'd written earlier in the evening.

As Rachel watched him, her face betrayed no particular interest in what the note might say.

Her father put on his spectacles. It was as if the message was of such import that he couldn't risk remembering it without reading it aloud. 'Mr Franwell rang at ten o'clock. He said whatever time you come in, will you please ring him. He says you already have the number.'

'Would you and Mother excuse me for ten minutes?' said Rachel. 'I'll get that call out of the way. Do you mind if I take that whisky with me, Dad? You might even feel on this occasion it could be topped up when I come back.'

She was radiant as she left the room and went to her bedroom. Soon after she had gone to work for Ben Franwell, Rachel had had her own telephone extension installed in her parents' house.

She turned on the light, closed the door, kicked off her shoes and lay on her bed, flat on her back. Then she picked up the telephone and dialled the unlisted number in London.

10

Inside the *Rampart*, Angela was at her desk. At a distance she might have seemed blasé – the exquisite makeup, crewcut, one of her City gent's suits. Close up her face was concentrated as she held her telephone with one hand and scribbled with the other. She was speaking with the wife of the newly appointed Foreign Secretary.

'But isn't it customary for the Foreign Secretary and his family to move into his official home in Carlton Gardens? ... We've heard your husband told the Foreign Office he's not moving because he has a perfectly good home of his own. Is that correct?' Having listened to the reply, Angela began to laugh, scrawling on a second sheet of copy paper. 'All right. Thanks very much for your time ... Goodbye.

'Hullo, Daisy. Let me just finish my notes on that phone conversation.'

Daisy perched on one corner of the desk.

'Right,' said Angela. 'What's new?'

'Who were you talking to about Carlton Gardens?'

'The wife of the new Foreign Secretary.'

'I wondered if it was her. Ben wants me to try and get an interview with her.'

'She wasn't that keen to have a few minutes' telephone chat with me. But then most politicians' wives are wary of newspaper diarists, not least if the diarist works for the *Rampart*.'

'Ben said to use the approach that she's an American journalist who finds herself married to the British Foreign Secretary – and I'm another American journalist who has just arrived in this country. Shall I write her or ring her?'

'Does it have to be for this week?'

'Not necessarily.'

'Then write her saying what you want. Say you'll ring her in a few days' time to see if it would be convenient to her. The more polite the approach, the more awkward for her to refuse – especially with the American journalist link thing.'

After her hour and a quarter interview with the Foreign Secretary's wife at the Holland Park home which he refused to vacate, Daisy took the Circle Line from Notting Hill Gate to Blackfriars. At a snack bar opposite the *Rampart* she bought a sandwich to eat at her desk.

As she had hoped, she found the other desks deserted; it was 1:30 in the afternoon. Having got coffee from a machine, she opened her sandwich and began reading through her copious notes of the interview, translating the most illegible scribbles while she could remember what they meant. She'd discovered that people she interviewed were less guarded when she took notes instead of using a tape recorder. Because they were amused by the intently scribbling young woman who patently had done a lot of homework? Or because they knew when they said something was 'off the record', it was more likely to remain so if it wasn't taped? Certainly she had found people talked quite freely with her.

She liked to transcribe the best parts of her notes onto her typewriter, and later start the actual writing, but she wouldn't begin any of that until everyone came back at three o'clock. Meanwhile, how would she best enjoy herself while no one was around?

Honest in her dealings with individuals, she shared the compulsion of most people who work for a large organization: she adored using the office telephone and postal service for matters that had nothing whatsoever to do with the office.

She'd observed before that while the males went out to lunch, generally returning with a receipt which they would claim back on expenses, one or two women often remained at their desks, making calls and writing letters they didn't want to have to deal with at the end of a long day. A recently married news reporter used a fortnight of her lunch breaks to write a hundred thank-you letters for her wedding presents, marking the envelopes 'First Class', and putting them in the *Rampart*'s outgoing postbag. 'Everyone does it,' she told Daisy.

With the assurance that comes from using stationery embossed RAMPART, Daisy now typed a stern letter to the telephone people, stating that a telephone had still not been installed in her flat, and that she needed it urgently for her work. She did not mention that the ground-floor hall at Lower Sloane Street had a coin box where tenants could receive as well as make calls. In the lefthand bottom corner of the letter, she typed 'DB/ek'. That should impress them, indicating, as it did, that Daisy Brewster had dictated the letter to her secretary whose initials were 'ek'. Daisy did not have a secretary.

From time to time she glanced at the moon-faced electric clock on the wall. At 2:30 she dialled direct to Princeton, New Jersey. Frances had told here there was talk of having the phones monitored so the staff couldn't use them to talk to their lovers halfway round the world. But so far this threat had not been carried out.

The telephone in Princeton rang and rang. She counted up the time difference again. It definitely had to be 9:30 in the morning there. Why wasn't Carl in his office in the Political Science department? Perhaps he'd had a late night. He never mentioned taking out other women. She went out with other men, yet somehow that seemed different because she was living in a new country. It needn't mean she loved Carl any less.

She redialled the number and let it ring twenty-three times, because that was how old she was and might be lucky. All the way on the Circle Line, with the anxiety of the interview behind her, she'd thought of surprising Carl after he'd opened his mail in his office this morning. Their weekly exchange of letters had become a little erratic lately. She needed to hear his voice.

'Are you all right, Daisy? You look a bit down.'

Frances had returned from lunch early.

'I thought I could talk to Carl, but no one's there.'

'That's too bad. Possibly the telephone is the most unsatisfactory instrument of communication yet invented. What are you doing tonight?'

'Nothing.'

'Shall we have a drink after work and an early meal somewhere?'

They hopped the number eleven bus to Trafalgar Square and walked up St Martin's Lane to a trattoria. At a quarter to seven only one other table was yet occupied.

'If Giles had been with us, we'd have come in a taxi,' Frances said. 'How did you get to your interview this morning?'

'I went directly from home, and there was plenty of time, so I took the underground.'

'I guessed right. And you took the underground back to the *Rampart*. And you'll put both trips down as taxis on your expenses sheet. I asked Giles why he doesn't do that. He said that he's so tense before an interview that he has to arrive in a taxi to bolster his self-confidence. And then after the interview, he's so relieved when it's gone well, or depressed when it's gone badly, that either way he has to sink back in a taxi.'

'Quite a few of the *Rampart*'s male reporters seem to go for that kind of self-bolstering – more than the women reporters, I think.'

'What gives me a pain is when the married male reporter takes one of us out for a slap-up lunch, claims it as expenses for entertaining an important source, and meanwhile his wife at home is hoiking his shirts to the launderette, their infants trailing behind her. I'm sure if it was the wife who was here, she'd devise some way to get the expenses in the clear to take home with her wages. It irritates me so much that I've stopped having lunch with any of the married blokes. Not that many of them ask me.'

Over their gin and dry vermouth Frances said: 'Have you had a lot of love affairs before Carl?'

'Only one that really mattered. With a guy in his last year at

Harvard. But it wasn't the way it is with Carl. I liked going to bed with the first one because it was him. I liked it a lot. But I didn't experience any of these amazing physical feelings until Carl. And the fact that he can make me feel like that reinforces everything else I feel for him. I go out with other men, but I don't want to get physically involved with them. Apparently I can sexually desire only one person at a time. I've always been like that. When I was at school and was allowed to date at weekends, I'd fall in love with some youth and kiss his acne-face passionately, and at the next weekend's party I'd fall for someone else and immediately be repelled by the acne-face I'd cherished the week before.'

'What Dr Eustace Chesser called "monoerotic".'

'Neat word.'

'He said everyone misuses the word "monogamous", because people might want to stay married to one person and at the same time like leaping into bed with other people. They're "polyerotic", he said. People like you are "monoerotic".'

'Who's Dr Eustace Chesser?'

'A Harley Street shrink. Just before the swinging began in the sixties, the British Medical Association nearly threw him out because he wrote a pamphlet titled: "Is Virginity Outmoded?" and answered the question by saying it was. All those unbelievable characters who run the BMA professed to be profoundly shocked – like high court judges. Absurd men.'

Frances's pale eyes remained fixed on Daisy's open face and its clear grey eyes. They made a striking couple. Several other diners kept looking at them.

'In between your body-and-soul attachment to Carl and any of his male predecessors, have you ever been attracted sexually to another woman?' Frances asked.

'Well, I can't speak for my subconscious, of course. But so far as I can tell, the answer is no. Unless you count when I was in the first grade at school and my best friend sometimes came back to play in the afternoon. Do you suppose those two little girls tickling each other were actually producing mini-orgasms?'

They both laughed.

Frances said: 'Let's order.'

She had studied her menu for a minute when she put it down. She leaned across the table and put her hand on Daisy's forearm.

'I've decided it would be a mistake to try and seduce you,' she said quietly. 'You and I are differently placed. But it doesn't mean we can't have a friendship.'

She withdrew her hand to pick up her menu again. She saw that Daisy showed no embarrassment at what had just been said.

'Have you noticed,' Frances said, 'how few men are at ease with one another – understand each other – when they have different sexual proclivities? I'm not just talking about the Ben Franwells of this world. I'm talking about most men. I think I'll start with whitebait. What about you?'

11

She walked round and round the pair of grey marble birds on the plinth where they copulated serenely. She was mad about the Epstein doves. Finally she turned away from them, nodded to the elderly guard watching her from his spindly chair by the wall, made her way to the front door and out into the late afternoon.

It was one of those almost balmy days that April suddenly offers as a true taste of spring. Sitting on the topmost of the tall steep stairs that serve as an enormous apron to the Tate Gallery, she gazed onto the shifting steely silent waters of the Thames.

Daisy felt intensely alive, aware of her body, and so conscious of the three-dimensionality of the world around her that it was almost like when she'd tried mescaline a couple of times at Radcliffe. She'd read a book several years ago about hallucinogenic mushrooms. It was written by that weird English archaeologist who said primitive people saw the red round sun as the tip of the sungod's penis as he rode over the sky and into the night. She was looking forward to this evening. They were meeting at Langan's Brasserie again. Andrew said he wanted to demonstrate to her that he could dine there without one of his relations falling off a bar stool.

She stood up, dusted the seat of her jeans, and set off down the long wide stairs, swinging her bag by its shoulder strap. Monday was her favourite day. She loved having it as part of her weekend while for everyone else it was the start of the working week. She could have a quick look at the Rodin sculpture in that garden just before the Houses of Parliament. She wondered if Andrew was this very minute somewhere inside the Commons. She still hadn't seen inside it, even though she'd been in London for three and a half months. Amazing how fast time moves. 'Time like an ever rolling stream bears all its sons away; they fly forgotten as a dream flies at the break of day.' She'd never cared for that hymn. Supposing that Carl suddenly died. He wouldn't be forgotten at the break of day. And her mother and father. And people's children who died, those unthinkable deaths, everybody says. They wouldn't be forgotten. It couldn't be so. Strange to think the Thames would go on flowing, flowing, perhaps forever. 'Time like an ever rolling stream...' When she took her bath before dressing to go out tonight, she'd have to be specially careful that her hair didn't get damp, because that always made it kink where it grew from her temples. She hated those two kinks. Why couldn't her hair grow straight like Frances's? Auburn hair looked really nice when it was straight.

'Why do you like that Epstein sculpture so much?' asked Andrew.

Daisy took another sip of her straight-up martini with its two olives and the twist of lemon.

'It's so tactile. You want to cup your hand over the back of the dove that's on top. And my response to it isn't only in my hands: it makes me feel excited deep inside...' She hesitated, then added, 'Generally.' She surprised herself with her own imprecision. She was accustomed to talking quite openly. Why should she have to be coy with Andrew Harwood?

'I've always found that when I'm moved by the beauty of some painting or sculpture, I feel sexually stirred as well,' she said. 'Okay, the Epstein doves were intended to be erotic. Yet there's this amazing serenity about them, even though they're screwing. Do you know, he was in his thirties when he carved four different versions of those doves, and he never did anything like them again.'

'When you find a sculpture stirs you sexually, what do you do then?' He found her directness amusing.

'Well, I don't instantly go out and throw myself into the arms of some goon who happens to pass me on the sidewalk,' said Daisy. 'But I have noticed that sometimes men try to pick me up when I've just left an art gallery, so maybe there's something about my expression that has misled them.'

Andrew smiled to himself. He lit a cigarette.

'Why don't you try and find a studio and do some sculpture in your spare time while you're in London?' he asked.

'There doesn't seem to be any spare time. On my days off from the *Rampart*, I like to sightsee – though I admit there are days when I don't do anything except lie around and give myself a beauty cure and read.'

'I liked your interview with the Foreign Secretary's wife – especially the bit about Dr Kissinger in his specially fitted 707, en route to make history in southern Africa, having to fly to an English fishing town he'd never heard of – because the British Foreign Secretary didn't want to interrupt his constituency weekend.' Thinking of his own constituency, Andrew began to laugh.

'Do you have any kind of social life with Labour MPs, or do politicians here stick with their own parties day in day out?' asked Daisy, who had just finished eating the first of her two gin-soaked olives, disengaging it from its stone in neat little bites.

'Most politicians do the second.'

'Isn't that boring – everyone agreeing with one another?'

'The recriminations *within* a political party are far more enthralling than the ritualized conflict between opposing parties. Actually, most MPs avoid one another when they're away from Westminster: we spend quite enough time together when we're in the House. But *if* I'm to dine with another MP, I'd prefer him to be a Tory: at least we could have an interesting argument about Margaret Thatcher and other colleagues.'

His eyes were on Daisy's mouth as she nibbled around the stone of her second gin-soaked olive.

'Last week,' he went on, 'I found myself at a dinner party where the hostess had also asked a Labour MP in the hope that he and I would provide a bearbaiting exhibition. Too tedious. We declined. Why on earth should one be expected to serve as a gladiator for a society hostess's guests?'

Her second olive stone now lay in the ashtray beside his cigarette.

'As we're nearing the end of the months with an R, do you think we should have a few oysters before the season's finished?' he said.

Over their coffee, his hazel eyes were slightly narrowed as he watched her through the smoke he'd just exhaled. She felt as if he was sizing her up. It made her pleasantly tense. He beckoned to a waiter to bring the bill.

'Giles tells me you know Carl Myer.'

She flushed, pleased – she was immensely proud of being loved by Carl – and also not so pleased.

'Yes. Why? Have you met him?'

'No. But if one happens to be interested in international relations, and one is mildly literate, one is likely to have heard of Carl Myer. He has a fairly cavalier attitude towards poor old Europe.'

Daisy found she didn't want to think about Carl just now.

Andrew settled the bill, and they got up from the table.

They walked down Stratton Street to the turning where he'd parked the tan Scimitar coupé. He unlocked the passenger side and opened the door. Just as she started to get in, he pulled her upright again so that she was facing him.

They both stood silent, each looking into the other's face, the expression in their eyes curiously similar: part query, part challenge. He leant over and kissed her on the mouth. She drew away from him but not far. He put his arms around her and drew her back to him, his mouth against hers. She started to push him away. He held her harder against him, his mouth pressing into hers.

They had stood together like that for several minutes, against the car's open door, when Daisy pulled back from him.

'This is not a good idea,' she said. 'I think that martini must have gone to my head.'

'I'm not so sure it did,' he said, drawing her against him again. She turned her face away.

Instantly he let go of her and walked around to his side of the car, unlocked it and got in. Daisy climbed into the passenger seat. Andrew started up the engine. He might have guessed she was one of those American cock-teasers. They drove in silence to Lower Sloane Street.

He walked with her to the outer door of the house, but this time when he kissed her lightly on one cheek, it was a sardonic courtesy. And this time he said nothing about ringing her next week.

In her room, Daisy got ready for bed. Once there she reached over to the drawer and got out the pad and pen. As she hesitated over the date, she realized it was a fortnight since she had last written to Carl.

'Dearest Carl,' she began.

She burst into tears.

12

Two days later Ben Franwell took Daisy to lunch. He told his driver to let them off at the corner of Greek Street which ran one-way from the other end. They walked the twenty yards to L'Escargot.

Daisy felt important as people inside the restaurant glanced up from their tables, first at Franwell, then at her, then at Franwell again. He paused at one of the tables where two men were deep in conversation.

'I'll give Jeremy Thorpe ten more days as your leader,' he said to them. 'Then he's had it. Quite a legacy to be left by a murdered dog.' He grinned.

One man gave a noncommittal smile, the other made a little debonair flourish with one hand, waggling the fingers in a way that defied interpretation. Politicians generally adopted an amiable manner when they encountered Ben Franwell, whatever they might say when he was out of earshot.

Nor did Ben care about their private censure of him. What mattered was that they feared him.

'They're Liberal whips,' he said to Daisy.

As she sat down opposite her editor at the small table, she felt uneasy. His ruddy face was not unlike an excited schoolboy's, and so far she'd found their conversation stilted as he paid her compliments to which there was nothing to reply. 'I'll bet you've always had a queue of men panting at your door. Do you think I should push my way to the front of the queue?' he'd said in the car. She preferred him in the office – in his element as the interfering emperor. As soon as they'd left the *Rampart* he seemed to feel awkward. She found the condition contagious.

Things improved once they'd ordered food and got through some claret. He asked her to tell him about the interview she'd had with a junior minister the day before.

'Whatever he said to you, Daisy, he's sick as a parrot that he's not yet in Callaghan's Cabinet. Has he asked you out to lunch, or is he waiting to see what you write about him?'

'I don't think it crossed his mind that I was of the slightest interest except as a journalist.'

'Come off it, Daisy. He's one of the House of Commons' great gropers.'

He asked her a bit about her background, but as she knew he wasn't all that interested, she kept it short.

'I liked the way when you first came to see me, Daisy, you pretended you were an old hand at journalism. I didn't believe it then, and I don't believe it now. But all I care about is that you keep producing work like the best pieces you've done so far. The fact is that as an American you seem to be better at disarming politicians than the British hacks that they're more familiar with. I like the way you don't comment on what people say – you let their asinine remarks speak for themselves. What do you think of Andrew Harwood?'

The abrupt change of subject made her wary.

'I hardly know him,' she replied.

'I saw you talking with him at Angela's party. Was that the first time you met him?'

'Yes.'

'I'll bet you he's hot on your trail. He's a great ladies' man, our Andrew. The only thing is that he tires of each lady he's laying and moves on to another. Still, I suppose he has to do something to make up for that pansy brother.'

Daisy was silent. She felt slightly sick.

Ben Franwell was watching her.

'I'll bet you're already soft on Andrew Harwood. He could go far if he quit bleating about how we should anoint with perfumed oil every layabout and murderer and black – all that balls-aching stuff which makes most Britons puke. The only reason Andrew Harwood didn't join the Liberals was because he wants to go to the top in politics, not just preach to the rest of us.'

'How do you know he wants to go to the top?' asked Daisy.

'That's where all those Whig nobs believe they have a natural right to be. They rabbit on about equality of opportunity and One Nation, but they start from the premise that everybody wants the opportunity to be *just like them*. They have not a doubt in their little heads that they're innately superior. Well, we'll see if a grocer's daughter can beat them at their game. You've arrived here at an interesting moment in the history of the Conservative party. Margaret Thatcher has been leader only a year. Wait until she gets into her stride.'

He emptied his wine glass and refilled it, then topped up Daisy's. He grinned at her.

'Now that the Bedford Forge by-election is sewn up for Rachel Fisher, I'll lay you a bet, Daisy. When the Tories come back into government, any job that is offered to Andrew Harwood will already have been turned down by Rachel Fisher.'

Ben saw Daisy's momentary frown.

'What did you think of Dempster's piece about Nelly Harwood in this morning's *Mail?*' he said.

'I missed it,' she said. 'What did it say?'

'The *Mail* lawyers had got the wind up, so you had to read between the lines. Nelly Harwood was punched in the nose by some creep outside one of those clubs for perverts. Both kinds. Male and female. So-called. God, it makes your stomach turn.'

Daisy fiddled with her wine glass.

She was relieved when Ben turned his attention to the robust man who strolled over to their table; he turned out to be the editor of the *Mirror*. After Daisy had been introduced, the two men talked about the Jeremy Thorpe affair. She was struck again by

how much more at ease Ben seemed when he wasn't with her
alone.

On their way back to Fleet Street, she sat in the right-hand
corner of the Jaguar, chatting more lightheartedly than she actually felt as she stared through the glass partition at the back of the
driver's head. From the corner of one eye she could see Ben
Franwell was looking at her knees; her skirt stopped just above
them. When she turned towards him, he looked away. As she
stared ahead again, she felt his eyes return to her knees. It made
her uncomfortable.

When she felt his hand on her left knee she was even more
uncomfortable. If she told him to remove his hand, there would
be an awful embarrassment between them – as if she was suggesting
he was about to rape her or something. Perhaps the best thing
was to pretend she didn't notice. Yet how would he interpret that?
For both of them knew it was impossible for her not to notice.

'Would you like to have dinner with me one evening?' he said.
'We could go to Annabel's.'

She turned and looked at his face. His eyes were on her knee
which he had begun to stroke with tentative clumsiness.

'The trouble is, Ben, I don't go out much at night. I'm involved
with someone in America.'

She looked ahead again at the back of the driver's head, hoping
Ben would remove his hand. Instead he pushed her skirt a little
higher. She felt the flat of his hand move up the inside of her leg.

She slapped his hand away.

He felt as if it had been scalded. And the way she did it was an
automatic reaction – like swatting a fly: she didn't even think of
it as a big deal. His face looked like a hurt child's, the large lips
pressed together. His ruddy complexion had deepened to scarlet.

The hurt showed only briefly. Then his expression turned into
a jeer.

'Perhaps your American fancy boy should be told his little Daisy
hangs around Langan's with one of London's great horizontal
joggers.'

There was nothing for her to reply. In the stiff silence between
them as the Jaguar drove round St Mary-le-Strand, she longed
for them to reach the other end of Fleet Street. Would he punish

her in some way when they were back in the office? Would he ask her out again?

Had she understood him better, she would have known Ben Franwell would never ask her out again: he would not risk a second rejection. But he'd never forget she'd swatted him like a fly, without a thought – and not, as she had pretended, because of some man in America. He was certain it was because she had fallen for Harwood. More fool she for preferring one of those sodding toffs to him. He was too proud to let himself be seen to punish her directly. He'd find another way to get his own back.

Inside the *Rampart*, he dropped into insolent banter with the director who shared the lift; he was back on his own territory.

Twenty minutes later Giles Alexander was summoned to the editor's office.

Daisy was not under the Friday pressure building up in most of the room: she didn't have to write her piece for this week. Standing at the file, she turned to Nigel Dempster's page. She winced at the skilfully written account of Nelly Harwood's humiliation at the hands of a man he had tried to pick up – innuendo but no libel.

Returning to her desk she felt downcast – silly, really, as she didn't even know Nelly Harwood. She wished she would hear from the brother she did know. It was two days since he'd given her that mocking kiss on the cheek when he left her at the front door. Anyway, why did it make any difference to her? Yet it did.

She grew aware that the atmosphere around her desk was charged. Giles's face was bent over his typewriter so that all she could see was the orange hair. He was subjecting the typewriter to something approaching mayhem. Suddenly he ripped the copy-paper out of the roller with such ferocity that she was amazed to see the paper still in one piece. He jumped up from his chair and in his loose-jointed way strode in the direction of the editor's office.

Rachel Fisher was at her desk

'Is the editor inside?' asked Giles. His face was white.

'I'll find out. Do you want to see him?'

'Yes.'

Rachel buzzed through. 'Giles Alexander is standing here. He'd like to speak with you.'

She spoke in that tone of voice which is so modulated it's almost insulting, though to whom Giles was not certain. Probably himself.

'The editor says he'll see you now,' she said.

Ben Franwell looked up from his desk and grinned as he reached for the single sheet of copy that Giles offered him. 'Wait while I read it,' he said. The big-featured face tautened into concentration.

When he finished, he put it down and looked up. His blue eyes were like ice, the menace of the grin undisguised.

'Thanks for such an amusing diversion, Giles. I've always said you're an entertaining fellow. But I think it's time you peddled your charms to another employer. I hope you have no difficulty in finding one.'

Giles turned on his heel and left the room. When he passed Rachel's desk, she didn't glance up.

As he reached his own desk, his face the colour of putty, Daisy looked up anxiously.

'What on earth's going on?' she asked.

'Do you know what that bastard Franwell wanted me to include in my column?'

Daisy waited.

'He pumped one of Angela's lackeys for a few more details about some trivial affray that Nelly Harwood got himself into last night. Ben said there was room to expand the piece that Dempster had on it this morning – that I could contrast Nelly's lifestyle with his big MP brother's "more calculating ambitions".'

Giles spoke the last words in Ben's Yorkshire accent.

'I said I had better things to do in my column than write totally irrelevant tittle-tattle about my friends. That great leering Franwell face said it was precisely this friendship that qualifies me to speculate effectively about "the embarrassment Nelly Harwood is causing his brother's cherished career as a public servant".'

Daisy noticed that mimicking the Yorkshire accent seemed to increase Giles's anger.

'I'm meant to be writing a political column, not a gossip diary, for Christ's sake.'

'So what did you put on that piece of paper I saw you abusing?'

'I added a little to the cast. I said that the fracas outside the gay club was no doubt a mild embarrassment for the overweening political ambitions of Nelly Harwood's brother. All that garbage. Then I added that on Thursdays the club has "mixed night for gay boys and gay girls". I invented the rest.

'I said that a woman who expects to be elected shortly to Parliament might also find the fracas unfortunate if it turned out, "as is now claimed by one of the people present", as they say on this sheet when they're making the whole thing up, that while Nelly was embroiled on the pavement outside the gay club, this woman politician was seen leaving it in the company of another woman. This woman candidate for Parliament, I went on, happens currently to be the very good friend and "personal assistant" of a distinguished Fleet Street editor, and we would have to wait and see whether we read anything about the matter in his great crusading newspaper.'

Daisy caught her breath.

'Because it was so ludicrous, I felt an overwhelming desire to say it.'

'What did Ben say when he read it?'

Giles gave his short laugh. The colour was coming back into his face.

'He thanked me sarcastically. Then he sacked me.'

'Oh Giles. Does he ever change his mind?'

'If it's in his interest. But even if he does, I've had enough. That may be why I did it. I don't want to be beholden to him any more.'

'What are you going to do?'

'I don't know.'

13

Ben Franwell was almost right: it was twelve days later, on the tenth of May, that Jeremy Thorpe resigned, brought down by a man who was an ex-stableboy and ex-model. At forty-six Thorpe had been leader of the Liberal party for nine years. The campaign for his successor had already begun.

While the whole of the British public was titillated by the scandal, more than a few were uneasy as well – some because they were ashamed that the homosexuality of a public figure should make him a target for blackmail, others because they too were in public life and knew that there but for the grace of God went they.

Towards the end of the week the news desk at the *Rampart* was rapturous over the clods being hurled between David Steel and John Pardoe in the fight to lead the Liberals. True, neither candidate was seen to do the dirty work; their henchmen did it for them. As Pardoe chose to fight a macho campaign, he was badly disconcerted when he discovered why TV cameras began zooming down from above: the Steel camp had let it be known that Pardoe wore a hairpiece.

Across the room from the news desk, Frances's mind was on something other than the leadership contest. Her chair was tilted back so that her head was against the wall that divided her cubicle from Rachel's office. Everyone knew it was Rachel's last day as Ben's personal assistant. The Bedford Forge by-election was to be held in three weeks.

Frances's usual deadpan expression altered. She caught her lower lip in her teeth. After a minute she tilted her chair back to its usual position at her desk.

Frances was silent as she and Angela and Daisy walked towards Blackfriars for their lunch. They liked the light food at the salad place, and the room was rarely crowded: the proprietor hadn't got a drinks licence. The three women had never seen any male journalist they knew there, and they suspected that the few male patrons were bank clerks. Today two thin men were at separate little tables across the room, both sitting tensely upright with their shoulders held high beneath their ears.

'What do you want to bet they each order the vegetarian salad?' said Angela. 'Ecologists and health freaks always look nervous wrecks.'

She lit a cigarette and exhaled languidly.

When their own orders had been placed, Frances said: 'Something rather terrible seems to be happening to Rachel. I never before thought of her as quite human. I was wrong.'

'What do you mean?' asked Daisy.

'Sometimes in the past I've heard her when she's raised her voice on the other side of the partition between our rooms. Even then she usually managed to keep that modulation. But this morning she sounded almost hysterical. I don't know whether she was talking on her telephone, or on that line into Ben's office, or whether she was standing in the doorway between their rooms. All I could hear was her side of the conversation. It was awful.'

'What was she saying?' asked Angela.

'She kept saying: "I don't care that they say if I'm going to do it, it must be done as soon as possible. I'm not going to let it be done until the last moment possible." There were other things, but she said that three different times. She sounded like someone in absolute agony.'

'What on earth was she referring to?' asked Daisy.

'I don't know. Whatever it is, it's not good. Odd that I should feel for her distress. I suppose it's the first time I've imagined she could be in real distress.'

All three said nothing further for a few moments.

Then Angela said: 'I wonder if I can discover what's happened from Ben. He's so protective of Rachel that I daresay I'd have to employ my special wiles to get it out of him.'

Each woman gave a small knowing smile.

Rachel's flat was in Morpeth Terrace, ten minutes' walk from Westminster. She'd taken its lease the year before: she knew it wouldn't be long before she needed to be near the House of Commons. She knew, too, that once she was elected, Ben's visits to the flat would have to be curtailed. Even now, he always asked his driver to drop him off in Victoria Street, and he walked the rest of the way, past several identical gloomy mansion blocks, their red brick made funereal by a hundred years of grime, before reaching the one he wanted.

So far he'd been lucky: he hadn't met up with either of the two Labour ministers who also paid regular visits to these outwardly sombre mansion blocks that flank Westminster Cathedral. Ben knew about them: they didn't know about him. He knew that one of them went to the block at the far end from Rachel's. The other called at a block on the opposite side of the Cathedral. Thus far these ministers had managed to keep their mistresses out of the press. Their wives knew, and, as is usually the case, neither wife nor mistress chose to make the matter public. Their ministerial private offices knew. Some other MPs and their secretaries knew. Political journalists knew. But the ministers' constituents and the general public did not know. No newspaper had yet found a way to reveal the matter and prove it in court if a libel action was brought.

Ben liked looking at the Cathedral as he walked past it presiding calmly in its close. Not that he was remotely interested in neo-Byzantine architecture. But he had to admit that the brick dome and single campanile looked dramatic against the pink night sky over London, and he liked the way the big stripes of stone decorating the brick walls shone eerily in the light from the street lamps. Most of all he liked the fact that this was where the Archbishop of the Roman Catholic Church hung out. Ben didn't like Catholics. It made him laugh to think what Cardinal Hume would say if he knew what was going on in these mansion blocks right under his nose. Bloody papist priests. He'd read once that 40 per cent of them were queer. Abruptly he turned and climbed the steps to the electrically locked outer door of number 64 where he buzzed flat twelve on the entryphone.

As it was a top-floor flat, the ceilings weren't particularly high. The entrance hall ran back to the big room at the front overlooking the Cathedral. It was her sitting room, study and dining room combined. The desk was at one side of the fireplace with its gas logs, and on the other side stood the small round dining table. The table was Victorian, its walnut veneer cut like the slices of a pie, but most of the other furniture was reproduction or modern, bought from the Army and Navy or Peter Jones. She'd chosen different shades of blues and brightly patterned cushions. On the wall to wall carpet lay a new Persian rug, wine red dominating the blues and whites and yellows. It was a Christmas present from her parents, proud to show they knew good quality when they saw it. The room might not be distinctive, but it was cosy. Rachel usually felt a warmth of contentment when she got back to her flat and walked into the big room just to look at it before going to her bedroom and changing.

The bedroom was off the hall, as were the bathroom and beyond it the kitchen. She had different shades of blue in the bedroom. Her mother had asked her why she wanted a double bed, and Rachel pointed out that it was only the standard four-foot-six width, which these days was not considered much bigger than a single bed, and she liked to have room to have the newspapers open beside her when she was reading in bed. An oval mirror from Peter Jones hung over the dressing table with its blue striped chintz skirt. A small armchair was covered with the same chintz. So was the scalloped headboard of the bed.

As usual they lay on top of the blue bedspread as they sipped whisky and talked. Some nights they turned back the covers and took their clothes off and made love. Just as often they remained dressed, Rachel in a casual skirt and sweater, Ben's jacket and tie hung over the back of the little chintz armchair, one of them getting off the bed from time to time to fetch another drink from the front room. To an outsider they would have seemed more like comrades than lovers. And the outsider would have been right.

Tonight their conversation was troubled.

Rachel said. 'I'm not going to let them do it until the last moment possible.'

Ben said: 'I didn't think you'd mind so much.'

'Nor did I.'

'Shouldn't we again go through the whole question of marriage?'

'No.'

'Why not?'

'You know why not. It's not right for either of us. When I marry, it will be to someone who is prepared to be secondary to my career. When you marry it will be to someone who looks after your house and children in one of the Home Counties while you concentrate on your Fleet Street career. I admire that in you.'

'Yeah.'

Both were silent, Ben resting his drink glass on his stomach.

Then he said: 'And there's also the other thing we've talked about before. If you were my wife, the *Rampart* couldn't give your career the support that I can give it if you're married to some anonymous pipsqueak. But by God, he'd better be bloody anonymous, whoever he turns out to be. Do you know, Rachel, if it weren't for the electorate's suspicions of single MPs, I'd hope you never married. For that matter, I wouldn't mind going through my own life unshackled, go on living as I do now in a plush service flat with meals laid on when I'm there. In the end, though, you're right: I'm going to settle for the little-woman-at-home setup. I suppose if I actually had children, I might grow interested in them. Most people seem to.'

Rachel screamed. She turned violently away and lay on her side, facing the wall alongside the bed. As abruptly as she had screamed she was silent again.

Ben put his glass on the side table and turned to her. He felt clumsy as he put his hand on her shoulder. After a while he smoothed her dark hair, though even that was done self-consciously. He remembered once when he was a boy, standing beside the bed where his mother used to lie down several times a day after she became ill. Once he had stroked her hair. He liked the way the chestnut was streaked with grey: there was something reassuring about it. 'Don't,' his mother said.

'Don't,' Rachel said.

He took his hand away from her hair.

Then she said: 'After fourteen weeks they'll be able to tell whether it's a girl or a boy.'

'You mustn't wait that long. Everything about it is dangerous.'

'I want to keep it inside me until I know which it is. You don't know what it's like. I never knew anything could make me feel this – feel what I do. All right. I know I can't keep it forever. "MP becomes unmarried mother."'

'For God's sake, Rachel, let's talk about the marriage thing again.'

'There's no point.'

She turned back and lay facing the ceiling. Throughout she remained dry-eyed.

'But they can't do it until I've found out whether I'm carrying a little girl or a boy. I think it's a little girl. I want to know. I need to know what I'm throwing away forever.'

Later that night as Ben Franwell walked back past Westminster Cathedral to find a taxi in Victoria Street, Rachel undressed. Turning out the light, she slipped into the bed. She lay facing the ceiling, one arm thrown out, the other hand held over her womb.

There was no sound other than the 'plip plip' onto the pillow-case, though mostly the salt water streamed soundlessly over her lips and throat or down into her ears, then silently onto the pillow.

After a while she turned the pillow over so that the sodden side was underneath.

14

Saturday – 17th May

Dearest Carl,

   Yes, I do find my life in London is increasingly absorbing. It's not that I don't miss you every day – and obviously every night. I do. Terribly.

Daisy put down her pen and looked at the top half of the plane trees. She'd rearranged the furniture so that while lying in bed, she could see out of the window. Her landlady had been reluctant to let her have an ordinary single bed instead of the convertible sofa-bed that the room boasted when first she moved in. But there was something disheartening about having to perform an engineering feat every time she wanted to go to bed. And if she left the sofa-bed stretched open during the day, it took up two-thirds of the room. In the end Daisy had convinced her landlady that a respectable case could be made for a bed that was a bed.

One reason she'd chosen this flatlet was that immediately across the heavily trafficked road was Sloane Gardens – a somewhat bleak little square, narrow, and surrounded by houses so tall that the sun rarely got a look-in. But Daisy loved it because it had trees that she could see from her two front windows. She liked to take her juice and coffee back to bed in the morning, and when she'd opened and read what little post there was, she would look out at the top half of the plane trees and daydream. She'd never understood why people seemed only to rave about trees that are dressed for spring and summer. She found their winter austerity appealing as well, especially the planes with their big flakes of two-tone bark and the branches reaching out like witches' fingers.

In those first winter months, she had daydreamed about Carl – sometimes looking back at their life together in New York, sometimes fantasizing a dramatic future when Carl, famed throughout the United States and Europe (not infrequently, he was famous throughout the entire world), would rescue Daisy from a precipice where she had somehow got herself stranded and about to plunge to her death (the logistics varied), other times imagining the reality of his planned visit to London.

Would they first see each other when he came through customs at Heathrow? Or would she wait in her flat for the entryphone to buzz and then open her door to him, close it behind them, then stand in this small room in his embrace? Probably he would book them into a hotel; they both were thinking in terms of two weeks together in July, half way through her year of trial, 'just to make sure that beautiful Daisy's thoughts do not become too filled with her London adventures', he had written soon after she began work at the *Rampart*.

Her parents also intended coming to London for two weeks in the summer. Seeing no reason to acquaint them of Carl's visit, Daisy had suggested they come in August, explaining elaborately that so many Londoners go away that month that the capital is less hectic than usual. She'd felt only a little mean when she gave this as the reason her parents should plan their visit after July. Definitely after July.

Now, looking out of the window at the tender green of the leaves that transformed the witches' fingers into lace-bedecked graceful arms, she had to remind herself to daydream about Carl. Was it natural after four months' absence – she counted them on her fingers again to make sure – that she should think less about him? It needn't mean she loved him less.

'Absence makes the heart grow fonder.' She remembered her mother once saying it wasn't so. Daisy tried to remember the reason given. Because she had occasionally, when the maid was on holiday, helped to make her parents' big double bed, she was certain they still had a 'full' marriage, as her mother would say if she was compelled to refer to such matters. Her mother's obliqueness in discussing anything sexual meant that her low-voiced pronouncements were clothed in ambiguity. But what Daisy *thought* her mother had meant was that if the person you love was away too long, unless you intended to moon about hopelessly, you had to think about other things, and that the other things might unexpectedly blur your love for the absent one.

Yet when she was with Carl, in his arms again, would not all her feelings for him be renewed and even enriched by what she'd learned in the meanwhile? It was two weeks – two weeks and five days – since that second dinner with Andrew. He still hadn't rung back. She frowned and picked up the pad and pen again.

> But there is so much to do in my time off from the *Rampart*. (Did I tell you that I hardly ever have to work on a Saturday? So I have three days off most weeks.) Last Sunday I went to the Victoria and Albert Museum, and when I couldn't take in any more I walked to Kensington Gardens and sat on the steps of that weird monument to Prince Albert. And Monday I took my Blue Guide and went to the Law Courts and the Inns of Court, even though they are near the *Rampart*, because there's not been time to see them when I'm in Fleet Street during workdays. Inside the Courts of Justice [she used their correct name because Andrew had used it when mocking them] the barristers are exactly as a friend of mine described them, bewigged, pompous, strolling through the spacious Gothic halls, enjoying their private jokes.

She looked out of the window again. She would finish the letter later; she must decide where she'd take her Blue Guide today.

Someone knocked at her door.

'It's a very good thing I happened to hear the pay phone ringing. There's a call for you,' her landlady said.

Tying a dressing gown over her pyjamas, Daisy ran down to the ground floor hall, thinking of the few people who ever tried to reach her at home, as most rang her at work. She picked up the receiver. 'Hullo?'

'You're very elusive.'

She recognized his voice instantly.

'I had to ring Giles before I could discover this number. Not sure he was wholly pleased. He said didn't I know that as he is no longer employed by a Sunday paper, he is asleep at ten o'clock on a Saturday morning. It's Andrew Harwood.'

She felt fantastically happy. She must be careful not to let it show.

'Is there any chance at all that you might be free for dinner this coming Monday? It's short notice, I know, but you told me that you like Mondays best, so I thought it might be a good evening to suggest. Is it possible that you're free?'

'As a matter of fact, yes.'

'Hooray. What time shall I pick you up?'

'Eight?'

'See you then. Goodbye.' He rang off.

Upstairs she made another cup of coffee and took it back to bed, lying on top of the multi-coloured Indian bedspread she'd bought in the King's Road market.

Was saying she was elusive his way of dismissing the fact that he hadn't tried to ring her before? For had he rung her at the *Rampart*, even though she'd been on an assignment, someone would have taken a message.

Had he not rung before so she would realize she couldn't just string him along? Or had he simply been occupied with someone else? The last thought caused her the same pang that she'd had whenever she'd considered that likelihood during the last two weeks and five days.

For some minutes her eyes had been gazing, half-seeing, at the top half of the plane trees. As she became fully aware of them, she thought that they were the most ravishing trees she'd ever seen in her life.

She leaned across him to stub out her cigarette in the crystal bowl on the bedside table. Lying down again alongside him, idly she watched the cigarette he was smoking: if he wasn't careful, the ash would break off and drop onto his chest.

'If it falls off and I rub it into those carrot-coloured hairs, do you suppose they'd turn grey?' she said. 'It would give one a momentary sense of you thirty years hence.'

'I've noticed before, sooner or later your morbidity surfaces,' he said placidly.

As far as Angela could remember, whenever she was in bed with a man she was aware primarily of herself. She observed that her body was even paler than Giles's. She was pleased that they were lying on her bed: she far preferred it to anyone else's. The Louis XIV headboard and footboard, long ago painted a delicate aquamarine scattered with taupe and sage-green flowers, suited her – pretty, elegant, like her. The silk curtains at the two windows – the same washed-out blue as the bed – that fell several inches onto the thick taupe carpet were drawn together and their sage-green sashes hung loose. Angela liked the way the curtains had been gathered into their top pleats by silk ropes of the same sage-green as the flowers painted on the bed.

As well as the more obvious things about being in bed with someone, she enjoyed the unguarded gossip that always – well, almost always – followed fornication. Sometimes she thought it was what she liked best.

It was odd: she loved undressing, loved making love, yet with none of her bed partners had she ever shared the big O which people went on about. Perhaps the reason she went to bed with so many men, she sometimes thought, was because she liked having her body admired. That psychiatrist could have been right when he said she was a classic narcissist. She was quite small-breasted. She rested her right hand on her right breast, enjoying the sight of the carmine-lacquered nails as she touched one of them against the tip of the nipple. Later, after Giles had left, she would use that same hand in her own way for herself alone. There was no hurry.

'Does Frances ever talk to you about her women?' she said.

'Sometimes.'

Giles propped himself on one elbow long enough to put out his own cigarette in the crystal bowl.

'Does it make you jealous?' Angela asked.

'I suppose it ought to,' Giles replied. 'Then again, it's not really competition, is it? It's a different ballgame. She says that bisexuality enhances her erotic feelings all round. Quite possibly it excites me too – the knowledge that she goes to bed with women. I've never known any woman so capable as Frances of showing one – me – how to give her pleasure. She says it's from women that she learned how to enjoy her own sexuality.'

Angela thought about the implications of this. Yet she was perfectly content generating her own sexual climaxes. 'Has she a regular girlfriend? Or is she promiscuous?'

'Frances and I have only recently become intimate, as they say. We've not yet got that far through our case histories. She may very well have told you more about her relationships than she's told me.'

'It's funny about Frances. She is so direct, apparently open. But when you think back on a conversation, you realize she's been reticent about the nuts and bolts. Do you think she fancies Daisy?'

'Maybe. But she knows about Daisy's great passion for Carl Myer. And I think she would be careful not to jeopardize her friendship with Daisy.'

'Do you ever miss the *Rampart*?'

'In a way. There was always the challenge between Ben and me: what could I get away with? Working for the *Statesman* where everyone flays right-wingers, I'm no longer writing against the grain of the paper – which means less bravura for me and fewer frissons for the reader. Some day I'm going to examine the psychology of why readers like to be enraged.'

'Meanwhile, you can feel self-righteous at not being in the pay of the enemy,' said Angela. 'Except that that's not part of your make-up, thank God. If you asked me what I find the biggest turnoff in most left-wing journalists, it's their holier-than-thou conceit – though the chaps aren't quite as bad as the chicks. One of the things I like about fascist bullies is that at least they are not self-righteous.'

'That's probably true. Whatever else I might call Ben Franwell, it wouldn't be that – as distinct from his being bloody certain he's always right.'

Giles propped himself on an elbow. He offered the half-empty pack of cigarettes to Angela, took one himself, and lit both with the purple Dunhill lighter that Nelly Harwood had given him when they were sozzled one night.

For another three or four minutes he and Angela lay beside each other, absorbed in their own thoughts. Then Giles stubbed out his cigarette in the crystal bowl, got out of bed and went into the bathroom with its aquamarine tiles and towels.

When he'd washed, he returned to the bedroom where Angela was still lying against the pillows. She'd lit another cigarette. As he picked up his clothes from the floor, she thought how much she liked the flowers painted on the footboard.

15

'Shall I come up and wait?' Andrew said into the entryphone.

'No. I'm almost ready.'

It was ridiculous. She'd woken up in a pitch of excitement that Monday was here. There'd been nothing whatsoever she had to do all day, and yet here it was, eight o'clock, and she still wasn't ready. Actually, it was a little after eight. Thank God he wasn't one of those people who arrive exactly on the appointed minute.

Tonight she blamed her unreadiness on her landlady's aversion to a decent lamp; Daisy would never understand the English passion for maroon damask lampshades with tassels. Even though she'd stood directly over the bedside lamp, a large mirror in one hand, the light was so dim that she'd stuck her mascara brush in her left eye. She didn't mind that it hurt: what mattered was that it had made her blink before the lashes were dry, and both eyes now had black smudges beneath them. With careful quick movements she smoothed cleansing cream under her eyes. What a mess. She couldn't go any faster, for Christ's sake. This time the final embellishment was completed without misadventure.

She looked out of the window. The tan Scimitar was still

standing at the kerb. She snatched up her jacket, slammed the door behind her, and ran down the stairs.

The car was empty.

Then she saw him strolling up the other side of Lower Sloane Street. He crossed over and opened the car door for her, smiling as he said 'Good evening,' with a quizzical glance at his watch.

The restaurant was in a turning off the Pimlico Road, small yet with enough room between the tables, run by a middle-aged Italian couple whose two sons were the waiters. All four greeted Andrew warmly.

'They won't be made as well as at Langan's, but shall we risk it and have a martini cocktail?' he said to Daisy.

He gave precise instructions, and when Luigi returned a few minutes later, he presented his achievement with a flourish. Along with the lemon peel in each glass were three olives. 'For good measure,' said Luigi, beaming.

Over their mussels, Andrew returned to the subject of the sculpture she'd told him she wanted to make one day.

'Are you sure you shouldn't try to get hold of a studio while you're in London? You can rent them quite cheaply, you know – to use, say, at weekends. Nelly belongs to the Chelsea Arts Club. He could advise you.'

Daisy's grey eyes were shining as she sipped her chianti. He seemed genuinely interested in her welfare.

'I think it's better to wait until I go home,' she said. 'This year is going so fast. Except for places nearby – you know, Kew, Chiswick House, Hampton Court – I've scarcely been outside London. Last week Frances and I took one of those boats from Westminster pier to Greenwich. Coming back it rained – water streaming down the windows as the Thames flowed below us. I loved it. In Philadelphia and New York it's so terribly hot and humid for months on end that one always is hoping it will rain. Londoners find rain dreary, but I associate it with relief, so I like it. Also it looks nice.'

Andrew smiled, half to himself, half at Daisy.

Only when they were finishing their veal escalopes did she raise a subject on which she'd been brooding.

'Some people at the *Rampart* were talking about politicians and their various ambitions.' She couldn't remember exactly what Ben had said over their strained lunch at L'Escargot – something about upper-class Tories assuming they had a natural right to run the country. 'What's your ultimate political ambition?'

He lit a cigarette, blew the smoke away from Daisy, looked across the room at nothing in particular. He turned back to her. 'I *think* what I probably would most like is to be Foreign Secretary. But I was quite struck when I read somewhere that Iain Macleod said any politician who claimed he didn't want to be Prime Minister was lying. I'm not sure he's right, but I take the point.'

'Why wouldn't you want to be Prime Minister one day?'

'Self-indulgence? There's much in life besides politics, and there's little evidence that a prime minister has time for anything except politics. Can you imagine being married to Number Ten Downing Street? Because that's what it would mean for a wife – or for a husband, as Denis Thatcher will one day discover.'

'But as you haven't got a wife, the problem is academic.'

'Who says I'm not going to marry when the right person comes along?'

'Well, Ben Franwell says you only like short-term relationships.' At last she had aired it. Immediately she felt better – though only for a moment.

'Does he?' Andrew said coldly.

She wasn't absolutely sure that's what Ben had said, but it was near enough.

'I must say,' Andrew said, 'one's impression of life on the *Rampart* is that extraordinarily little time goes into actually writing the bloody paper. Why did you choose to go there instead of somewhere else in Fleet Street?'

Under the freckles, Daisy's face had gone pink with pique. Having set out to criticize him, if only implicitly, *she* was the one being criticized by him.

'Because I'd heard of it. And as it turns out, it's about the only paper where you can start without already belonging to the union. And the *Rampart* pays well enough for me just about to support myself for the year I'm in London. It irritates me when newspapers – or anyone else – think they're so wonderful that people working for them shouldn't mind being underpaid. If the *Rampart*'s farther right politically than you approve of, I don't really care. I'm not all that interested in who is where on the political spectrum.'

Andrew burst out laughing. 'Very sensible. No one except a politician is interested in politics.'

That disarmed Daisy. Immediately her resentment evaporated.

'So why then do newspapers and television go on all the time about it?' she said.

'Because they see politicians as public entertainers. At the same time the media want to display their own *gravitas*, so they have to blather on about policies as well. The truth is that apart from a few lunatic party activists, no one is remotely concerned with the detail of policy – except, of course, when they see it affects them directly. Like schools. Social security. Income tax.'

'Why then do you bother to be a politician?'

Andrew laughed.

'Well, however boring the nuts and bolts, the fact is that political decisions *do* affect how people live in this country.'

He looked at his watch. Politics was not uppermost in his thoughts. He beckoned to Luigi to bring the bill.

When Andrew let Daisy into her side of the Scimitar and she watched him walk round the front, she found she was almost breathless.

He started the engine, then switched it off and turned to her.

'It's not late. I live in a flat around the corner. Would you feel like having a brandy before I take you home? If your description is anything to go by, my flat is rather bigger than yours. We'd be able to sit sedately on opposite sides of the drawing room with at least fifteen feet between us.'

The image made Daisy laugh, and that made it possible to agree without conclusions being drawn.

'All right.'

He started up the engine again.

It was a second-floor flat in Eaton Place. There was no lift. She walked ahead of him up the marble staircase with its ornate wrought iron railings painted black. Conscious of her high heels and the swing of her hips as she mounted each step, she wondered what he was thinking as he came up behind her. If he was four stairs behind, his face must be almost on a level with her hips. What was that like for him? She felt slightly sick. She was sure it had nothing to do with what she'd eaten. It was the sexual tension between them. Carl had once told her that tension meant both the attraction and strain between two poles. Throughout the evening, even though they were always talking about other things, Daisy had felt Andrew's preoccupation with how it would end. Perhaps the best thing was casually to mention straight away that she had her period – just to get rid of the uncertainty so they could think about something else. There was no way he could know it wasn't true.

On the second landing he unlocked a panelled door. Inside was a hall where he went ahead to switch on the lights in the drawing room.

Three big windows looked down on Eaton Place. Daisy's eyes went to the chandelier. The ceiling must be twelve feet high. Over the mantelpiece was an elegant gilt mirror. Late eighteenth century? An enormous worn Persian carpet of coral pinks and faded turquoise covered much of the floor. The sofa was a chesterfield covered in bottle-green velvet, and the pair of rather battered armchairs were clumpy and looked comfortable. Two other armchairs were Victorian and seemed at home. She recognized the portrait of a woman as an Augustus John; Daisy liked the romantic vigour of his early work. The room had a strong presence – as if it was all of a piece.

'Did you choose the things here?' she asked.

'Most of them,' he said. 'Various bits came from Long Green – that's our house in Shropshire; there's far more stuff there than anyone needs. I bought the Kitaj. There's a bathroom at the other end of the hall if you want to restore yourself. Not that you look as if you need restoring.'

Walking down the hall she glanced into a kitchenette, then into what appeared to be a small study, before coming to the bathroom. Just beyond it, the door at the end was open into what she saw, even though it was dark, was the bedroom.

Closing the bathroom door behind her, she looked around at the ink-blue tiles and wine-red towels. She was absolutely sure a woman had chosen them as appropriate for a man's flat. At once she was stabbed again with the pang that had become familiar in the last fortnight. What was it Ben had said? 'He's a great ladies' man, our Andrew. The only thing is that he tires of each lady he's laying and moves on to another.'

Daisy turned on the cold-water tap. It was stupid to be self-conscious about the sound of her own peeing, yet she was acutely aware of being alone with Andrew in this silent flat. Next she emptied her small handbag onto the slab beside the basin; she began touching up her makeup. It was nice not to have to hurry. She noticed the fluttering within her was almost like a throb. She would sip her brandy in a perfectly civilized manner and then he could take her home.

When she returned to the drawing room he got up from one of the armchairs that stood either side of the fireplace. 'Brandy? Whisky?'

She stood beside him at the drinks table, looking at all the bottles.

'Could I have a whisky and soda? I'd never seen one of those syphons until I came to England.'

'They're convenient. Is that about right?' he said.

'Yes.'

Instead of handing her the glass he carried it across the room to where the chesterfield stood, an inlaid marble coffee table in front of it.

'I'll put it here,' he said. 'I told you we could sit with fifteen feet between us. Will you feel safe enough?'

Daisy laughed. She was deeply excited as she sat down on the sofa, Andrew returning to his armchair which was in fact ten feet away.

'Actually,' he said, 'I'm not sure I can carry on with my own charade. Do you mind if I sit beside you?'

It was the same old predicament, and she was sure that's why he had put the question. If she said yes she did mind, then immediately she had declared that she expected the man to make a pass at her, which was presumptuous on her part. If she said no she didn't mind, within five minutes the man always did make a pass at her. And the thing tonight was that she wanted Andrew to sit beside her. She didn't answer his question.

He put his own drink on the table with hers and sat down at the other end of the sofa. He lit a cigarette and leant back, blowing the smoke in short puffs – *pfft, pfft* – towards the opposite side of the room. Neither of them seemed prepared to select a subject for conversation. He turned sideways on the sofa to look at her.

Daisy gave a small nervous laugh. The carriage clock on the mantelpiece chimed once. It's half past eleven, she thought. She could think of absolutely nothing to talk about. It wasn't that they'd run out of things that interested them: it was that now her preoccupation matched his. The fluttering deep inside her was almost unbearably delicious.

He reached over to an ashtray and put out his half-smoked cigarette. Then he got up and walked around the table to stand facing her. He took her glass from her hand and put it on the table, then leant over her, putting one knee on the sofa against her thigh. He kissed her lightly on one cheek. Outwardly it could have been the same sardonic courtesy that she remembered when he'd coldly said good night that last time, but the molten sensation in her loins told her there was all the difference in the world. He put his hands either side of her face and kissed her again and again, always lightly, on her mouth. Then he stepped back and stood looking down at her.

Neither of them said anything. He drew her to her feet. As they stood silent, looking into the other's eyes, each wore an expression different from the night when they'd faced one another on the sidewalk after they'd left Langan's. Here in Andrew's flat there was neither query nor challenge, but a mixture of collusion, tentative tenderness, and hard desire. He thrust one knee between her legs and pushed them farther apart as he put his arms around her, and his mouth fastened on hers. This time she did not draw away from him.

16

The lunchtime traffic was nearly solid before her taxi even reached the top of Fleet Street. Everybody knew about the English weekend, but this was crazy: it was not yet one o'clock on Friday afternoon.

Looking past the driver's tweed cap she could see St Mary-le-Strand ahead in Aldwych, the tip of its tower outlined prettily against a sapphire-blue sky. She slid across the seat so she could look out of the right-hand window as they passed the Law Courts with their illusion of snow – was it mould? – whitening the grey stone walls. She never could pass them without smiling as she visualized Andrew's vain fellow barristers.

How many weeks had passed since that first dinner? She had no difficulty remembering its date: March 21st. Today was May 27th. She would count the weeks on the calendar when she returned to the *Rampart* after lunch. This must be the slowest taxi ride in history. No point in looking at the meter. Anyway, today was pay day, and she wouldn't be expected to pay her share of lunch. She could eat a lot and then have only an egg or something at home tonight. That's about all there was in the smallest fridge in the world.

She and Andrew had had dinner together twice since the night she first went back to his flat, and that was only eleven days ago, so he couldn't have spent many evenings with anyone else he was taking out – was it that odious actress dressed all in white? He couldn't have had that much time to go to bed with her, because he'd been at the House of Commons quite a number of evenings, he said. And he'd been to his constituency. He'd be there tonight and tomorrow – in the West Midlands, as she now proudly called that area.

Two weeks ago she hadn't had the faintest idea where the West Midlands was, though she supposed it was pretty obvious once you thought about it. She'd borrowed Angela's road atlas. Waymere was printed in such tiny letters that you needed a magnifying glass. But she finally found it, left of Crewe, near the white blob called Peckforton Hills. If you went further left you were in North Wales. When she thought of Andrew in his constituency, she thought of those tiny letters near the white blob.

On their second night 'together', as she thought of it, he'd come back to her flat after dinner: he wanted to see where she lived. But it *was* a small room, and she thought probably they were both glad when he left an hour later.

On their third evening together, they went back to his flat. She loved Eaton Place. Also, he had a proper big double bed. She never spent the night there; instinct and tactics were linked when she did not presume he would want her there in the morning, and he'd done nothing to persuade her to stay. She liked to lie in his bed watching him dress so he could drive her home. He didn't bother with a tie at that hour. There was something about a man's shirt unbuttoned at the throat that always pulled at her heart; even when she was surfeited, she found it sexy. When Andrew returned from the drawing room with the campari soda for them to share while she dressed, she put her face inside his open shirt collar. She loved the contrast between the rougher skin of a man's face and the tender skin of his throat. She loved the way Andrew smelled. She'd loved the way Carl smelled, but she quickly averted her mind from that thought.

She was glad Giles had suggested meeting at L'Escargot – fun to see what it would be like when Ben was not being gratuitously unpleasant about Andrew. She was looking forward to meeting Nelly Harwood. He'd asked to meet her, Giles had said. She knew they were friends from schooldays, and she gathered that this bond survived their different views of the world. Nelly, apparently, was this thing called something in the City – on the face of it, a far cry from Giles's concern for society's underdogs. Giles had talked with her about the wide social divisions – of class and income and access to resources. He'd said that not only did this mean less freedom for the have-nots, but after a certain point these wide divisions didn't add to the freedom of the haves: 'John Paul Getty doesn't consume his fortune. It consumes him.' It was the first time this particular concept had been put to Daisy. She tucked it away in her mind, taking it out from time to time to think about it.

'I'll get out here and walk the rest of the way,' she said.

Their taxi had been almost stationary in Charing Cross Road for the last five minutes. In her high-heeled shoes she click-clacked the remaining hundred yards to Cambridge Circus where she took a shortcut as the taxi driver had instructed. Sure enough, after one minute she saw the picture of the snail hung only twenty yards along Greek Street.

At a corner table in the first-floor back room, Giles and a sandy-haired man got to their feet.

'Hullo, Tulip. This is Nelly Harwood.'

He had something of Andrew about him, though he looked more than two years younger. The corners of the hazel eyes crinkled into a friendly smile. Daisy warmed to him straight away.

'What are you going to drink?' asked Giles.

'If you're having wine with lunch, I'll wait.'

Once their orders were taken, Giles said: 'We were talking about how commonplace our kings become when they're without their crowns. Prime ministers, in this instance. When I was at the House this morning, I passed Harold Wilson in Speaker's Courtyard. He was alone, no one else making the slightest effort to walk over and speak to him – yet only two months ago he was the PM. He looked small and grey – reduced, as indeed he is.'

Over their gulls' eggs, Daisy asked Nelly what he actually *did* in the City.

'One of the American phrases I love best is that one,' Nelly said. 'Straight to the point: "What do you do?" the lady asks. In this case, it's a particularly apposite question. What on earth do I do, Giles?'

'He is one of society's parasites,' said Giles. 'He contributes bugger all, and then creams off the rewards of other people's work.'

Nelly laughed. 'It's true, Daisy. Andrew is the one who operates on the principle that we have an obligation to give back to society some of what we've received free of charge. I agree – absolutely – with the principle. But I can't seem to apply it to my own life.'

'Why not?' asked Daisy.

'Oh dear. Let me think. There must be a reason apart from idleness. Can you think of one, Giles?'

Giles gave his thin smile.

'Was Andrew ever idle?' asked Daisy.

Giles glanced at Nelly who didn't answer for a moment.

Then Nelly said: 'Andrew used to lark about a lot. Yet he always had a *capacity* for hard work. He made an effort – throwing himself into things that I would never do. Long-distance running. Student politics. He was actually curious to learn from his studies. I was the feather-brained one of the three of us.' He smiled at Giles. 'At Marlborough, Giles was in the year between Andrew and me. Giles became my friend because he has a soft spot for puppy dogs.'

Nelly turned back to Daisy. 'But Andrew could also be idle, certainly. And he often was. I suppose that changed a bit after the accident.'

'What accident?' said Daisy.

'Oh.' Nelly looked briefly at Giles. 'Perhaps he hasn't mentioned it.'

'He hasn't said anything about an accident.'

Nelly turned his attention to pouring them out some more claret. His face was expressionless.

Giles said: 'You know, don't you, that there was a brother five years older than Andrew?'

'I thought it was just you two,' Daisy said to Nelly. His eyes now reminded her exactly of Andrew's.

'No. There was Donald. He was the golden boy.'

Daisy found this an odd statement: for her Andrew was the golden boy.

Almost as if he could read her mind, Nelly said: 'Donald was effortlessly good at everything. He walked away with every prize at school. Our parents assumed he would go to the top in whatever he did. Everybody expected him to become the great politician. He'd just been selected for a safe Tory seat. He and Andrew were driving to Shropshire late that night. Our parents hadn't yet been told the good news. Somehow the car went off the road. All pretty messy. Donald died. There was no way that Andrew could have saved him. Not the most agreeable lunch conversation, I'm afraid.'

Nelly emptied his wine glass and got out his cigarettes.

'Who was driving the car?'

Nelly looked at his empty glass as he answered Daisy.

'Andrew. Unfortunately for him.'

That evening, as she cooked herself an omelette, she felt unaccountably depressed. There was no reason why Andrew should have told her. God knows there was plenty she hadn't told him. Nonetheless, she was apprehensive. She felt isolated from his fundamental feelings. When a door banged suddenly in another flat, she jumped. Perhaps she'd better write to Carl. She still hadn't answered his last two letters. But what was she to say?

There was no division at the House of Commons the following Wednesday evening. She was to meet Andrew for dinner at a restaurant half way between her flat and Westminster. She'd come home from the *Rampart* on the number eleven bus, which she preferred to the tube if there was time: while she saw others employing their journey in reading, she liked looking out of the window. Sometimes she concentrated on the buildings that she passed and the people walking by. More often she daydreamed. At the bus stop just before Sloane Square she jumped off, pausing to admire the plane trees that now wore their full verdure, then remembered there wasn't much time to bathe and dress.

It was past eight when she flagged down a taxi and jumped in, the late spring rain so soft that it scarcely spotted the taxi's windows. She loved the way rain turned the pavement shiny black. It also made her hair close to her temples draw up into the tight curls she didn't like, damn them. When she got out in Pimlico Road, she put both hands flat alongside her ears, holding the wanton hair in place as she ran across the pavement to the restaurant door.

There was so much to ask Andrew and tell him, about things and thoughts encountered since they'd been together six nights before, that it wasn't too difficult to prevent herself from asking the question until they were having coffee.

Then she said: 'Nelly says you had an older brother. Why didn't you ever mention it?'

'Why don't you mind your own fucking business?' he replied.

He said it in such a quiet, flat voice that the people at the nearby table heard nothing untoward.

She felt as if she'd been slapped across the face. She looked down at her hands lying still on the red and white checked table cloth.

After perhaps a minute of the silence between them, Andrew said: 'That was rather a crude reaction on my part. I'm sorry, Daisy. It's just that I don't want to talk about it.'

'That's okay.' Her voice was subdued, and for the first time since they'd met, their conversation became desultory.

In the car, they drove in silence towards her flat.

The traffic around Sloane Square was light when he pulled over to the kerb outside W. H. Smith and let the engine idle. 'Look. This is no way to finish an evening. Let's go back to my flat and have a drink and try to recover the situation. Or do you want to have an early night?'

'I'd prefer the recovery programme,' she said quietly. She looked quite wan.

He pulled out from the kerb, drove round the square, and headed back towards Eaton Place. Spatters of rain appeared on the windscreen. Again the street turned shiny black.

This time she found the enchantment of the high-ceilinged drawing room was overlaid by her anxiety. He poured them each a whisky and soda.

'Let's sit down,' he said.

They sat in the armchairs that faced each other across the

fireplace. 'You want to know. All right. I'll tell you.

'My mother adored Donald. He must have been conceived when my father was on leave early in the war. It wasn't so much that Donald was the first-born: he was the only one there for five years – if you count the nine months that my mother carried him, nearly six years. My father was posted to Burma. He ended up in one of the Japanese prison camps. He came out of it, evidently, more intact than some of the others. When he got back to Shropshire he found his wife and his unknown son were very close to each other. Not easy at first for my father.

'But then he too fell in love with Donald. That may seem a strange expression to use, but everybody fell in love with Donald. He had *everything*. Intelligence. Charm. Physical strength. He was dark-haired, like my mother. Really strikingly good-looking. In some extraordinary way, he was entirely unconscious of how attractive he was. From earliest childhood, I suppose I idolized Donald.'

Andrew stopped speaking.

Daisy, her eyes on his face, still said nothing.

He lit another cigarette.

'Since first I became involved in student politics at Oxford, I thought of becoming an MP, but it was so obviously Donald's role. I became a barrister instead. The only surprising thing was how long it took him to get selected for a winnable seat. Absolutely absurd he should not have been in Parliament when the Tory government came in in 1970.

'Then in '72, the sitting MP in a safe Tory seat suddenly died. Donald was selected to replace him. At the time, Donald was about to marry the woman he'd had a long affair with. Nice woman. Complications, though, about her divorce. It was like Donald that on the night he was selected, he opted to drive to Long Green to tell our parents.'

Andrew stubbed out his cigarette. He drank some more of his whisky and soda.

Although he had kept his face impassive throughout, Daisy thought she had rarely seen anyone look so sad.

He lit another cigarette.

'I'd gone along on the selection evening as a kind of lark. I was sitting in the lounge of the local hotel, having a couple of beers, reading the weeklies, looking at television, while he and the other candidates were undergoing the selection. As soon as he walked into the lounge, I knew from his face that he'd won. We had a celebration whisky. Then we set off for Shropshire. It was raining.'

He talked in slightly jerky sentences.

'Nelly told you, I expect, that I was driving. It was going across that barren part of the Shropshire hills that we went around a bend and came on the tree fallen into the road in front of us. Donald said: "Watch it, Andrew." I can hear his voice now – calm and intense. I swerved to miss the tree. Donald's door came open. He was thrown out. The car turned over. When I climbed out, I found him caught under the car. He gave a kind of half smile. I tried to lift the car off him. People say that in a life-or-death crisis, you can perform physical feats you could never do ordinarily. I still couldn't get the car off him. He said: "Take it easy, Andrew." I heard another car coming. I ran back and flagged it down. The two men in it helped me lift the car off Donald. While we were doing it, he died. Apparently he was haemorrhaging internally.' Andrew put out his cigarette.

After a minute he lit another.

Daisy got up from her chair and crossed over to his. She sat on the floor alongside him, her knees pulled up and her arms wrapped around them, one cheek laid on her knees. Except for sitting against his left leg, she didn't touch him.

After five or six minutes, he put his left hand on her neck and rested it there.

Later, in his bedroom, she told him that she didn't want him to touch her the way he usually did, she didn't want to be aroused, she just wanted to receive him. When she'd last been with him, she'd begun to get used to the sound he made – something like a drawn-out, low shout – as he went into his own climax. This time he was silent, and his final spasm was like a shudder. He fell asleep while he was still inside her.

After a while she pulled herself out from under him, drew up the bedclothes, and lay down again, one arm around him. She lay like that, awake, until he turned over in his sleep and put an arm around her. Then she too fell asleep.

17

On the following Monday she was introduced to the Mother of Parliaments.

Andrew had got her a ticket to the Chamber, the proper name, she now knew, for where the great debates were held. At 2.15, alongside other favoured guests, she stood eagerly in the Central Lobby, Sir Giles Gilbert Scott's neutered version of Victorian Gothic rising coldly above them as they waited for what her programme notes billed as the Speaker's Procession.

At 2:20 exactly a colossal bellow issued from a policeman: *'Hats off, Strangers!'* What sounded like a regiment was heard approaching, hard soles slapping marble floor in military precision. Past the 'Strangers' tramped a figure in wig and black knee-breeches, shoe buckles agleam, supporting on one shoulder a great gilt mace. Behind him trod another figure wearing his wig slightly askew, the black gown billowing out over his breeches and buckles suggesting to Daisy that he must be the Speaker. Two more figures brought up the rear. That was it. She blinked.

Having climbed up to the gallery of the Chamber and been shown to her seat by someone wearing sinister clothes – pitch-black morning dress fronted by a huge brass disc which hung on a chain suspended from the executioner's neck – she looked down on a second anti-climactic scene.

At the other end sat the figure who wore his wig askew. Green leather benches were banked either side of the central gangway. On them lounged a few men and a scattering of women, mostly talking among themselves despite the fact that a man from the government front bench was standing at the dispatch box answering questions. Occasionally people seated behind him said: 'Hear, hear,' in a low sound very like a belch, she thought. In vain she looked for Andrew. He'd said he hoped 'to catch the Speaker's eye' – Daisy inwardly preened herself on knowing the phrase – and speak in the trade debate that would follow; a small wool industry in his constituency had an interest in one clause of the bill.

She tried to decide whether the Tories looked more like gentlemen than those on the Labour government's benches. Apart from the Tories' lapels being sharper and their pin stripes more pronounced, she could see little to distinguish one unexceptional exterior from another. She said to herself that any gathering of people in the same business usually looked pretty unimpressive – journalists, for instance. Even so.

Just before the questions were due to end at 3:30 and the debate begin, more MPs began wandering in from behind the Speaker's Chair. Daisy was sorry the new prime minister, James Callaghan, was not among those who now settled on the government front bench.

Suddenly Rachel appeared from behind the Speaker's Chair. Daisy watched, fascinated, as Rachel, looking relaxed and assured in her perfectly-cut Oxford grey suit, laughed at some aside made by a male colleague as she went up the stairs to the top row of opposition benches.

Then Andrew appeared. Pausing to chat with one or two people, he strolled up to the third bench. For Daisy the atmosphere now was charged.

The first time he stood and waved his order paper to catch the Speaker's eye, someone else was called instead. The second time the Speaker shouted: 'Mr Harwood.' Daisy didn't yet know that the Speaker was the only person in the Chamber who called

MPs by their names rather than their parliamentary titles.

She couldn't take in a word of what Andrew was saying about the wool industry in Waymere: she was totally absorbed in the graceful yet confident way he stood and spoke – far the most attractive person in the place, obviously.

After he sat down again, he glanced up at the gallery. Seeing her, he wrote a note and handed it to a page. A few minutes later, an executioner handed the folded paper to Daisy. 'Can you meet me in the Central Lobby at 4:45?'

When Andrew looked up, she nodded.

Together they walked down a wide splendid staircase with polished dark oak banisters to the next floor which opened out onto a terrace overlooking the Thames. Here there was no anti-climax, watching the barges moving quietly on the indigo-blue water that glittered in early June sunshine, then looking up at the ornate Gothic towers rising above her. Several other MPs came over to their table to say something to Andrew and be introduced to Daisy. She felt proud.

After tea they sauntered back through the dark warren of the House before crossing New Palace Yard and then Bridge Street. Like most recently arrived Members, his room was in the Norman Shaw building, a few minutes' walk from the Palace of Westminster.

'Americans are always taken aback when they see our so-called offices,' he warned her. 'Some MPs have to share a room, so believe it or not, I'm lucky in having a shoebox all my own.'

He was hardly exaggerating: his room was so pinched that it was virtually filled by a desk, three chairs and a filing cabinet. His secretary, who worked for another Tory backbencher as well, had to hike from some remote part of the building. When she appeared, Daisy made her own way out.

Modest as a backbencher's life might be, Daisy found it glamorous: it was all part of Andrew.

'You'll have to tell him something one of these days,' Angela said.

'I know,' said Daisy.

It was Tuesday, and they were lunching at the salad place.

'Do you realize it's turned out the way my parents hoped it would?'

'Just as well you're fond of them. Otherwise you'd have to marry Carl to spite them, even though your doting heart has now turned elsewhere. As you're not the world's most brilliant actress, I daresay Carl has already detected a change in your letters.'

'But what am I going to say? "Dearest Carl. I do not want to marry you after all. This is because I have fallen in love with an Englishman called Andrew. And as my friend, Frances, informs me that I am monoerotic, I also do not want to make love with you again. Meanwhile I haven't the faintest idea whether this same Andrew will still desire me next month."'

Daisy looked gloomily at her chicken salad.

Angela gave her inward smile. 'Once you wrote it, at least you'd feel better. Draft the letter first on your typewriter: something about the machine's physical separateness helps one to detach emotionally a bit. Or so I find – not that I have any great difficulty in achieving detachment. As for Andrew, he's the type who actually wants to settle down. Supposing he decides he'd like to do so with you. Would you marry him?'

Daisy frowned. 'It's so disgusting. One minute I am saying to myself what marvellous children Carl Myer and I could produce together. The next minute I'm saying the same thing about Andrew Harwood. But that's how I've always known if I'm serious about someone: do I want to have his child? It's not that I envisage myself as a great sow suckling piglets for half my life. But the child thought always comes into my mind when I'm wondering how much I love a man. Do you ever think like that?'

'Not that I can recall. Certainly not in my current mild preoccupation.'

'What's that?'

Daisy was delighted to be distracted by someone else's life.

'If I marry,' said Angela, 'it will be because I see the prospect primarily as an entertainment. Take Ben Franwell as a possibility.'

'*What?*'

'It's not to be ruled out. I like living on the outside of things. I doubt that I'm even capable of a grand passion. Certainly I don't want one – all that inevitable pain.'

'Yes, but Angela, you'd miss all the happiness that would balance the pain. I'm sure these things are in balance.'

'Do you suppose our neighbour will mind if I light another cigarette?'

Having done so, Angela said: 'I daresay you're right about the balance. But unlike you, I prefer mine to be at a low pitch. I'd rather forgo your heights of emotion than risk having all my eggs in someone else's basket. I want to be the one who controls my feelings, be they ever so low-key as a consequence. I don't wish to care greatly whether an Andrew or a Ben or anyone else is head over heels in love with me next month as well as today. I expect I am cut out for the marriage of convenience.'

'Has Ben asked you to marry him?'

'No. But I think he's turning it over in his mind. He lives on the outside of his emotions too. I enjoy watching power politics – and I mean in everything, not just Westminster and Fleet Street: power politics in the art world, business, other people's marriages, sex generally. Ben likes wielding power. My network would provide some handy inside information. I'd be quite useful at the kind of entertaining that would suit his purposes. I wouldn't be a drag about his general lack of interest in home life, because it doesn't interest me either. Ben and I might very well suit one another. We'll see.'

18

On Thursday evening Daisy was back in the House of Commons. She and Frances and Giles were Andrew's guests for dinner in the Members' Dining Room. The room soared above them, as tall as it was wide, its walls covered with a handsome claret-coloured flock paper embossed in gold, the pattern repeating one that Daisy had noticed elsewhere in the House.

'I do enjoy Pugin's wallpapers and all that inventive decoration,' Frances said. 'Too bad most of his work burned down in the 1941 bombing. Enough to put one off the Germans. How do you like being surrounded by our esteemed legislators, Daisy? You're looking a teensy weensy bit bemused.'

Most of the legislators were temporarily absent, having, like Andrew, abandoned their guests after a singularly noisy bell had clanged and a stentorian voice had shouted '*Division!*'

'It's all right, I suppose.'

'Why don't you come out and say it baldly, Tulip: they look like a bunch of pricks.'

Daisy began to laugh wildly. 'It's not that. It's just that they're treated so prominently by the media. You're always writing about them, Giles. Then when one is actually with them, they look so ordinary and at the same time seem so pleased with themselves.'

'That's what I said, if more succinctly.'

'But you don't think of Andrew like that.'

'The Andrews in this place are pretty thin on the ground, whichever party they belong to. Most of these characters are humbugs: they'll tell you they want to serve the community, improve society, all that pious stuff. How many of them will say they want power for its own sake?'

'They don't always,' said Frances. 'I can think of politicians who've made a genuine contribution to society.'

'Okay. So you have a few sincere fascists like Mosley.'

'Honestly, Giles. What's the point in your preaching to us week in week out that first Wilson's government, now Callaghan's, lacks the true blood of socialism if in fact you dismiss all politicians as mere egomaniacs?'

'What about Roosevelt?' Daisy had been racking her brain to think of some politician she'd heard of who was genuinely interested in altering society.

'I accept that he was out of the ordinary,' Giles replied. 'And I daresay there are two or three blokes and blokesses today who are not purely opportunistic. Andrew actually imagines he might make things marginally better for his countrymen when he achieves a strong enough position. But then everyone else *says* that to themselves – whatever their party – and most of them believe it, strangely enough. That's another reason for thinking they are mad.'

'Do you think Andrew's mad?' Daisy found it easier to consider any concept in terms of an individual. Also, she loved talking about Andrew.

'I've known him – and Nelly – since Marlborough. Andrew is intelligent, generous, ambitious. You could say he's a bit cracked in his obsession that he must contribute for two people – himself and Donald. But mad? No.'

'He's a bit mad to have invited you to dine here tonight,' said Frances. 'After what you wrote about the blessed Tory leader last week, most Tory MPs would find a good reason not to consort so openly with the enemy.'

She turned to Daisy. 'MPs see journalists all the time in Annie's

Bar or somewhere else considered an acceptable venue for "keeping in touch". But they shy away from entertaining to dinner here the very hacks who have attacked their leader, no matter how much they agree with the attack.'

'That's another reason I like Andrew, even though he's a Tory,' Giles said. 'He's not always watching his back. Though if he's going to get anywhere in this game, he should glance over his shoulder occasionally.'

He looked beyond his table companions. 'Our legislators are returning.'

Andrew had just sat down again when Rachel Fisher appeared in the doorway and looked around the dining room until she spotted the opposition spokesman on housing. She crossed over to his table to speak with him.

Giles watched her.

'I'm about to start doing a proper stint in this place,' Andrew said. 'I gather I'm to be taken onto the opposition's housing team any day now. Hullo, Rachel.'

Having finished her conversation with the opposition spokesman on housing, she had come straight to their table.

'Hullo, everybody,' she said. 'I was in the Chamber when you were called this afternoon, Andrew. Good speech.'

'Thanks. Do you want to join us?'

'Thanks. I can't. How's life on the *Rampart?*'

'Much the same,' said Frances. She held up one hand. 'Look at that bruise. That's where the big white chief cracked his whip just because my review of Macmillan's autobiography included a gratuitous jibe at Mrs Thatcher's hard heart.'

Rachel laughed. 'Give Ben my love. I'll see you, Andrew.' She gave a small wave and moved towards the door.

'Like a benediction,' said Giles.

'In fact, I've never known her so friendly before,' Daisy said.

'That's because she and Andrew now belong to the same club,' said Giles. 'You always speak to the other member's guest. Even when you are trying to do each other down.'

Daisy thought back on the MPs who on Monday afternoon had come up to their table on the terrace.

Andrew laughed. 'There is not the slightest evidence that Rachel is trying to do me down,' he said.

'You wait. She will,' said Giles. 'How much do you want to bet?'

19

Once Daisy had got her interview with the Foreign Secretary's wife, it was easier to get other VIPs to see her. She discovered quickly that if you quote people in context and make your criticisms wittily, you can get away with a lot.

On Friday she had written to the Health Minister asking him for an interview, adding that she would ring his office in a few days' time to see if something could be arranged. 'Don't give his private office a chance to send you a letter turning you down,' Ben had told her.

Sloane Square looked quietly cheerful on Sunday as Daisy walked to the newsagent outside the tube station and returned to her bedsitter, the *Rampart* tucked under one arm. Having made a cup of coffee, she stretched out comfortably on the multi-coloured Indian bedspread, looked at the top of the plane trees beyond her windows, then opened the newspaper.

She turned first to the page that had her interview with the Chancellor's wife. She had seen the proof sheet of the page before leaving the *Rampart* on Friday evening. (Most features went to press Friday night so that on Saturday the presses would be free for the ever-changing news stories.) But like most journalists, she lived in terror that a typographical error would reverse the meaning of what she had written – 'he is not trying to undermine the Prime Minister' becoming 'he is now trying to undermine the Prime Minister'. Were it ever to be found that the embarrassing typo was made on purpose by a mischievous sub-editor, Ben would have sacked the culprit on the spot. (If the typo was made intentionally by a linotype operator, even Ben could not have sacked him out of hand. But then it never could be proved anyhow: the kindliest of the printers showed a mafia-like loyalty to their less kindly brothers.)

Relieved and quite pleased with the end result, she turned back to the front page to start going through the paper in order. It was a good ten minutes before she reached the leader page. Immediately her eyes fell on the name that kept reappearing in Ben's column.

There's a bright new gleam of hope in the eyes of the Member for Waymere this Sunday morning. For two years Mr Andrew Harwood has languished, neglected, on the Tory backbenches.

Lo, an angel is about to transport him to sit in relative glory as the opposition's junior spokesman on housing. But should not the angel first ask if this baronet's son begins to comprehend the nation's housing problems?

Mr Harwood might think no one better understands the poor's desire for an indoor toilet than a toff raised in the twelve-bedroom splendour of Long Green, Shropshire. Picture for yourself the local grocer delivering to the back door the weekly lavatory rolls that you can bet your bottom dollar are not destined for an outside toilet.

. . .

I have no objection to Members of Parliament earning an honest buck in their spare time. No doubt Mr Harwood can be the smoothest of barristers.

And when he can tear himself away from more private activities, he even deigns some days to call in at the Commons.

. . .

But would it not make more sense to add to the housing team an MP who knows how ordinary people live – and one prepared to make

a proper job of parliamentary work? Why not appoint the Member
for Bedford Forge, Rachel Fisher?

*This newest addition to the Tory benches knows all Britons must put their
shoulder to the wheel if they are to regain their freedom from the unholy consensus
of Labour bureaucrats and Tory patricians.*

Would the Conservative party and the country not be better served
if it was Rachel Fisher who joined the housing team – and Mr Harwood
left to pursue his private activities outside the House?

Daisy flung the *Rampart* to the floor, her face hot with outrage.

What was it Andrew had said about Ben's column? 'He says
such frightful things about people that he makes me laugh – so
far.'

She picked it up and read it again.

Ten minutes later she reached for her newly installed telephone
and dialled Frances's number at the Barbican.

No answer.

She dialled Angela's number.

'I wondered if you might ring. The first thing is that it doesn't
matter, Daisy.'

'If it doesn't matter, then why does Ben bother to do it?'

'Well okay: it doesn't *really* matter. It won't have the slightest
effect on Andrew's career. It's not as if there had been any
suggestion that he is corrupt.'

'But it's so horrid.'

'Too true.'

'One is left with the impression that Andrew is an idiot. And
what are the "private activities" referring to?'

'Ah. That is one of the great Franwell techniques. Does he mean
off-stage money-making? Does he mean having an affair with
you? Does he mean beating up his mother?'

The last image made Daisy laugh, and momentarily she forgot
her indignation.

'Anyone who knows Andrew will realize Ben is just having a
go. Anyone who doesn't know Andrew will forget what was said
within two minutes.'

Daisy only half believed it.

'Did I ever tell you, Angela, what Ben said to me when he took
me to lunch that day at L'Escargot? He said when the Tories get

back into government any job offered to Andrew would already have been turned down by Rachel Fisher.'

She heard the click of the cigarette lighter.

Then Angela said: 'Ben will no doubt do what he can to promote Rachel. Politics being politics, if you want to put someone up, you need to put someone else down.'

While Angela drew on her cigarette, Daisy waited.

'And we both know that Ben has it in for Andrew.'

'Why?'

'Ben thinks of everything in personal terms, Daisy. When you made it plain you didn't fancy him, it would have cut him to the quick. He had to blame your sexual disinterest on someone other than himself, and Andrew was an obvious candidate – because no amount of success will ever remove Ben's chip about Tory aristocrats. He'll still be bearing it on his shoulder in his coffin.'

'Does he carry on his vendettas forever?'

'That's his tendency, I fear. Even when he can't come up with a charge that will in itself damage – destroy – his quarry, he finds the endless pursuit can eventually demoralize the victim.'

'What happens then?'

'The victim loses his own balance and falls off the tightrope.'

Daisy was silent.

Angela said: 'As far as Andrew goes, I'm sure you mind today's piece much more than he does – though he won't like it. Who would? Perhaps you ought to consider whether you want to get too involved with a politician, Daisy.'

After she had put down the telephone, Daisy looked out of the window towards the plane trees, but all she could see was Ben Franwell's face, grinning.

20

By the middle of June, Britons were complaining of the extra-ordinary weather: by nine in the morning the temperature was high in the eighties, the humidity reminding Daisy of the wet blanket of heat which sank upon Philadelphia each long summer.

Even though it was a Monday, she woke early. Lying naked on her bed – a sheet was too much; she'd left her curtains open to any current of air in the night, but they hung limply still and her room remained stifling – she lifted her hair off her neck, spreading the damp curls over the pillow.

Then she remembered what day it was. She propped herself on one elbow to look at the Baby Ben ticking calmly on the bedside table. It was nearly seven o'clock. Oh God. She'd been taken aback when he had rung last week to say he didn't want to wait until the fortnight they'd planned for late July: he was making an extra three-day visit in June.

As she lay there, hot, anxious, resentful – she had to remind herself that *she* wasn't the one who should feel resentful – the plane from New York was approaching Heathrow.

All he could see out of the window was the thick white mist of

clouds banked together. Then a ragged chink opened, and through
it he recognized the fairy-story crenellated ramparts of Windsor
Castle. After a moment the thinned edges of the clouds, with their
false appearance of drifting in the opposite direction to the plane,
interlocked again.

Not much more than an hour later a taxi deposited him at the
front door of Brown's Hotel. Apart from his brief case, he had
only one bag with him, and that was compact.

At one o'clock, Daisy jumped off the number fourteen bus in
Piccadilly, less jaunty than she usually felt when she found herself
near Green Park. Other times she was touched by the people lying
on the grass, seizing each moment of sunshine as if it were a rare
gift. Today she scarcely noticed them.

Walking the half block of Albemarle Street, she faced the fact
that she was extremely nervous.

The man behind the reception desk at Brown's Hotel rang
Professor Myer's room.

'He says he has booked your lunch table for 1:30, madam, and
would you care to come upstairs for a few moments? It's room 242
on the fifth floor.'

'Tell Professor Myer, please, that I'll wait in the lounge.'

She sat on a damask-covered sofa and looked at the people
dotted around the big, handsome, impersonal room. Impossible
to place them in any one category. It really was intolerable of
Carl to put her in a position where she seemed silly when she
declined to go to his room. She then taxed herself: why couldn't
she just have gone to his room? He wasn't going to rape her.

'Hullo, Daisy. Did you think I was going to rape you?'

She had forgotten lately how attractive he was. His smile was
good-humoured, the brown eyes twinkling, as he looked down at
her. She found she was glad to see him. She liked the two deep
vertical lines that transected the narrow cheeks.

'We're a bit early, but I daresay we'd find our table ready – if
you think it's safe to sit with only a tablecloth between us. I asked
the reception desk to book us a table at that restaurant you seem
to like so much. Langan's. They said it's just five minutes from

here. I've been cooped up in that plane for seven hours. Do you feel like walking?'

Their table was several along from the front door, above them three Hockney gouaches of a swimming pool. As soon as he'd placed their order, Carl said: 'You're looking ravishing. But then that's not new.' He watched her closely.

'I love London,' Daisy said.

'So I gather. I didn't think much of your last letter. If it comes to that, I didn't think much of any of your letters for the past few months. But I decided it was better for you to get some of these newfound excitements out of your system. Was I wrong?'

Daisy was staring into his face. She'd never been physically attracted to two men at the same time. Was she now? Or was it nostalgia? Or was it simply that she *liked* him so much?

'I met someone earlier this year. The whole thing is altogether surprising. I've got rather involved with him.'

'Anyone I might know?'

'He knows who you are. He's a Tory MP. He was elected in 1974. Did you know Britain had two general elections in 1974?'

Carl Myer laughed. 'The politicizing of Miss Daisy Brewster continues apace. I suppose this person has a name?'

Daisy was torn between discomfiture and the desire to say the name.

'Andrew Harwood. He's also a barrister.'

'Never heard of him. So what has Mr Harwood in mind?'

'What do you mean?'

'You know exactly what I mean.'

Delicately she began to twist her napkin into a long cone. The fact was she didn't know what Andrew had in mind.

'I *don't* know what you mean. All I know is that something that was unimaginable when you put me on that plane six months ago has happened. I find him very attractive.'

'Are you saying you don't want to marry me?'

'I don't know what I'm saying.' She felt miserable. 'I suppose that is what I'm saying.'

'Have you told Mr Harwood that I am the man who taught your body how to feel things it had never felt before, that I opened your mind to thoughts, concepts, you'd never considered before?'

'Oh Carl, don't.'

'Why not? You can't go through life, Daisy, imagining that you can pick up and put down other people's hearts as if they were bonbons.'

'You make me sound like the Daisy in *The Great Gatsby*.'

'You're not essentially self-absorbed as she was. But there is a marked similarity between her frivolous attitude to life and – from time to time – your own.'

With some other man she would have bristled at being called frivolous just because her feelings had changed. In this instance she accepted there was a validity in what Carl said.

'I didn't think it possible that I could be attracted to anyone except you. I didn't want it to happen.'

'Then why don't you take a relaxed attitude to whatever it is that has happened? Look, Daisy, we've talked a little about this before. And since you've been away, things have moved forward. If Ford is re-elected in November, the chances are better than good that I'll be on my way to Washington before the year is out – though I couldn't actually leave Princeton on sabbatical until the first of the year. Maybe I'd start with an advisory job at Defense. Maybe in the State Department – though Henry-the-K may not want another intellectual standing quite so close. When he first took his sabbatical from Harvard to go to Washington, he was seen by some intellectuals already there as a threat – and they were right: within a year he had assumed power over and above theirs.'

'And you're going to follow in his tracks?'

'Why not?'

In some moods, Daisy remembered, she had found his arrogance could infuriate her. At this moment, however, she acknowledged he had grounds to be arrogant. She was proud of Carl's intellectual prowess. She was intrigued by the political power he intended to be his. She smiled at the boldness of the brown eyes watching her response.

He went on: 'Think of the life we could lead together in Washington – I operating from within power politics, you operating as a portrait sculptor with senators and congressmen lining up at your door. And one thing could be guaranteed: we would never bore one another.'

He kept his eyes fixed intently on her face. 'Okay, so you – and maybe I – might sometimes want to add a further dimension to our experience – like this year of yours in London. Your little theory that you are "monoerotic"' – he turned down the corners of his mouth in mockery as he used the word she had recently learned – 'is crap. Anyone claiming to be monoerotic is simply repressed. And you are not. I should know: I developed your sexuality.'

He saw Daisy look down at his hands where they rested on the tablecloth. He was careful to make no gesture towards her with his hands. He looked at her mouth – the soft full lips – and then back to her eyes as he said: 'Why should you keep yourself corseted all your life? There's a whole range of plural experience that can actually make a marriage stronger as well as more entertaining. That presupposes, of course, that it is a good and interesting marriage – which ours would be. Have your adventure. Then come back to me.'

He could see she was at any rate turning the thing over in her mind.

'Why don't you just relax and enjoy your London love affair?' he said.

Then he overplayed his hand.

'Far better to treat it as a transient pleasure in itself than to throw overboard all that I am offering. You can't really want to settle into domestic obscurity with some little MP in a country that's going down the drain.'

Her face flushed with anger.

But Carl was often lucky. At that moment a couple appeared at the bar end of the room. They must have been lunching upstairs. The young woman wore a flowered silk dress without a petticoat so you could see the full length of her marvellous legs. The man with her was Andrew. At the same time as Daisy realized this, Andrew saw her.

He spoke to the vision with him, and she went ahead towards the front door. She was not the actress dressed in white, which made it even worse.

Apparently unperturbed, he came over to the table beneath the Hockney swimming pools.

'Hullo, Daisy.'

'Hullo.'

She hoped she sounded bright and chirpy. 'This is Carl Myer. This is Andrew Harwood.'

Carl got to his feet, and the two men shook hands. They were the same height, but otherwise their physical types were different – the one sandy-haired, sturdily built, the other wiry with pale skin that contrasted with his black hair. Each looked with open interest at the other. Each smiled faintly.

'Daisy has spoken of you,' Andrew said. 'I've read some of your work – and with much interest.'

'Yes,' Carl said, declining to return a conventional pleasantry.

'I'll give you a ring next week, Daisy. Goodbye, Professor Myer.'

'Goodbye, Mr Harwood.'

Daisy said nothing.

Andrew turned and walked to the door.

Carl sat down. He looked at her. His eyes were twinkling. 'Perfectly presentable young man, I agree.'

Daisy still said nothing.

Carl beckoned to a waiter, and when the bill was settled he said: 'Look, we can't lapse into permanent silence just because your young man has another lady on his arm today. I've booked us tickets for the National Theatre tonight. *Othello* is playing at the Olivier. You'll want to go back to your flat before then and "freshen up", as your mother would say. But first let's walk back to Brown's for half an hour. I want to show you an article I wrote for the *New York Times* last week. It's about something you were asking me not long before you left the States.'

Daisy was not remotely interested in his article in the *New York Times*, but she decided to go back all the same.

As they turned the corner into Albemarle Street, Carl started to cross to the sunny pavement on the other side.

'I don't like walking in the sun when it's so hot and I'm wearing clothes,' Daisy said.

She sounded petulant.

They stayed on the shady side until they were opposite Brown's, and there they crossed over.

Although she hoped it didn't show, inwardly she was in turmoil – angry and depressed. She had no reason to think Andrew didn't see other women. She hadn't asked him, because she didn't want him to feel claustrophobic. Anyhow, she had other dates, so why shouldn't he? But the point was that as far as she was concerned, her other dates were purely platonic. Ben's words came back: 'Andrew gets tired of each lady he's laying and moves on to another.' She felt quite ill.

Room 242 was big, with two beds wider than most single beds. She sat in the armchair by the window reading the extract from the *New York Times*. She tried to concentrate. Part of Carl's influence on her stemmed from his skill in selecting reading that caught her interest and taught her something new. Damn, damn Andrew and his gorgeous woman. Presumably they were this very minute in Andrew's bed.

Carl stood in front of the armchair. He took the newspaper from her and put it on the table. Then he put his hands under her arms and pulled her to her feet. He gripped her hard by the shoulders as he looked down at her.

'You're wrong, you know,' he said. 'You haven't really got over me. It's just been too long. Perhaps I should have come sooner. I suppose I wanted to demonstrate that my presence wasn't necessary to hold you. Well, I'm holding you now.'

He released her shoulders so he could undo the tiny pearl buttons running down the front of her silk T-shirt.

She pushed away his hand.

'I don't want to,' she said.

'Yes you do.'

'I don't,' she said.

'Yes you do.'

He had decided not to make any reference to what Andrew Harwood might be doing at this same moment. Why risk it backfiring? She would already be thinking about it without his having to point it out. Her pride was hurt. No need for him to do anything except what he was doing.

Again he began undoing the little pearl buttons.

This time she was more tentative when she pushed his hand away. He took both her hands and held them flat against her thighs.

Then he removed his hands from hers and resumed unbuttoning her silk T-shirt.

Afterwards she turned away from him and lay on her side, looking out of the window at the blue sky that framed the top of a grey stone building. Two enormous pigeons were perched on its rooftop.

Carl pulled her back so she was facing him. Unlike six months earlier, she didn't like lying with her face against his chest; she was no longer besotted with all those black curls. The familiar smell of his skin no longer suffused her with love. It wasn't that it smelled unpleasant: it was that it didn't smell like Andrew's skin. Carl made her body do all those things. But where before she had adored him for it, now she didn't feel anything. She'd never had that happen before – her body acting quite separately from her mind. Perhaps that's what it was like for women who slept around a lot. Maybe Angela felt those fantastic sensations without their having any connection with her emotions. Though she thought Angela had once told her – hadn't she? – that she didn't get a big charge out of the actual act of intercourse. Perhaps she never had the feelings Daisy had before the actual penetration – when Carl seemed to be delicately removing layer after layer until he caused a swell of desire so overwhelming that it was as if she were inside the desire. She wished she hadn't felt like that. She didn't feel anything at all now.

'Don't move. I'll order us some tea.'

'I don't want any tea, Carl. I'm going to get dressed.'

'Why?'

She was silent for a moment. 'You can make me feel like that. But I don't feel the same in other ways.'

'You're wrong.'

'How can you say that? I'm the one who must know how I feel.'

There was no reason now for him not to refer to Andrew Harwood. Carl was holding a stronger hand than he had thirty minutes earlier.

'Daisy, when I first met you, you didn't dream what pleasures lay within you, waiting to be developed. But now you know. I don't expect you to lock yourself in a sexual prison for forty, fifty years. What possible purpose would it fill? When your Mr Harwood and his other lady have completed their pleasure together, perhaps you will want to have a turn in his bed. That's all right. I'd have a stab of jealousy. But I'd understand it. The point is that it wouldn't diminish what I can offer you. You like the image of me as your teacher – out of bed as well as in it. I've only started the tutoring process. Before next year is out, you'll be in Washington with me. You'll love it. And that will be only the beginning.'

'I've got to go to the bathroom.'

When she returned to his bedroom she began to dress. He lay, naked, on one elbow, watching her.

Stepping from the cool of Brown's Hotel lobby, she noticed the whole of Albemarle Street was now in shadow. But when she reached Piccadilly, the white sun was still throwing its heat onto London town.

In Green Park quite a few couples lay in one another's arms. She not only felt detachment towards them: she felt detached from what had taken place in room 242. It was not a nice feeling.

21

Carl Myer was in London for three days and nights. On Tuesday and Wednesday Daisy had to be at the *Rampart*, but she spent all three nights in room 242. Perhaps her emotions were not as detached from him as she had thought. It was obvious she greatly enjoyed Carl's company – though it was hard to judge how much this satisfaction gained from her determination not to be dependent on Andrew's caprice. She felt she was defying Andrew.

At the disagreeable meeting in Langan's he had said he would ring her next week, yet she'd hoped he would telephone her the next day at the *Rampart*. She had intended being coldly reserved, but she wasn't given the chance: he didn't get in touch. Each evening when she entered room 242 she thought: 'This will show Andrew.'

Carl liked to play with her body and bring her almost to her climax, then abruptly check her as he drew back and surveyed her. After a few moments he would begin again, from the beginning, then stop and turn her face towards him. As soon as he let go of her face she turned it to one side on the pillow, her eyes closed while he gave his attention to her nipples, first one, then switching to the other. Without again putting his hand between her legs he could bring her almost to a frenzy of desire.

Yet immediately afterwards she felt the detachment. Outside their sexuality, she experienced none of the rapture that once she had known with him. That had been transferred to Andrew. She wished she could transfer it back to Carl. Perhaps she could if she never saw Andrew again. She resented loving Andrew when he was able to forget about her.

Minutes after Daisy arrived at the *Rampart* on Tuesday of the following week, her telephone rang.

'I don't know whether you're still tied up, but I thought I'd give a ring to say hello,' Andrew said.

She was determined to keep her words cool.

'Oh hi,' she said casually.

There were a few moments of silence which she did nothing to break.

'Is there any chance you would be free for dinner tomorrow night? There's only a two-line whip, so I can get away from the House.'

'The trouble is that I'm tied up tomorrow evening,' she lied.

'What about Friday evening?'

'I can't, Andrew. I'm sorry.'

After a pause he said: 'Is Professor Myer still here?'

'No. He left last week.'

'I see.'

Again she made no effort to break the silence.

'Had you been free for dinner this week, I'd intended raising something that I thought you might enjoy next week.'

Daisy remained silent.

'Thursday – nine days from now – will be the final evening of President Giscard's state visit. There's to be an after-dinner reception at the French Embassy. I hoped you might find it entertaining to come with me. We could have a quiet dinner first.'

After a short pause Daisy said: 'That sounds very nice.'

'Good. Are you absolutely sure it's impossible for you to be free for dinner tomorrow or Friday?'

'It's a shame, but I'm tied up. But I look forward to next week.'

After a pause he said: 'I don't suppose you'd be free for dinner on

Monday? It seems a long time since we saw each other properly.'

She weighed up her desire against tactics, and decided one week of declining to see him was sufficient.

'All right.'

When she put down the telephone she was nearly ecstatic – with exaltation that he had rung, pride that her self-control had made it possible to decline to see him for six days, joy at the prospect of next Monday and Thursday. Did his invitation to go with him to the French Embassy mean he put her in a different category from the woman who'd been with him at Langan's?

They had decided to meet at Walton's. Other diners' eyes followed her as the head waiter led her between the tables, and from the corner of her own eye she recognized five or six faces: Walton's was popular both with London's intelligentsia and show biz.

Glancing up from the wine list he was studying, Andrew's face lit with pleasure when he saw her. Despite her intention at least to start off with a distance between them, her face glowed with the happiness of being with him again.

The first taste of her martini made her tongue tingle. All of her tingled.

'You're looking ravishing,' he said.

The fact that Carl had used the same words a week before in no way reduced her delight at hearing them from Andrew.

'Thank you.'

He smiled as he kept his eyes on her face.

Daisy looked down. She didn't want her resolve to crumble: they could not take up where they had left off without any explanation from him. She had persuaded herself that her behaviour with Carl was a consequence of Andrew's promiscuity, a punishment of Andrew.

'What have you been up to since last we met?' he said.

'Oh, different things.'

'I see.'

He lit a cigarette, blew the smoke away from her, and watched her. He was not entirely certain how to proceed.

'There are some things we should talk about,' he said.

Daisy looked at him briefly and then turned her attention to her martini. One of the olives had been stabbed with a toothpick which she had removed but now re-inserted to lift out the gin-soaked olive and begin nibbling it away from its stone. As Andrew watched her, they both felt the enjoyable tension tightening.

'How hungry are you?' he said.

'Not very.'

'It's so hot, what would you think of having the gazpacho or a plate of smoked salmon? We could have a glass of champagne with it. Then we could have an interval – leave here and go some-place cooler to have our serious talk – at Eaton Place or your flat, whichever you preferred. Impossible to have a serious conversation among all these sweltering diners. We could ask if a table might be free for us to come back for our second course.'

Despite her resolve to be reticent, Daisy burst out laughing. It was such a lovely idea. And it *was* too hot to eat two courses, one right after the other.

Like the first time she had mounted the marble staircase, she was acutely aware of him several stairs behind her, his face on a level with her swinging hips. They had agreed that Eaton Place would be cooler. He had made no attempt to touch her.

He threw wide the windows in the drawing room.

'It's nearly the longest day of the year,' he said. 'Unless you yearn for more light, I shan't switch any on just yet.'

'At home in the summer we never switch the lights on until we have to. They add more heat.'

'Do you mind if I take off my jacket and tie?'

Daisy watched him undo the top button of his shirt. Something deep within her moved. She tore her eyes away.

'I have some champagne in the fridge. Do you think that would be a pleasant accompaniment to our serious talk?'

They sat facing each other in the armchairs either side of the fireplace.

'Who begins?' he said.

'I think you should.'

'In one way it was too bad that we should have collided like that at Langan's. On the other hand, I'm glad to have met Carl Myer. You've been pretty reticent about him. You could say it was none of my business. Of course I knew from Giles that you and Myer have been very involved with each other. As he came to London to see you, I assume that still is the case.'

'I assume you are involved with any number of women,' Daisy said with asperity, the thought of it having immediately made her bristle. And she resented that *she* should be the one put on the defensive.

'I wouldn't describe my side activities as involvement,' Andrew said. 'Self-indulgence, yes.'

He was entirely open in his manner with her.

'I've never told you that I don't go out with other women, because I do – though less and less, I might tell you. But it's an agreeable habit more than anything else. And it has nothing whatsoever to do with my feelings for you. As it happens, I love you.'

Daisy's eyes were fixed on his.

'You've never said that before.'

'I'm saying it now.'

After a minute they looked away from each other, both taking a sip of their champagne.

'I'm not sure I want to know about your life with Carl Myer,' Andrew said. 'But I need to know this: Are you in love with him now?'

When she answered it was in a low voice. 'No.'

'Do you love me?'

Her voice remained low. 'Yes.'

'Will you come and lie on my bed?'

She hesitated before saying: 'All right.'

The moist heat of the room made her think of New Orleans and *A Streetcar Named Desire*. Or was that image stirred by the liquid lilting voice of Ella Fitzgerald as it drifted through the open window, singing 'Basin Street Blues' on a stereo in another house in Belgravia? Daisy felt a delicious tremor at her heightened awareness of being alone in another country in this man's bedroom.

As she stood watching him, he threw the cover and top sheet over the foot of the bed. Kneeling, he removed one of her high-heeled sandals, then the other. It had been too hot to wear tights.

He took down her lace panties and she stepped out of them. Then he stood up and looked into her face.

'Why are you smiling?' she said.

'Pleasure.'

Her sleeveless silk blouse was tied at the front with half a dozen silk ribbons. At the same time as the slight smile played over his face, his expression was concentrated as he untied the ribbons, starting with the top one.

He tossed the little piece of cloth onto the carpet and put his arms around her to unfasten her lace bra – the same champagne-colour as the silk that now lay on the floor. His hands were moist from the heat as they moved over her moist body to remove this last small piece of covering.

He stepped back and looked at her.

'So,' he said.

He laid her on his bed, on her back, and as she watched him he took off his own clothes.

He placed his hands flat against the inside of her thighs and parted them. Kneeling on the bed with one knee between her thighs, he placed one of her arms almost at a right angle to her body, the sensitive inside of the arm facing up.

'I think I'll begin here,' he said.

As the fingertips began the tantalizing, she felt the steady pressure of his knee between her thighs, and her entire body quickened. He didn't hurry.

'We have all the time in the world,' he said.

22

President Giscard d'Estaing began his state visit in the fourth week of June. He and his wife and entourage had flown to Gatwick airport in time to board a train to Victoria Station and be disgorged at twelve-thirty sharp. Everyone knew the British Queen was obsessed with timetables. It was paramount that their horsedrawn coaches arrive at Buckingham Palace at precisely one o'clock; otherwise lunch would be delayed.

The President had to admit that the British equalled the French when it came to ceremonial pomp and splendour. He looked with admiration at the gleaming chestnut flanks of the four horses drawing the carriage in which he sat beside the British monarch, President and Queen each deigning to lift one hand to the crowds lining the sidewalks, both wishing their panoply wasn't stuck to them in this unbelievable heat. It was one of the hottest summers recorded in Britain.

Very soon it was plain that this visit was going to have more than the usual tribulations. The President had never known such inadequate security as was provided for him and his entourage at Buckingham Palace. And he was astounded that he should be asked to give two of France's highest awards of merit to the

Queen's Lord Chamberlain *and* a lady-in-waiting.

Yet he had to say that the first evening's banquet at the Palace was quite splendid, the Royal Marines band alternating French and British melodies and marches. Even in this land which he privately detested, he found that as he stood at the top table in front of these enthralled people, he enjoyed the sense that he was God. A spirited rendering of 'La Marseillaise' always produced that effect on him.

But the essential English gaucherie manifested itself the next day at Downing Street. At lunch he, Giscard d'Estaing, President of France, found himself seated facing a painting of the Duke of Wellington. Had the British Prime Minister been honoured with lunch at the Elysée Palace, Napoleon's painting would have been covered with a curtain. A century and a half after Waterloo, the English still had not grasped these fundamental courtesies.

Lunch at Downing Street the following day was less offensive. The President's staff had conveyed his displeasure. This time the seating arrangement was inverted: the President sat with his back to the Duke of Wellington.

Now here he was hosting a return banquet for the British monarch in his own French Embassy, and one might as well be on the equator. The temperature must be ninety-eight degrees. Intolerable that his ambassador had been so preoccupied with his bourgeois snobberies that he'd never thought to have air-conditioning installed. And it did seem strange that they were compelled to have the curtains drawn against broad daylight merely because an interior decorator had told the ambassadress that this would show the rooms – newly refurbished for the state visit – to better effect. The airless drawing room was more uncomfortable than anywhere the President had yet found himself incarcerated by duty. Women, fanning themselves, at least had the good fortune to wear low cut gowns. The men were wedged into white tie and tails, some appearing uncertain of survival as sweat dripped steadily onto their starched white fronts.

Most of the garden was filled with an enormous marquee. Here, while the honoured guests sealed in the house were coping with their *framboises frappées*, lesser mortals were gathering, at least a quarter of them household names. Politicians, journalists, television presenters, famous actors, along with the usual crowd of high-ranking civil servants and ambassadors and their ladies, sipped champagne and sweated from the heat as they looked over the shoulder of whoever they were talking to.

Inside the house the Queen's lady-in-waiting frowned at her discreet platinum watch. The French were impossible: no sense of time.

At eleven minutes past the appointed hour of ten o'clock, everyone under the marquee looked up as the central doors onto broad stone steps descending into the garden were thrown wide. Through them stepped the Queen, tiara sparkling, beside her the French President, imperial and imperious.

'Oh look,' said Daisy. 'The woman coming down the steps just behind the Queen: the one in the pink dress. I interviewed her. Do you remember? Do you think we could go say hello?'

'We'll see you later,' Andrew said to the broadcaster and his wife whom they'd been talking to just before the doors had opened.

'Hullo. I came to interview you last month. I'm Daisy Brewster,' Daisy said.

'Of course I remember you. This is my husband.' The woman in the pink dress turned to the Foreign Secretary. 'This is my fellow American who did the interview for the *Rampart*. You actually enjoyed it.'

The Foreign Secretary looked at Daisy quizzically over the cheroot which he held in his lips, exhaling little clouds of smoke. Then he removed it to say: 'My wife was quite wrong to tell you that I am perverse. I cannot think of a more accommodating husband. Hullo, Andrew. I'm afraid,' he said amicably to his wife, 'that Andrew Harwood is a Tory. These things happen.'

After two minutes of chat, the Foreign Secretary looked at his watch. 'We must be going,' he said to his wife. He gave a friendly smile to Daisy. 'Goodnight. Goodnight, Andrew.'

'I didn't realize you knew each other,' Daisy said.

'We don't. But MPs know one another's names and faces. When we meet outside the debating chamber, we are usually polite, certainly when a wife or child or' – Andrew hesitated – 'chosen companion is along.'

At 11:30 on the dot the Royal Party withdrew.

By midnight the marquee was nearly empty.

The telephone rang insistently. Andrew turned on the bedside light and looked at his watch. 2:15. An hour ago he'd taken Daisy back to her flat.

He reached for the telephone. 'Yes?'

'It's Nelly. I'm in a difficulty.'

The words weren't slurred. What was it that was odd about them? He realized: Nelly was enunciating with unusual care. Immediately Andrew was wide awake, intent.

'Where are you?'

'In dear old Chelsea Police Station. I thought it best to give my lawyer a ring. I don't suppose you could come along?'

'Yep. Tell me first: what's happened?'

'Their view is that I was not driving my best. They have also got it into their heads that I may have been using illegal substances.'

'They're holding you on suspicion only?'

'Yes. They want me to take a saliva or blood test. I don't want to.'

'I see.' He sounded neither critical nor sympathetic. He assumed the police could be listening on another line.

'They're wrong about the drugs, Andrew.'

'Then why won't you take the saliva or blood test?'

'It's so undignified.'

For the first time Andrew smiled, if only faintly.

'I'll be along as soon as I can. It's been at least a year since I've called on you at Chelsea Police Station. Mustn't get out of practice.'

As they'd have a record of the last time, best to refer to it, he thought as he put down the telephone. He'd better shave.

At 4 am Nelly agreed to give a blood sample: though he couldn't remember how to calculate the percentages, he knew his alcohol level would have fallen by then. At 4:15 the Harwood brothers left the police station and got into Andrew's car. By now Nelly seemed quite sober.

'Well, *will* the test show you were using drugs?'

'No – assuming you are not referring to the demon drink. True,

I *might* have been smoking a substance considered even more reprehensible than nicotine. In fact I wasn't.'

'Why did they think you were?'

'Oh, Andrew. You know what they're like. Nark and grass. Everybody who goes to that gay club knows there are plainclothes police there, looking for an excuse, any excuse, to pick up a gay on suss and then have a feel up, allegedly to discover if he's carrying a kilo of dope or an arsenal tucked behind his balls.'

For the thousandth time Andrew was irritated by the usurping of the adjective 'gay': there was no satisfactory substitute for it in the English language.

'I'm sorry to have involved you in this,' Nelly said. 'I suppose it would be better if I got another lawyer one of these days. But with luck no reporter will choose today to call in the station on the off chance of finding a familiar name on the charge sheets.'

Andrew said nothing.

'When a copper takes it on himself to ring a press contact and volunteer a tidbit, what do you suppose is the copper's payoff?' Nelly asked.

'A case of whisky? I don't know. Ask Giles. "Institutionalized minor corruption" is what he calls it.'

'Well, with luck the boys in blue won't have recognized you.'

Andrew said nothing.

'What do you think of young Master Nelly's latest escapade?'

Daisy jumped. When Ben came up behind her chair like this and announced his presence, it felt like Jehovah. She turned to see him standing there, grinning.

He thrust the early edition of the *Evening Standard* onto her desk, folded over so that instead of the departing French President being on top, looking up at her was a photograph of Nelson Harwood. *'MP's brother "over legal limit".'*

'You'll enjoy reading between the lines,' Ben said, 'especially the bit about his being stopped as he drove away from that perverts' den.'

'Will you be referring to it in this Sunday's *Rampart?*'

Ben's laugh was insolent.

'Worried about his big brother? You needn't be – this time.

There's no further news value in Nelly's drink charge until it comes before the court. And frankly, Daisy, I can't be bothered to give Andrew Harwood free publicity in my column so soon after he last had the honour to be mentioned there.'

Her face was expressionless.

'But you might tell him something, Daisy, when next you see him. If he goes even half as far as he thinks he's going in politics, he's carrying a time bomb. Before Nelly Harwood is done, he'll blow the floor out from under his brother's public career. Mark my words.'

23

Mr and Mrs Brewster came to London for the first twelve days of August. They too chose to stay at Brown's Hotel – something about its discreetly expensive solidness, presumably. Daisy was thankful that at least they were not in room 242.

She waited on the same damask-covered sofa where she'd waited six weeks earlier. She remembered how she had advised her parents not to come until August, imagining she and Carl would be together during July. In the event, she had written asking him not to return in July – though she did not acknowledge the parting as final. Carl saw no reason why when Daisy returned to the States next year they shouldn't take up where they'd left off last January. She knew it wouldn't happen.

'Good evening, dear,' her mother said.

'Hullo, darling,' said her father.

They were an elegant couple, and something in their manner made it immediately apparent to strangers that they enjoyed each other's company. Daisy always felt proud when she was with them.

Yet this evening she experienced anxiety. Was she more concerned about how they would feel about Andrew, or how Andrew would see them? At any rate, after the way they had carried on about Carl, they could hardly find much fault with Andrew.

The taxi driver let them out at St Stephen's entrance. The only time Mr and Mrs Brewster had previously dined at the House was with the Lord Chancellor in the last Tory government.

'Where are we to meet your young man?'

Mrs Brewster employed that phrase when she was speaking of a specific admirer of her daughter, otherwise referring to them as 'beaux' (with the exception of Professor Myer whom she managed not to call anything). Nothing could have induced her to speak of 'boyfriends'.

Although her daughter hadn't said so, it was evident that the man they were to meet tonight was someone special in her life. Mr and Mrs Brewster shared the same mixed feelings: if this meant Carl Myer was now a thing of the past, thank God; but it would be sad if his replacement, however suitable, lived on Europe's side of the Atlantic.

When they reached the Central Lobby, there was no need to ask a policeman to telephone Andrew: he was already there, talking to another MP who rested one hand on the outsize shoe of Gladstone standing sternly on his plinth.

Andrew came forward to greet them. Together they strolled past the Pre-Raphaelite frescoes, Mrs Brewster noting to herself that the three Cabots kneeling to receive their charter from Henry VII were ancestors of her mother. At the foot of the great double staircase that Daisy loved, they went through the door to the terrace. There, with the river flowing past, the sun's red deepening as it approached Chelsea's turrets and towers, all four started to relax over a drink. Mr and Mrs Brewster began to size up Andrew while he in turn felt them out, acutely aware that they were Daisy's background. She acted as mediator, introducing subjects in which they might have a common interest.

By the time they went into the Members' Dining Room, all four were confident their evening would prove a success.

The day after Daisy's parents flew back to Philadelphia, satisfied with the way their daughter's life seemed to be going, though uncertain how her relationship with Andrew Harwood would turn out, Parliament at last rose for the summer recess.

Two days later Rachel Fisher went into a small private nursing home in Surrey: her gynaecologist didn't like the vacuum method for aborting fourteen-week-old embryos.

Her name was entered on the hospital form as Mrs Sarah Green. The nursing staff were polite in a distant way.

Early the following afternoon, some hours after she came out of the general anaesthetic, the surgeon called in her room.

'Everything went well, Mrs Green. You can go home tomorrow morning. I want you to take things easily for six or seven days. Even though you may not feel it now, these things are a shock to the system. You'll be glad to know there is no reason why you should not have another child when your life is better able to handle it.'

'The scan showed it was a girl. I just want to make sure.'

'I don't understand you.'

'It *was* a little girl?'

'Oh. Well, yes.'

The surgeon looked uncomfortable. Even when an embryo was malformed, it wasn't an agreeable operation. And there appeared to be nothing whatsoever the matter with the fourteen-week foetus he had just extracted – except that the mother didn't want it (he didn't care to personalize with a gender the neatly formed pathetic little creature he'd removed).

He was a tolerant man: he genuinely believed that the mother should have the right to decide. Even so, when the decision was taken simply as a matter of convenience, it did seem a bit bloody much for the woman then to take an interest in which sex she had just consigned to the rubbish bin.

Though she was booked in as Mrs Green, he knew perfectly well it wasn't her name. The doctor who had made the referral was required to tell him her real name was Rachel Fisher. Then by chance, reading his *Daily Telegraph*, he'd seen a reference to a new MP of the same name – Rachel Fisher, unmarried – and a small photograph of her with other MPs.

He looked down at the woman lying before him, her pale distressed face surrounded by damp dark hair that lay limp on the pillow. He'd yet to see a woman come round from a general anaesthetic with hair that had kept its bounce.

'Let me know if you are worried about any side effects. I shouldn't think there will be any. Everything was perfectly normal.'

He opened the door and went out, shutting it firmly behind him.

Rachel lay with her hand on her emptied belly, her eyes closed, tears seeping from under the lids. She was sure the loss would have been less had it been a boy. A girl is so much more vulnerable – even, she felt, in the womb. Long before the scan – from the beginning – she had guessed it was a little girl. She always thought of her not as a girl, but as a little girl.

When a nurse came in an hour later to take her blood pressure, Rachel didn't open her eyes. There were no visitors and no telephone calls. For the rest of that day and evening she spoke to none of the staff who entered her room.

Nor did she ever speak again of the daughter she had thrown away, though once, much later, she would allude to it, strangely, in a letter to Andrew Harwood.

II

In The Limelight

24

'Jameson's broken body, still attached to his shredded parachute, was found earlier this evening on the north Wales mountainside by a shepherd, Mr Elwyn Martin. Mr Martin contacted the police who immediately went to the area and sealed it off. The pilot was making the final tests on the Raider fighter which was due to be delivered next week to the Ministry of Defence. There is no trace of the plane itself.'

'Christ.'

Ben could actually feel the rush of adrenalin as he saw a big story at his fingertips. For in his left hand he held the tearoff sheet of the Press Association news flash, his right hand resting against the slanted wooden stand on which lay a shiny facsimile front page. The huge cellar room in which he stood had the acrid smell of newsprint and was always called the stone, even though the electricians' method of printing had nothing in common with the stone used by the old linotype operators.

The absence of windows made the atmosphere airless, like a vault, and as usual Ben had left his waistcoat and tie in his office upstairs. His shirt was undone at the throat, the sleeves rolled up. He carried his forty-eight years lightly. His burly frame appeared little altered, and while the brown hair had thinned, the face had the same ruddy fleshiness. Entirely unchanged was the disconcerting intense blue of his eyes.

He had just directed a sub-editor to make a last change before the front page was ready to roll when the deputy news editor, Joyce Barlow, appeared on the stone and handed him the flimsy sheet that had glided from a fax machine, unfolding soundlessly the fact of the Raider pilot's violent end.

Ben turned to the sub. 'You'll have to hold the page.'

He strode over to where the news editor, Tommy Lowell, stood in front of a facsimile page two. Ben handed the sheet to Tommy who read it and at once turned away from page two.

As the three got in the lift, Ben said to Joyce: 'You write the story. I want to see it by 10:25. It's got to be subbed by 10:30 and off the stone by 10:45. You can improve it for the later editions.' She looked at the clock on the wall of the lift: five past ten.

He said to Tommy: 'You ring Harwood. We've got all his telephone numbers. If you can't reach him, get one of his junior ministers.'

They stepped out directly into the immense open-plan newsroom. The architects had exploited the unpartitioned original interior of an East End warehouse when the *Rampart* joined the exodus from Fleet Street.

Once Rupert Murdoch had made the midnight flit to Wapping in 1986, breaking forever the print unions' grip, it was only a matter of time before the other national newspapers followed suit. Most editors – Benjamin Franwell a conspicuous exception – were too mealy-mouthed to say publicly how grateful they were that Murdoch had ended the tyranny which enabled the old-style printers, at 10 pm, to demand cash in unmarked envelopes if the morning paper was to appear. Now operating costs could be quartered, and cheaper premises were possible. Soon all newspaper proprietors had no option except to leave Fleet Street a ghost street: there was no other way to compete with Murdoch.

Journalists, whether they voiced it or not, welcomed the knowledge that their own work would no longer be wrecked by the caprice of a few linotype operators. But they groused about leaving the familiar watering holes of Fleet Street for the alien dockland, long emptied of ships, which spread east from Tower Bridge. Lunching with a Cabinet minister or anyone else in the West End now entailed half an hour's travel each way. Midday trysts weren't easy.

The *Rampart* stood within a huge four-storey warehouse, its brick shell built in 1820, the gleaming white interior and fluorescent lighting installed in 1988. The windows on one side looked out on the occasional barge gliding past. Across the Thames, behind the Victorian warehouses converted into swanky *pieds-à-terre* for executives in the City, rose the new high-rise blocks with their high-price flats. To the west, past the first bend in the river, Tower Bridge was outlined against the sky, and immediately beside it the turrets of the Tower of London.

The newsroom took up almost the entire top floor – nearly a hundred desks in all, each with its keyboard and screen for direct input. At one end was a door. Beyond it was an office for the editor's two personal assistants. Beyond that was Ben's room.

It was almost a carbon copy of his room in Fleet Street – white walls, thick black Wilton carpet, black furniture except for the massive mahogany desk, the outsize chesterfield lately re-covered, the black leather of the two Eames chairs and their ottomans slightly dulled from a decade and a half of use. Fixed to the wall behind the desk was the square of steel engraved with the blown-up map of Britain.

This late on a Saturday night no more than twenty newsroom journalists were still at their desks, almost all – except the subs – using their telephones. The secretaries had packed up for the week. Most of the hard core of top journalists were downstairs on the stone.

When they stepped out of the lift at six minutes past ten, Joyce Barlow went straight to her desk with its keyboard and screen. Tommy Lowell followed the editor through the door at the end.

There was no one in the first room: one of Ben's personal assistants usually left at seven on Saturday evenings, the other at nine. The connecting door to his room stood ajar.

'Telephone from out here,' he said to Tommy. 'If you can't

reach Harwood and you can't reach one of his junior ministers, get *anybody* at the MoD and get 'em to say *anything*. I'll start a new leader.'

Ben's signed column, his lethal toy, was in the middle of the leader page. Above it, running across the top quarter of the page, was the unsigned leader, sometimes written by a deputy under Ben's direction, more often written by Ben.

He went into his own room, leaving the door open.

Daisy was lying on her back, waiting. The top sheet was turned back so that it covered her only up to the waist, and one leg was thrown outside it. She wore a fine-mesh gold coiled necklace that looked a little like a snake. Otherwise she was naked.

Through the wall that divided the bedroom and Andrew's study, she would hear when he opened the study door to walk through the hall to their bedroom. He would 'join her', he had said with mock formality, in ten minutes.

She loved it when he came to bed before they were so tired that they wanted simply to put their arms around each other and fall asleep. What he often called, with the same self-mocking formality, 'an early evening' had become an infrequent luxury. She remained intrigued by everything about Andrew. She was proud of his work as a senior Cabinet minister; nonetheless there were times when she looked at the ministerial red boxes he'd brought home and she hated them.

After her bath when she had been smoothing oils into her body, thinking about her own sexuality had produced the delicious awareness of the place within her loins opening slightly and then the excitement of its being poised, faintly quivering, waiting to open further.

Outside the bedroom door she had propped the seven-by-nine-inch sign, rather crumpled from use, that Sophie had made as a Christmas present some years before. Though Daisy had asked for the present, the design was entirely Sophie's. She had chosen various poster paints for the birds that fluttered around the edge of her cardboard sign; the hearts were painted in bright pink; the message was written in large scrolled turquoise letters, each carefully filled in with pink: 'DO NOT DISTURB'. Lest Matty feel left out, he had been asked to make a sign to go outside his parents' bedroom in the Waymere farmhouse, but as Matty was a year and a half younger and less artistic than Sophie, his sign was not so beautiful, though the message was the same: 'DO NOT DISTURB'. Daisy didn't like to lock the door against the children, and their painted signs had seemed a viable alternative. Only once – soon after the advent of the signs – had Matty come barging in, and while it hadn't been too embarrassing a moment, Andrew was sharp with him, and Matty had not ignored the sign again. Daisy might also say to the children: 'If the telephone rings for Andrew or me, could you take a message? We're going to have a rest and don't want to be disturbed.' But as it was after ten this evening she hadn't bothered. On the whole the children appeared to regard themselves as colluders in their parents' desire for some 'rest', though Matty occasionally pulled a face.

Daisy heard the study door open.

Immediately the government's scrambler telephone in the study rang.

The wall muffled Andrew's voice so she couldn't hear what he was saying.

Five minutes later the bedroom door finally opened.

He looked at Daisy, waiting for him, closed the door behind him, and lay down in his clothes on his side of the bed, propping himself on his left elbow, reaching over with his right hand to touch the golden snake.

'I'm sorry, Daisy. That was the resident clerk at Defence. Something has come up. So much for our lovely early evening.'

He gave a rueful smile, leaning over to kiss lightly the breast where the snake lay, before he got to his feet. They could both hear the ordinary telephone ringing in the study.

'Do you terribly mind answering it, Daisy, while I think for a moment?'

She reached for the bedside extension and switched it on again. 'Hullo?'

'Is that Mrs Harwood?'

'Yes.'

'It's Tommy Lowell at the *Rampart*. We've not seen each other for getting on to fifteen years. I hope you're keeping well.'

'Hullo, Tommy. Yes. What about you?' She pulled the bed sheet up to cover her breasts.

'I feel pretty much the same. What I look like is something else, I expect. Look, is your husband there? Something important has come up and I need to check it out with him.'

Daisy hesitated. 'Could you tell me what it's about, Tommy?'

She looked at Andrew standing in the doorway.

'It's about a fighter that Stockton Air Space is due to deliver to the MoD. It's disappeared. The pilot's body has been found. This is the third body of someone working for Stockton that has been discovered in the last three months.'

'Oh. Hang on.'

Andrew left the bedroom and went into the study. Daisy put the telephone on the pillow, draped around her a shirt he'd earlier left hanging over the back of his bedroom armchair, and followed him.

'It's the *Rampart*'s news editor, Tommy Lowell,' she said. 'I used to know him. He says that a pilot testing a plane for you has been found dead. He says the pilot's body is the third one to be found in the last three months.'

'Actually, the other poor blighters weren't flying the planes. You mentioned one of them to me when you read about it at the time because his death was so bizarre.'

He picked up the regular telephone that stood beside the red scrambler. 'Hullo.'

Daisy returned to the bedroom and replaced the telephone extension before exchanging the shirt for her own coral silk dressing gown, her auburn curls gleaming a deeper shade of the silk. Ah well.

In the hall she glanced up at the next floor. She couldn't tell whether the voices were coming from Sophie's room or Matty's – whichever it was, they'd closed the door. Along with their two voices she heard 'Eleanor Rigby'. Funny that once again children had fallen in love with the Beatles. Was it too late for Matty still to be up? Not really. He was almost twelve. And she had to admit that she was glad to have Sophie occupied on a Saturday evening. Since Sophie had turned thirteen, the question of her Saturday evenings had become a thorn in the flesh.

Daisy opened the door to the study and closed it behind her. The armchairs standing either side of the fireplace were rather more battered than when she had first seen them in his Eaton Place flat fifteen years earlier. She sat down in the one facing his.

He kept his eyes fixed on a middle distance as he concentrated on the voice at the other end of the telephone line. Daisy watched him.

'Yeah. We are all worried. But you know there is absolutely nothing I can say until MoD investigators have given me a report. They've only just got to the scene where Jameson's body was found. We'll have to leave things at that for now.'

Tommy Lowell must have accepted that this was all he was going to get out of the Defence Secretary. He thanked Andrew.

'Goodbye,' Andrew replied in a friendly manner.

As he put down the telephone he looked at his wife. 'Do you feel like making us a highball?'

The red telephone rang – the scrambler.

'Hullo? ... Martin. I thought I'd be hearing from you.'

Martin Thrower was the principal private secretary to the Defence Secretary. While the two men were talking on the scrambler, the ordinary telephone rang. Andrew frowned.

Daisy put down the soda syphon and went into the bedroom to pick up the extension there. 'Hullo?'

It was the *Sunday Times*.

'He's on the other line.'

'I'll wait,' said the *Sunday Times* news editor.

As usual on Sundays, the children fended for themselves at breakfast time. Andrew remained asleep until Daisy reappeared with a large tray and set out fresh juice, bacon, and a teapot on a small table by the window: early in their marriage he had persuaded her that he couldn't eat in bed. She got back into her side of it, propping up the pillows, her breakfast and coffee pot on the table beside her. They shared the five newspapers.

The short news accounts, most towards the bottom of the front page, were much the same. Only the *Rampart* led with the story. Tommy Lowell was exact with the facts.

Ben Franwell's unsigned leader used the facts for his own purpose:

> Less than four months ago a Stockton Air Space engineer was found decapitated in his car. He had been engaged on an 'entirely conventional' secret project for the Ministry of Defence. An inquiry concluded the engineer had decapitated himself. Rather an odd way to kill yourself. And if he was working on something entirely conventional, why was it kept secret?
>
> Two months ago a Stockton scientist's car was found under twelve feet of water in the River Tees, the scientist inside it. It was mere coincidence, we were told, that this man too was engaged on secret MoD contracts.
>
> Yesterday evening a test pilot's body was found on a north Wales mountainside, his shredded parachute now his shroud. John Jameson was making the final tests on Stockton's Raider fighter, the first of the seventy-two aircraft ordered by the MoD for its ES6 programme.
>
> Where is the plane this morning? Why is its pilot lying on a slab in Bristol Mortuary?
>
> We all know Mr Andrew Harwood enjoys the trappings of high office. Is it asking too much for the Defence Secretary to turn away from these vanities long enough to remember he has a job to do?
>
> Or does Mr Harwood find nothing strange in three people, all working on MoD contracts, meeting mysterious and violent ends?
>
> As he reposes in his bedroom this Sunday morning, basking in his wife's affection, should he not spare a thought for the wife – now widow – of John Jameson?

Passing her the *Rampart*, folded inside out, the leader page on top, Andrew said to his wife: 'Ben Franwell hasn't lost his touch.'

25

On Wednesday morning a Bridgwater trawler was fishing in the Atlantic off southwest Ireland. The boatswain noticed strips of silver-grey sparkling as they bobbed on the waves. As the trawler chugged closer, the linesman keeping his eye on the cables drawn taut by the net dragging five hundred feet below, the boatswain saw that the silver-grey strips floating on the water were bits of metal fabric. Most of them had jagged edges.

'How deep is the sea where the wreckage is lying?' Andrew asked.

'About two thousand feet,' Martin Thrower replied to his Minister. 'There's a chance the black box can be retrieved.'

'And the cockpit? And its canopy? And the pilot's seat? Unless some more stuff is found on that Welsh mountainside, it means that nothing came out of the plane with Jameson except his shredded parachute.'

'Our people and Stockton are scouring the mountain,' said Martin. 'Odd to think of the plane flying nearly four hundred miles on autopilot before coming to its own end.'

Andrew didn't reply. Both men were imagining what could have happened had the plane been pointing the other way when

John Jameson, for some reason, was ejected, and the Raider flew in a straight line until its fuel ran out and it plunged from the sky. Andrew found himself visualizing Sophie on her way to school. Immediately he switched his mind to the pilot's parachute. When was it torn to bits?

'The team of crash investigators say there's no reason to think Jameson was inclined to suicide,' Martin said.

'How long is it likely to be before any of the wreckage in the sea can be salvaged?'

'It's too soon even to guess, Minister. Fighter aircraft's director says they'll start negotiations with private contractors next week.'

'I want to see Cartwright today.'

Charles Cartwright was the civil servant in charge of F-section which dealt with private contracts for fighter aircraft.

'And you'd better ask Barthmore to come along at the same time.'

Austin Barthmore was the Permanent Under Secretary, or PUS, the top civil servant at Defence.

The Ministry of Defence had none of the majesty of the Foreign and Commonwealth Office on the other side of Whitehall. The FCO was designed to impress nineteenth-century ambassadors from the far-flung empire: Britannia ruled the waves. The MoD was strictly utilitarian, constructed in the prewar 1930s. Its present occupants called it 'East Berlin style'. You could drive past its boring concrete facade in Richmond Terrace without noticing it was there.

Martin Thrower had been principal private secretary to Andrew's predecessor, an Old Harrovian who thought you got your way by shouting. Martin knew that Andrew's style was the more effective. In the fifteen months he'd served Andrew, he had become fond of the man. Had that not been so, Martin Thrower would still have been loyal to his minister – though as always in this situation, the loyalty would have been split.

For the civil servants who make up a minister's private office are curiously placed: they are double agents. One loyalty, transferable, is to their political boss. The other loyalty, continuous, is to the department's civil service head, the PUS. How the private secretary balances the two depends largely on his personal feelings for the minister.

There were four private secretaries junior to Martin, two men, two women. All five had desks in the office immediately outside the Minister's room.

Because Martin Thrower both respected and liked Andrew, he talked to his minister with an intelligent discretion which was invaluable to Andrew, enabling him rapidly to discover strengths and weaknesses of the Ministry.

Andrew was unconvinced that Charles Cartwright was the right person for his job. He had already raised the question with Barthmore who was responsible for the personnel side of the department. Barthmore had said that he himself would keep a close eye on the director of F-section.

'How long, Charles, do you expect it to take for the contractors to submit their estimates for the job?'

'I'd like to be able to give you an answer, Minister. But what's left of the Raider is lying two thousand feet beneath the surface of the Atlantic. No doubt it is fortunate that the sea at that point is only a sixth of the depth of where the *Titanic* rests. Nonetheless, salvaging is not certain, let alone easy.'

Andrew beetled his brows. He did dislike Cartwright's schoolmaster manner, at once obsequious and all-knowing.

'And you have stressed, Minister, that when we give out our contracts, we must get value for money. Once I have the submissions, I'll begin negotiating between them.'

'You do realize that there is some urgency about our retrieving the seat of the aircraft and the black box?' Andrew said. 'Until then the entire ES6 programme has ground to a halt. There's a limited amount we're likely to learn from what remains of the pilot.'

Martin Thrower glanced up from the note he was making.

Barthmore's bland face gazed impenetrably at the man he'd put in charge of handling fighter aircraft.

Cartwright said: 'I shall arrange for invitations to submit tenders to be on the desks of appropriate salvage firms on Monday, Minister.'

Andrew turned to Barthmore. 'Am I right, Austin, in thinking today is Wednesday?'

The PUS said to Cartwright: 'I'm sure F-section can provide a list of appropriate salvage firms by tomorrow – which is the Minister's day for answering questions in the House. As these begin at 2:30 in the afternoon, I see no reason for the necessary letters not to be on the desks of the salvage firms by then. You will need to fax them.'

The four men were sitting in the Minister's enormous room on the sixth floor. On two of its walls hung pictures selected by Daisy from the government's picture collection for use in ministers' departmental rooms. Andrew had asked her to choose pictures appropriate to the MoD. The curator had turned down her first choices; the best pictures and sculptures, he said, were earmarked for the Washington and Paris embassies. Only those few Cabinet ministers who had official homes, like the Foreign Secretary and the Chancellor, qualified for the finer quality works of art.

On one long wall hung poignant coloured engravings of First War trench-fighting. (There was no depiction of what took place when the generals ordered their officers and men out of the trenches and into the fields of the Somme, Passchendaele and the rest.) On another wall hung three big oil paintings by war artists of the Second War – two Spitfires, one crippled, over Dover; 8th Army tanks lurching towards Rommel's Panzers; a 2nd Parachute Brigade soldier making his lonely reconnaissance just below the rubble that housed German headquarters on top of Monte Cassino. Maps were pinned to the wall behind the desk. The fourth consisted of windows looking across the Embankment and the Thames, St Paul's dome rising beyond a bend in the river.

Most Cabinet ministers' rooms had a marvellous view but a wholly unremarkable assemblage of Heal's furniture chosen by the Public Services Agency. When Michael Heseltine was Defence Secretary, however, his private office staged a coup during the twenty-four-hour hiatus after the 1983 election: the matching Georgian furniture which once had graced the room of the First Lord of the Admiralty was whisked into the Defence Secretary's room – where it would remain long after Heseltine gathered up his papers and walked out of the Cabinet Room and out of his job.

At the top end of the room, facing the door, was the elegant Georgian desk with a kneehole on either side. Nearby stood the mahogany bookcase – damaged where Churchill, when First Lord, had kicked it.

Under the First War engravings was the chesterfield with its buttoned blue leather, flanked by two matching armchairs. Two dozen straight blue leather chairs stood against the walls, ready to be placed in three arcs facing the sofa when the Defence Secretary held large meetings with his generals and admirals and their staff. (Two of the straight chairs had arms for service chiefs just below armchair rank but above those who sat in the other straight chairs.)

In front of the windows was the hexagonal table for smaller meetings.

For some meetings, particularly with his junior ministers and other MPs, Andrew moved over to the sofa. For this one he remained at his desk. Across from him the PUS sat in a straight chair with arms, the director of F-section in an ordinary straight chair. Martin Thrower's chair was placed in a kind of no man's land at one side of the desk.

'The autopsy should be completed tomorrow, Minister,' Martin said.

'And Stockton?'

'They are taking apart the ejector seat in similar aircraft, Minister,' said Cartwright.

'We'd better get Stockton's chairman in here tomorrow evening or Friday morning. We've not had the pleasure of his company for at least a month.'

Martin looked up from his note-taking in time to see something like a small smile, were it not so bleak, flicker on Andrew's face.

'And will you ask him, Martin, to bring his chief designer with him?'

At 12:30 the next day, Downing Street was crowded with fifteen black Rovers and four Jaguars as their drivers waited for Cabinet to end. Beside each Jaguar with its bullet-proof windows stood a

Special Branch detective. Unlike the Rover, the XJ6 was fast despite the weight of the armour against landmines. The Jaguars belonged to 'Grade A' Cabinet ministers.

One detective, Inspector Denis Spearman, stood beside the only Jaguar that was not black. Its driver was Ollie Brown. When a Cabinet minister changes jobs, he can take his government driver with him. Ollie had driven Andrew when he was Industry Secretary. Ollie now drove the dark blue armoured Jaguar of the Defence Secretary.

Cabinet finished just before one o'clock. A few minutes later the front door of Number Ten opened, and eighteen men and one woman came out and went to their cars.

Andrew handed his red box to Ollie.

'I'll walk,' he said.

With Denis Spearman keeping pace a few feet behind him, the Defence Secretary strode the short distance to the MoD for a sandwich lunch and coffee at his desk.

At 2:15 he left the Ministry and got into the back of the dark blue Jaguar outside the front door. Denis took the front seat alongside Ollie. Martin Thrower climbed in the other back door.

As they drove to the House of Commons, Andrew rested one hand on the door panel, and Martin noticed the knuckles were white. Each time he accompanied a minister to Question Time in the House of Commons, Martin thought afresh how glad he was not to be a politician.

The police at the gate saluted and waved the car through into New Palace Yard.

At 2:28 the Defence Secretary appeared from behind the Speaker's Chair in the Chamber and took his place on the government front bench. At 2:30 the Speaker called out: 'Mr. Harwood.'

The first question was a routine one from a Labour unilateralist concerned about the new base north of the Humber. The second question was asked by an obscure Tory backbencher concerned to get his name in his constituency's local paper.

The third question, from another Labour MP, was the first to reflect a phrase of Ben Franwell's leader:

'Can the Right Honourable Gentleman tell us whether he shares the concern on all sides of this House for the three recent and entirely unconventional deaths of Stockton Air Space employees engaged in "entirely conventional" projects for the Ministry of Defence, and has he enquired into the circumstances surrounding the death of the test pilot, John Jameson?'

Andrew, having sat down as usual during the question, resumed his place standing at the dispatch box.

'As the House already knows the answer to the first half of the Honourable Gentleman's question, I'll take the House's time only on the second half. Appropriate salvage firms have received a letter from my office informing them that by Monday morning they must submit tenders for the salvage of the Raider which is lying on the ocean bed. Until the black box and the ejector seat have been recovered, it would be irresponsible for me to make a statement on the cause of Mr Jameson's death.'

Later questions from opposition Members came at the thing slightly differently, and most used innuendo based on phrases in Ben Franwell's leader.

As Ollie turned into Cheyne Street, Andrew looked at his watch. 10:45. Denis hopped out and opened the back door of the car.

The red box in one hand, Andrew glanced up at the first-floor light: Daisy must be reading in bed. The second-floor windows were dark: Sophie was asleep. Probably Matty was as well, but his bedroom was at the back. Andrew stepped lightly up the four steps to the front door, his key already in his hand. God it was good to be home.

Ollie pulled the Jaguar away from the kerb. He would drop Denis at the tube station and then return to the government car park and swap the Jaguar for his own Ford saloon. At this time of night he should get to South Norwood in twenty minutes. He'd left there sixteen hours ago. God he'd be glad to get home.

Andrew changed into pyjamas and his dressing gown before he and Daisy went into the study.

'I've taken a major decision,' he said as he poured two whiskies and added a lot of soda.

She waited.

'I'm not going to open that bloody red box tonight.'

Daisy curbed her desire to ask about the Raider drama. Instead she told him about the distinguished director of one of the nation's great art galleries: when he'd come to the house that morning for the first of his sittings, he'd asked her whether he had to keep all his clothes on.

'He said he didn't want to have that buttoned-up look. For the present we settled on his removing his jacket and waistcoat and unbuttoning his shirt to the waist.'

'How much of this chap do you intend to include?' asked Andrew.

'I'd expected to stop somewhere around his shoulders. I may change my mind. It depends what he takes off next time.'

It was the first subject the Defence Secretary had heard all day that made him laugh.

26

'Grade A' Cabinet ministers were determined by security risk rather than rank. Thus the Prime Minister, Foreign Secretary, Home Secretary, Defence Secretary, Northern Ireland Secretary were Grade A, whereas the third-ranking member of the government, the Chancellor of the Exchequer, was Grade B.

Special Branch's job was made easier if the detective slept under the same roof as the minister, which worked out well enough if the house was grand and there was staff. But while the Harwoods lived comfortably and in style, the family liked privacy. They preferred having Denis under another roof.

Like many Chelsea houses, especially the elegant terraces built at the end of the eighteenth century, the Harwoods' house was larger than it looked, three rooms running back on each of the three floors, with a big kitchen and fair-sized dining room in the so-called garden basement. Daisy did much of the cooking. She would have liked it better if the kitchen and dining room had been entirely above ground. The only thing she really missed in London was the sunny openness of the big house where she'd been brought up. Americans, she said, even when they live in town, use the basement for hanging up sheets to dry; the ping-pong table is down there, the sink to wash the dog. But you cook and eat above ground, for heaven's sake.

However, as Daisy's home was central to her life, and she preferred not to yearn for what she didn't have, she rationalized the situation by saying she supposed she wouldn't enjoy their farmhouse in Shropshire so much if the London house was equally bright.

They'd moved to Cheyne Street two months before Matty was born. Before that, for the first two years of marriage, they'd lived nearer Sloane Square. Though it wasn't in the division bell area, it was less than ten minutes' drive from the House of Commons except when traffic was bad. The three bedrooms were enough, just, after Sophie was born. But Andrew grumbled about his dressing room having turned into the room for the 'mother's help', the young woman who was half nanny, half au pair. 'It's not,' he had told Daisy, 'that I particularly want an extra room in order to sleep alone. It's the idea of having an option.' She would never understand why the English went on about Americans' need for euphemisms when they themselves described a separate bedroom for the husband as a dressing room.

At Cheyne Street, their bedroom, Andrew's study and the famous dressing room were all on the first floor. The children and the mother's help (later an au pair) each had a room on the second floor. The ground floor consisted of the drawing room and Daisy's sculpture studio, the small room between used by her sitters to change their clothes. The studio had windows high up on three sides, making it impossible to see anything outside except the top half of the ash trees in the garden. For the same reason, no one in the garden could look into the studio. The house had been built for a sculptor two centuries earlier, and no subsequent owner had altered the studio's structure.

Along its walls Daisy's maquettes stood ghostlike on their wires. Sometimes she used them for the models of birds which end up larger than life-size, horses smaller than life-size, though one day, she said to herself, she would undertake a full-size horse like those by Elisabeth Frink.

Where Daisy excelled was at portraiture. She was no Epstein, but she had a gift for catching the likeness and imparting the sitter's vitality. She modelled the heads in clay, and then they went off to the Fulham foundry to be cast in bronze. Most sitters commissioned them for their homes or offices. Extra casts had been made of a dozen particularly successful busts, and these were on display in Oxford and Cambridge colleges and a couple of City boardrooms.

In the last three years, the National Portrait Gallery had bought two of Daisy's portrait sculptures, and one was on permanent display. Whenever she visited the gallery, she took a quick peep at her own work and thought afresh how well life had treated her — and immediately touched the wooden plinth. Andrew was immensely proud of her work.

Their weekdays at Cheyne Street usually began with the same routine. Ingrid, this year's au pair, dealt with the children's breakfast. Only after Daisy had made breakfast for herself and Andrew and carried it upstairs, the morning newspapers tucked under one arm, did he concede the day had begun and put on his dressing gown, settle in the armchair and fold *The Times* so he could read it as he ate. When he returned from shaving, she was still propped up against the bed pillows, having moved on from the *Daily Mail* and the *Guardian* to the *Independent*. Even after fourteen years of marriage she liked watching him dress. 'You're very graceful,' she sometimes said. 'Thank you,' he always replied. It wasn't until he finished knotting his tie that she'd get out of bed finally.

Anyone seeing this peaceful scene would not have guessed that it was regularly followed by thirteen, fourteen, fifteen hours of intense concentration and activity on Andrew's part and a less systematic, shorter but productive day for Daisy.

By the time the Jaguar had reached the bottom of Cheyne Street and headed towards Whitehall, she was in her jeans and T-shirt, and was starting on her face. Even though she was certain of seeing only Ingrid and Mrs Salmon, the daily, Daisy always put on some makeup before she went downstairs to her desk to deal with the more urgent post. Sooner or later somebody always leant on the doorbell, and she was convinced that whoever it was, that person would have a more helpful attitude if her face was looking reasonable. She remained a strikingly pretty woman with almond-shaped grey eyes set off by the dark auburn hair.

Unless it was for work – and after attending half a dozen government lunches she put them in the work category – she rarely went out during the day, preferring to make the most of solitude before the children came home after school. Sophie and Matty went to private day schools a short bus ride away, and both made their presence known when they got back soon after four. Still, that meant seven hours without the family around, and Daisy often wondered why she managed no more than four hours, often less, in her studio. Mrs Salmon looked after the house. Ingrid looked after the practical side of the children – though as they got older an au pair had less and less to do. If sometimes Ingrid seemed more like an adolescent-sitter than anything else, that single capacity made her invaluable when Daisy was in the constituency or on an official trip with Andrew or simply out for a dinner party or an evening with Angela or Frances.

A puzzle to her was why being a senior Cabinet minister's wife should take so much time. True, since Andrew had been made Defence Secretary, she had to host more obligatory lunches than during the two previous years he'd been Industry Secretary. Other countries' defence ministers often brought their wives to London with them, and although Government Hospitality made the arrangements, Daisy was expected to be hostess. She found a two-hour formal lunch took four hours out of the day – by the time she'd washed her hair and dressed properly and travelled both ways.

It was a great help that in her official role she was allowed the use of Andrew's car, though she sometimes felt an irrational hostility to the back of Ollie's cap. Ollie never, of course, commented to Daisy about her tendency to set off from home at least ten minutes late, so that he had to drive through yellow lights – once up on the kerb in Piccadilly – to get her to the destination on time. But he noted the passing minutes when he waited outside the house in Cheyne Street, and later he groused to Denis. Daisy sensed all this when she was finally inside the Jaguar and looking at the back of Ollie's cap.

If someone else was to blame for her being late, she didn't mind in the slightest. It was when she alone was responsible – usually the case – that she suffered a burst of paranoia: Andrew had an army of civil servants to look after him – private office, driver, detectives – while she had to fend for herself. In such moods, fortunately shortlived, she asked herself why no one in the government thought spouses might also be the object of a terrorist's attention. She thought of the minister's wife who had been killed – and Margaret Tebbit paralysed – by the IRA bomb in the Grand Hotel at Brighton duries the Tories' 1984 conference, though she had to admit they were with their husbands when the bomb was detonated. At that time Andrew was a second-rank minister, and he and Daisy had been allocated a room well back from the front bedrooms that collapsed like cards when the bomb went off; they were lucky.

What else did she actually *do* as a Cabinet minister's wife? She suspected she felt more anxiety on Andrew's behalf than he did, and she wondered if that used up some of her time as well as energy.

And she always felt uneasy if she had a drink with Frances or Angela and afterwards drove home in her own Volvo estate car. For like all ministers' spouses, Daisy knew she was a target for the press. If she was waiting patiently in traffic and some bus driver bumped into her 'sensible' Volvo and she was the one who'd had a teaspoon of whisky and therefore had it on her breath, she would not only be breathalysed, never a dignified procedure, but the incident would be splashed across the tabloids. No matter that she was not over the legal drink limit: what most people would remember was that the Defence Secretary's wife was breathalysed after her car was in a collision. As yet this baleful scene had not transpired, but whenever Daisy read about something similar happening to a politician's wife, she imagined her turn would come.

If she was already in a bad mood, she could resent this sense of being constantly under surveillance. 'Caesar's wife must be above suspicion.' When at school she'd first read that pompous statement, she'd felt annoyed on Caesar's wife's behalf. Nonetheless, she could not pretend that emulating Caesar's wife actually used up her time. Perhaps she was just chronically unpunctual. Could it be a disease?

Finally Ollie got across the lights on the north side of Parliament Square and turned into Whitehall, stopping at the barrier into Downing Street. One of the police bent down to look at their passes. He gave Daisy a friendly nod and waved the Jaguar through into the little street whose physical modesty is at odds with its fame.

So narrow is Downing Street that it is impossible properly to see the Foreign Office looming on the left. But the simple houses built in a single terrace on the right, their seventeenth-century bricks restored so many times that their age has been almost erased, are in scale with the street. Just before the cul de sac where the Foreign Office Stairs descend to Horse Guards Parade, Ollie pulled to the kerb in front of Number Eleven. He looked at the digital clock above the gear box. One o'clock. Not bad, considering she had been twelve minutes late in coming out the front door of Cheyne Street.

The policeman outside Number Ten strolled several paces to stand by the step of Number Eleven. The front door was opened by an aged attendant who greeted Daisy pleasantly and hobbled ahead of her up the stairs on the left to the white painted door leading to the Chancellor of the Exchequer's private apartments. His wife was giving a small lunch party for the controversial post-feminist writer who happened to be married to the French finance minister.

On the other side of Whitehall, inside the bleak block of concrete in Richmond Terrace, Andrew was having a whisky at his desk. The porter put down a silver tray with sandwiches and a pot of coffee. The Minister's morning had been entirely taken up first with the Anglo-German dispute about deployment of conventional forces, then the question of his own tactics in dealing with British unilateralists, and finally the strained relations with the Department of Industry over whether to order components – for the ES 7 programme – from Stockton Air Space or Bedfordshire High Tech or a plant in the United States.

Rachel Fisher was undeniably an effective Industry Secretary. Andrew asked himself whether it was his imagination that the tension between their departments seemed to have an element of personal antagonism. He didn't think he felt any particular hostility to Rachel. Perhaps he was mistaken in sensing a private antipathy on her part. Impossible to know how much was simply Ben Franwell's use of the *Rampart* as advocate for Rachel Fisher's ministerial ascent. In the current pecking order, Defence ranked above Industry. Only the Foreign Office and the Exchequer and the Home Office ranked higher than Defence.

He'd set aside lunchtime to read the latest brief on the dead pilot. The autopsy had been completed the day before. The chairman of Stockton Air Space was to arrive with his chief designer at 2:45.

At two o'clock the porter returned and removed the silver tray.

At 2:30 when Martin came through the door, followed by the PUS, they found Andrew pacing the room.

He nodded to Barthmore and moved to the blue leather chesterfield under the engraving of the soldier on lonely patrol at Monte Cassino, Austin Barthmore settling in the blue leather armchair near the trenches of the Somme. Martin, his notepad at hand, sat on a chair under the Spitfires, the crippled one beginning its deathfall above his left shoulder.

Andrew sat forward, his hands clasped loosely between his knees, frowning. 'You've seen the autopsy report, Austin. Poor blighter.'

All three men were silent.

Then Andrew went on: 'Do you feel the three deaths can be dismissed as coincidence?'

'I know, Minister, that you find Charles Cartwright's personality irksome. But I've always found his judgement good. Cartwright accepts our investigators' conclusion that no outside sinister intent was involved in the earlier macabre deaths. Whether the three together reveal some flaw of judgement in Stockton's personnel management is something else. But Stockton's production record for us has been excellent – until this latest mystery brought our ES6 programme to a halt. Cartwright is examining the competition offered by Bedfordshire High Tech.'

Andrew gave a wry smile. 'I suppose one should not blind oneself to Bedfordshire High Tech's possibilities just because the Industry Secretary is pushing them. No doubt in due course

Cartwright will give us a tutorial on the matter. The extraordinary thing is that usually I rather like tutorials. Must be something the matter with Cartwright's and my chemistry.'

At that moment the diary secretary came into the room. 'Are you ready for Cartwright to join you, Minister?'

'Yep.'

'And the Stockton team have arrived two minutes early.'

'They might as well all come in together.'

The Stockton chairman's big forehead gleamed faintly from perspiration.

'We meet again, Mr Manning,' Andrew said as they shook hands.

'I wish the circumstances were less tragic, Minister,' replied Manning.

He was shown to the other blue leather armchair, his chief designer given a straight chair with arms.

Andrew opened the meeting. He addressed the designer, Lionel Barker.

'Jameson was carrying out the final tests before you delivered – were due to deliver – the first of the Raiders this week. Until last Saturday, what was your opinion, Mr Barker, of your new ejector seat?'

'It has different components from its predecessor, sir. But its reliability is beyond dispute.'

Manning cleared his throat.

Barker adapted his statement: 'We had every reason to think its reliability was beyond dispute. Unfortunately we do not yet have access to the seat or any of the plane. When – if – that is salvaged, we will know more.'

'The autopsy indicates that both of Jameson's shoulders were broken before he hit the ground. What do you think happened to him, Mr Barker?' Andrew was entirely courteous in his manner.

'Speaking privately, I feel certain, Minister, that unlike the two previous deaths of Stockton engineers, Jameson did not commit suicide. I believe that somehow the rocket in his headrest fired and punched a hole in the canopy above him. The suction would have wrenched him out of his seat, breaking his shoulder straps – and his shoulders. This has been known to happen once before, four years ago, when British Aerospace lost a pilot – and the plane – in similar circumstances. In that case, the wreckage lay so far beneath the ocean surface that it could not be salvaged, but before the plane ran out of fuel and crashed, it was seen flying without its pilot. What set off his ejection was never firmly established.'

Cartwright interrupted: 'You may recall, Mr Barker, that the MoD inquiry four years ago drew conclusions, albeit speculative ones, about that regrettable incident.'

'Yes,' said Barker, 'and until we know more, I make the same speculations about Jameson. When he was dragged through the broken canopy, its jagged edges would have shredded his main parachute. So he plunged 30,000 feet to the ground. As you will know from the autopsy, he was dead when he hit the ground. Or so they believe.'

For half a minute no one spoke.

Andrew then asked: 'What is the purpose of the rocket in the headrest?'

'It is an improved design intended to deal with a Raider that is falling vertically at such a speed that the normal small parachute might not inflate in time. If the special rocket in the back of the seat is fired, it can force the main parachute to inflate more quickly. The design assumes, of course, that the plane's canopy has been thrown off in the normal way so that the main parachute is not shredded.'

Andrew said to Manning: 'The MoD investigators who have been at Stockton all week are speculating along the same lines. They agree that nothing can be deduced until the aircraft is salvaged.'

He turned to Cartwright. 'In your view, Charles, how does this halt in the ES6 programme affect our plans for the ES7 programme?'

'It is most unfortunate,' Cartwright said with something like self-satisfaction, 'that we cannot assess the impact of the delay on the ultimate timing of the ES6 programme. In the meanwhile,' he paused magisterially, 'Stockton would have to put up a very compelling case before we could consider giving it the contract to make components for our ES7 programme.'

Andrew turned to Manning who took the white handkerchief
from the breast pocket of his striped jacket and lightly patted his
forehead before putting the handkerchief in a trouser pocket.

'Is there an urgency,' Manning asked, 'in the MoD deciding
on the ES7 contract before the Raider has been salvaged?'

'I'm afraid there is, Mr Manning,' said Cartwright. 'The Minister is committed to a tight timetable. The salvage operation
could take months.'

Cartwright was more than sanguine in his manner. He seemed
positively pleased to deliver this bad news to Stockton.

Thinking about it in the back seat of the Jaguar on his way
home that evening, Andrew could see no reason for Cartwright's
satisfaction that the Raider mystery must be prolonged.

It held up the important ES6 programme, which Cartwright
would not wish for.

It almost ruled out Stockton as a bidder for the ES7 contract.
Why should Cartwright take a personal interest in that?

27

'How long, though, did it take him to die, Dad?' In vain had
Daisy tried to get the children to call him Papa as she had called
her father.

'No one can say for certain, Sophie. The change in air pressure
at that height would have knocked him out pretty fast.'

'But he was a top test pilot, Dad.' Matty's face was intense.
'Aren't they trained how to hold their breath until they've dropped
down into air that's okay for them?'

'When he hit the canopy, that alone could have knocked him
unconscious. It was all so fast, Matty, probably he never knew
what hit him.'

Both children seemed to feel Andrew had personal responsibility
for what happened to anyone who worked directly or indirectly
for Defence.

The four of them were sitting on the four sides of the big kitchen
table at Stony Farm, their Shropshire farmhouse near the base of
the Peckforton Hills, on the edge of the village of Waymere. The
general management committee of Waymere's Conservative party
had not actually stipulated that their MP should have a home in
the constituency, but it was implicit.

It was also convenient. Andrew held a surgery for his constituents two Saturday mornings out of each month. His parents
still lived at the family house, Long Green, which was only thirty
miles farther west into Shropshire. Sometimes Daisy and the
children spent the long weekend with Lady Harwood and Sir
Edward, and Andrew joined them late Saturday evening. More
often, after school on Friday, Daisy made the three-hour drive to
Stony Farm, Andrew following later in the government car. One
reason he and Daisy had bought this particular nineteenth-century
farmhouse was that only an acre or two of garden remained
around it: it was an easy place to run.

Special Branch positioned Denis at the nearest point, which
was the local pub at the centre of the small village. The alarm
system throughout the farmhouse – 'Press the button and freeze,'
the police chief had said – rang through to the pub as well as to
the police station. The children had been extremely excited when
the system was installed after Andrew went to Defence. So far no
one had pressed a button by mistake, let alone intention.

Ollie took the Jaguar back to London, generally returning to
Stony Farm on Sunday afternoon to collect Andrew and Denis so
that the Minister could work during the three-hour journey.
Sometimes all four Harwoods, with Denis, made the return drive
together in the Volvo estate – 'rather crowded', Andrew invariably
pointed out when they all piled in.

He liked to add other engagements to these visits to Waymere,
both to keep in touch with his constituents and to be seen to be
doing so. Like any intelligent MP, Andrew made a point of being
on good terms with the provincial newspaper and local radio
station that were part of his constituents' daily lives. When their
reporters rang him at home or at Defence, he always took the call
or else returned it as soon as possible.

From across the big kitchen table where they were having
Sunday's late lunch, Daisy watched Andrew. She took a positive
pleasure in looking at him, scrutinizing his features once again,
enjoying the subtle changes of expression. It was partly that she
had a sculptor's interest in looking at his head, partly that she
remained intrigued by Andrew. Sometimes she asked herself how
much the continuation of their romance was a result of their joint

effort not to lose it. Early in their marriage she'd been struck by Andrew's saying: 'You have to look after love. It doesn't look after itself.'

They both enjoyed good health, and this added to their good looks. Daisy saw in the mirror that her skin was not impervious to time. Did one's face really age suddenly every seven years as folklore claimed? But others looked at her less critically and found her changed remarkably little. Occasionally she had the curls cut short. Once she'd had them straightened, but Andrew said he missed them, so she didn't repeat the experiment. Currently they bobbed on the tops of her shoulders.

His sandy hair seemed blonder because of the grey in it. She was glad he didn't have black hair: she found it sad to look at the first white strands in black hair. She wasn't sure whether this was because of the visual evidence of mortality, or whether it was simply an aesthetic regret.

Watching him now from across the pine table, she knew what was going through his mind: his own unease about the manner of the pilot's dying, together with his wish to allay the children's anxiety without deceiving them. He and Daisy both took the view that children's natural resilience makes them able to accept unpleasant facts of life without necessarily brooding about them, though Sophie tended to turn things over in her mind and then re-raise them with her parents – especially with Andrew these days.

In some phases of her thirteen years, Sophie had been closer to Daisy. But over the last couple of years she'd grown nearer to Andrew, discussing things with him at weekends as if she were on his level. Daisy was glad: the children had so little time with their father that she welcomed any evidence that their relationship with him could surmount the obstacle of his absence during most of the week. For even when he got home for a late dinner, the children rarely did more than come down to say hello: Andrew liked having time alone with Daisy, and after dinner he would have to open the red box. At weekends, however, they tried to have lunch *en famille* and sometimes the evening meal as well, especially when they were at Stony Farm.

'The *Rampart* says that his shoulders were broken,' said Sophie.

Despite himself, Andrew's unhappiness showed in his face. Thank God none of the newspapers had described fully the body that the shepherd had found attached to the shredded parachute.

'When the small parachute went through the broken canopy and inflated, it would have pulled at him with such force that his shoulder straps broke. And his shoulders,' Andrew said truthfully, even if it was only part of the story. 'It all must have happened in less than three seconds, Sophie.'

'But that would have been long enough for him to *know*, Dad.' As she said it, Sophie imagined the pilot had been her father. 'The *Rampart* says he had two children.'

'Yes.'

'Could you have done anything to stop it happening?'

'I don't see what, Sophie.'

'The *Rampart* says you could have stopped the ES6 order after the first two deaths at Stockton.'

'Sophie, I wish you'd stop saying "The *Rampart* says". I worked for the *Rampart*,' said Daisy. 'The editor I worked for is the same editor today. He's not God. A lot of what he writes is intended simply to make mischief between politicians.'

'It's not the gospel, Sophie,' said Matty, disinclined, just because he was younger, to accept a junior role. Often when Daisy watched her son, she imagined how Andrew must have looked when he was a boy – the same hazel eyes, the sturdiness, the well-made hands which when he was in repose were half closed in a way that was both relaxed and controlled. In Lady Harwood's morning room at Long Green there were framed photographs of each of her three sons. Daisy and Sophie were fascinated by these pictures. More than once Sophie, studying the one of Andrew, said: 'Don't you think Dad looks there the way Matty does now?'

And quite often, if they were alone, Sophie then asked her mother: 'Has Grannie got over Uncle Donald's death yet?'

Daisy tended to reply that she thought Grannie had got used to it.

Sometimes Sophie asked to be told again how Donald had died.

Daisy told her once again, invariably adding: 'It's such a sad subject for your father that he doesn't really like to discuss it.'

'I know,' Sophie always replied as if she didn't need to be reminded to behave like a grownup.

Sophie herself looked so like an adolescent Daisy that Andrew could find himself gazing at his daughter in astonishment. The same clear grey eyes, almost almond-shaped, and the lightly freckled skin, the same pert face with the big mouth. At times Andrew felt such a rush of love for Sophie that he wondered if it was unhealthy. Her hair had more gold in it than Daisy's, and it fell in loose curls, gleaming like molten butterscotch, six or more inches below her shoulders. Sophie hated the curls. She wanted dead straight hair.

'But could you have stopped the order so the pilot would never have had to test the plane, Dad?'

'There was no reason to do so, Sophie. The other two men who died earlier this year were working in another section of Stockton Air Space. They had no connection with the ES6 programme.'

'But what about now? Do you now think maybe those other two deaths weren't suicide?'

'All the people who made the investigations agreed they were suicides, Sophie.'

'But how could anybody decapitate himself?'

It was a good question. It had always seemed to Andrew that the engineer's death might not have been suicide, even though that is what Special Branch had concluded. It was such an extra-ordinary way to kill yourself – tying a wire between two trees and then driving your open car at high speed at the wire, standing up as you drove. Inwardly he winced as he thought of it.

'You've clearly read the *Rampart* in gory detail, Sophie. Well, the man could have decapitated himself like that. I agree, it was rather unusual.'

'Supposing somebody else had already made him unconscious and then held him up above the windscreen so the wire would cut his head off? Why couldn't that have happened, Dad?'

'This is absolutely the last time I spend an hour cooking Sunday lunch,' said Daisy, putting down her knife and fork.

Andrew smiled wanly. 'Special Branch considered that, Sophie. They decided it was far less likely than that the chap had managed it by himself.'

All four were silent, all thinking there must have been simpler ways available.

'And the Stockton scientist in the car that was upside down in the River Tees? How did the Special Branch know he'd driven the car into the river, Dad?'

'They didn't *know*, Matty. They couldn't find evidence of anything else. The man's wife said he'd been worried and depressed.'

'I'd be worried and depressed if I thought someone was out to get me, Dad.'

'So would I, Sophie. But the man's wife said he had never specified why he was worried – just that it had to do with work. At this rate I am going to be so worried and depressed that when we get back to London this evening I may drop the rest of you off in Cheyne Street and then drive myself into the Thames.'

He said it good-temperedly. All four laughed. Daisy asked Matty about a crisis with one of his schoolfellows, and the conversation moved on.

But Andrew felt slightly ashamed of himself. He'd brought the black interrogation to an end without answering the real question. Was there something in the *Rampart*'s innuendo? Was there some cover-up in his own ministry, perhaps in F-section, and he was blind?

28

Ben Franwell burst out laughing with the pleasure of it. 'I expect Master Andrew's Sunday was spoiled before it started. It won't have escaped his mind that the Prime Minister is a faithful reader of the *Rampart*.'

For the length of time it had taken him to write his column, he'd convinced himself that Andrew Harwood was both a lightweight and morally suspect man. Ben had deployed the skill for which he was renowned: selecting dubious evidence first to mock the man, then to plant the seed of suspicion about his integrity – not just in the general readers' minds but particularly in the corridors of Westminster and Whitehall.

When the Prime Minister promoted Andrew from head of Industry to head of Defence, the appointment was applauded on the whole. The superpowers' reduction of their nuclear arsenal had shifted many Britons, who previously deplored unilateral nuclear disarmament, to an open desire for more arms reduction. Where Andrew's predecessor at Defence had shared the generals' conviction that the best way for a nation to discourage attack was to bristle with arms, Andrew thought some of the bristling unnecessary and simply a drain on the country's resources.

One reason he'd enjoyed running Industry was because he could make a strategy for the nation's economic development – encouraging industries not only for their productivity, but as part of a wider scheme to provide employment in underused, poorer parts of the country.

This ability to look beyond his own department – not common in Cabinet ministers – earned him some admirers at Westminster and in the media. But a number of his own civil servants regretted that he declined to put his department – *their* department – above all other considerations. Even Austin Barthmore, who understood Andrew's concern for the economy as a whole, felt aggrieved when Andrew relinquished a tiny part of his Defence budget on an understanding with the Chancellor that it would go to the meagrely funded Housing Minister.

As for his personal standing with the Prime Minister, that was a mystery. The Prime Minister's promotion of Andrew was unaccompanied by any demonstration either of affection or coolness – as distinct from confidence in his capabilities as an administrator. If Andrew Harwood's reputation as an administrator could be tarnished, his political career would crumble.

Thinking about how he had opened his column, Ben grinned.

As the Defence Secretary rests a languid hand on the dispatch box, no doubt he will tell us again how happy he is to pass on taxpayers' money to Stockton Air Space where – in three months – three people working on MoD contracts have met grotesque deaths, one still under investigation?

Should we not ask the elegant Mr Harwood to open his mind to the existence of other companies competing in Britain's highly advanced aeronautics industry, for instance Bedfordshire High Tech, before he regally bestows the multi-million-pound order for his ES 7 programme?

It is, after all, our money that this lofty administrator is complacently dishing out. *Would you give a contract to a company that just might be guilty of incompetence to the point of criminal neglect?*

When Ben skirted close to libel, he wrapped the innuendo in slightly obscure sentences that could be defended by the *Rampart*'s lawyers, yet whose thrust was crystal clear to readers.

He glanced at the empty glass resting on his crotch. He was propped comfortably against one of the pillows scrunched up against the blue quilted headboard. 'Shall I get us another whisky?'

Rachel reached over to the small table on her side of the bed, smiling as she handed him her own empty tumbler. More than fifteen years after she and Ben Franwell had first met, they remained more comfortable with one another than with anyone else in the world.

There had never been a doubt in her mind why she'd kept the Morpeth Terrace flat as her *pied-à-terre* in London: patently it was too small for a family, and even a husband's presence could be discouraged. It was perfect for her to live there alone during the week, concentrating not only on her ministerial work but also on being 'seen around the House', MPs' vernacular for the show of camaraderie in the Commons that is useful if a minister is to build up a supporting group of backbenchers. And Morpeth Terrace was perfect for Ben's visits. Though these were no longer weekly – sometimes not for a month at a time – they were the focal point in Rachel's personal life.

When she'd married George Bishop twelve years ago, she had no illusions of being in love with him. She had approached matrimony as an investment. She told herself that all but Western marriages – and probably more of those than was acknowledged – were undertaken in a businesslike spirit and appeared to be none the worse – possibly even better – than those based on inevitably shortlived romance.

Rachel had never intended to be handicapped by the stigma that attaches to unmarried politicians. She'd got away with it initially, and she did not push her luck. The problem was to find a man who would be a suitable husband for a Tory MP without being a demanding one. George Bishop had appeared to fill the bill.

He was chairman of his own insurance business in Bedford, only ten miles from Rachel's constituency. Although he was nearly forty when they met – seven years older than Rachel – he was a bachelor: he had not met the right woman, he said, though he had once been engaged. His father had been a run of the mill barrister who had married slightly above himself – 'county' was how his complacently overbearing wife liked to describe herself. George had been sent to a minor public school and then to Cambridge. He was well-spoken, rather handsome, intelligent enough, and respectable. His humour was wry. Like Rachel, George was an only child.

His top priority and Rachel's were one and the same: her career. George had no doubt that she could and should go far in politics – one day, he hoped, to the top. She needed a man like him in the background.

Their two sons came along fairly rapidly: Rachel knew her childbearing time was running out. She was neither religious nor given to superstition, yet the thought had lurked in her mind that she might be 'punished' for what had taken place in the private nursing home in Surrey. She wanted children, ideally two. Howard was born in the second year of the marriage, James a year and a half after that. Both times George had been taken aback when Rachel went to pieces as soon as she learned the baby was a boy. She'd been quite stoical during labour – admittedly she'd been heavily drugged – yet as soon as the doctor held up the little creature and said, 'You have a healthy baby boy, Mrs Bishop,' she'd turned her face away.

George wasn't present at the births: neither he nor Rachel saw the charms of the father taking part in this messy episode. But afterwards, when Rachel made plain her distaste for holding her baby – there was no question of her breastfeeding – one of the staff had taken it upon herself to discuss the thing with George. Although some of the junior nurses had been indignant at Rachel's coldness to her newborn son, this more experienced woman told George that other mothers were sometimes repelled at the outset and then became fond of their children. George's personal secretary at the office had put everything else aside until she found an absolute gem through a London agency. When Rachel left Bedford Hospital on George's arm, the gem walked behind with Howard in her arms. George drove them home to Bedford Forge – to the turn-of-the-century substantial redbrick house that stood in the wide street flanked by old limes and adorned by the mansion housing the Conservative Club.

Both the Bishop boys were raised initially by the live-in gem who then stayed on as general housekeeper when Rachel agreed to a trained nanny joining the household. None of this suggested to the Bishops' neighbours in Bedford Forge, nor to the mothers of other small boys at the private day school the children attended in Bedford, that Rachel was lacking in maternal instincts: it was the way many members of the Conservative party aspired to live.

George was extremely fond of his sons. He took pleasure in driving them to school in the morning, dropping them off on his way to Bishop Insurance Company. In the afternoon, the gem drove the Bishops' second car into Bedford to collect the boys again. Soon after Howard's ninth birthday, he went off to boarding school. James would follow in due course.

Rachel fell into family life at the weekend and enjoyed it, in between her constituency duties, though these days Howard was away during the school terms. She liked to go up to London on Sunday night so that she could get into the department in good time on Monday morning.

The Department of Industry was only two minutes' drive from Morpeth Terrace. At ten minutes to nine her government driver double-parked outside, keeping the Rover's motor idling. At five minutes to nine, the electrically locked outer door of the sombre mansion block opened, and the Minister stepped out, a crocodile handbag under one arm, the other swinging the red ministerial box.

She too was a good administrator. Her progress was watched with interest. For Margaret Thatcher had shown precious little inclination to appoint other women to the Cabinet. When Rachel was made Industry Secretary, it was considered a bold appointment.

Women still had barely crossed the threshold of industrial boardrooms; the chairmen were all men, competing with one another and negotiating with their workers' unions. How would they respond to a woman presiding over them when they went to number one Victoria Street to argue their case for government support?

Their feelings were mixed. Most developed a grudging admiration for Rachel. The reluctance stemmed from the fact she was a woman, the admiration from her being so unlike their idea of a woman: she put her arguments in a detached, unemotional way. The industrial chairmen who came to the Minister's room had to admit that when she took her place at the head of the long refectory-style table, she had always done her homework. She was a quick reader: she mastered every brief before she considered how she would handle it.

Although she was not tall, she had a distinct presence. She held herself particularly erect, and the dark, not quite black, hair was cut in a bob that was becoming yet did not blazon her femininity. She looked her best in the dark narrow-skirted suits that she usually wore for work, pinstriped like the suits of her male colleagues, and yet subtly feminine. Her shirts were as well cut as those of any Tory's who had his own shirtmaker in Jermyn Street, but she wore hers open at the throat in a way that both looked brisk and flattered her face. Her manner always conveyed the sense that she knew what was right.

Propped against a pillow upended against her side of the blue quilted bedhead, she sipped the whisky Ben had handed her and then put the tumbler on the bedside table. Its top was protected with a bevelled piece of quarter-inch glass, so she never had to worry about those white rings that tumblers seemed to leave on wood.

Over the years she had redecorated the bedroom twice: she liked it to look fresh as well as tidy. But Ben never noticed the change, because Rachel found it simplest to use the same colours she had already found successful. The blue of the striped chintz that covered the small armchair was only a shade or two deeper than its predecessor, and although the skirt of the dressing table had not got shabby, she replaced it so that it would match the chair exactly.

'The Prime Minister doesn't want to play musical chairs too often,' Ben said.

He and Rachel were both wearing comfortable casual clothes as they lay on top of the blue bedspread.

'The ideal,' he went on, 'would be for Harwood to be demoted at the end of this year. By then you'd have had nearly two years at Industry. We could say you had put in process most of what you'd set out to do there and someone else could now take over, while the requirements of Defence really had to be met by a minister whose competence was not under question.'

As he said it, he could imagine using much the same words when the time came to write that leader.

'I like the idea of running Defence,' Rachel said.

'It's irresistible. All those man-hating harpies in their smelly anoraks would be stymied. God they make me sick. If they had their way, the British army would be carrying toy pistols and the navy would consist of boats barely able to float from one end of a bathtub to the other. If a woman was head of Defence, they'd be flummoxed. And the normal, decent women in this country would say it's no bad thing to have someone dealing with this nation's defence who also understands how mothers feel.'

'The funny thing is I'd be good at Defence.'

'I know. Has George said anything further about my new friend Charles Cartwright? I haven't got in touch with Cartwright while I'm using this line of attack on Harwood – in case Cartwright told me I was barking up the wrong tree.'

'After George had completed his nine holes on Saturday, he ran into Cartwright in the clubhouse. Over a drink, George asked him what the hell is going on at Stockton Air Space.'

'What did Cartwright say?'

'I'm afraid he definitely thinks the deaths are coincidental. He told George it would be months before the Raider can be salvaged, but Cartwright says the crash investigators expect to find the pilot was ejected by some freak accident – like that case four years ago.'

'And the other two grotesque deaths?'

'He told George there is no MoD cover-up involved. He said Special Branch is certain it's a rerun of those high-tech scientists' suicides several years ago – which led to the electronics industries supposedly reducing the stress that their employees work under. You remember.'

Ben's face grew sullen.

Both sipped their whisky.

After several minutes he said: 'Okay. So I've got all I'm going to get out of Plan One. I'll have to abandon that line of attack. But there's more than one way to skin a cat.'

His face brightened. 'We'll move on to Plan Two. Does Cartwright know that George is an insurance broker for Bedfordshire High Tech?'

'I think so.'

'Right. The time has come to talk with the director of F-section again about the merits in giving the ES7 contract to BedHiTe. I feel sure that this time round I can persuade him.'

Ben grinned at the thought.

He went on: 'George will have to make the approach to BedHiTe's president. I'm sure George can think of reasons why Nelson Harwood should join the board of directors. We've got to get Nelly Harwood in place before Andrew Harwood announces that BedHiTe has the contract. At the same time, we must make sure Nelly Harwood doesn't know the contract is in the pipeline. Otherwise he could mention it to his brother, and Andrew would immediately make a public statement declaring a family interest in BedHiTe – or he would say the contract had to go somewhere else.'

Ben chuckled.

'The beauty of it, Rachel, is that we can exploit George's connection with BedHiTe only because you are not yet Defence Secretary. But when that happens, then George should end any insurance links with companies that have – or want – Defence contracts. If we're going to manoeuvre Andrew Harwood into the position of appearing to favour his family when he gives out contracts, then we've got to be doubly careful that nothing like that can ever be pinned on you.'

'I've already discussed it with George. He points out that as an insurance broker for BedHiTe, he would make no direct profit if BedHiTe secured an MoD contract. Even so, he says he would be happy to give up handling any insurance policy that could conceivably be used against me by an enemy. If I get Defence, I think we should make a big noise about how George Bishop is so highminded that he has personally sacrificed an independent business contract so that the public can be absolutely confident no member of my family will ever benefit – even indirectly – from a government connection.'

'Caesar's husband must be above suspicion,' Ben said, laughing as he realized he had the intro to another leader. 'It shouldn't be too difficult for me to draw a contrast with Andrew Harwood's family.'

'George said something else that will interest you.'

She reached over for the tumbler on her bedside table. One of the pleasures she and Ben shared as they lay talking on top of her bed was a sense that in this oasis there was no hurry. She sipped her whisky, then replaced the glass and made herself comfortable against her pillow.

'He said that the directorship is coming up earlier than expected: the outgoing director wants to retire in June.'

'Christ. That's in less than two months' time.'

'When can you see Cartwright?'

'I'll make a lunch date within the week. He won't have that many engagements he wouldn't break to have a freebie at the Savoy with the editor of the *Rampart*.'

'Shall I go ahead and tell George to suggest to BedHiTe's president that Nelly Harwood would make a good director?'

'George could float the idea, so long as the BedHiTe president doesn't approach Nelly until we're ready. Never did I think the day would come that I'd be discreetly promoting a poof for an easy job. But as this poof happens also to be one of the world's greatest innocents when it comes to politics, he's just the trick we need.'

'The timing won't be easy.'

'We always knew that.'

As he closed the front door behind him and heard the electric lock snap, Ben glanced up at the dome of Westminster Cathedral outlined against the night sky. A full moon made the pale stripes of stone gleam against the wine red of the brick stripes. Under a street lamp, he looked at his watch. 1:30.

In Victoria Street he hailed a taxi, giving the address of his London *pied-à-terre*. His penthouse in St James's Place was big, modern, dramatic. Tonight, as on many nights, Angela would not be there; she was staying down in Sussex until Wednesday. But when she came up to London, she liked to entertain in style. That was part of the deal.

29

'Do you tell Ben?' asked Daisy.

'It depends,' said Angela Franwell.

She had entertained in style the previous evening. Tonight she had come to Cheyne Street for a quiet dinner with Daisy – Shrimp Newburgh at the big Victorian table in the kitchen. Before Andrew had left home that morning, he'd suggested they all have a drink together if he got back early from his dinner with lobby correspondents.

The two women had brought what remained of the bottle of white burgundy up to Daisy's and Andrew's bedroom, its pair of big sash windows facing the terrace houses on the opposite side of Cheyne Street. The narrow street had been made one-way, and some drivers hurtled past the parked cars at too high a speed for town. When brakes squealed outside as Andrew was having breakfast with Daisy, he would beetle his brows and grumble: 'You'd think it was a racecourse. One of these days there's going to be an accident.'

'I quite like Ben,' said Angela, 'so I don't mention a little fling if I think it would make him miserable. On the other hand, he's always known I have my pastimes, and sometimes he gets ...

what? Vicarious pleasure? He definitely gets a kick when someone who is front-page news is quietly having it off with wifey – and only he, Ben, knows about it.'

'Andrew wouldn't take that view. So it's just as well I don't feel like toddling into someone else's bed. Sometimes I think it might be interesting if I did. But when it comes right down to it, I don't actually want to.'

'Perhaps you really are what Frances calls "monoerotic".'

Daisy laughed. 'I hadn't been long on the *Rampart* when Frances introduced me to that word. I'd never heard it before.'

Angela's exquisite face was impassive as she neatly screwed a cigarette into an amber holder.

'You've put your eggs in one basket,' she said. 'One day it's bound to break. With luck you and Andrew will be in the same plane when it falls out of the sky. Otherwise one of you is in for a rough time. I don't want to feel that degree of pain.'

She lit a cigarette, drew on it, slowly let the smoke out between her lips.

Daisy looked away before she said: 'I've always known that sooner or later emotional heights have to be balanced by the depths. I'd still rather put up with the depths than be sort of neutral all the time.'

'Yeah.'

Both women were silent, thinking their separate thoughts.

Then Daisy said: 'Will Ben carry on his vendetta against Andrew forever?'

'God knows. But it could be worse, Daisy. Look what he did to the hapless Health Secretary.' She removed the remaining third of the cigarette from its amber holder and delicately stubbed it out. 'Ben will always resent Andrew's privileged background. And not that far back in the recesses of Ben's mind is his resentment that you turned down his sexual overture. He'll hold a grudge against Andrew for being the one you preferred.'

'Ben never indicated any great passion for me.'

'He's much too unsure of himself with women ever to press his suit, as they say. But in his gauche way, he made a pitch for you, and you turned him down. He'll always remember that, and he'd rather blame it on Andrew than think that he himself may have been insufficiently attractive.'

She inserted another cigarette in the amber holder. 'And it rubs salt in the wounds, I'm sure, that along with Andrew's political success he has the "ideal marriage". It's funny, that, when you think of it. All those years of being London's eligible heart throb, and then, so far as I can tell, Andrew settles down to hearth and home.'

Daisy touched the wooden table beside her.

'As if all that were not enough for a Franwell vendetta,' Angela went on, 'there's Rachel. As Ben's relationship with her has a sexual component – God knows what exactly it is – it's all wrapped together in his mind. Putting Rachel up at Andrew's expense has everything going for it.'

'If Ben wasn't editor of the *Rampart*, how do you suppose he'd vent his psyche?'

'Interesting question. Don't know.'

They were silent again.

Then Daisy asked: 'Have you seen Frances lately?'

'I bumped into her and Giles the other night. At Green's Champagne Bar. They had Frances's current paramour with them. At least I assume that's who it was – attractive in a short-haired butch way.'

Angela gave a slight, self-deprecating smile. She had recently had her own nearly black hair cropped as short as when Daisy had first seen her sitting on the desk at the *Rampart*. No one had ever mistaken Angela's parodies of male dress as remotely butch.

'Some youngish new novelist whose name escapes me,' Angela went on. 'Frances is her literary agent. When we were all together on the *Rampart*, I used to think she fancied you.'

'We once had a general conversation around the subject. It was a nice feeling – being able to talk about our separate proclivities, accept the difference and go on from there.'

'Can you imagine Ben having a close friendship with a man he knew was homosexual?'

The thought made Angela laugh. Like her voice, her laugh was low, yet sometimes a steeliness could be heard in it.

'Has Giles ever had a go in his column at Andrew?' she asked

Daisy. 'Usually he takes Tory ministers apart, limb from limb.'

'Never that really personal abuse. But when he and Frances were here one night for Sunday sups, Giles announced it's only a matter of time before socialist principle compels the tribune of the people to strip the Defence Secretary to the bone.'

Daisy burst out laughing. She was very fond of the left's most widely read polemicist. 'Sophie sat there wide-eyed – torn between her adulation of Andrew and her fascination with Giles. She's already begun trying out some pacifist views on Andrew. I see a trying adolescence looming before us.'

She slid off the bed. Pulling back one of the curtains, she looked down on the blue Jaguar stopped just before the maple tree that grew on their side of the road. She'd recognized the sound of its engine slowing down. 'It always makes me feel I'm one up on the detective when I can look down at the top of his head.'

Angela lit another cigarette. 'If Andrew's not in the mood for a quick drink, I'll push off.'

'Actually, someone has got out of the back of the car with him. I think it's Giles. ESP has been active again. I suppose he was at that dinner. Let's go down.'

Andrew Harwood and Giles Alexander were still in the entrance hall with the detective.

'Do you mind, Denis, if you and Ollie wait for a quarter of an hour and then give Mr Alexander a lift home? It would take you a few minutes out of your way,' said Andrew.

'Certainly, Minister. I'll be in the car with Ollie.'

In the drawing room, Andrew poured out drinks. The four friends were amused to find themselves together, rare enough these days. Giles seemed to be very somewhat tight, though his loose-jointed gait could give that effect when he was entirely sober. With his fairly tall frame now slouched in an armchair, he spread out his thin legs comfortably. He had put on no weight over the years. The carrot-coloured hair had faded slightly, but it still looked aggressive as it shot from his head. Two deep lines grooved the narrow face that always reminded Daisy of a hungry wolf, yet the humorous expression prevailed when he smiled with his lips closed.

'How is the big white chief, Angela?' he said.

'As always: happiest in his work. Biding his time from Sunday to Friday before getting down to Saturday's assault and battery. Do you know, when he wakes up on Sunday in the quiet of the domestic scene over which I preside so graciously in Sussex, I think he might actually die if the *Rampart* was not lying on the table.'

'Doesn't he still read every word of copy before it goes to the stone?' asked Giles.

'Yeah. But he likes to re-read the bits that will cause the most acute anguish to his current enemy.'

'Like his column on Andrew last Sunday?'

'I saw him read that twice. I told Daisy, Andrew, among the great cluster of feelings that Ben feels for you, he is jealous of your happy marriage.'

Andrew laughed. 'I wonder, Daisy, if you'd consider going off with some bloke to see whether that might get Ben off my back?'

Giles said to Angela: 'Do you ever feel embarrassed by some of the more *outré* Franwell assaults on your friend's husband?'

Angela shrugged. 'What's the point? We all know what Ben is like. The question really should be put to Daisy and Andrew: do they ever hold it against me? Lots of people would.'

'You know what I would hold against you?' said Daisy. 'If these days you passed on to Ben any conversation you and I had together when I'd asked you to keep it private. That would cut me to the quick. But then you never would. That's one of the differences in our relationships with our husbands. Even if you told me not to tell Andrew something, probably I would.'

Angela gave her small smile. 'That's why I'd never tell you anything I didn't want Andrew to know. I must go. The Minister's red box is sitting by the door, waiting for his attention. May I give you a lift, Giles?'

Before he could answer, a terrific squealing of brakes was instantly followed by the crunch of metal and glass shattering. Andrew ran into the hall and flung the front door open.

A red Mini was crammed into the right front bumper of the Jaguar where Ollie had carefully manoeuvred it into a tight space between parked cars. Denis was already out of his side of the Jaguar, his right hand inside his jacket.

From the Mini's only door that still functioned stepped Nelly Harwood. He had lately bought the Mini in the belief that, unlike its larger predecessor, it could do no damage.

'For God's sake, Nelly,' Andrew said, momentarily angry like someone who has been frightened and then finds there is nothing to fear.

Nelly, swaying only very slightly as he surveyed the mess, said: 'Do you suppose I was in charge of this disorder?'

Ollie now stood alongside Nelly. Denis removed his hand from the holster strapped across his chest inside his jacket.

'This is my brother who has made a somewhat dramatic arrival,' Andrew said to them.

Across Cheyne Street windows were thrown open and neighbours peered out.

'I'd intended to see if your lights were on before going home and ringing you,' said Nelly. He gave the impression of taking pains to enunciate clearly. 'The reason I wanted to discover if your lights were on was that I didn't want to disturb you if you'd gone to bed,' he explained.

'As unfortunately our lights are still on, you'd better come in,' said Andrew.

He turned to Ollie and Denis. 'Running into the Jag appears to be like hitting a stone wall. I doubt that the Mini can be driven.'

'I left the keys in it,' said Nelly. 'I'd be awfully grateful if you could find a few free feet of kerb to park it, assuming it can still move at all.'

'Would that be possible, Ollie? It would certainly make life easier if we didn't have to get a garage pickup truck here tonight.'

'Let us have a go at it, sir,' Ollie said.

Inside the house, Daisy went down to the kitchen to get black coffee for her brother-in-law. Nelly sat in an armchair in the drawing room, looking rueful. With his slim body and unlined face, he made Giles think of Dorian Gray.

'Should we try a second time to make our own exit?' Angela said just before the telephone rang.

Giles gave his short laugh. 'What do you want to bet that is one of my fellow jackals?'

Andrew picked up the telephone. 'Oh hullo, Ben. Angela's just here. Hang on.'

Although Benjamin Franwell knew his wife was spending the evening at the Harwoods' home, he had not rung to speak with her.

'It's you I wanted to speak with, Andrew. The *Rampart* has just received a call saying the Defence Secretary's car has been rammed by a Mini. What's happening?'

Andrew had already asked himself whether this ludicrous episode was bound to appear in the press. Now he knew the answer. He said into the telephone: 'The Mini belongs to my beloved brother. He just dropped in for a chat.'

'It doesn't sound too disastrous,' Ben replied, 'though of course you'll understand that I have a reporter and a photographer on their way to Cheyne Street.'

It was two o'clock when Andrew and Daisy got to bed. Six hours later they opened Friday's newspapers. The story about Nelly was played in various ways.

But the one Daisy minded did not appear until two mornings later. Opposite the *Rampart*'s leader page was an enormous photograph of Ollie at the wheel of the crumpled Mini while Denis pushed it free of the government Jaguar. In extra bold type the caption under the picture said: 'Is this why taxpayers' money goes to Defence?'

The leader on the episode was short – written in the 'detached' style Ben sometimes adopted for his unsigned leaders:

> Late Thursday evening the Defence Secretary's car, waiting outside the Minister's Chelsea home, was rammed by a car driven by his brother, Nelson Harwood. Nelson Harwood has been charged with dangerous driving when over the legal alcohol limit. As he refused to come to the front door of his brother's house and speak with our reporter, for the moment we must concern ourselves only with Mr Andrew Harwood.
>
> We can guess at Andrew Harwood's thoughts when he instructed his detective and his driver, both employed by the Ministry of Defence, to assist in making it appear nothing untoward had just occurred in a quiet Chelsea street.

Any of us could have a brother who, not for the first time, will be appearing before a court of law. But few of us are public servants receiving great emoluments from this nation. Should such a public servant really think nothing of instructing his MoD staff to cover up what is, after all, a criminal offence?

30

When chained to the House of Commons in the evening, Andrew
liked to use the time between division bells to work quietly through
the red boxes that Martin Thrower, at the end of his own work
day in Richmond Terrace, had packed up and locked and given
to Ollie to bring over to the Minister's room at the House.

After Andrew had first joined the Cabinet as Industry Secretary,
Daisy could scarcely believe her eyes at the contrast of his
Commons room with the 'shoebox' he'd had as a backbencher,
and the Defence Secretary's room was grander still. Like others,
not least MPs themselves, she was struck by the infinite gap
between a Cabinet minister and other MPs – not only in status
but in amenities. She'd begun to understand why some politicians
held onto high office just for its trappings.

Ollie had left two red boxes on the massive oak desk. Unlocking
them, Andrew realized he was extremely curious. The Pentagon
had rung through that afternoon to tell him that the President was
appointing a new Secretary of Defense and that the announcement
would be made on the evening news Eastern Standard Time.
Andrew glanced at his watch.

Just as he'd seen his outgoing American opposite number regularly, he was bound to see a lot of the incoming one. The official visit to London already lined up for next week would presumably be carried out by the new appointee.

Among the files coded with blue tabs he lifted out the one marked: 'Secretary of Defense, United States of America: Dr Carl Myer'.

On the top sheet, Martin Thrower had written: 'Minister: The following is scanty. We will of course have a fuller biography shortly. M.T.'

Andrew turned the page. One thing about Martin Thrower's style: if not elegant, it was to the point.

Carl Reuben Myer was born in 1942 in Boston, Massachusetts, the fourth of five children of Reuben and Myra Myer who emigrated from Russia during Stalin's pogroms in the mid-1930s. Reuben Myer became a wholesale tailor in Boston.

Carl Myer was educated in Boston's public schools and won a scholarship to Princeton University where he took his BA degree, his master's degree and his PhD. He then became a Professor of International Studies at Princeton.

By 1975 his articles in *Commentary* and the *New Leader* had been drawn to the attention of a wider audience, and his Princeton lectures became a focal point for visiting intellectuals and specialists in foreign affairs and, in particular, defence policy. By 1976 his hardline hawkish views were well known in Washington, and it was said that his *Commentary* articles had been closely noted by the then Secretary of State, Dr Henry Kissinger.

When President Carter came to office at the beginning of 1977, there was wide speculation that Dr Myer might be appointed as a presidential advisor. This did not take place.

During President Reagan's two terms of office, Dr Myer's writing and public statements received close attention in Washington. Mr Caspar Weinberger, the Secretary of Defense from 1981 to 1987 and regarded as the most hawkish member of President Reagan's Cabinet, was said to have drawn on specific policies advocated by Dr Myer.

When President Bush took office at the beginning of 1989, it was again rumoured that Dr Myer might be invited to take a political appointment. So far as is known, none was offered until now. Long reputed to be one of the cleverest men on the periphery of American power politics, today Dr Carl Myer moves to centre stage.

He will take an indefinite sabbatical from Princeton University in order to move to Washington. He will be accompanied by his wife. In 1983 he married Miss Jocelyn Randall, daughter of Mr Elliott Randall, scion of a New York banking family. Dr and Mrs Myer have no children.

If Andrew was honest with himself, which he usually was, he had to admit that when he first knew Daisy he'd been rather impressed that this young woman was the object of Professor Myer's private pursuit. Supposing Daisy had married Myer instead, this man who was now Andrew's most important opposite number – indeed the most important defence minister in the world.

He glanced again at the date in the last paragraph: 1983 – six years after Daisy had married Andrew. Carl Myer must have found her hard to replace.

He smiled to himself. He was looking forward to telling Daisy about the new American appointment. It would amuse her.

As he stepped from the Jaguar, he looked at his watch. 11:10. Not bad. He'd finished one red box and left it locked on his desk; Ollie would collect it in the morning and take it over to Richmond Terrace. He had the remaining box in one hand. Glancing up, he saw the only lights were behind the two pairs of curtains drawn in their bedroom.

When he reached the top of the stairs and opened their bedroom door, Daisy put aside the book she'd been reading and smiled happily at him, watching him as he took off his tie and swapped his shoes for the soft leather carpet slippers. She'd hoped he might come straight to bed, but the red box was standing by the door.

'Would you feel like having a drink next door before I get down to tomorrow's Cabinet on the American bases?' he said.

He poured out a highball for each of them, and they began their day's exchange of news.

'You'll be interested in the new American Secretary of Defense,' he said. 'You'll read about his appointment in tomorrow's news-papers. It's your old friend, Carl Myer.'

'Oh,' Daisy said. She sipped her drink.

'I thought you'd be entertained,' said Andrew, beetling his

brow as he saw she was not. He'd had a long day, and he'd looked forward to relaxing with Daisy before he opened that bloody box.

'I am, I suppose. It's just that I'm always slightly resistant to having my American life and my life here overlap.'

Surprised at finding herself so irritable, she looked down absently at the arm of her chair as with thumb and third finger she delicately twisted one of its velvet-covered buttons, now faded and a bit grubby. For sentimental reasons the pair of armchairs had been allowed to remain much as they had been when they stood on either side of the drawing-room fireplace in the Eaton Place flat.

He watched her. For fifteen years she had twisted that button when she was ill at ease. Good thing she wasn't ill at ease more often or the bloody button would long since have come off. He was annoyed by her reaction to his news.

'I suppose it's that one of my pleasures is the fact that you, the children, the friends who matter most to me are all to do with my life since I came to England. My life here has nothing to do with half-forgotten friendships – and so on – that are sort of inherited from one's own family and school – and all that,' she added lamely.

Andrew's pique was that of someone whose little gift is not appreciated.

'Had I known the complex of emotions my news would generate, I'd have delivered it less lightheartedly,' he said drily.

She hated it when he went cold like that.

'I'm being boring,' she said. 'It will be amusing to see Carl in his new role as your opposite number.'

Neither of them liked quarrelling. Anyhow, she didn't know why she felt such unease. Really quite irrational. She shook it off.

31

As he stepped out of Temple underground station, Charles Cartwright looked at his watch. 12:50. Good. He had the civil servant's
punctuality. He had meant to walk from Richmond Terrace but
the 11:30 meeting ran on longer than expected. He told himself
that walking to Westminster tube station and taking the first train
east would be quicker than a taxi in lunchtime traffic, even though
it would mean doubling back on foot to reach the Savoy Hotel.
In fact, a taxi would have had no difficulties had it gone by way
of the Embankment, but Cartwright begrudged the fare. If you
look after the pennies, the pounds will look after themselves, he
liked to say. His mother had been given to old saws. Glancing
again at his watch, he quickened his pace.

At the Embankment entrance to the Savoy, he nodded to the
doorman as if this was an habitual lunch venue for the Assistant
Secretary in charge of F-section at the Ministry of Defence. Inside
as he mounted the serpentine staircase rapidly, his thin, pale face
maintained a bland expression to suggest he was light on his feet
rather than concerned that he might be late for his meeting with
the editor of the *Rampart*.

Franwell's secretary had stressed that they would be lunching in the Restaurant – 'not the Grill which the editor finds too close quarters'. Cartwright recalled how gratified he had been to be taken to the Savoy Grill by a defence correspondent of the *Washington Post* two years ago. He had recognized at least eight people lunching there. Now he knew it was smarter to eat in the main restaurant, and when he found himself in it, he could see why: tables were set so far apart that an air of leisure was created and, more important, no one could overhear your conversation.

'You have a reservation, sir?'

Hard to know the status of this man in his black swallow-tailed coat and black bow tie. Cartwright adopted the patronizing manner which came quite easily to him. 'I'm meeting Mr Franwell.'

Instantly another figure came forward, this one dressed in swallow-tailed coat with a tie made of silver and black silk. 'Good afternoon, sir.'

Clearly the undertaker was the chap in charge.

'Let me show you to Mr Franwell's table,' he said.

The ten tables along the window wall looked particularly luxurious with their direct view over the Thames. Cartwright was shown to one almost in the middle. It was laid for two, glasses sparkling, silverware gleaming against the pink starched cloth with matching napkins, one of which another waiter, with a flourish, shook open and offered to Charles Cartwright's lap.

'Would you care to have something to drink while you wait, sir?'

'Not for the moment.'

When the head waiter had withdrawn, Cartwright examined the posy that embellished the centre of the table. The blue corn-flowers and white roses looked fetching against the pink cloth. With a long-fingered hand he neatly extracted a cornflower, snapped its stem in two and inserted the blossom in his buttonhole. He left the discarded stem lying beside one of his wine glasses. When he'd had lunch at the Reform with a Deputy Secretary, Cartwright had observed the senior official help himself to a buttonhole in this *grand seigneur* manner. Cartwright had been particularly impressed by the way the unwanted stem had been left openly on the table for the waiter to remove; that showed real confidence and style.

'Hullo, Charles. You found your way.'

Cartwright looked from the corner of his eye at the undertaker figure who had shown Ben to his table. Why did Franwell have to suggest that Cartwright was not perfectly familiar with the Savoy Restaurant?

The answer was that during all these years of success, Ben Franwell had made not the slightest effort to acquire tact. He took pride in being a rough diamond. And it meant he could exercise a subtle bullying superiority over striped-pants milksops like Cartwright with their fussiness about doing things the correct way, even when they were corrupt.

Ben's eyes took in the bowl of flowers and the buttonhole and the stem lying on the starched tablecloth. Smarmy arsehole, he thought to himself. Where'd he pick up that trick? 'What are you going to drink?' he said.

'I'll have a dry sherry,' said Cartwright. 'Tio Pepe?'

Wouldn't you know? Ben would have bet £10 that Cartwright would ask for sherry or a gin-and-tonic. 'We'll have one Tio Pepe and a double whisky,' he said to the waiter hovering at his elbow.

Having no interest in exchanging idle anecdotes with Cartwright, as soon as their food order was placed Ben came straight to the point.

'Who's going to get the contract for the ES7 components?'

Cartwright didn't intend to be hurried. He reminded himself that it was he, the Assistant Secretary in charge of fighter aircraft, who held the ace when it came to bestowing multi-million-pound components contracts on Bedfordshire High Tech or anyone else.

'There are three bidders on my shortlist.'

'Including BedHiTe, I trust. We've discussed this before.'

'Oh yes. You know already, Benjamin, that I have a lot of time for BedHiTe.'

'You've ruled out Stockton?'

'Not yet. They have an established reputation for top-quality workmanship at reasonable cost. And so long as the Raider remains on the seabed, we have proof that any fault lay in Stockton's new seat design.'

'Do you think that's where the fault was?'

Ben wanted to make absolutely certain he was right to abandon Plan One.

'Yes and no.' Cartwright sipped his sherry, swallowing rather more than his fastidious manner suggested, then pressing his lips.

Ben waited. One of the reasons why he found the man so tedious was the perpetual schoolmasterly drawing out of a perfectly simple answer with this pompous we-must-consider-all-aspects-of-the-thing crap.

'We are virtually certain that it was a freak accident – not sinister intention – that produced such unhappy consequences for the pilot.'

Cartwright was very fond of Tio Pepe. He held his glass against the light to enjoy the lustrous glow imparted to the remaining drops of amber.

'But of course it remains a possibility that Stockton's new seat design has a crucial fault in it. We must wait for the salvagers' work to be completed.'

Jesus, Ben said to himself. Get to the point for Christ's sake.

'I have almost ruled out Stockton – but not quite.' He, Charles Cartwright, would show that he could not be twisted around Benjamin Franwell's little finger.

Ben glanced at the waiter nearby and gave a curt gesture with a forefinger to Cartwright's empty glass. The waiter nodded.

'Who's the third on your shortlist, Charles?'

'Samson in Somerset. You may know them.'

'I know that our aeronautics man is lukewarm about Samson. He says they are unreliable on delivery dates. Why are you considering Samson?'

'Ah, Benjamin,' Cartwright began, then gave a light, dry little clearing of the throat to manifest discretion as the waiter put down a second glass brimming with Tio Pepe.

He took an initial sip in the manner of a wine buff tasting a 1961 Haut Brion brought up specially from the Savoy's cellars.

Then he continued: 'Even your specialist chaps on the *Rampart* don't always have full inside information on these things. I must tell you that Samson's recent record on deliveries is equal to BedHiTe's.'

He paused again as two waiters simultaneously placed two plates of smoked salmon on the pink starched cloth.

Then he said: 'As you know, I share your view that BedHiTe could be the coming aeronautics company and we should get an order in soon. However . . .'

He pressed his lips to indicate the seriousness of the words to follow. 'One does not like interference from another department. I must tell you, Benjamin, that the Department of Industry has been making its own representations to me on behalf of the contract going to BedHiTe. It occurred to me that the Right Honourable Rachel Fisher's constituency might stand to benefit from BedHiTe's further expansion, but in fact BedHiTe is outside her constituency. Could the lady have some other personal interest in the matter? "Miss Fisher has her own fish to fry,"' he added archly, pleased with his little play on words.

Ben's naturally florid colour deepened. He waited, his intense blue eyes on Cartwright's pale face.

'The smallness of this world has once again been demonstrated – this time at my golf club,' Cartwright went on. 'I was talking just the other day to a member called George Bishop. He happens to be married to the Industry Secretary. And I happen to know he also handles the insurance for BedHiTe.'

'It's well known that Rachel Fisher has a husband who does something or other in insurance. So what?'

'I mention it, Benjamin, purely as a coincidence, nothing more.'

'You can bet your last rise on the civil service ladder that it is purely coincidence. Rachel Fisher has one interest only in BedHiTe – and it is the interest you would expect from a first class Industry Secretary. She wants deserving firms rewarded. That's what this government is about.' You cruddy jerk, Ben added to himself.

'Indeed.'

Cartwright knew he shouldn't have drunk that second sherry so fast on an empty stomach. He must abandon this thorny conversation and devote himself to the superb Scotch salmon sliced so generously, unlike those slivers he'd been given last month at the Reform. Everyone knew it was infra dig to combine eating and business. Franwell had been crude in raising the subject at the outset. A gentleman would have waited until coffee and cigars. Cartwright turned his full attention to the smoked salmon.

At least they would get through the meal fairly fast at this rate, Ben said to himself.

When Cartwright had finished the last morsel of the chicken breast poached in cream with brandy, Ben said: 'When will you be making the decision on who gets the ES7 contract?'

'I expect to do so in May,' said Cartwright.

Ben said pleasantly: 'Shall we have a brandy with our coffee?' When the end required false bonhomie he was prepared to turn it on.

'I don't suppose, Charles, I could interest you in doing a bit of background research for the *Rampart*? We're planning to run a series on jetsetters' resorts. I'm suggesting an expenses-paid three-week holiday for several non-journalists – whose judgement is good – to book into fashionable hotels in different countries. Each of them would be expected to take along a wife or friend, naturally – unless they preferred taking a holiday alone.'

Ben rarely got involved in this sort of thing, but when he did, he was adroit. By saying that the *Rampart* was sending three non-journalists on these expenses-paid luxury holidays, the deal sounded almost like normal newspaper practice.

He went on: 'If the *Rampart*'s travel correspondent were to stay at any of these five-star resorts, he'd be recognized and given preferential treatment: we wouldn't be able to get an objective assessment. What we want to find out is how much service an unknown holiday-maker gets for a large amount of expenditure. If you were interested in being one of our anonymous jetsetters, the most we would want from you would be your impression of the place – purely for background, not attributable. And of course, in the end, we might shelve the series – but that would be my lookout, not yours.'

'I see.'

'To cover travel and three weeks' expenses at one of these top-notch resorts – you could say which country you preferred – we'd be talking in five figures. I'd be delighted if you felt like casing one of these playboy spots for me. What do you think?'

Cartwright revolved the brandy balloon slowly. He felt quite hot.

'I think I'd be interested in that,' he said.

'Good. Think about where you'd like to go. The world is yours. You and I could make firm plans about your trip a little later – talk about it again in May or June.'

Cartwright took another swallow of his brandy.

'And by the way, Charles. You'll be ringing me before you send up your ES7 decision for ministerial approval, won't you.'

It was a statement, not a question.

'I'll be glad to, Benjamin – purely in the capacity of personal friendship.'

'I'd appreciate it if you rang me before anything about the ES7 contract is actually formalized on paper. It would help me clear my mind.'

'Nothing could be easier, my dear chap.' Cartwright gave a languid wave with one hand. He'd always been proud of his slender hands.

Ben looked at his watch. 'I must be off in two minutes. How are you getting on with Master Andrew?'

Cartwright hesitated. Although his job entailed his calling on the Minister from time to time, communication between them was usually on paper. Like most civil servants, he had no personal relations with the Minister. Yet he wanted to impress Ben Franwell.

'Between you and me, Benjamin, he's not the kind of minister I like to see in charge of Defence. He let the Housing Minister, if you please, have some of the budget he should have demanded for the MoD. What's it got to do with him whether the Housing Ministry is underfunded?'

Cartwright suddenly felt indignant just thinking about it.

'Politicians shouldn't let emotion get in the way of their work. They'd do a lot better if they had the civil servant's objectivity. Actually, I don't care for Andrew Harwood. Who does he think he is?'

Ben didn't press him. There was nothing to be got from Cartwright in this area: he was only on the periphery of Andrew

Harwood's life. It was mere chance that made Cartwright a useful pawn in another area.

The two men left the table together and crossed the restaurant. In the lounge Ben stopped.

'You'll be going back to Richmond Terrace. I'm going in the opposite direction. My car's waiting for me at the Embankment entrance, so I'll say goodbye here. Nice to see you, Charles. You'll be ringing me.'

They shook hands, and Ben turned right and made for the serpentine staircase, while Cartwright strode purposefully towards the front door where the doorman would be waiting to beckon to the taxi rank just beyond. Before reaching the front door, he turned into the men's cloakroom. When he emerged from it a few minutes later, he went back to the lounge and walked across it to the serpentine staircase, its brass rail gleaming as it wound down to the Embankment entrance.

Outside the revolving door, he nodded casually to the doorman before setting off on foot for Temple tube station. He looked at his watch. Even if he had to wait five minutes for a train, he'd be back at his desk comfortably by three.

32

'Welcome, Mr Secretary.'

Andrew had gone down to the Horse Guards entrance of the Ministry of Defence to greet the American Secretary of Defense on his first arrival.

The band of the Grenadier Guards blew their horns and thumped their drums as a full Guard of Honour marched down Horse Guards Avenue and came to attention before the two defence ministers. Secretary Myer stepped briskly down the front stairs to inspect the Guards.

Back inside the building, the two defence ministers took the lift to the sixth floor, leaving most of Secretary Myer's security agents on the ground floor.

In his room, Andrew motioned towards the blue leather chesterfield and the armchairs. Both men were at ease as Martin Thrower left the room, closing the door behind him. It was half past six.

'Would you like a drink?'

'No thanks. How's Daisy?' said Carl Myer.

'Putting up philosophically with marriage to a politician. You may know that she's become a success as a sculptor of portrait busts. One's on show now,' Andrew added with pride.

'I shall make it a point to see it. Probably not this visit. As it's my first time officially, the schedule's pretty tight. What do you think of the American ambassador?'

'Seems a competent chap. Certainly very friendly. There's been no reason for us to have more than what are effectively social relations. How's life at Claridge's?'

'My God. I can see why Claridge's stopped putting up the American Secretary of Defense for several years. Quite a hassle for them. Still, it keeps the staff on their toes. I'm not clear how one would handle a clandestine affair – not that a Secretary of Defense would ever go in for that sort of thing.'

Carl's brown eyes twinkled. 'The business of having to be always obtainable by the President has certain disadvantages – such as having an agent standing outside your hotel suite day and night.'

He shrugged.

Andrew laughed. 'How do you find Washington after Princeton?'

Carl Myer chuckled. 'Everyone says that Washington is a provincial town. True. But its provincialism is not in the class of a university town. Nothing can be more parochial than Princeton, however many distinguished visitors arrive to exchange their brilliant ideas on international affairs.'

'I gather you want to increase your defence spending.'

'That's right. I believe you are more relaxed than I am about the threat from the East.' Again the brown eyes twinkled.

Watching him, Andrew could see why Daisy had been charmed. When he and Myer had had their brief encounter fifteen years earlier, not only had they both been unprepared for it: they had been rivals. Andrew could remember vividly the contrast between Myer's pallor and his black curly hair, the intentness with which Myer had studied him, the way they had smiled faintly at one another without any effort on either side to suggest the slightest warmth.

Yet now Andrew recognized friendly feelings in himself, and, he thought, in Myer. When the American Defense Secretary got up to leave, each used the other's first name.

'Good night, Andrew. You'll see me in this room again almost before you've turned around.'

The British Defence Secretary laughed. 'Good night, Carl. Business between us begins, I believe, at 10:30. I know Daisy will want to see you when your time is less pressed. If not this visit, the next.'

'What's he look like?' she asked.

They were sitting in the study. There had been only the one vote at ten, and Andrew was home by 10:30.

'I liked him. Dry humour. I expect I'll see the intellectually arrogant side tomorrow. I'm rather looking forward to that.'

'Why?'

'Intellectual curiosity on my part? He *is* one of the cleverest men to enter American politics in fifteen years.'

'But does he *look* different from the way you remember him? He's nearly fifty.'

'Forty-nine.' Like all politicians, Andrew was exact about another politician's age. 'As we're in London this weekend, shall I ask him to call in here on his way to the airport?'

Daisy was surprised by her excitement. 'All right.'

At 10:30 the next morning Martin Thrower led Secretary Myer and two of his officials into the Minister's room. Austin Barthmore was already there.

Six blotters and six pens had been placed on the Georgian hexagonal table in front of the windows.

The first item on the agenda was got through in five minutes.

The next item concerned Satyr. Everyone present had a neat summary before him, though there was no need to refer to it.

'As you know, Carl, Britain needs a new series of satellites – Satyr – for military communications. We want it to be entirely independent of America's Sun system.'

'As Satyr will be used only for communications, why is it so important that it be unavailable to contact with our Sun system? We're not the Soviet Union.' Carl smiled.

'We've taken a political decision.'

'I see. I take it that doesn't rule out some of Satyr's components being made in the United States if one of our companies, say US Solar Space, could do the job more efficiently than a British company.'

'We want all parts of Satyr to be made here.'

'Because you don't trust us not to make a one-way link with our own system? Or because you have sentimental reasons?' Again Carl Myer smiled. He was leaning forward on his folded arms.

Andrew replied amiably: 'We want Satyr to be independent – in every respect – from start to finish. Satellite components are one of the things we are best at producing in this country. You know we like to encourage British industry. Satyr would be a conspicuous symbol that we were doing so.'

'I envy you your defence budget,' Carl said. 'I wouldn't be able to afford to spend a billion dollars when I could get the job done for two-thirds of that cost. If you go in with us on the production, maybe we could launch the satellites for you at a reduced price.'

Andrew was amused by the affable manner in which Myer put his case for an American company to share in the gravy.

'If we could work out something which would save you money, would you consider having some of Satyr's components made by US Solar Space?' Carl asked.

Andrew too was now leaning forward on folded arms. 'I wouldn't rule it out.'

'Could one of you children please answer the doorbell?'

Daisy was wearing a pale blue lace bra and underpants. A large pink towel was over one shoulder. She was drying her hair.

'*Sophie. Matty!*' she shouted up to the next floor.

The already high volume of the Beatles singing 'Eleanor Rigby' grew louder as an upstairs door was opened. Over the banisters, Sophie's head appeared.

'What's the matter?'

'Someone's been leaning on the doorbell for the last five minutes. Can you please answer it? Carl Myer isn't due for another half an hour.'

'All right.'

In her bare feet Sophie pattered down the stairs, jumping the last three steps to land with a clonk on the first floor landing.

Passing her mother in the hall she said: 'Where's Dad?'

'Gone to the newsagent. Where's Matty?'

'Dunno,' Sophie called back, jumping the last three steps to land with another clonk on the ground floor.

Holding the towel around her bra, Daisy peered over the banisters and waited.

A minute later she saw the top of Sophie's head reappear, her hair hanging nearly straight; she must have spent the morning ironing out the curls. Looking up at her mother she said: 'It's the fuzz. They're American. They want to search the garden.'

'Oh God, I forgot about them,' Daisy said. 'Private office told me they'd be coming.'

A man's head now appeared and looked up at Daisy.

'We're security agents, ma'am.'

He held up a badge which she couldn't see from that distance.

'We need to look around this floor and the lower floor and garden, if you don't mind, ma'am, before Secretary Myer arrives.'

Daisy burst out laughing. 'I'm drying my hair. Sophie, could you show them around?'

When Andrew returned fifteen minutes later, the security agents were standing outside the front door.

Inside the house the only sound came from the top floor. Good thing he liked the Beatles, Andrew said to himself as he went up to the first floor where he found Daisy standing in front of the bathroom mirror, a mascara brush in one hand. With her white silk trousers she was wearing a pale turquoise silk shirt, cut like a man's, its three top buttons undone. Her toenails were painted coral pink. She wore pearl earrings, and her curls were caught up by tortoiseshell combs. Andrew imagined looking at her through Carl Myer's eyes. She was a very pretty woman. He felt the pleasure of a man confident of a woman's exclusive love.

'How long have those two chaps been hanging about?' he asked.

'Half an hour? They've checked out the garden and downstairs. I hope they didn't think it necessary to taste my Chicken Diable in case I intended poisoning their precious Secretary of Defense. Why are they so much fussier than your detectives?'

'You know as well as I do: at the best of times your compatriots make a special show of security. And the latest Middle East incident has put Americans everywhere on high security alert.'

At that moment they heard the roar of outriders approaching.

Daisy looked out of one of the bedroom windows as two BMWs braked beside the maple tree. Behind them came a police car from which three more Metropolitan Police and an American agent got out and stood on the pavement. Walkie-talkies crackled. Across the street, windows were thrown open and neighbours leaned out to watch the show.

Sophie appeared beside her mother. 'What a commotion. Is all this to do with Dr Myer?'

Daisy laughed. It was rather absurd that a fortnight ago he was a Princeton professor, and this week the whole of Cheyne Street was about to be sealed off.

The lead car now appeared at the top of the street, barely coming to a halt before more police and another American agent jumped out.

Security these days dictated that the car carrying the American Secretary of Defense be inconspicuous as well as armoured. Behind the lead car a pale grey Opel Senator drew up. Behind it came the follow car, a black saloon whose doors opened as soon as it stopped, British agents and one American agent stepping out.

'The pavement is certainly getting crowded,' Sophie said.

Then the back door of the Opel Senator opened. What had been the beginning of a tonsure when last Daisy saw him was now a bald patch and then the short thick curls began. She could see where they grew low on the back of his neck, only a quarter of an inch of white skin showing above the collar. 'That lovely unmarked part of the neck that looks so vulnerable just before the armour begins.' The unbidden words flashed through her mind, giving her an odd feeling.

'Did you used to know him really well?' asked Sophie.

'I suppose I did,' Daisy replied.

Andrew appeared on the pavement and shook hands with their guest. Then a smaller sandy-haired figure appeared. Even from above Daisy could tell that Matty was proud as he shook hands with Secretary Myer.

'Let's go down,' she said to Sophie.

When they walked into the drawing room, Andrew was at the drinks table pouring out two whiskies. Matty had disappeared. Carl was standing with his back to the fireplace. She saw the colour come into his face.

'Hullo, Daisy.'

'Hullo, Carl.'

She remained just inside the drawing-room door. She hadn't considered in advance whether they would kiss on the cheek. She found she wanted to keep a space between them. 'This is Sophie.'

'I can tell that. Hullo, Sophie,' he said in a serious voice, crossing the room to shake the daughter's hand before kissing the mother on the cheek.

As he stood back again, the brown eyes, twinkling, returned to Daisy's face. Andrew was behind him, and Carl glanced down at the shirt where it was unbuttoned. He looked up again to her face.

Piqued by his brass, she blushed. Perhaps it wasn't pique. Was it pleasure? She wasn't sure.

Lunch was relaxed. Rather than running back and forth to the dining room, Daisy had laid the Victorian table in the big kitchen with a starched tablecloth and linen napkins. 'People always prefer eating in this room,' Andrew invariably said when they entertained there.

Both Harwoods were acutely curious about Carl, he was acutely curious about them, each of the three alert to the reactions of the other two.

As his plane was due to depart from Heathrow at three o'clock, they didn't linger at the table.

Upstairs Andrew said: 'Daisy, why don't you show Carl your studio?'

'Do you want to see it?'

'Very much.'

'Give a shout when you come back,' Andrew said. 'I'm going to make a quick call from the study.'

Daisy led the way back past the small room where her sitters sometimes changed. Inside the studio, Carl closed the door behind him.

The first thing he noticed was that the windows were set so high you could see only the treetops. Moderately knowledgeable about trees, he recognized these as ash; he liked the intense vividness of their Maytime green before soot began to dull their foliage.

His eyes went back to Daisy who had turned to face him. Standing between the ghostly maquettes on their wires, she looked even more vibrant than she had when he'd watched her across the kitchen table.

He was silent as he stood with his back to the closed door, watching her face. Then again he looked down at the silk shirt unbuttoned to just above her bra – if she was wearing one; he wasn't sure. She was tensely aware of the direction of his eyes. He looked back at her face.

'You are even more beguiling today, Daisy, than when I unbuttoned your shirt in room 242.'

He spoke in a low voice. Andrew had said he was going upstairs. The studio door was thick and had a green baize cover on both its sides. Even so.

He moved away from the door into the centre of the studio and stopped three feet from Daisy. 'You pushed my hand away. Do you remember? You said: "I don't want to." I said: "Yes you do." You pushed my hand away again, that time more tentatively. I took both your hands and put them flat against your thighs. Then I resumed unbuttoning your shirt. I was right. You did want to.'

Daisy remained standing where she was. A torrent of memories of that hot July afternoon in Brown's Hotel rushed through her mind: her jealousy of the glamorous woman she'd seen with Andrew, anger with Andrew, her abandoned physical response to Carl's sexuality, her distaste afterwards because there'd been no connection between her body and her emotions. With crystal clarity she saw the two enormous pigeons perched on the rooftop opposite the window of room 242.

It was the last image that broke the beam between her eyes and Carl's. She turned away and walked to the back of the studio. On a wooden plinth was a larger than life-size clay model of two birds, one's neck turned around the other's in what was like an embrace. During the previous month when she'd modelled the birds, she had supposed they sprang in part from the Epstein marble doves copulating at the Tate. Now she realized what the relevant memory must have been: the pigeons on the rooftop outside the bedroom where she had lain, surfeited and naked, beside Carl, surfeited and naked. She remembered the smell in room 242. It hadn't been that his sperm and his skin smelled unpleasant: it was that they hadn't Andrew's smell.

She put out a hand to rest it on the back of one of the pigeons. The clay, still moist, felt cool.

'You're meant to be taking an interest in my work,' she said.

'You always did that, Daisy.'

He remained standing in the centre of the studio, his hands at his sides, watching her.

'What do you mean?'

'When you were embarrassed by the way a conversation was going, you always turned the subject as if you hadn't noticed what was being said. What is it about me that embarrasses you, Daisy?'

She kept her hand on the cool clay. What was so odd was the combination of feelings, half annoyance, half attraction. Was it the situation more than the man that accounted for her excitement? If he wasn't the American Secretary of Defense would she feel the same? How could she know? He *was* the Secretary of Defense.

'Why don't you take your hand off that bird and answer me, Daisy?'

Carl walked towards her.

Footsteps could be heard coming down the hall. Immediately Carl turned around. The studio door opened. Andrew laughed.

'One of your convoy is in the front hall. He seems to think you should set off for Heathrow.'

'They fret so. Still, I expect I should go. Perhaps the Harwood household will allow me to pay another visit? There can't be many defence ministers who have a genuine personal interest in each other.'

Andrew felt pleasure as the three of them walked to the front door. It was true: Carl was the first of his opposite numbers with whom he could envisage a private friendship.

He turned to his wife. 'On one of Carl's trips to London, why don't you and he try to find a couple of hours for him to sit for you?'

He turned to Carl. 'It might take a number of official visits before the bust was completed. But it would make a nice addition to the Pentagon, don't you think?'

'An excellent idea, Minister.' Carl's eyes twinkled.

He stepped into the open back door of the grey Opel Senator. Instantly the quiet Saturday afternoon in Cheyne Street was disrupted as in unison the two outriders on their BMWs rammed a foot down on the starting pedal.

33

'What do you actually do there, Uncle Nelly?' asked Sophie.

'An excellent question,' Nelly Harwood replied. 'Let me think.'

Having done so, he listed his daily routine as a stockbroker for Rothburg Investment Trust.

'I arrive at ten o'clock and open my post. I call up on my data screen the European stock-market prices relevant to the accounts I handle. I decide whether to buy, sell or quietly hang on. This is more complicated than you may think, Sophie. Each client's portfolio has its own individual requirements. Naturally I have either to consult my clients or, where they have given me a free hand, dictate a letter informing them of what I have done in their name. After this stressful morning, I go off to lunch. Ordinarily this would demand three hours out of my work day, depending on the traffic between the City and the West End. Then I return to my office by which time Wall Street has been awake for an hour or so, and I call up the latest share prices on my screen. Throughout this flurry of activity on behalf of my clients, I have to give some concentrated thought to my own portfolio.'

There was nothing the matter with Nelly's IQ. He was a good deal brighter than many who worked in the City. But he resembled the traditional City chap rather than the eager yuppie of the 1980s: essentially he was an indolent man. And he had now been with Rothburg for five years.

His dream was to acquire enough directorships so that in a not too distant future he had a substantial salary without spending more than two hours a day at hard labour. So far he had only one directorship – in a timber firm in Surrey run by a friend from Marlborough.

The morning after his conversation with Sophie, he stepped out from Monument underground station into a bright May morning, glancing up at the gilt flaming urn atop the great Doric column designed by Wren, the sun glinting on the flames that the Monument commemorates. Whenever he thought of the Great Fire of London raging 325 years ago where now he walked, it gave him an odd feeling. He couldn't decide whether it was a sense of his transience in this world or a sense of continuity. Perhaps a mixture of the two.

He stepped off the kerb and strode across Eastcheap before the next burst of traffic bore down. At the end of Mincing Lane he turned right, and when he came to the wide marble stairs of Rothburg, he took them two at a time. He was feeling good.

When these warm summer days were bestowed on England in May, his heart was always light. Perhaps he should have a new adventure. He hadn't been to Heaven for at least a month. Strange to remember how ten years ago there were three thousand men at a time cruising in their palace under the arches of Charing Cross. Last month only a couple of hundred had been there, and great clouds of coloured gases had been puffed all over the place to make it seem more animated. He remembered the first time he'd seen the notice for Body Positive Night: he had supposed it was an evening when pumping-iron freaks, oiled and rippling, would be on display. They were not to his taste, but he'd gone along for the laugh, and it had been a shock when he walked into Heaven. One glance at the chaps, subdued, some emaciated, revealed what he would have discovered if he'd read the small print of the notice: Body Positive was a euphemism for HIV positive. God. Poor devils. He'd been lucky. But then he was careful. And it must help that he wasn't wildly promiscuous. He had never gone in for that compulsive cruising, day in, day out. Could you imagine anything more *boring* than to be burdened with an obsession?

His office was on the twelfth floor, two from the top. As he went through the anteroom, he swept off his bowler hat and gave a little bow to his secretary. Inside his own office he sent the bowler skimming neatly onto the sofa. Sitting at his desk, he was half way through his post when he came on the letter from the president of Bedfordshire High Tech. It said:

> Dear Mr Harwood,
>
> As you will know, BedHiTe is one of Britain's fastest growing engineering industries. Of our twelve directors, one is retiring rather earlier than expected. We shall be appointing a new member of the board as soon as possible.
>
> It has been brought to our attention that you can offer qualities that we are looking for in our directors. I should be pleased if we could meet to discuss what the job would entail.
>
> If you are interested, as I very much hope will be the case, perhaps your secretary could ring my office so that a meeting can be arranged. I would suggest that we hold our conversation over lunch at a restaurant convenient to you.
>
> BedHiTe is anxious to decide this matter by 20th May.
>
> Yours sincerely,

The letter was signed by BedHiTe's president, Brian Burford.

Whistling lightly through his teeth, Nelly gazed out of the window at the sun's reflection on the glass jungle that Richard Rogers had designed for Lloyd's. He'd never seen why such a fuss was made about the building being at odds with its older neighbours in 'The Square Mile'. Rogers's creation was dramatic with its functional organs on display outside instead of being tucked discreetly inside a conventional exterior; funny to think what human beings would look like if they were made like that. What would BedHiTe offer? Fifteen thousand pounds for three afternoons' work a month? Twelve times three was thirty-six.

He got out his pocket calculator. That meant £416.66 an hour. Not bad. Who could have recommended him to BedHiTe? Another Marlborough chum? Someone from Oxford days?

Usually chaps told you when they were about to put your name forward for a freebie, not least because you'd then want to return the favour one day. Good chap, whoever he turned out to be. How many directorships would be needed to say goodbye to his present daily grind at Rothburg? Five? Six? He pressed the buzzer for his secretary.

When they met the following Monday at Claridge's restaurant, Nelly found the president of BedHiTe was an urbane product of Manchester Grammar School and Edinburgh University. Brian Burford had taken his degree in engineering. Somewhere along the way elocution lessons had erased the evidence of his origins. The two men exchanged small talk until they reached coffee, when they got down to the basics.

Nelly had guessed right about the hours that the directorship would involve, wrong about the price: he'd overvalued himself by £1000. Fourteen thousand pounds was on offer. Perhaps he could push it up to £15,000 there and then, but that seemed a bit squalid. Anyhow, he should have a second chance next week when, before finalizing things, he was to have a look around BedHiTe – 'to familiarize yourself with what you'd be taking on,' said his host.

As they walked together across Claridge's lobby to the front entrance, Nelly said, 'By the way, who recommended me for your board?'

Brian Burford had expected this offhand query earlier. George Bishop had been precise: under no circumstances was Burford to say the suggestion had come from George. 'Under no circumstances,' George had repeated.

George had explained that he personally did not know Nelson Harwood, but that Harwood had been highly recommended by an old friend from Cambridge. That was a good enough reference for Brian Burford. George Bishop had handled BedHiTe's insurance for ten years, and the two men liked each other. George's wife being up in London during the week meant he got lonely some evenings. Burford's wife liked George, and the three tended to dine together regularly. Solid man, George.

George had said: 'One thing you've got to remember: Nelson

Harwood, I'm told, will turn the directorship down out of hand if you give him any inkling that you might be offering it because his brother is Defence Secretary. So you must be careful how you handle him. *We* know that his family connection can prove useful to BedHiTe: he's bound to know people who know how things are done in Whitehall, how to get round a corner to get a contract. But if *he* knows our interest in him is related to who his brother is, Nelson Harwood will be off like a shot. If for some reason the family connection comes up, act as if you didn't know about it. Or if you think that makes you seem too unworldly, act as if you'd half forgotten the fact.'

Burford had asked George: 'Won't Nelson Harwood's being one of our directors mean the Defence Secretary will have to declare an interest when he is deciding who gets the ES7 contract?'

George had replied: 'That's why, to be on the safe side, you should get the directorship verbally agreed as soon as possible, and then formalize it in writing just *after* the ES7 contract is signed. There's no reason to expect a great public announcement of either thing, but you never know. My MoD contact tells me he expects the ES7 decision to be brought forward earlier than we had expected. He says it could be signed, sealed and delivered to BedHiTe on the twenty-third of May. That's just ten days from now. So you ought to get a move on.'

As they approached the revolving door into Brook Street, Brian Burford replied to Nelly's question: 'Your name has come up before. Various people in the business have said you've got the qualifications that a rapidly rising engineering firm wants in its directors. Now this opening has suddenly made it possible to issue an invitation. But we do need the answer next week.'

Nelly was not an overweening person, but he had his share of vanity. He knew he was coolheaded and, in his way, reliable. He would turn up for each of the monthly meetings, which was more than could be said for some of his friends who held directorships and boasted of attending a maximum of four or five meetings a year. Burford's answer seemed reasonable enough to Nelly.

Thinking about the £14,000 – possibly £15,000 – made him quicken his gait as he walked towards Bond Street in the warmth of the mid-afternoon sun. Before hopping a taxi back to old

Rothburg, he'd just pop into Sulka. The thing about Sulka's shirts was that in their expensive way they were flashy – just right for dropping in at Heaven this evening. He approached shirt-buying much as he approached Heaven: don't decide in advance exactly what colour and design you want or you're likely to fail in the quest; always shop with an open mind.

On reaching Bond Street he turned south and walked along swiftly, whistling 'Springtime in the Rockies' through his teeth.

'Perfect.' Ben grinned. 'What else did George say?'

'Not a lot. We're not given to long telephone calls.'

Rachel smiled. She was fond of George.

'It's important always to remember that George is not a natural conspirator,' she said. 'He's a gentleman. He prefers to be decent. He and I talk about this arrangement in a matter-of-fact way – as if it were all above board.'

Ben chuckled. 'The beauty of the thing is that it *is* above board as far as the three main participants are concerned. Brian Burford doesn't realize the implications. The Harwood brothers are in the dark. And yet with a bit of skill we can raise such a stink about nepotism that the MoD will have to grab their oxygen masks. If Britain was the Philippines, no one would think twice about a minister handing out a billion-pound contract to a business connected with his family. But Britain is not the Philippines. We have a gut reaction to the merest whiff of nepotism in government.' In his mind he had begun the leader he would write in the *Rampart*.

Rachel sipped her whisky as she reflected. 'What's to keep Nelly Harwood from mentioning to Andrew that the BedHiTe directorship has been offered him? Andrew would see the risk and avoid it.'

'Okay. But the time span is so short that it would be sheer bad luck if Nelly Harwood had both occasion and inclination to discuss his latest wheeze with his big brother. Always play your hand as if you expect good luck, Rachel. And supposing Nelly does go chatterbox. At worst, Plan Two would come to nought. But my bet is we'd simply have to change our tack.'

He looked down absently at the glass balanced on his crotch as he considered the options.

'Let's just imagine, Rachel, what Andrew would do if he learned Nelly was about to become a BedHiTe director. He could instruct Cartwright to look for another engineering company. Or he could ask Nelly not to take the directorship – though that's a fairly indefensible thing for a man to ask when he is enjoying his own cushy salary. Or he could make an inconspicuous written state-ment to the House of Commons, announcing the contract and mentioning the fact that his brother is about to assume an interest in BedHiTe. Any one of these things – not least the last – could be made to look damaging.'

Ben altered his voice so that it sounded stern: 'Slipping infor-mation which embarrasses him into a written Commons statement is the uneasy minister's traditional device to cover himself against future censure – without anyone noticing what he has said. But *we* have noticed. And we do not intend to let the Defence Secretary get away with shabby subterfuge.'

Rachel reached out a hand and rested it on Ben's thigh. She turned her face towards his blunt-featured profile as he lay propped up against the pillows on his side of the bed. She burst out laughing.

'I love it when you start writing your leader right in the middle of a conversation.'

Ben grinned.

They sipped their whiskies.

Rachel said: 'The Prime Minister can be very loyal when one of the government is under attack from the press.'

'That didn't stop me getting the Health Secretary out on his well-cushioned arse.' Thinking of his hapless victim now languish-ing on the backbenches, Ben chuckled. 'When one of your col-leagues is constantly portrayed as lurching from one suspect episode to another, the Prime Minister can be forced to conclude, no doubt reluctantly, that the minister is a bloody albatross whose usefulness has come to an end – at any rate in the same job.'

'Too bad you can't actually demonstrate that Andrew has misused his office.'

'I told you, Rachel: always play your cards as if you'll be lucky. BedHiTe is a nice hand to be holding. And if we can't demonstrate misuse of office, we have other tricks up our sleeve. You'll see.

There are only so many banana-skins that Andrew Harwood can step on – no matter that the *Rampart* strewed them in his path – before the public says: "For Christ's sake, do we have to have a Defence Secretary who is so accident prone?"'

Rachel smiled.

Ben grinned. 'I'd settle for Andrew Harwood being moved to a lower-profile job so long as we get him out of Defence and get you in,' he said,

Noticing Ben's glass was empty, the Industry Secretary took it from him, swung her legs off the bed and picked up her own nearly empty glass in her other hand.

'My turn,' she said.

34

'Are you reasonably content with Cartwright's recommendation of BedHiTe for the ES7 contract?' Austin Barthmore asked.

Andrew finished lighting his cigarette and snapped the lighter shut.

'His summary of the findings was hard to fault. I've approved the recommendation: I initialled it an hour ago.'

The Permanent Under-Secretary was having an early evening drink with the Minister in his room – a once-a-week habit that gave Andrew a chance to keep some sort of tabs on civil servants whose advice was sent up to him.

He drew on his cigarette and slowly exhaled. 'Too bad we reached the stage of final commitment before a report could be made on the Raider. Until that last unhappy episode, Stockton's performance for us had been excellent.'

'I agree. But with the ES6 programme still on halt until the Raider can be salvaged, we had no recourse except to get started on ES7. And you felt, as I did, that we couldn't give it to Stockton when we don't yet know why that pilot was skinned alive.'

Andrew frowned. A few defence correspondents had learned

about the condition of the body catapulted through the jagged hole in the Raider's fiberglas canopy. But even the *Rampart*, with its standing as a family newspaper, stopped short of a full account of what the shepherd had found attached to the shredded parachute.

Barthmore switched back to his usual non-emotive style. 'The latest study from BedHiTe indicates to our aerospace technologists that the company can produce even more refined components than anyone expected when the programme was conceived four years ago.'

'Yep.'

In outward manner Barthmore seldom showed he had registered his Minister's irritation, but his words conveyed awareness.

'As it happens, Minister, I would have preferred that the decision had not come down in favour of a company being pushed by our friends at Industry. One always feels resistant to interference from another department. You already know that Martin Thrower replied fairly sharpish to Rachel Fisher's private office. Unfortunately, Cartwright found the case made for BedHiTe was convincing. And I could find nothing to question in Cartwright's reasoning. He's been our man in aeronautics negotiations for eight years.'

'So there we are.'

They moved on to discuss that afternoon's meeting with the generals.

On Friday, the media's defence correspondents received a routine handout from the MoD press office announcing that the ES7 components contract had been awarded to Bedfordshire High Tech. The quality newspapers at the weekend carried matter-of-fact short summaries. The *Rampart*'s equally impersonal piece by its defence reporter probably went unnoticed by most readers.

On Monday Nelly Harwood countersigned his five-year contract to become a director of BedHiTe at £15,000 a year, subject to increments in line with inflation. He was pleased to note that the contract was dated to run from the previous Monday when, at the end of his visit to BedHiTe, he had told Brian Burford he'd be happy to become a director. Always a good sign when a company made a generous gesture to start with. And nearly £300 a week for doing fuck-all wasn't to be sneezed at.

Afternoon had always been her favourite time to make love.

She loved the all-absorbing pleasure in the response of their bodies, which afternoon gave leisure to draw out. She loved the way the pleasure – their shared desire to keep it intense – coloured everything else in their life, whether everything else was directly shared or not. She loved the sense that they were on an oasis, the rest of the world cut off.

All these feelings were enhanced by its being not night-time, nor morning, but lovely, lovely Saturday afternoon.

She parted her legs, half-seeing the azure sky beyond the bedroom window as he bent over her.

While Daisy was in bed with Andrew at Stony Farm, Ben was editing the defence reporter's story. It was to have pride of place under the headline: 'Defence Secretary's Brother May Benefit From MoD Contract'.

> The *Rampart* has in its possession photocopies of two documents that suggest a link between the brother of the Defence Secretary and the award to Bedfordshire High Tech of a Ministry of Defence contract.
>
> One document reveals that on 20 May, Mr Nelson Harwood, younger brother of the Defence Secretary, Mr Andrew Harwood, was appointed a director of Bedfordshire High Tech, an aeronautics company that until now has not quite made it into the big league of defence contracts. Mr Nelson Harwood will be paid £15,000 a year for occasional attendance at meetings of the board. So far as can be ascertained from public records, Mr Nelson Harwood has no previous experience of work on behalf of the aeronautics industry.
>
> The second document reveals that three days after Mr Nelson Harwood's payments as a director began, Mr Andrew Harwood awarded BedHiTe the £1 billion contract for the MoD's ES7 programme.
>
> The award of the MoD's prestigious ES7 contract will, of course, hugely enhance BedHiTe's standing and earning capacity – two boosts

that will give satisfaction to its directors, not least the director whose appointment coincides with the award of the contract.

Alongside the spread was a photograph of the letter of contract from BedHiTe to Nelson Harwood, dated 20 May and countersigned by Nelson Harwood. Beside it was a photograph of the advice sent up from F-section, through the chief procurement officer, to the Defence Secretary. In the margin alongside Charles Cartwright's summary, Andrew had written in red ink beside the name of Bedfordshire High Tech: 'I think BedHiTe would be best.' The submission he approved was dated 23 May.

Having finally satisfied himself that nothing libellous remained in the front-page story, the *Rampart*'s legal chief had approved it. Long experience had convinced him that Cabinet ministers only sue when there is factual misrepresentation – not when a false impression is conveyed to readers. He turned his attention to the editor's unsigned leader: as usual Ben Franwell had come within an inch of libel and then skirted it.

The leader appeared under the heading: 'What Are We To Think?'

> In view of the extraordinary deaths at Stockton Air Space earlier this year and the recent, cruel and unexplained death of the pilot testing the company's new Raider for the MoD's ES6 programme, the *Rampart* has suggested that the lucrative contract for the ES7 programme should be awarded to another competitor in Britain's advanced aeronautics industry. Bedfordshire High Tech was a name we put forward for consideration. Its recent achievements made it a strong contender. And we imagined MoD contracts were awarded in the interests of this nation.
>
> What we had not imagined was that only after the Defence Minister's brother became a BedHiTe director would the Defence Secretary give the contract to BedHiTe.
>
> Andrew and Nelson Harwood were given the privileged upbringing of English gentlemen. Within that elite there has always been a strand that put the interests of its own class above the public weal. We would welcome a statement from Andrew Harwood that he and his brother do not belong to that strand.
>
> For Andrew Harwood is a Minister of the Crown. His handsome salary, his army of assistants, his car, his first-class international travel

sometimes accompanied by his sculptress wife, a large measure of his entertaining: all these are provided for him out of the public purse. And the £1 billion contract between BedHiTe and the MoD? It will be paid for out of this same public purse – i.e., by you.

What are we to think of the Harwood brothers?

At Stony Farm the children had gone upstairs to their bedrooms. (Like most sensible au pairs, Ingrid had chosen to stay in London for the weekend.) Daisy and Andrew were sitting either side of the fire that crackled cheerfully on the hearth of the small study. She had her feet tucked up under her as she read a Peter Carey novel. On the floor beside his chair, one of the three red boxes was open; he found it relaxing to do what he called the 'easy' reading in the evening.

The scrambler rang.

Daisy looked at Andrew. He looked at his watch. 11:30. He picked up the red telephone on the table beside him. 'Yes?'

'It's Martin. I'm sorry to disturb you this late, Minister. The resident clerk has just rung through. The Press Association is trying to reach you. No one answers in Cheyne Street. The PA has your Waymere number, but apparently it's out of order.'

'I took it off the receiver an hour ago so my wife and I could have a quiet evening together.'

'I'm sorry, Minister. But you may feel you want to make a comment to the PA about tomorrow's lead story in the *Rampart*. The first edition has already appeared in the West End. The PA has faxed it over to me. Shall I read it to you?'

'What's it about?'

'The BedHiTe contract. Apparently your brother became a BedHiTe director last week.'

'*What?*'

'The *Rampart* has gone to town.'

'You'd better read it to me. How long is it?'

Daisy laid her open book face down on the arm of her chair, cupping her chin in one hand as she watched him.

'There's the front-page piece and then the leader,' said Martin Thrower.

'I might as well light a cigarette. Hang on.'

When he'd taken a long drag on the cigarette Andrew said: 'I suppose you'd better start with the front page.'

Daisy left her chair and picked up his empty glass, taking it into the dining room and pouring out a light highball. His first one, he'd said, was going to be the only one as they'd be having an early night.

She put the drink down beside him, returned to her chair and watched him. He was silent while Martin finished reading from the *Rampart*.

'Is that it?'

'Yes.'

'I'll just think for a moment, Martin.'

He took a slow swallow of his highball before putting the glass back on the table.

'I wonder if you could read the opening of the front-page piece again?'

Martin Thrower did so.

After the first four sentences Andrew said: 'Okay.'

Martin waited.

'I'm going to leave the regular telephone off the receiver, Martin. Perhaps you could give me a ring on the scrambler tomorrow morning? 9:00. You'll be getting back now to the resident clerk to say I'm not available for comment.'

'Yes.'

'I'll say goodnight then.'

Andrew put the scrambler back on its receiver. His short low laugh was mirthless.

'What is it?' asked Daisy.

'That bastard Franwell must be unable to believe his fucking luck. Nelly has become a director of a company that just received an enormous contract from the MoD.'

'Does it matter?'

'Franwell has produced one of his more brilliant innuendos making it appear to matter a lot.'

He looked at his watch. 'Can you remember Nelly's number? It's unlisted, isn't it?'

'730–1001. I've never known why he is unlisted. Do you think he'll be there on a Saturday night?'

Andrew didn't answer. He picked up the red telephone, but instead of pressing the scrambler button, he dialled in the ordinary way.

After the seventh ring Nelly's quite sober-sounding voice said: 'Hullo?'

'It's Andrew. I'm sorry to disturb you. Are you alone?'

'Not exactly. But I'm alone in spirit, you might say. Wait a sec.'

Daisy could not read Andrew's expression. Was it exasperation? Detachment? Resignation?

'I'm back,' said Nelly.

'If some of our wonderful press can get hold of your unlisted number, you're in for a disturbed evening. When did you become a director of BedHiTe?'

'It was finalized a few days ago. Why?'

'How long have you been involved with them?'

'Depends how you define involvement. The BedHiTe president gave me an excellent lunch at Claridge's about a fortnight ago. I remember I was quite pleased that he chose a particularly agreeable bottle of Clos de la Roche. 1979. After that I went up to Bedfordshire to have a look around the place. Then they sent me the contract which they had pleasantly backdated to my verbal agreement with them. That's my involvement to date. Is something the matter, Andrew?'

'This BedHiTe president. You will have asked him who recommended you for the board.'

'He said that my name had come up before – that various people had told him I had the right qualifications for a rising firm.'

'Did he discuss with you the negotiations that have been going on for more than a year with the MoD?'

'Not a peep.'

'Nothing about our ES7 programme?'

'De nada.'

'Did you happen to read – it was Friday of last week – that the MoD has given the ES7 contract to BedHiTe?'

'No. But then I don't peruse the newspapers as systematically as perhaps I should. What's the matter?'

'The editor of the *Rampart* is running a piece as good as saying that BedHiTe has made you a director because you and I colluded to get the ES7 contract for BedHiTe.'

'What a cheek.'

For the first time Andrew gave a bleak smile. 'That's one way to put it.'

'Has this made a difficulty for you, Andrew?'

With his free hand Andrew lit a fresh cigarette.

'Look, Nelly, I'm sorry to be a bore, but let's just go through this again. Did you approach BedHiTe or did they approach you?'

'They wrote to me. They had a director's place that had become available. This president bloke and I met for lunch to discuss it. Then I went up to Bedfordshire "to familiarize myself" as they say. Quite a big organization, really. Buildings with small machines blinking their lights and humming away. Operators dressed in white. Other buildings with much bigger stuff.'

'Did they say why they'd invited you to become a director? Electronic engineering is not really your scene, is it?'

'I know as much about it as I do about the timber industry, i.e., bugger all. That doesn't stop me being a director of a timber business. The BedHiTe chap said they'd heard of me, and they wanted me to take on this £14,000 herculean task.'

'£15,000.'

'That's where it finished up.'

'I think you'd better get hold of an early edition of the *Rampart* – it's already in the West End – and then ring this BedHiTe president first thing in the morning – wherever he may be this weekend. Ask him how he thinks photocopies of your contract and the MoD document got to the *Rampart*. Ask him what the hell he's up to. Then give me a ring. Use the scrambler; you have the number. The regular telephone is off the hook. I know it's Sunday, but could you manage this before 8:30? I've got to say something to the bloody press, if only "No comment." And I need to learn what BedHiTe says to you before I can hold a conversation of my own with the MoD. What's this president called?'

'Brian Burford.'

Andrew wrote it down. 'Did he mention the name Charles Cartwright?'

'Never heard of him. What am I going to say to the press if they get hold of my number?'

'Let's think for a minute.'

Andrew took a last drag on his cigarette before putting it out. He didn't look at Daisy: he didn't want his concentration broken.

'Tell them you haven't yet read the story and to ring you back in the morning. Then leave the telephone off the hook. But for God's sake remember to ring me at 8:30.'

'Why can't I tell them the truth – that this is the first I've heard of the MoD contract?'

'You may have to. But wait on it. It might seem a bit odd that you should become a director of a company, at quite a decent fee, without knowing anything whatsoever about the biggest fucking contract they've probably ever negotiated.'

'I see what you mean.'

Neither brother spoke for a moment.

Then Nelly said: 'I'm awfully sorry, Andrew, if this lands you in the shit. I had no idea.'

'I know that, Nelly. Give me a ring in the morning at 8:30, even if there's nothing much to say. Goodnight.'

He looked at Daisy. They both sat in silence.

After a while he said: 'It's a bloody bore.'

'Is it going to affect your job?'

'Hard to say. Nelly has done nothing wrong. So far as I'm aware, I am not guilty of corruption. Yet in this sort of thing, denials often simply keep the story running.'

He was silent again.

Then he said: 'Prime ministers rarely give you the boot because of an accident that then gets blown up by the press. But I must say, I find it fairly unpalatable to read that I and members of my family are involved in graft.'

Again he was silent.

Then he said: 'I must say, it *is* rather a striking coincidence of events in one week.'

'What is?'

'Nelly's signing a contract with BedHiTe. My department giving a contract to BedHiTe.'

Both lapsed into silence again.

After a while Daisy got up and put another log on the fire. It had nearly gone out.

'Why don't you go to bed, Daisy? I'll be up in a little while. I'm going to have one more cigarette. Don't stay awake.' He looked at his wife. 'And don't fret. I daresay the whole thing will seem much less dire in the morning.'

35

At 8:30 in the morning, despite its being Sunday, the local paper's political reporter, a photographer beside him, pressed the bell. The reporter explained to Daisy that they couldn't telephone first because the Harwoods' number was continually engaged.

'Oh. Well, my husband isn't available at the moment. Perhaps you could come back after lunch?'

The two men retired to the wooden gate at the entrance to Stony Farm and stood just outside it. Daisy could see them from the kitchen window.

Sophie, still in her pyjamas, came into the kitchen.

'Does everyone know the sitting-room phone is off the hook?' she said. Just as she and Matty knew they were not to touch the scrambler in the study, they also knew they shouldn't assume the regular telephone was disconnected by mistake.

'Leave it off the hook, Sophie,' Daisy said.

Andrew appeared in the kitchen doorway.

'You better not go near the window, Dad. There are some geeks by the gate. I think they want to talk with you.'

Andrew smiled rather wanly at his daughter.

'The whole thing is very odd,' he said to Daisy. 'Nelly says that Brian Burford – he's the president of BedHiTe – is totally baffled by the *Rampart* story. He tells Nelly he has absolutely no idea how the photocopy of the contract could have got to Franwell. The BBC has already been on to Nelly and Burford.'

'Is the BedHiTe president upset by the story?' said Daisy.

'He's horrified, Nelly says. But that's not the point.'

Matty appeared. 'The scrambler's ringing in your study, Dad.'

Andrew went back to the study and closed the door behind him.

Twenty minutes later when he returned to the kitchen, Sophie and Matty were standing by the window.

'I can count eight guys now,' Matty said. 'And six cameras.'

'Did you know Denis is now standing outside the front door?' said Sophie.

Daisy was sipping from a large coffee cup. She sat at the big kitchen table strewn with the Sunday newspapers, the *Rampart* not only crumpled but smeared by the marmalade that Matty had intended to put on his toast.

'Has Uncle Nelly done something wrong, Dad?' he said.

'No. But a peculiar chain of events makes it look as if he and I have been in cahoots in giving a big contract to a company called BedHiTe.'

'The *Rampart* says ...'

'Sophie, the *Rampart* has a personal interest in doing down your father. The *Rampart* is only pretending that they think Andrew and Nelly are guilty of some heinous crime.'

'The trouble is, Sophie, that the coincidence is extremely awkward,' said Andrew.

He turned to Daisy. 'That was Martin Thrower. I've asked him to get Barthmore and Cartwright into the Ministry at four o'clock. I'll meet them there. Martin had already told Ollie to be here by eleven in case I wanted to return to London earlier than we'd planned. You three will have to do the best you can. If I were you, I'd get off before any more press are stationed at our gate.'

'If they ask us to say something, what shall we say?' said Sophie.

'Don't say anything. Just smile,' Andrew said.

'That's all very well for Mama and Sophie,' said Matty. 'I'd look stupid smiling and smiling as they ask their questions.'

'That's sexism, Matty,' Sophie said. 'If I can smile at them, so can you.'

Daisy and Andrew went upstairs while he collected his things. The regular telephone remained disconnected.

At four o'clock when Daisy drove the Volvo into Cheyne Street, the pavement in front of their house was crowded with reporters and cameramen, most conveying an air of festivity.

'They're using our front steps as a sort of picnic table,' Sophie said. 'Take your time, Mama. Nobody can ever park the first time when a bunch of people is standing around staring. You're not going to touch the car in front: you've got plenty of room.'

'Don't forget to smile,' Matty said.

Under the maple tree two men in lightweight anoraks raised their television cameras onto their right shoulders as the three Harwoods climbed out of the car and took their weekend belongings from the back.

'Is your husband going to be making a statement today, Mrs Harwood?'

'How long have you known your brother-in-law was involved with BedHiTe, Mrs Harwood?'

'How do you feel about people saying your husband was looking after his brother when he awarded the contract to BedHiTe, Mrs Harwood?'

It's funny, Daisy thought to herself as she looked at the young woman reporter who had put the last question: I'm always surprised when another woman homes in like that. Stupid of me: inverted sexism on my part.

'Goodbye, folks,' said Sophie, smiling until she closed the front door on the crowd. 'Jerks. You'd think they might have something better to do.'

Ingrid came down the stairs. 'What's going on? When I came home an hour ago they asked me a lot of questions.'

'It's all because of a newspaper story this morning. About Dad. What did you say?' asked Matty.

'I told them I didn't know anything because I just live upstairs.'

Daisy gave a small smile. 'Could everyone please stay away

from the windows at the front of the house?'

'Can you throw any light on this, Charles?'

Andrew was still in his faded shirt and old tweed trousers, but he had put on a tie. He was sitting behind his desk. In the blue leather chairs facing him were Austin Barthmore and Charles Cartwright. Martin Thrower sat slightly apart – almost alongside the desk so that he as usual was neither with the civil servants nor with the Minister.

Charles Cartwright's pale narrow face was expressionless. Sometimes when he was under stress a tic appeared just below his left eye. It was all very well for ministers to adopt any casual position that they liked – leaning on their elbows with their hands either side of their face in some sort of parody of concentration; if they had a nerve which commenced its tiny tremor under the eye, they could cloak it with one hand until it settled down. An official had to sit correctly, his face fully exposed. Cartwright was pretty sure that he always felt it when the tic played up. So far he could feel nothing.

'The difficulty about any document, as you know, Minister, is that however scrupulously the office monitors the copying machines, the document can be taken from the building and photocopied elsewhere – if someone in the office is prepared to embark on such an unpleasant endeavour.'

'Have you any idea who might have wished to embark on what you call an unpleasant endeavour?' Andrew had to remind himself that his chemical reaction to the director of F-section could cloud his own judgment. If anyone else had used that phrase, probably it would not have grated.

'I have no idea, Minister. Tomorrow morning we will begin a post mortem.'

'How many photocopies were made of the submission that was sent up to the Minister, Charles?' said Barthmore.

'So far as I've been able to ascertain since you rang me this morning, sir, two. Matters have not been assisted by the fact that my secretary chose this weekend to go to Paris. When she returns to the office tomorrow morning, I shall be in a better position to give you a firm answer to that question.'

'Under what circumstances, Charles, does the office photocopy a document *after* it has been approved by the Minister's red pen?'

Barthmore's face retained its usual bland impenetrability as he gazed at his junior official.

'Normally that would not occur, sir.' Cartwright wished he could be absolutely certain the tic was not displaying itself.

'Have you any idea how it might be in BedHiTe's interest to send the *Rampart* a copy of their contract letter to my brother? Presumably the public furor that has been stirred up could jeopardize their contract with the MoD.'

Cartwright forced himself to keep looking at the Minister: eye contact showed confidence.

'We might find ourselves in a difficulty, Minister, if we cancelled the contract. Unless it can be proved that the president of BedHiTe or someone on its board is responsible for this leak, we could be opening ourselves to a lawsuit not only for breach of contract but for damages to BedHiTe's reputation.'

No one said anything further for a minute. Andrew and the PUS kept their eyes on Cartwright. Cartwright kept his eyes on Andrew. Martin Thrower looked up from his note-taking to glance at all three.

'As nothing further looks like being learned until tomorrow, we might as well call it a day,' Andrew said. 'Austin, would you like to stay behind for five minutes?'

Cartwright and Martin Thrower stood up, nodded to the Minister and the PUS, then left the room.

Andrew and Austin Barthmore remained silent.

Then Barthmore said: 'I know that pedantic manner is tiresome, but he is good at his job. I'll have to come back to you on this, but I expect the best thing would be to switch Cartwright with someone else of the same grade. I'd like to think about it. F-section requires highly specialized knowledge.'

Andrew lit a cigarette and exhaled a thin cloud of grey smoke, watching it as it dissipated.

'We'll meet in the morning, Austin,' he said. 'Sorry your day has been disrupted along with mine. Not to mention my family's. I expect they've already had to run a gauntlet when they returned from the country.'

Barthmore gave his enigmatic smile.

Both men got to their feet.

As it was a Sunday, Charles Cartwright had a fifteen-minute wait on the westbound platform of Westminster underground station. From time to time he raised one of his graceful hands and with the middle finger touched the tic. It was now playing up.

The carriage was nearly empty. He looked absently at the red alarm button as he reflected. Had he actually done anything immoral? If he analysed events, he might almost be seen as an innocent party. True, when the document submitted to the Minister had come back with his decision in favour of BedHiTe written in red ink in the margin, Cartwright had taken it with him when he went out to lunch. After making two photocopies at a stationery shop, he had folded them and put them in the inside pocket of his jacket. When he had then returned a little early to his office, he had clipped the original to the appropriate ES7 file. His secretary had collected it along with other files in his out-tray, at 4:30.

That evening at his flat in Ealing, writing in small neat block letters, he had addressed an envelope to Benjamin Franwell at his London flat, marking it private and confidential, with no covering note. The next day he had posted it from the letterbox outside Westminster underground station. The following morning Franwell had rung him to say thanks. That evening when Cartwright got home, he had destroyed the remaining copy.

As he continued westward on the District line, though he didn't like contemplating it, he nonetheless had to ask himself why he had been so ready to accommodate Benjamin Franwell. Why should he, Charles Cartwright, feel flattered by the attentions of the *Rampart*'s editor? Did it make the slightest difference to him if the head waiter of the Savoy restaurant showed him special respect? Or had it more to do with the wonderful sense of power he derived from being able to hurt his political master? Andrew Harwood had started off with advantages that he, Charles Cartwright, had had to earn for himself. Not only that, the more efficient he was at F-section, the more credit the Minister took.

Anyway, how could photocopying a document whose advice was originally submitted by himself be regarded as immoral let alone illegal? All it meant was that a perfectly normal document had been made available to the *Rampart*. Everyone – except ministers – wanted more open government. The British press had been campaigning for it for years. In the United States there had been a Freedom of Information Act since 1966 – and a much wider act since 1974. If one thought about it, one could see that he had behaved entirely in the spirit of the times.

As for the luxury holiday whose tab would be picked up by the *Rampart*, what was the matter with that? Ministers took luxury trips all the time at the expense of taxpayers like himself. No taxpayer would be footing the bill for his three weeks in a West Indies paradise. If the *Rampart* chose to pay for the jaunt, that was its lookout. If he'd had a wife the bill would be twice as big, so the *Rampart* should consider itself lucky.

He felt his cheek just under the left eye. The minuscule throbbing had ceased. As the train came to a halt, he glanced through the grimy window: Turnham Green. Two more stops. He liked Ealing Common. It would be nice to be home. Ludicrous that the Minister hadn't been able to wait until Monday for his meeting. It wasn't as if anything had been accomplished by insisting on breaking up Sunday afternoon like this. Interesting to know whether the PUS too had found the exercise a silly charade whose single purpose was to feed the Minister's ego.

He extended his left hand, turning the wrist inward to look at his watch. Just after six. His mother had always said: 'You have beautiful hands, Charles.' When he got back to his flat, he'd relax with the brochures he'd collected from three different travel agents.

In the study of the brick house in Bedford Forge, George Bishop was alone with the Sunday papers and a weak whisky. As the gem had taken the weekend off, George and his younger son would have a cold supper that Rachel had left on two trays, everything covered with clingfilm so as not to dry out. After tea she had gone back to London so that she would have an early Monday morning start to her week at Industry. James was now upstairs in his room, doing his homework. Howard was away at boarding school.

Try as he might to get on with the *Sunday Times* and *Sunday*

Telegraph, George kept returning to the *Rampart* and looking afresh at the two photographs on its front page. Something about the photocopy of the MoD document made him think of the Vassall scandal when he was a boy. George was not absolutely certain that when he copied BedHiTe's contract letter to Nelson Harwood, he had realized how it would be used. Hard now to be sure. Had there been any explicit discussion with Charles Cartwright over their last drink together at the club? Or was it with Rachel? Or a bit of both? He had been prepared to photocopy the copy of BedHiTe's contract with Nelson Harwood because, after all, he himself had advised Brian Burford on making the appointment. And directorships were open to public scrutiny.

What with handling BedHiTe's insurance, and his friendship with its president, George often had access to the files kept on the directors. He'd felt a little odd as he made the copy. By nature he was an honest man. He was also a loyal man. And his prime loyalty was to Rachel. She had told him her path to higher office could be expedited if Andrew Harwood was moved from Defence. Anyhow, there was nothing illicit in copying a BedHiTe letter. It wasn't as if he had forged it. When he gave the copy to Rachel, he hadn't asked her what she intended doing with it. Now he knew.

George had met Ben Franwell only at the occasional government reception. Although Franwell was friendly enough, there was something ill-at-ease about his manner. George could never make out what Ben thought of him. But then there were lots of people in Rachel's London world of politics whose attitude to George was unclear. He knew she was particularly fond of Franwell. She spoke sometimes of having lunch with him. But then she had lunch regularly with parliamentary colleagues and he thought nothing of that. In any case, Franwell had been a kind of patron since Rachel had worked as his PA. How many years ago?

The thought of Rachel in bed with Ben Franwell flashed suddenly into George's mind. Instantly he blanked it out. He believed bed played little part in Rachel's thoughts. Certainly it had not appeared to worry her that he was not all that keen on sexual intercourse with his wife. He'd done what was expected of a man

and fathered two sons. But he'd found foreplay embarrassing if
not outright disgusting. He'd been greatly relieved when he found
on their honeymoon that Rachel did not appear to expect anything
very adventurous in that line.

In the top flat at 64 Morpeth Terrace, Ben's jacket hung on the
back of the chintz chair. The thought that had flashed through
George's mind was not quite accurate: Ben and Rachel were not
in bed. Having taken off their shoes, they were lying on top of the
bedspread, Rachel's ankles crossed, Ben's knees bent and his feet
set comfortably apart. He had loosened his tie but not taken it off:
he only had forty-five minutes.

He'd come up to London a night early, because the *Rampart*'s
proprietor was giving his once-a-month Sunday supper party. The
last time Angela had attended one of these occasions was, she said,
sufficient for a lifetime: she had been seated between the only two
boring men in the room, she said. Tonight she had stayed in
Sussex, and would come up to London as she normally did on
Tuesday.

'Has Brian Burford been on to George today?'

'Not before I left.'

'Are you absolutely sure, Rachel, that George won't end up by
spilling the beans to Burford? George has all the marks of the man
who cannot tell a lie.'

'The only beans he has to spill are that he photocopied the
contract-letter between BedHiTe and Nelly Harwood. And he
would lie about that, however much he'd dislike doing so. George
would never point the finger at someone else at BedHiTe: nothing
could make him that sort of shit. But he doesn't need me to tell
him what would happen to my career if his part in all this came
out – first his suggesting Nelly's appointment as a director, now
the leak.'

'As long as he plays the innocent with Brian Burford, there is
not the faintest reason why either thing should ever come out.
That has always been the beauty of it. Plus the fact that Burford
has no idea of Cartwright's interest in recommending that
BedHiTe get the ES7 contract.'

They both were silent, reflecting.

Then Rachel said: 'I laughed aloud when I read your leader this morning.'

Ben turned his head on the pillow propped up behind him. He grinned at her. 'Which bit did you like?'

'Wait a minute.'

She swung her legs off the bed. When she returned from the other room with the *Rampart* already turned inside out, she stood beside the bed and read aloud in a voice parodying righteousness:

> 'And we imagined MoD contracts were awarded in the interests of this nation.
>
> 'What we had not imagined was that only after the Defence Minister's brother became a BedHiTe director would the Defence Secretary give the contract to BedHiTe.'

She skipped down to the leader's end:

> 'What are we to think of the Harwood brothers?'

She folded the newspaper and placed it at the foot of the bed as she lay down again on the blue bedspread and crossed her ankles.

'Very neat, Mr Franwell.'

36

Standing outside the modest entrance to 10 Downing Street, you would never guess how large a building lies within. For behind the front door other doors open into various annexes used as offices and added on after the original houses were built in the late seventeenth century. In 1732, when Number Ten was joined onto an enormous mansion that stood in a garden at the back, it became the Prime Minister's official residence.

When you pass the policeman on the front step and first enter the house, you can look straight through three pairs of doors standing open in the corridor to a fourth door, usually closed, at the end. The fourth is a double-door to make it soundproof, as it leads directly into the Cabinet Room.

The inside of the Cabinet Room door is painted white, as are the panelled walls and cornices and a pair of Corinthian columns which stand as sentinels before the huge Cabinet table stretching most of the room's length. The table, covered in dark brown baize, is boat-shaped (some think of it as coffin-shaped) so that each member of the Cabinet can see and hear every other member. Half way along the table stands the Prime Minister's chair, the only one of the twenty-two red leather chairs to have arms, its back to the small grey marble fireplace over which hangs a portrait of Sir Robert Walpole in his horsehair wig.

Prime ministers vary in the way they conduct Cabinet. This prime minister liked to get through discussion in two hours flat. The hour hand of the clock on the mantelpiece had rarely reached one when discussion was drawn to a close. Ordinarily, the only ministers asked to speak were those whose departments were relevant to the subjects on the agenda, though others chipped in when they had a strong view on the matter. The tradition of addressing one another by title helped depersonalize issues. Except in emergencies, the Cabinet met only on Thursday mornings. Unlike the Commons, debate in Cabinet was genuine, no need to entertain public galleries, no childish exchange of Party insults.

Some Cabinet ministers, feeling insecure, took decisions to Cabinet that they should have handled within their own departments. Andrew Harwood preferred to take the absolute minimum to Cabinet, but redeployment of British troops in West Germany was a policy matter which had to be agreed by his colleagues. Over breakfast that morning he had told Daisy he welcomed the opportunity to remind the Prime Minister and his colleagues that despite the BedHiTe shambles, he was on top of his job.

'Defence Secretary,' said the Prime Minister.

His chair was three along on the opposite side to the Prime Minister. Leaning forward as he spoke, his hands clasped on his brief, Andrew set out his argument simply and cogently.

When he had finished making his case, the Prime Minister said: 'Foreign Secretary.'

Immediately across from the Prime Minister, the Foreign Secretary sat in the habitual stolid hunched posture which cartoonists liked to depict as a toad's. He proceeded to give his support to the Defence Secretary's objective and the method Andrew was proposing to achieve the end.

The Prime Minister said briskly: 'I think we are all agreed that this can now be left with the Defence Secretary.'

The next subject on the agenda was the proposed amalgamation of Britain's remaining nationalized industry and a private company.

'Industry Secretary,' said the Prime Minister.

Five places down on the same side as the Prime Minister, Rachel
seemed erect even though she had to lean forward slightly to speak
directly to the Prime Minister. Dispassionately she put the case
for accepting the financial terms offered by the private company.

While Cabinet members prefer it when a colleague conducts
debate with clarity, something about Rachel's overwhelming self-
certainty could jar. This was probably one reason why others –
not the Defence Secretary – chipped in to make points against her.
After half an hour the Prime Minister 'interpreted' the consensus
opinion as being in general support of the Industry Secretary,
moving on smartly to the next subject on the agenda.

At 12:45, the doors were opened and the ministers closed their
folders and began their departure, gossiping to one another as they
moved down the long corridor towards the front door.

'Andrew.'

He turned back and saw the Prime Minister standing alone.

'Shall we just have a word?'

Andrew went back and the two of them stood alone outside the
Cabinet Room.

'I just wanted to say,' said the Prime Minister, 'that I am
appalled by the suggestions the *Rampart* has made about your
brother's appointment to the BedHiTe board. I have no doubt
that the *Rampart* is mistaken in its assumptions. You will know
that my private office has already discussed the matter with your
private office. These irritating stories in the press usually turn out
to be seven-day wonders. My private office tells me this will almost
certainly be the case with BedHiTe. If there is, however, any
question in your mind about continuing with the ES7 contract,
I'm sure your private office will raise it with mine, as we would
need to consider the public implications.'

'Thank you, Prime Minister. Defence Questions in the House
are this Thursday. I daresay I'll be asked more than once to rebut
the *Rampart*'s innuendo. I shall be able to add little to the press
statement my office issued yesterday. There is no known reason
to terminate the ES7 contract, and therefore the MoD expects to
honour it – not least because of the fantastic damages we might
otherwise have to pay to BedHiTe.'

'I see that. And although the *Rampart* is a loyal supporter of my government, I would not like its editor to feel his rhetoric could influence my own assessment of my ministers.'

'Thank you. The fact remains we have no idea who sent the photocopies to the *Rampart*. Nor do we know whether the timing of my brother's appointment as a BedHiTe director was a coincidence or whether in fact there was malicious manipulation by an unknown party.'

'I fully understand your sense of frustration, Andrew. Let me know if you would like a further talk.'

That night when he got home after the ten o'clock Commons vote, Andrew told Daisy of this enigmatic conversation.

'On the one hand, it could be read as a message that the PM regards the *Rampart* piece as rubbish,' he said. 'Equally, it could be read as a message saying: "You're on trial, mate."'

Daisy's expression became so sombre it made Andrew laugh.

'Things aren't that desperate,' he said, getting up from his armchair and crossing the study to her chair. He leaned over and kissed her and then went over to the drinks tray and poured each of them a highball. 'If one reflects on it, the fact is that every member of Her Majesty's government is on perpetual trial with the PM. So the only new thing in my situation is that it has been brought so dramatically to the public's attention. When did the press disappear from our front door?'

'The last of them had gone when Sophie got back from school. Is that because once you issued your statement there was no point in hanging around?'

'Presumably.'

'Nelly rang on the scrambler an hour ago.'

'I wish he'd ring on the regular telephone.'

'He said he'd tried to for an hour, but it was perpetually engaged.'

'I thought we'd agreed to put it back into action as soon as things had quietened down a bit.'

'I think Sophie was on it. She and her young man seem to have a lot to say to one another.'

A fleeting scowl passed over Andrew's face. He said nothing. Daisy noticed both these things.

'Mind you,' she said cheerfully, 'Jason is all of fifteen years old and has a bad case of acne, so I expect he and Sophie have long discussions about homeopathic cures.'

Andrew pressed his lips.

'What did Nelly want?' he said.

'He wanted to talk to you again about whether he should resign his BedHiTe directorship. He said you told him yesterday not to consider it. But he still wonders if it would make things less embarrassing for you.'

'I never can remember his telephone number.'

Daisy reeled it off.

'Brilliant.' Andrew punched the seven digits. He put the thought of Sophie and her young man firmly out of his mind.

After the telephone had rung ten times in vain, he replaced the receiver. At the same time there was a tap on the study door as it opened. Sophie came in.

She was in her pyjamas. When she had walked home in the rain that afternoon, a headscarf had been insufficient: her hair, ironed that morning – she'd got up early to do it – had resumed its natural curls. Daisy felt warm compassion for this child, so like herself in many ways, who yearned to have straight hair.

'I'm still awake. May I come in for a few minutes?'

'Of course,' Andrew said.

Sophie perched on the edge of a chair.

'What sort of day have you had?' said Andrew.

'All right. A girl in my class asked me about Uncle Nelly. She said her father had said why didn't Uncle Nelly resign from being this Beebite executive or whatever he is.'

'BedHiTe, though I like your version. And he's called a director. We were just talking about that.'

Andrew's face was filled with love as he looked at his daughter. Usually by the time he got home during the week he only wanted to see Daisy. Tonight he found he was glad Sophie had come downstairs to join them.

'Is he going to resign, Dad?'

'When we spoke yesterday he offered to. I told him not to.'

'Why?'

Andrew finished lighting his cigarette. 'It would make little difference at this stage: the damage has been done. It might even suggest he is guilty of something. And I am hardly the person who should place any guilt on my brother.'

'What do you mean, Dad?'

'I was the person who deprived him of our older brother.'

Daisy looked up in surprised silence. He'd never before alluded to that reason for his indulgence of Nelly.

Immediately Andrew veered away from his introspection about causing Donald's death. 'But the main thing is that there are limits on what I should expect of my family just because I am a Cabinet minister,' he said, 'though I'd be obliged, Sophie, if you didn't turn our home into a reception centre for thieves and addicts.'

'I wish you wouldn't call my friends thieves and addicts.'

Sometimes Sophie was offended by her parents. But tonight she was feeling so good after her telephone conversation with Jason that she felt only pleasure as she sat on the edge of the chair looking at her father. She knew he hadn't meant it about her friends. She liked to play the game with him.

He smiled at her.

Sophie got up. 'Goodnight. It's nice being able to walk up Cheyne Street again without having to thread my way through all those geeks.'

At 2:20 the next afternoon as they rode together in the back seat of the Jaguar, Martin Thrower again noticed his Minister's hand as it rested against the door panel: the knuckles were white.

At 2:30 the Speaker called out: 'Mr. Harwood.'

The supplementary questions, always the tricky ones, turned out to be neither more nor less unpleasant than can be expected after a newspaper has given the Opposition some bricks to throw. On all sides of the House, there was a mixture of smirking and sympathy. Andrew was regarded as an honest man, and his statement of his ignorance of his brother's recent appointment was accepted. At the same time, Tories jealous of a minister, along with Opposition members always glad to see the government embarrassed, were bound to take some pleasure in the affair. Simultaneously, they knew one of them could wake up in the morning, open a newspaper and find himself in Andrew Harwood's shoes.

Because he played it straight, it turned out to be – as the Prime Minister had said it might – a seven-day wonder. Most of the dailies carried a cartoon about the Defence Secretary and the BedHiTe imbroglio along with summings up and some sanctimonious advice. And then the British media lost interest.

On Sunday only the *Rampart* made further comment on the matter, and Ben Franwell played that with a light hand. For while he would never have acknowledged it publicly, he knew he'd lost this round. He'd still have to let Cartwright have his luxury holiday: a deal was a deal.

Yet it hadn't been a total loss. A residue would have been left in the public consciousness – and, more important, at Number Ten: the man in charge of Defence was accident-prone. Ben grinned at the thought of who had manipulated that impression.

He was not a sour man; he approached a vendetta as if it was hardball: you hurt and you got hurt; it was all part of the game. He had not yet devised Plan Three, but give him time. You never knew what would turn up.

37

'You will be on time, won't you?' Andrew had said just before he'd stepped out of their front door that morning.

As usual he'd given her the card listing his day's main appointments – a courtesy provided by the diary secretary in his private office. The last engagement said: '8 for 8:30–Dinner at No. 10. Black tie.' Immediately preceding it and written, unlike the rest, in large block letters was: '7:30–MRS HARWOOD DEPARTS IN CAR FROM CHEYNE STREET.'

Daisy had never made up her mind about the significance attached to her part of the official day being typed in those big black letters. Was it a further special courtesy to her? Or was it a hint?

She looked at the clock on the bathroom wall: 7:28. There was no need to look out of the bedroom window: Ollie always arrived ten minutes early – as if that might bring some psychological weight to bear on her ill-formed sense of time. It was the knowledge that he was certain already to be there which had made her once again stick the mascara brush in her eye so that she blinked and made a smudge and now had to clean the whole lot off and start over again. Carefully she did so. 7:34.

She rushed into the adjoining bedroom and slipped into the top layer of clothing: white organdy blouse cut low, black silk skirt, jet-embroidered belt. At other times she might fling her jewellery into her handbag and put it on in the car. Tonight she had to stay in front of her dressing-table mirror while she carefully fastened the diamond and peridot necklace and the matching earrings she'd got out of the vault that morning; they had belonged to Andrew's grandmother. Daisy was wearing her hair up to show off the pale green of the sparkling peridots.

7:44. She snatched up her bag, her white boa, Andrew's clean shirt, the clothes hanger with his dinner jacket and trousers. Thank God she'd put the tie in the jacket pocket earlier. She hoped the boa wouldn't shed plumes onto the black serge. Still, she could pick them off while she was in the car.

As she reached the ground floor she shouted down the stairs to the kitchen: 'Goodbye everybody.'

Sophie's and Matty's and Ingrid's voices returned a little chorus of 'Enjoy yourself.'

Ollie's face was expressionless as he stepped out from the driver's seat to open the back door for her. Apart from saying 'Good evening, ma'am,' he was silent.

As he drove the Jaguar across two Embankment traffic lights after one had turned yellow and the other was already red, Daisy tried to avoid looking at the back of his cap which managed to convey a sense of grievance. Not for the first time she thought how fortunate the Prime Minister was to live in a flat at the top of Number Ten and have only to walk down a flight of stairs to reach the State Rooms.

Ollie cut the Jaguar in and out of the traffic that moved laboriously around Parliament Square. Daisy looked up at Big Ben. Two minutes past eight.

'You've made marvellous time, Ollie.'

Ollie said nothing.

When he swung the Jaguar into the kerb in front of the MoD, he was instantly out of the car and had its back door open for her. She got out carrying the Minister's clothes. Hoping she looked composed and unhurried, beneath her long skirt she took the largest steps that her high heels could manage.

At the top floor Ollie went ahead to the Minister's room. When Daisy reached the private office, she suspected that Ollie had already said his piece, though of course Denis and four secretaries nodded to her politely as they half rose to their feet, and Martin Thrower appeared amused as he came forward to open the door into the Minister's room. The clock over the door said seven minutes past eight.

Andrew was signing letters at his desk. He didn't look up until he'd finished the last two. Then he glanced at his watch and for the first time appeared to notice his wife had at last arrived.

'Good evening,' he said as he got up, unhurried, and came round the desk to take his clothes from her. He seemed relaxed rather than irritated, she was relieved to see. 'Do you want to sit down while you wait?' he said.

The engraved trenches of the Somme above her, Daisy stared at the clock over the inner side of the door. 8:10. The MoD certainly liked to be reminded of the time. Perhaps they were right. Why on earth had she not left her sculpture studio twenty minutes earlier? She never knew what Andrew's mood would be when she was late. She thought it probably depended on whether or not he too was running behind schedule, though he seldom acknowledged that this might be the case lest she be even later for their next meeting.

He reappeared from his bathroom, still apparently unfussed. She thought how handsome he looked in his dinner jacket. As they left his room together, she glanced again at the clock. 8:15.

He said goodnight to the private office. 'Martin, will you kindly see that when Ollie comes back for the box he also collects my other clothes? I'm afraid I left them in something of a heap in the bathroom. We seem to have cut our time a little close this evening.'

Everyone smiled.

As the Jaguar pulled away from the kerb in Richmond Terrace, Daisy skimmed the two sheets of paper Andrew had just handed her, potted biographies of the principal guests who were not members of the British government. No civil service provided this meticulous detail as well as the British.

At the entrance to Downing Street members of the Diplomatic Protection Group opened the barricade. Outwardly DPG dressed like ordinary policemen, though Daisy could just discern the bulge under the left side of one officer's jacket. Half a minute later, the Defence Secretary and his wife stepped into Number Ten.

'Good evening, madam. Good evening, sir.'

She never pretended to herself that she was blasé about going to a dinner party at Number Ten. Her smile was one of genuine friendly pleasure as she returned the greeting of the elderly custodian who had opened the door.

Just to the right in the entrance hall stood several members of DPG and Special Branch, who nodded to the Minister and his wife in a polite detached way. Above them was the red electric eye of a security device. Behind them Daisy saw a clock on the wall. 8:24. At least it wasn't yet half past. Would she always be the last guest to arrive anywhere on earth?

Yet when she and Andrew reached the lobby in front of the Cabinet Room and turned right towards the eighteenth-century staircase with its polished mahogany banister and S-curved iron balustrade, she immediately forgot how close they'd cut the time. She forgot the reason for the DPG and Special Branch men in the entrance hall, each with a Smith and Wesson in the holster strapped under his jacket. As she lifted her black silk skirt and started up the stairs to the historic State Rooms, she really was entering another world.

'You asked me to tell you when we're coming to Gladstone. He's just ahead where the staircase turns,' said Andrew.

Some day Daisy intended to have time to examine the engravings of the prime ministers one by one. She wondered whether the White House had a similar display of past presidents.

Beneath the Waterford glass chandelier that cast its subtle light onto the White Drawing Room, the Prime Minister and the American Vice-President stood chatting with several guests, waiting to receive the last arrivals. Only once had Daisy ever seen anyone actually sitting on the damask-covered Adam furniture. She hadn't realized how tall the Vice-President was. When the usual courtesies had been exchanged – Daisy always felt the Prime Minister found it a slight effort to hold even a short conversation with her – they all went through to the Blue Drawing Room.

Daisy looked up at the second of the pair of Waterford chandeliers, this one suspended over Chippendale furniture. She loved the fairy-tale effect of cut glass and mirrors. She looked at the dozen guests in the room. She recognized the Foreign Secretary and his wife and the director of the National Gallery. Andrew was already talking with someone on his other side when she became aware of being watched from the third drawing room. She looked ahead. Just inside the Pillared Drawing Room stood Carl Myer.

Even before she had read the guest list, she knew he was going to be there. He and Andrew had met at Richmond Terrace earlier that day. All the same, she felt surprise at seeing him suddenly in this setting. He bowed. Daisy gave a little bow in return. Then she joined Andrew's conversation with the Governor of the Bank of England.

'One of us,' Andrew said to his wife, 'ought to look out for the Myers.'

'I think I saw him in the next room,' said Daisy.

'Let's go through.'

As there were fifteen or twenty more guests in the Pillared Drawing Room and waiters carrying their silver salvers bearing glasses of champagne and whisky and orange juice, she didn't see Carl at first. Then again she became acutely aware of being watched. He was standing near one of the Ionic columns. Beside him was a tall woman in a floor-length red dress with short sleeves, its V-neck cut low; it flared at the bottom – like Carmen's – the flares moving with her. A mass of shiny blonde hair was heaped on top of her head where it was caught into a knot. As the Harwoods approached, Daisy could see that the woman was – what? Not exactly beautiful. But certainly dramatic in an elegant, slightly sinister way. Perhaps she *was* beautiful.

Carl Myer smiled at Andrew and kissed Daisy on the cheek before introducing his wife. 'This is Jocelyn.'

As Daisy shook hands, she was aware of hostility emanating from Jocelyn who smiled with small, very white teeth. Daisy also recognized a feeling of hostility within herself. But then usually the response of one stranger to another is mutual.

Almost immediately people began moving into the State Dining Room. The Prime Minister appeared at Daisy's elbow. 'My dear, will you take Dr Myer in with you? Andrew, perhaps you'll show Mrs Myer the way?'

Protocol being protocol, Daisy found the Foreign Secretary seated on her left, Carl Myer on her right. She looked around the room. She loved the painted vaulted ceiling, a bit like cake frosting, rising above the honey-coloured panelled walls. In the centre of the wall facing her loomed the full-length portrait of Wellington standing proudly with a red silk sash across his chest.

Not until the second course could Daisy talk with Carl. Almost immediately she asked about Jocelyn.

'How long have you been married?' she said, even though she remembered the brief file that Andrew had shown her when the American Secretary of Defense had been appointed in May. She already knew he had married 'the daughter of Mr Elliott Randall, scion of a New York banking family', in 1983. One of the Randall family had been at Radcliffe with Daisy. A cousin? She and Daisy hadn't been friends.

'Eight years?' said Carl. 'I'm not sure that you and Jocelyn will like each other.'

'Why shouldn't we?'

'Jocelyn and I are well suited. Each of us can give the other something the other does not have.'

Carl always shaped his conversation to suit himself, though there was inevitably a purpose in it, and he never failed eventually to answer whatever question had been asked. Daisy heard in her head something Angela had said long ago: 'Ben and I might very well suit one another.'

Carl went on. 'Jocelyn is the rich New York aristocrat. I am the second-generation American Jew who has made it. She was born into top-drawer society. I commanded a place in the intellectual world – and sooner or later I was pretty certain to be at the top table in Washington. So I was able to offer her the entrée into two worlds she didn't have before.'

'Is the exchange symmetrical? I can see what you could offer her. But did her money and all that mean so much to you?'

'It means a lot, Daisy. It makes daily life much more attractive. I enjoy the elegance of our house in Georgetown, the New York apartment overlooking Central Park. Jocelyn has made them the way they are – not just because her money helps pay for them, but because of her taste in decorating them. You could have done the same thing.' As he talked, Carl looked directly into Daisy's face. 'Though I never expected your father to give you a large dowry if you married me.'

'There wasn't that huge a dowry on tap for anyone I might have married.'

'You know what I mean, Daisy. You were brought up with money in an upper-class Philadelphia family. Your family wouldn't have me. And then things changed.'

Daisy looked down at the half eaten *boeuf en croute* on her plate.

'I asked myself more than once if you would have fallen in love with Andrew if he had been another Jewish immigrant's son.'

'For me that had nothing to do with anything,' said Daisy.

'I'm not so sure. You were still a student. I think you found the situation with me rather romantic. For a time,' he added. 'And then you reverted to norm.'

Daisy said nothing. It was offensive. But there was no response she could make that would not sound defensive.

'Then I met Jocelyn Randall. Her father accepted me for what I was – a distinguished academic with a future in Washington. It's even possible that he enjoyed my company. Perhaps New York aristocrats are that much more worldly than Philadelphia ones.'

Daisy's face hardened with anger. Yet there still was nothing she could reply without seeming on the defensive. And the fact was that Carl was right – about her family, anyhow.

'I'll tell you why you and Jocelyn may not like each other,' he said, now ready to answer her question. 'You think that she may have behaved better than you. She knows I was in love with you in a way that I have never been in love with her.'

'Oh Carl, don't say that.'

Daisy's anger had been replaced by a different emotion. It was not remorse: falling in love with Andrew had had nothing to do with the reason that Carl gave. But she felt something like humility – because he was prepared to be so open about his feelings. As she looked at him now, there was none of the teasing laughter in his eyes. They were sombre and sad.

'Will you be going with Andrew on his trip to Moscow?' asked a deep voice on her left. The waiters had removed the dinner plates and replaced them with a set of Wedgwood dessert plates, each painted with a different British bird in its habitat. Several waiters were carrying round silver platters of strawberries heaped in an enormous meringue, while other waiters poured champagne into the glass waiting among the cluster of crystal at each guest's place.

Daisy shifted to her left. This course it was her turn to talk to the Foreign Secretary.

At ten o'clock sharp the Prime Minister rose from the table. The doors leading to the Pillared Drawing Room were thrown open. Beyond them Daisy saw that the guests invited for after dinner were already gathering. She was likely to know more of them than Carl did. She led the way.

Beside one of the two Ionic columns stood Angela and Ben. Seeing her, Daisy laughed. In one hand Angela had a six-inch-long cigarette holder. She exhaled an enormous cloud of smoke immediately past the head of a woman whom Daisy recognized as the television star exhorting the nation on the evils of tobacco.

'You probably won't remember, Carl, but one of my friends on the *Rampart* was called Angela. We're still friends, even though her husband is a bastard. He's the editor of the *Rampart*.'

Daisy was bound to encounter Ben at various functions. She always hid her resentment at his trying to undermine Andrew. She didn't want Ben to have the pleasure of seeing he had hurt her. When she introduced the Franwells and Carl, Angela gave her small smile.

'The great Dr Myer,' she said. 'I've been yearning to meet you ever since first hearing of your compelling charms.'

'I'm delighted someone so described me. When was that?'

'1976?'

Ben said: 'I'm not sure which compelling charms my wife has in mind. But for me the principal one is your disinclination to believe everything the Russkies tell you. My God, what was the matter with your predecessor?'

Before Carl could answer, another couple joined them. The woman's blonde hair was so pale that it was almost the colour of silver. Bone straight, the front strands were pushed back behind her ears, and it was all cut to end in a razor straight line an inch above her shoulders. The pale eyes were amused.

'I hope Daisy will introduce us,' Frances said to Carl Myer. 'My husband harbours grave suspicions that you are proposing to bring the world to an end.'

As Daisy introduced them, Carl took in the carrot-coloured hair and the narrow face with its two deep grooves. Even before becoming American Secretary of Defense, Carl had been a regular reader of Giles Alexander's column in the *Vanguard* – in recent years the most influential of the British political weeklies. Carl had taken a perverse pleasure in Giles's attack on him last week – the gratuitous insults interspliced with a closely argued case for reducing defence forces in Europe.

'I gather that you enjoy an optimistic nature, Mr Alexander,' Carl said.

Giles gave his short laugh. No one had so described him before.

'I have merely suggested,' he replied, 'that we might as well take another step towards disarmament as march in the other direction and go straight over the precipice. What are you planning to do, for example, about that little nuclear bomb that has now been developed by our charming friends in the Middle East?'

At that moment Jocelyn materialized at Carl's side. Everyone looked at her. Her height, the piled-up blonde hair, the scarlet gown: unquestionably she was a striking figure. For a fraction of a second, Angela's eyes flicked from Jocelyn to Daisy and back to Jocelyn again. Daisy made the introductions.

'The *Rampart* is my favourite newspaper when I'm in London,' Jocelyn said to Ben.

While the others resumed their own conversations, Ben grinned at Jocelyn. The grin was boyish without a trace of the potential menace. Despite being more at ease in the company of men, something about Jocelyn took his fancy.

'I've often wondered what sort of woman would be the wife of an American defense secretary,' he said. 'Not that your husband is typical of any secretary except himself. Nor, I see, are you typical of anyone except yourself.'

He might be gauche with women, but he could make his meaning clear. He liked her.

Jocelyn was accustomed to people being guarded with her. She took Ben's arm.

'I don't suppose we would be permitted to sit on that rose damask settee over there?' she said. 'I always feel William Kent designed such things for the purpose of being sat upon. And that dusky rose should look rather unexpected with my red satin, don't you think?'

Ben grinned.

A quarter of an hour later Daisy glanced at the pair who sat on the William Kent settee. The red satin dress was indeed stunning against the rose damask. Ben was sitting forward, listening closely to what Jocelyn was saying.

For no reason whatsoever the thought came into Daisy's mind: two enemies joined together more than double the strength of either alone.

38

Ben Franwell was in New York for three days. Angela Franwell was at their London flat, in bed in the spare room. She thought the English word more appropriate than the American 'guest' room. The English one conveyed more possibilities.

She and Ben slept in twin beds at home and anywhere else such an arrangement was possible – which these days meant nearly everywhere. Sometimes when he snored she moved into the spare room in Sussex or here in the St James's Place penthouse. Occasionally she chose at the outset to go to bed in the spare room simply because she wanted to be by herself.

She was lying on the Louis XIV three-quarter bed from her Pimlico Road days. She still preferred it to anyone else's – the aquamarine painted headboard and footboard scattered with faded taupe and sage-green flowers whose irregular brush strokes added to their charm. Beyond the window she could see the lush foliage of Green Park's plane trees in June. She loved going to bed in the afternoon. She loved the awareness of herself on the bed. When she entertained during Ben's absence, she always did so in the spare room. Angela was not without a sense of propriety.

She looked down at the thumb resting on one breast as the third finger circled, then rubbed the hardened nipple. She rested one of her hands on his: she liked feeling his hand while it felt her. It was as if they both were making love to her. When he took away his hand and turned his back on her to spread her legs, languidly she pulled him back. She took one of his hands and covered her left breast with it, opening his fingers so her nipple would protrude between them and she could touch it with the tip of one red-lacquered nail.

'I'm not absolutely sure how long I can go on like this,' Giles said.

Angela gave her small smile.

'Do I gather you would like to come inside me, sir?'

Afterwards he lay on his back beside her, looking at the foot-board.

'Are you sure it's been two years since I last saw those taupe flowers?' he said.

'Umm.'

'They seem the same. So do you.' He turned his head on the pillow and looked at her. One of her hands was resting on one breast.

Giles propped himself on an elbow as he reached over to the bedside table for his pack of cigarettes and the lighter Nelly had given him years ago. Lying again on his back, he took out two cigarettes and handed one to Angela, flicking the lighter twice. They watched the two little clouds of smoke appear above their heads and separately dissolve.

'I don't know what your dear husband would make of this,' Giles said. 'One night last week – Frances was out with her latest chum – Nelly and I had dinner at Green's. We got pretty sloshed. He asked me if I wanted to call in at a place called German's. It's not a bit like Heaven where I once went with Nelly and never wished to go again – absurd place. German's is smallish, almost subdued, some men arriving in couples, others quietly looking each other over before settling into one of the booths for two. Nelly and I were sitting at the bar. The light at German's is dim, as you would imagine. Even so, when a couple got up from a booth and walked to the door together – a middle-aged man dressed soberly in grey flannels and a blazer, with him a snake-

hipped youth dressed entirely in white except for his gold jewellery – I recognized the man in the blazer. I've seen photographs
of him with Rachel Fisher, and he was with her at a Downing
Street reception last winter. It was George Bishop.'

'Shall we have another cigarette?' said Angela.

When Giles had snapped his lighter closed he went on: 'The
manager of German's was there that night. I got Nelly to find out
if he knew the man in the blazer. He didn't know the man's name
but said he'd been in a number of times. Like many patrons of
German's, the bloke in the blazer was always quiet, the manager
said, and he always paid cash at the bar.'

They watched two more clouds of smoke dissolve.

'Do you ever worry about getting AIDS?' said Angela.

'I suppose everyone thinks of it. But only very very infrequently
do I find myself in a high risk situation, as they say. Do you think
about it?'

'Only when there is another great burst of publicity about its
being spread amongst us clean-living heterosexuals. That's why
you were invited this afternoon to adorn yourself in what I still
prefer to call a French letter. But then as soon as we're told that
it's only propaganda to share out the blame, I stop thinking about
it.'

'What would Ben think?'

'About George Bishop consorting with a lovely lad?'

'Yeah.'

'He'd flip.'

'But how?'

Angela studied the faded flowers on the footboard.

'Hard to say. It would be extremely awkward for him. He
couldn't advise Rachel to leave George: that could end in scandal.
He might advise her not to sleep with her husband again; but she
may not be doing so now. Perhaps his greatest worry, apart from
whether he would throw up whenever he thinks of the revealed-
as-he-really-is George, would be whether this information about
Rachel Fisher's husband will get into one of the tabloids.'

'It's your last thought that had already occurred to me,' said
Giles. 'I shall brood upon it.'

He looked at his watch. 'I must go.'

When he returned from the bathroom, she was still lying on the bed. She lit another cigarette. As he dressed, she watched the solitary clouds above her disappear into the air.

She was particularly fond of Giles, but she would not be sorry to have her pretty bedroom to herself.

Carl had taken off his tie and undone the top button of his Brooks Brothers shirt. From where he sat comfortably on the sofa he could see the June lushness of the treetops beyond the windows. He dropped his eyes to the figure in faded denim. Her shirt and jeans had evidently been through the washer quite a few times. Her hair was pulled off her face with two big yellow butterfly grips. Although she'd made up her eyes, the rest of her face was *au naturel*. Her feet were bare.

'Do you mind if I put my feet up?' said Carl. 'I think my right leg is going to sleep in its present position.'

Daisy laughed. 'All I'm interested in is your head. Can you keep it facing more or less this way?'

Carl grunted.

Ten minutes later he spoke again. 'How many of your male sitters, gazing at you two hours on end – okay, so you allow two five-minute breaks – how many of them get an erection?'

She reached over to the heap of damp clay on the big deal table beside the plinth. With a short blunt knife she scooped out a dollop and pressed it on the right cheekbone of the clay head on the plinth. She put the knife down and used her thumbs and forefingers to model the cheekbone. Her lower lip was caught in her teeth as she concentrated.

'I asked you a question, Daisy.'

'Umm.'

'What I asked you was whether other male sitters looking at this particular sculptor find they have an erection'

She picked up the short blunt knife again. Then she put it down.

'Look, Carl, this wasn't my idea. First it was Andrew's bright thought. Then Jocelyn chimed in. So here we are. And I hope my artistic prowess will be appreciated by the Pentagon. But in the meantime could you please talk about something besides the state of your genitals. I'm not interested in them.'

She picked up the knife again, took another dollop of damp clay and smacked it onto the left cheekbone.

Eight feet away where he lay on the sofa with his feet now propped on one of its arms, his head turned partway to the right so he was still facing Daisy, the flesh-and-blood Carl was enjoying himself.

'All right. We can have a philosophical conversation. You told me that it keeps my face from going rigid if I talk from time to time.'

Daisy wiped her hands on a piece of wet cheesecloth, drying them on the back of her jeans.

'Let's have our other five-minute break,' she said. 'Do you want a cup of coffee? There's some left in the percolator.' A single-ring electric burner stood on a table along one wall.

'No thanks. I'll take a walk around the room.'

He got up and stretched his chest, his arms lifted with the elbows bent. In his wiry way, he was muscular.

He strolled to the other end of the studio from where Daisy was sprawled in an armchair covered with a multi-coloured Indian Madras bedspread that had seen better days. It was left over from her pre-marriage bedsit off Sloane Square.

Carl put out a hand and rested it on the larger than life-size clay model of two birds with their necks turned as if in an embrace. No moisture met his touch; the clay had dried. He removed his hand and swivelled on one heel to recross the studio, skirting several wooden plinths, each supporting the unfinished bust of another sitter half-visible through the plastic bag tied over it to keep the clay from drying out. Something in the way the bags were knotted around the throats made Carl pull down the corners of his mouth.

He stopped when he came to the back of the armchair where Daisy was still stretched out, resting. Leaning over her shoulder, he slipped his right hand flat inside her denim shirt with its two top buttons undone. She was wearing a bra. He pushed the tips of his fingers under it. It was all done in one movement.

Daisy slipped lower down on her spine and twisted to one side, removing herself from his hand as she got to her feet.

'You don't understand, Carl.'

She strode over to the mantelpiece cluttered with jars and brushes. Standing with her back to it, she said: 'I don't want to have an affair with anyone.'

'That's what you say, Daisy.'

'That's what I mean.'

He remained standing beside the armchair she had vacated. He lifted a corner of the hemp bedspread thrown over it, examined the pattern idly before letting the rough cloth drop again.

'Plurality enhances appreciation of the loved one,' he said with mock solemnity, as if he were opening a lecture.

He then became matter-of-fact. 'You know as well as I know, Daisy, that however considerate – however imaginative – a couple may be, things get a little repetitious after a decade. Any truly sensual person will have plural relationships – for their own sake and to increase the routine pleasure with the loved one.'

'I wish you'd stop saying "the loved one" as if you were talking about one of those embalmed corpses in Evelyn Waugh's novel.'

Carl laughed. He stayed where he was.

'I am not suggesting anything that would diminish your relationship with Andrew.'

'Yes you are. The fact that it's only Andrew who arouses the sexual side of me is important to him – and to me.'

'He needn't know. Do you know if he has the occasional adventure?'

'I think he would tell me if he did. Or if he didn't tell me at the time, he'd tell me afterwards. Probably,' she added. Occasionally Andrew had talked about his surprise that though he remained very conscious of attractive women, when it came down to doing something about it, he found he couldn't be bothered. He would smile when he'd add to tease her: 'But you mustn't let it go to your head. I'm sure the explanation is that this bloody job doesn't leave much time to stray.' She chose to believe him. Perhaps it wasn't so. She had never asked him explicitly, and, now that she thought about it, he had not stated explicitly that he never strayed. She wasn't sure she wanted to know if he had.

Watching her, Carl said: 'People who have the closest of marriages have discreet affairs on the side, especially if they are interested in heightening one of the greatest pleasures God has bestowed on us – our sensuality. That doesn't mean we have to go around discussing the thing. No one else need ever know.'

'But *I*'d know.' Daisy's voice was momentarily a wail. 'I like having him provide all that side of my life. It makes everything else we do together richer – and more fun. The fact that all this emanates just from him heightens our relationship.'

'How touching. But you know you're being silly, Daisy. You talk like some little Radcliffe sophomore who knows nothing whatsoever about the world.'

Daisy stamped one foot. It really was intolerable to be lectured like this.

Carl burst out laughing. He walked around the armchair and sat down in it, his legs spread straight and apart. He lifted an edge of the hemp bedcover and rubbed it over one cheek as he watched Daisy standing with her back to the mantelpiece.

She was embarrassed that she had stamped her foot: it showed he had got under her skin. He was so bloody cocky that he would no doubt interpret her brief loss of control as physical passion for him. Why on earth did Carl Myer have to turn out to be the American defense secretary? Yet if she was honest with herself, she had to admit that there was a glamour in the situation. But she didn't want to go to bed with him, which is what this whole conversation was patently about.

'Look, Carl. My relationship with Andrew is the most important thing in my life – though obviously I'm not talking about the children when I say that.'

'Naturally.'

'And the relationship with me is more important to Andrew than you may realize. Sometimes we've talked notionally about what would happen if I had a fling with someone. He says even if I didn't tell him, it would change things between us, because I'd feel differently about him. It's true.'

'On the contrary. I am perfectly aware that Andrew loves his wife. What I'm suggesting could actually increase that love, because you would find Andrew even more interesting if you forgot all the puritan rubbish you were taught. You should allow yourself a little diversity. It would be good for both of you.'

'But I'd be different then. I told you. I don't want that.'

'You're wrong.'

He got up from the chair and walked to where she'd remained standing. He stopped two feet away from her.

'This is what I suggest we do,' he said.

Someone was knocking on the studio door.

Carl turned and took rapid quiet steps away from Daisy.

'Come in,' she said.

The door opened. It was Sophie. Her hair was twisted up on the top of her head and held by a green butterfly hairgrip she'd borrowed from Daisy's dressing table.

'Hullo, Dr Myer. Hullo, Mama. Those two geeks who were standing outside the front door when I came home from school are now standing in the entrance hall. They rang the bell and I let them in. One of them says to ask you, Dr Myer, what time you think you should be leaving for the Embassy. Has Matty come home yet?'

'Not so far as I know,' said Daisy.

Carl was looking at his watch. 'They're right, I should go. How are you, Sophie?'

'I'm all right.'

She watched Carl Myer as he picked up his tie and put it around his neck, lifting his chin as he began to tie the knot. She liked him. 'How can you do it without looking in a mirror?' she said.

'Experience. I have been talking to your mother about that very thing.'

Daisy had disappeared. Carl and Sophie walked down the passage towards the front of the house.

Daisy was in the entrance hall with the two security agents who now moved outside where the lead car and the grey Opel Senator had been manoeuvred between cars already parked at the kerb. Two policemen in helmets and boots stood by their BMWs. A black saloon roared forward from the top end of Cheyne Street and stopped alongside the motorcycles, blocking the road as the American Defense Secretary stood on the pavement saying goodbye to the mother and daughter.

From the bottom end of the road where the red pillar-box stood on the other side, the short figure of a boy crossed the street. He broke into a run, reaching the house just as Carl was about to get into the car.

'Hullo Dr Myer.'

'Hullo Matty.'

Carl shook hands as if he had all the time in the world.

'I was hoping I'd get a glimpse of you, Matty,' he said. 'I look forward to seeing you next time.'

The back door of the Opel Senator had hardly closed when the outriders rammed down their starter pedals. As the cavalcade reached the bottom of Cheyne Street, from the top end the Post Office van rushed past.

Sophie watched it stop by the pillar-box, its engine ticking like the crocodile in *Peter Pan*. She never understood how Post Office drivers got to each pillar-box four times a day almost on the minute scheduled, even though it was the same schedule all over London. She bet when she and Matty and her mother got back in the house, the grandfather clock in the hall would say 5:31 exactly.

It did. There was no reason for her to imagine a day when the Post Office van would arrive too late.

39

Facing the windows, Carl saw the afternoon sky darken and then split when the lightning flashed down. June had become unsettled. His back to the windows, Andrew heard the single thunderclap and then the rain gusting against the glass. In less than half an hour, the summer storm had abated and both teams had advanced in a trade-off of non-nuclear forces in Europe.

It was the next subject that was awkward: Satyr.

Andrew set out the three parts of his equation.

Carl replied: 'Let us suppose, for the moment, that I can convince you no American-made component would contain a chip enabling the Pentagon to eavesdrop. If you divided the production work between British companies and US Solar Space, I can guarantee we would launch the satellites for you at an even lower figure than was previously discussed.'

Andrew put his elbows on the table, the heels of his hands under his chin. He looked quite comfortable – which was just as well. The long hand on the clock over the door jerked onto seven o'clock as the meeting finally broke up

'I'll see you at Buckingham Palace,' Andrew said to his opposite number.

'Do you always lead this dizzy social life?' asked Carl.

'No. Monarchs and statesmen from foreign lands have an unaccountable passion for visiting Britain in June.'

The long hand jerked onto 7:35 as Daisy walked through the door.

She was radiant in a sulphur-yellow silk gown cut so narrow that even with the slit to the knee she could only take small steps. Her white kid court gloves nearly reached her shoulders. As well as her sequinned handbag she carried a starched shirt in the laundry's transparent envelope. Behind her came Ollie bearing the wooden hanger from which hung black trousers, tailcoat and white waistcoat, a white tie draped around the hanger's neck.

Daisy beamed with pride: she had left the house and climbed into the Jaguar only five minutes after the appointed time.

'Brilliant,' said Andrew.

He was sitting at his desk. 'I'll just finish signing these. Ollie, why don't you unload your precious burden onto the sofa? Daisy, make yourself comfortable.'

When the Minister emerged from his bathroom in his white tie and tails, he surveyed his wife. 'You look delicious,' he said.

Ollie drove round Parliament Square and into Birdcage Walk. At its other end he swung right towards the gilded figure of Victory and a proud Queen Victoria seated below, looking with satisfaction towards Trafalgar Square, her back to Buckingham Palace.

One of the elaborately wrought iron gates stood open. As the Defence Secretary's car went past, sentries in red tunics and black bearskins presented arms. Ollie drove across the forecourt, stopping behind three other official cars waiting to decant their bedecked passengers.

'Do you remember,' Daisy said, 'the first time you brought me here for that cocktail party for Margaret Thatcher, and the courtier who took us upstairs said it didn't matter in the slightest that the Queen had already gone in?'

Andrew laughed. 'Actually, I'm not sure I'd realized until then that even when the Queen is hostess, one is meant to arrive before her. Strange people, royalty, when you think about it. We'll get out here, Ollie.'

Half a dozen DPG and two members of Special Branch stood near the portico in the middle of the Palace front. The Harwoods entered the door that leads into the Grand Hall.

Daisy looked up at the huge gilt capitals that crown the marble columns of the Grand Hall. A courtier was standing in front of the ornate fireplace, its overmantel displaying a magnificent gilded clock flanked by Victories.

'Hullo, Andrew. Good evening, Daisy.'

Daisy scarcely knew the courtier, but Andrew had been with him at Marlborough. Except for his knee breeches, his evening clothes were like Andrew's. He walked with them up the sumptuous staircase which sweeps up to the facing wall, then forks right and left before returning on itself to complete the march upwards. Her gown was so narrow that Daisy had to hitch it up to climb the stairs. Reaching their top, she glanced up at the assemblage of white marble sculptures and the dome above.

'Come on.' Andrew put a hand on one of her elbows.

The thing about Buckingham Palace, she found, was that once she entered the Green Drawing Room or the Blue Drawing Room or any of the other drawing rooms, there were always people standing about. She couldn't talk with them and at the same time have a proper look at the room. She was aware of ceilings soaring far above, walls hung with lavish silks of crimson and sapphire, green and lemon yellow, festooned with heavy garlands of gold. But she couldn't take in any details of the paintings and sculpture and furniture and no doubt priceless bibelots.

'Good evening, Minister.'

'Good evening, Field Marshal.'

Andrew introduced Daisy and the Chief of the Defence Staff. The top half of the Field Marshal's dress uniform was encrusted with row upon row of medals. He introduced his wife, a formidable figure in stiff green taffeta and a tiara. A footman proffered a silver tray from which Daisy took a glass of champagne. Andrew took a large whisky.

As it appeared unnecessary for her to make conversation with the Field Marshal and his wife, Daisy looked around her. There must be fifty people in the room. She knew or recognized about half of them. Although most seemed to be engaged in some sort of conversation, there was an air of expectation.

From the far end of the room where a back door suddenly opened, a rustle began and moved like a wave across the White Drawing Room as the guests nearest the door saw the royal party enter, and other guests sensed it and turned that way. Daisy and Andrew were still at the opposite end of the drawing room, all the other guests standing in between.

'Daisy. Andrew. I've been asked to present you to the Prince of Wales.'

The courtier led the way to where the Prince of Wales stood talking with two people Daisy recognized as the National Theatre's director and his wife. She and Andrew and the courtier waited a few feet away. Glancing around her, Daisy saw three other members of the royal family positioned several yards from one another, each honouring a different guest with the royal attention. By the time the evening was over, almost every guest would have talked with one royal personage, or, if they were very special guests, two. It was funny. However informal some members of the royal family liked to think themselves, they never expected you to treat them informally. Even Prince Charles, with all his concern for mankind and so on, would not expect a guest at Buckingham Palace to speak to him until he spoke first. And he would ask Daisy questions without expecting her to ask him any about himself.

Without any pause that Daisy could discern, Prince Charles suddenly ended his conversation with the National Theatre's director and his wife – by simply turning away from them and moving a step towards the courtier who immediately had a word with the Harwoods.

The courtier presented them. Daisy gave a little bob. Her American upbringing made it impossible to emulate one of those English women – almost always they wore tiaras, she had noticed – who sank to the floor in the deepest of curtsies, vain of their graceful – and to Daisy's eyes obsequious – display. The Prince shook hands with Andrew, who bowed his head for a moment. The Prince then opened conversation in the voice that always slightly surprised by its rich depth – though Daisy wasn't sure why it should be surprising. Because the Queen and Princess

Margaret and Princess Diana had such tight, rather high voices? Or because, absurdly, she didn't expect a man with the Prince of Wales' slight build to have such a deep melodious voice?

'How long did it take you, Mrs Harwood, to complete the bust of Sir Julian Staverton?'

The Prince looked with intent interest at Daisy, as if nothing in the world could be more fascinating than her answer. Clever of him to have noticed the bust at the National Portrait Gallery and then remembered it, Andrew thought to himself.

'Goodness, Sir, it went on forever,' said Daisy. 'Sir Julian was the most restless human being I have ever encountered. He was meant to come to my studio for several two-hour sittings. But after half an hour he was always pacing up and down the floor, and it was impossible, I found, to trot alongside him, peering at his features, and model my lump of clay at the same time. So it went on for months.'

Prince Charles laughed appreciatively. Daisy had noticed before when engaged in one of these never quite relaxed conversations with royalty that if you said anything even remotely humorous, they seemed to find it hilarious. Must be something to do with the constrictions of their life.

'Whose features are currently on lumps of clay in your studio?' asked the Prince.

'Oh. Well, Auberon Waugh is swathed in one plastic bag at the moment, Andrew Lloyd-Webber in another. And I've just started on a head of my husband's opposite number – who, I think, is here this evening.'

'Ah. The great Dr Myer,' said the Prince. 'One rather gathers that the ecological balance of our environment is not his uppermost consideration.'

He's well briefed, Andrew thought to himself, not for the first time. The Prince turned to him.

'I was interested in your speech at Trinity House a fortnight ago. Jolly difficult thing to gauge how far to trust others' apparently well-intentioned offers, how far to view them with a little skepticism.'

As it was Andrew who was now the object of the Prince's attention, Daisy could take a turn at reflection. She was mildly surprised that the Prince had made even an indirect reference to Carl's much publicized argument in favour of a limited nuclear strike under certain provocations. She'd thought one of Prince Charles' frustrations in being middle-aged and still without a real job was that he was never meant to talk about politics or defence.

The Prince turned away. Another rustle moved through the room. Two hundred people from three drawing rooms were going into dinner.

Among them Daisy noticed Rachel Fisher. She was dressed in silk the colour of tawny port. Beside her walked a quite good-looking man who must be George Bishop. Daisy had met him once before at a Buckingham Palace reception.

Entering the State Dining Room, her eyes flicked up to its three saucer domes. Then she looked at the card she'd been handed when she and Andrew had first arrived: her place was part way down one wing of the U-shaped table. When she reached it, Carl was standing alongside.

'Allow me,' he said, pulling her chair back before a footman could help her seat herself.

Peering at the place card to her left, she recognized the foreign name from the two pages of potted biographies she'd been given to read on the short drive to Buckingham Palace. It was one of the persons accompanying the dapper little monarch on his state visit to London. But which one? She'd forgotten.

An elegant figure bowed low to her and took the seat on her left. She wondered if he spoke English. The only other language Daisy knew well was French, and she found that rather tiring. She leaned forward so she could see past him: thank God the next woman along was not talking to her other dinner partner. Daisy sat back and quickly turned to her right.

'You don't happen to know who the person is on my left, do you, Carl? His card says he's Commander Dorocco.'

'He's the *chef de cabinet* of the guest of honour,' said Carl. His eyes twinkled. 'You'll be glad to know he speaks English, though it's not as good as he thinks it is. Do you realize, Mrs Harwood, that you and I are flying in the face of numerical expectation? Protocol dictates that I find myself seated between two usually unscintillating ladies who just happen to have husbands of rank

equal to mine. They do their best. I do my best. No one could say
it is fun. But all that changes when I come to London. Lo, the
wife of the British Defence Secretary happens to be the most
attractive woman living in this scepter'd isle. How are you?'

Daisy laughed. She was glad to see him. Half her dinner conversation was bound to be enjoyable.

'I'm very well,' she said, looking down as she began the business
of unbuttoning her gloves, removing her hands from them, and
then rolling the empty kid fingers up until she could tuck them
into the wrists of the gloves before a footman reached her with the
first course. Carl watched her doing it. He was always interested
in how women managed the *petit déshabillé des mains*.

'But I have such ignoble thoughts,' she went on. 'Do you see
that woman with the dark curly hair and tawny-coloured dress
sitting across the table? Just down there to the left.' Without doing
so conspicuously, Daisy indicated where Rachel was sitting. 'Have
you met her?'

'No. She looks interesting.'

'I suppose she is. She's the Industry Secretary.'

'Is that Rachel Fisher?'

'Yes. Do you remember my introducing you to the editor of
the *Rampart* that night at Number Ten? Well, he's constantly
promoting Rachel Fisher at the expense of Andrew. So I don't
like her. And seeing her down the table, I find I have unworthy
thoughts.'

'Let me guess.'

Daisy waited.

'You could be hoping one of those footmen will spill the hol-
landaise sauce over her shoulder.'

'I hadn't thought of that. It's an idea, though.'

'You could be pleased that you're higher up the table than she
is.'

'That's exactly what my unworthy thought is. Isn't it
disgusting? It's so petty. Now that I've told you, I've exorcised
it.'

Carl smiled. 'You're right: it is petty. But all of us are petty,
Daisy. Shall I tell you who is pettier than anyone else I know?
My colleagues at Princeton. To be precise: the Jewish intellectuals

at Princeton. They cannot stand it that I am the one who is the Secretary of Defense.'

'But isn't it that you are more conscious of them than anyone else? I'm sure other people also have feelings of jealousy.'

'Logically that is so, Daisy. But they haven't the sustained resentment. Henry Kissinger told me he experienced the same thing. He said that the Jewish group at Harvard would have preferred anyone to be Secretary of State rather than another Jewish intellectual. That they could not forgive.'

The footmen in their red livery, gold buttons embossed with a crown and ER, were already clearing away the Royal Worcester plates. The Queen did not like to linger over the courses. In any case, most of the plates, individually painted with British flora, were scraped nearly clean: the lobster had been excellent. Daisy looked at the gilt underplate and the goblets at each place; two of the four goblets were gilt. She would have to ask Andrew why you were meant to drink the other two wines from crystal: if the Queen had this many gilt goblets she must have some more put away somewhere that she could have used as well had she wished. From Daisy's left came the deep voice of the *chef de cabinet*.

'Shall I tell you, Mrs Harwood, the secret of boiling the lobster so he remains full of tenderness like Her Majesty's – rather than his muscles becoming stiff, rigid?'

Daisy turned to her left. Social demands were made easier by an innate curiosity.

'Rigid,' she said encouragingly, *Roget's Thesaurus* flitting across her mind, not absolutely certain whose muscles were under discussion.

The *chef de cabinet* gave a long dissertation on how Her Majesty's chef must have heated the water slowly and lulled the lobster to sleep. Because of the word in his title, Daisy envisaged the dignified figure beside her wearing a white apron and tall white hat as he stood over a large saucepan. He was looking at her intently, his eyes of such a deep chocolate brown that she could read nothing whatsoever in them. But then there was a theory that the actual eye is expressionless, that it is the muscles of the face around it that produce our expression.

She looked at the Queen, who sat in the middle of the table

which joined the two wings. Even had Daisy not been long-sighted, she would have been fairly sure the Queen's court gloves, their fingers neatly tucked up, weren't made of elegant kid. Daisy had been profoundly impressed when last July she'd been a guest in the royal box at the Royal Opera House in Covent Garden. Everyone knew that most of the royal family infinitely preferred horses to opera, and therefore the royal box was usually occupied by lesser souls. But, perhaps because Placido Domingo was singing, the Queen had been inveigled to attend. What particularly struck Daisy when they met in the private dining room immediately behind the box was that the Queen wore a diamond and ruby bracelet over one of her long white gloves. In Daisy's Philadelphia girlhood, she'd been told by her mother that it was vulgar to wear jewellery over one's gloves. But the most notable thing of all was that the Queen's court gloves looked uncannily like cotton fabric. It had been one of those steaming Julys, and Covent Garden was like a sauna. Daisy's arms, like those of the Queen's lady-in-waiting and the chairman's wife who was hostess, were encased in white kid, than which few things can be hotter. Only the Queen had made herself comfortable in lightweight gloves.

When the banquet under the three saucer domes concluded, the *chef de cabinet* bowed to Daisy, and Carl escorted her into the White Drawing Room. She spotted Andrew and crossed the room to join him. Ten minutes later the familiar courtier was at their shoulder. He'd been asked to present them to Her Majesty.

As they waited for the monarch to complete her conversation with two other guests, Daisy scrutinized her. She looked fresher and far less stern in the flesh than in newspaper photographs. Her smile was bright and infectious. If her social small talk was somewhat ritualized, who could wonder? Imagine being expected to converse with strangers on a thousand different and drawn-out occasions a year. Daisy would go mad.

The Queen must have decided she had bestowed enough energy on the other two guests. Abruptly she turned her back on them. With her good memory, it was not necessary for the courtier to remind her she'd met the Harwoods before. Daisy did her little bob, Andrew his small bow.

'Prince Charles tells me you have a statue in the National

Portrait Gallery,' said the Queen. 'The last portrait bust made of me was the most exhausting experience I can remember. The artist appeared to think one had absolutely nothing to do but sit for two hours, unblinking.' The Queen smiled brightly.

When their car drove out of the courtyard of Buckingham Palace and Ollie headed for Cheyne Street, Daisy put a kid-gloved hand on one of Andrew's hands. She spoke in a low voice.

'I was thinking earlier about how our life is more complicated and grander than it used to be, yet our marriage hasn't got pushed to the wayside. Our children are healthy. You enjoy your job. I enjoy my work. And on top of that we have the bonus of a glamorous evening like tonight: it's not *important*, but it's fun to dine at Buckingham Palace.'

When they were undressing in their bedroom, Andrew pulled off his white tie and loosened his collar and waistcoat and then stopped. He sat down in the armchair and watched Daisy as she stepped out of her sulphur-yellow gown and stood in her saffron lace bra and her tights and high-heeled sandals. She hadn't yet taken off her necklace and earrings: she knew he was watching her.

'Each time we were making a transition to a new phase in our life, you thought it would be less good than the previous one,' Andrew said. 'Yet each phase has been happy – different but happy.'

He went on looking at her.

She still had not removed her sandals and underclothes and jewellery.

'Would you like me to put on my court gloves again?'

'Why not?'

When she had done so he got up from the armchair and crossed the room to where she stood. He unfastened her saffron bra.

40

Because of the number of Mondays in the month, school had broken up a little earlier in July than usual. She was wearing an old shirt of Andrew's over her cut-off jeans. She had difficulty keeping its sleeves rolled up. He certainly had long arms. She liked it because she wouldn't have to pull it over her head when she was ready to change into her new dress.

The thing about ironing your hair straight is to start while it's still wet, iron it flat, then wind it round and round your head as tight as you can, fastening it carefully with tortoiseshell pins, but you must be really careful or even tortoiseshell will make a kink that spoils the whole thing. What made Sophie most anxious was having to wait at least an hour while it set straight, she hoped, before being able to undo it and discover whether she'd succeeded or whether she'd have to start the whole process again. Even when it worked, she had to be sure not to let it blow about or expose it to any dampness or it would begin to curl. So she'd had her bath first. She'd meant to leave time to do the process twice if need be, but when she glanced at the clock she saw it was already 5:20. And Jason was calling for her at six. It was amazingly dark for July. Then she realized that rain clouds must have blotted out the sun. She looked out of her window onto Cheyne Street. The street had turned that lovely sleek black from the first drops. The maple tree's leaves were wet. She loved the whispering sound that rain makes when it falls gently on leaves. The rain was so sudden that with any luck it would be finished before she and Jason set out. Gently she began unfastening the pins. Two long flat ribbons of auburn hair hung straight down in front of her shoulders. So far so good.

'Sophie?'

Mama was calling. From the timbre of her voice Sophie could tell Daisy was outside her bedroom on the floor below. She'd just have to wait a minute.

'*Sophie.*'

Damn damn damn damn. 'What?'

'Please come to the top of the stairs. I need to speak to you.'

'I can't, Mama. My hair is at a crucial stage.'

'Sophie, I mean it. I need you.'

Walking very straight, Sophie went out into the hall and looked over the banister, both hands alongside her ears, holding in place the next two big hunks of hair that she'd just unpinned. 'What's the matter?'

'Look at me. I'm stark naked. My hair is dripping wet. The car is collecting me at quarter to six. And I never posted the letter I promised Andrew I'd get off to his mother today. *Please* take it to the corner for me. There's still two minutes before the van comes.'

'I can't, Mama. My hair's at the really crucial point. If I let go of it it'll be ruined. And it's raining outside. And I haven't time to do it again.'

'*Please*, Sophie. You look pretty whatever you do to your hair. Put something over it.'

'Why can't you go?'

'Look at me for God's sake. And that hateful car is coming in fifteen minutes. And it's an official thing that I don't want to go to. And you know how your father feels about my being late. And I have got to get that letter posted. I said I would. *Please* help me. The van will be here in a minute.'

'Oh all *right*. Where is it?'

'On the hall table.'

Sophie ran down the stairs. The half unpinned ribbons of hair began to cascade down. The whole thing was ruined. She burst into tears. 'Why is your party more important than mine?' It was half a shout and half a sob as she passed the open door to her parents' bedroom.

'God how I hate family quarrels,' Daisy said aloud as she half dried herself and pulled the towel around her long enough to go down the corridor to Andrew's dressing room where she kept the convector heater under the bed. If she just concentrated she could get her hair set and dried in six minutes and still have nine minutes to dress and make up. But how could she concentrate when Sophie was so upset? It *was* rather hard on Sophie. God, how Daisy hated that bloody bloody bloody car and the way that everyone in Andrew's office thought she had nothing to do but spend the day getting ready to step into it on the exact minute decreed. She was half way to the dressing room when she heard the tearing scream of brakes.

She ran back and flung up a bedroom window. Near the bottom of Cheyne Street, between cars parked on either side, a car was standing with its door thrown open as a man jumped out and disappeared in front of it. Daisy could see the red pillar-box at the corner beyond. Except for the whispering sound made by the rain falling on the maple leaves, everything seemed silent – and strangely three-dimensional, as if fixed in time.

She snatched her jeans off the floor, pulling a T-shirt over her head as she ran down the stairs.

A second car was being driven too fast down Cheyne Street. This man at the wheel also had had a long day and was in a hurry to get home. He saw that a car was stopped at an odd angle just before the corner ahead. Some idiot had left the door open. He could just get past it, but he'd better slow down. As he did so, a woman appeared from nowhere and ran into the road in front of him. He rammed on the brakes, and the slippery surface made his car slew to one side just short of her. He noticed her hair was wet. She never saw him. As she ran past the open door of the car that half-blocked the street, he saw she was barefoot. Starting up his engine again, the man, angry as someone is who's been frightened, rolled down the window and shouted ahead: 'You crazy woman. Are you trying to kill yourself?'

Half a second later he realized. He eased his own car up to the open door so that the entire road was blocked. He cut his engine and opened his door, wondering how he would keep charge of himself. Then he walked to the front of the other car where a man was leaning over something lying on the shiny road while alongside knelt the woman with wet hair.

At the top end of Cheyne Street the postman's red van came around the corner. He was one minute late.

'We'll wait here for a little, sir. You may find you need us for something.'

'All right,' Andrew said.

He took his time as he walked beside Daisy to the front steps. She was still in her jeans and T-shirt, though she had put on some shoes. In one hand Andrew carried his red box. He counted the front steps: one two three four. The hand that put the key in the door seemed to have nothing much to do with him. He closed the door behind them.

Inside, Matty was sitting on the bottom step. He got up. 'Oh Mama. Oh Dad.'

Daisy touched Matty's cheek with her open hand. Then she went upstairs.

'Is she dead?'

'No.'

'Is she going to get well?'

'I don't know, Matty.'

With his face against Andrew's shirt front, Matty could feel the cotton cloth get wet. Then he felt something dripping on his hair. After a few minutes he stepped back out of Andrew's arms and looked up. Andrew's tears now poured directly onto his already sodden shirt front. Matty wiped the palm of one hand across his nose and mouth.

'If she doesn't die, will there be something the matter with her?'

'I don't know.'

Andrew wondered whether he said that in order to break the news slowly to Matty or whether he didn't want himself to acknowledge what the surgeons had said. They couldn't predict when – they didn't say 'if' and he hadn't been able to bring himself to ask if they meant that, though he knew they did – when she would come out of the coma. Until the oedema had gone down, they could not consider operating. They explained that oedema meant fluid swelling the brain. This usually happened when there was a skull fracture. It was too soon to say how much paralysis there would be. The human body was a remarkable instrument. These spinal fractures had been known to respond to treatment, or perhaps partially respond would be a more accurate way to put it. Of course she would not be left alone in the intensive care unit. But it was important that her mother was not present while they made the early tests. They would be making tests throughout the night. There was no reason to think from the heartbeat that Sophie would suddenly die. Whatever happened was not going to happen overnight. She might remain unconscious for weeks. Her parents could return first thing in the morning. It would certainly be possible for Mrs Harwood to stay near her daughter once things became clearer. But there was no question of her daughter regaining consciousness tonight. Mrs Harwood was in shock and it was in everyone's interest that she should go home tonight and get a few hours' sleep. Did they need sleeping pills? Of course if anything changed someone would immediately ring the Harwoods' home. The hospital was only fifteen minutes' drive from Cheyne Street. And the Minister could ring them at any time during the night. Things might become clearer in the morning.

'Uncle Nelly should be here at any moment,' Matty said.

Andrew leaned over to pick up the red box. He didn't remember putting it on the floor. He put one foot in front of the other. When he reached the top of the stairs the bedroom door was closed.

He went into his study. The lights hadn't been turned on. In the dark he crossed the room to his chair. He put the red box on the ottoman in front of it. He started to turn on his light and then stopped. He recrossed the room and went out of the door.

He opened the bedroom door and went in, closing the door behind him. The curtains were drawn so there was no light from the street: the room was entirely dark. He walked over to his armchair and took off his jacket and hung it on the back of the chair. He folded his tie and put it on the mantelpiece. His eyes had got used to the dark, and anyhow he knew where everything was. He walked to Daisy's side of the bed and put his arms around her.

It seemed much later when he said: 'What happened?' He knew only that Sophie had been hit in Cheyne Street. Neither at the hospital nor in the car had he asked Daisy how it had happened.

She told him. It took a long time because of the wrenching sobs between almost every word. When she came to the part about how she'd called for Sophie when Sophie was just finishing ironing her hair, Daisy could not go on for some time.

There was not a lot of difference between the sound of the woman crying and the man.

Then Andrew spoke in a terrible strangled voice. 'Why did you make her post the letter?'

Daisy pulled herself away from his arms. She turned on her right side with her back to him, her left arm across her face. She lay silent and still.

Andrew climbed the stairs to the next floor. He wondered who had turned the light on in Sophie's room. It had a purple lampshade which turned the bedspread a bruised colour. He lay on the bed and looked at the ceiling. There were two considerable cracks in it. Perhaps they should get the builder in.

Some time later he left Sophie's room and went down to the next floor. He turned on a light in the study and walked over to the drinks table. There were no glasses. He went down the other two flights of stairs. Matty and Nelly were at the kitchen table. There were a lot of coffee mugs. Nelly was smoking. They were listening to an old Beatles tape. 'Eleanor Rigby'.

Nelly got up and pressed the back of one hand against Andrew's cheek. 'How's Daisy?'

'It's a bad business,' Andrew said.

'I'll be in here with Matty if you want me. If the telephone rings I'll take it,' Nelly said.

Andrew took two tumblers from a cupboard and returned upstairs. In the study he noticed that the chairs each had an individual presence, as if they had been there for a long time. They looked unusually three-dimensional. He drank half a tumbler of whisky straight off. Then he half-filled both glasses, put a splash of soda in them, and carried them next door.

'I'll just turn on one of the lights across the room,' he said.

He then walked to her side of the bed and sat on the edge of it. He put one tumbler on her bedside table and held the other one out to her. She was lying on her left side so she was facing the wall.

'Daisy. Darling. You must understand I did not mean what I said. How could I? It was meaningless. It would be unforgivable if it made any kind of sense. But it was senseless. You must understand that. It was the totally meaningless cry of someone momentarily deranged.'

She said nothing. She didn't seem to see the glass that he was holding for her. He drank some whisky from it and put it down beside the other one. He walked around the bed and lay down on his side of it. He rolled over and put his arm around his wife, holding her. With her back to him, she made no movement or sound.

Some time later, Andrew got up and walked round the bed to Daisy's side. He picked up the glass that was part empty. He turned off the light. He closed the bedroom door behind him.

Later that evening when Nelly opened the study door, he found his brother sitting in the armchair with a full glass of whisky in one hand. On the ottoman lay the red box. Nelly noticed it was unopened. They exchanged a few words. Nelly was slightly surprised when Andrew called him Donald, but Andrew only said it once and didn't notice it, Nelly was pretty sure.

He closed the study door and went down to the drawing room. He poured himself a tumbler of gin which he drank. He filled half the tumbler again and drank the gin more slowly. Then he poured gin nearly to the top and went down to the kitchen to add some water.

Matty was still at the table. It sounded to Nelly like the same Beatles tape he'd heard earlier. He fried some eggs and they ate them with bread and butter. Not much later Nelly got some more gin and he and Matty went up to the top floor. He'd sleep in the spare bed in Matty's room.

At midnight Denis shook Ollie awake. 'We might as well go.'

Ollie straightened up behind the wheel and started the engine. As the Jaguar approached the corner, they both glanced at the red pillar-box across the street. 'Jesus,' Denis said.

41

Some nights Daisy stayed at the hospital. Most of each day she was there.

The Jaguar collected Andrew from Cheyne Street in time for him to see Sophie on his way to Richmond Terrace. In the first weeks he often went back to the hospital a second time during the day, sometimes again in the evening.

After the operation, Sophie had been returned to the intensive care unit. A fortnight later she was moved into a small room off the neurology ward. She remained in a coma. A narrow bed was squeezed into the room so that Daisy could lie down some of the time she was there. She began staying the night on this bed rather than on one of the half dozen beds tucked away on the top floor for 'guests'. She talked to Sophie and read aloud.

When Andrew arrived, Daisy always left the room and went for a walk through the endlessly stretching hospital corridors. If it wasn't raining, she went outside and walked over Westminster Bridge, stopping half way to lean on the railings and look down on the Thames flowing below. 'Time like an ever rolling stream bears all its sons away ...' She always hated that hymn, she remembered, yet looking down at the grey water slipping under the bridge, she didn't feel anything so positive as hate: she felt leaden. The water seemed leaden. She looked up at the sky over the Houses of Parliament: it was cloudless. She thought it was probably blue, yet it seemed leaden. She stepped away from the railings and started back to the end of the bridge where she'd come from. As they hurtled past her, several drivers felt an instant's irritation with this woman who walked so near the kerb, looking down. A lorry's protruding side missed her by inches. Daisy didn't notice.

She spent some nights at Cheyne Street and was there during a part of each day. Most days Matty was at a friend's house, but if he was home when Daisy was there, each was glad to see the other. Yet she found that even being with Matty was draining. The household still had to be run, letters answered, bills paid. The most draining effort of all was making a telephone call. Andrew's mother was one of the few who understood this. Lady Harwood dropped a note to her daughter-in-law once a week, but it was Nelly that she would ring at his Rothburg office when she felt she simply had to talk to someone about Sophie's progress, even though Lady Harwood knew the reason why neither Andrew nor Daisy had rung her was because there was no progress to report.

She and Sir Edward had been informed of the accident within an hour of its happening: Martin Thrower had rung them so they wouldn't learn of it from a news report. When Lady Harwood and Andrew were speaking together the next day, she had told him she'd like to come and stay at Cheyne Street to help out. 'I could be there, dear, so that Daisy would be free to come and go without worrying about someone being at home with Matty,' she had said. 'You know I would not expect you or Daisy to spend any time with me. I could deal with things like the telephone. You have Ingrid, but it's not the same thing.'

'Thank you, mother,' Andrew had said. 'I think it's better for now if we are by ourselves. When you can help us, I'll let you know.'

He didn't have to spell out that there wasn't enough energy to deal with anyone else, however unobtrusive he knew his mother would have been. Lady Harwood didn't need it explained: when she allowed herself to do so, she remembered Donald's death as if it were yesterday.

Daisy's sister-in-law as well as her mother had wanted to come from America and stay at Cheyne Street. It was half past five in the evening in Philadelphia when Martin Thrower had rung Daisy's parents to tell them what had happened at half past five London time. It was the following afternoon before Mrs Brewster and her daughter were able to talk on the telephone.

'Thank you, mother,' Daisy had said. 'I think it's better if you come later. I'll let you know as soon as there is something you can do. For now, we need to be by ourselves.'

During the first fortnight Nelly stayed at Cheyne Street several nights a week. Matty was glad to have him around. Despite the view that children adapt to events rapidly, Matty felt odd. He was unable to distinguish how much of his unhappiness was because of Sophie, how much was because of his parents' unhappiness. When he visited the hospital and sat on the edge of Sophie's bed as he talked a little with his mother, in one way it came to feel natural. In another way it was like a dream.

Then Matty went to Shropshire to stay for the rest of July with his grandparents at Long Green. It was arranged that in August he would go to Italy for most of the month with one of his school friends whose family had a villa outside Verona.

In the first days after it happened, when Daisy was at home she went into the studio. She untied the plastic bags which encased the three half-finished busts. Absently she checked the clay's moisture before she retied each plastic bag. One day she didn't bother to tie the bag tightly around Carl's clay throat. Then she stopped going into the studio. By the middle of the second week the clay of his head was as dry as a bone.

Andrew's private office still put in his red box the daily card for Daisy to know his main appointments. He left it on the table by her chair in his study. If it was still there when he came home the next night, he put it in the wastebasket, leaving the following day's card in its place.

There was a good chance of his getting home for dinner once or twice during the week. In July while Matty was there, Andrew would find Daisy at home preparing the evening meal. It was quickly established that Matty had his dinner with them, unlike the many years' habit of the children eating early and their parents having some time together alone.

Weekends were variable, but when Andrew went to the constituency, Daisy was never with him. If his Waymere commitments were finished off Saturday evening, he sometimes drove to Long Green for the night.

When Daisy stayed the night at Cheyne Street, generally she and Andrew slept in their bedroom. Often Andrew slept with his arms around her. She never slept with her arms around him.

Twice they talked about the distance between them.

'Neither of us is in any kind of normal state,' he said. 'If we were, you might find it in your heart to accept that what I said to you was meaningless.'

'When you said it, you meant it. I saw your face.'

'Daisy, if you were being physically tortured and when it became intolerable you said: "Do it to Andrew," you wouldn't mean it. I know you wouldn't mean it. What I said to you was *meaningless*. What makes it so unforgivable is that what I said to you was what you were thinking: "Why did I make her post the letter?" It's a lunatic question. We both know it's a lunatic question. We both know that people always charge themselves after an accident.'

'In that Orwell book, when Winston said under torture: "Do it to Julia," nothing was ever the same between him and Julia again.'

'That was a book. We are two living human beings who love each other. We need each other more, not less, at this time. Can't you open your heart to me, Daisy?'

'I'd like to. I don't know how to,' she said.

After his second attempt to reach her was rejected, he began sleeping in his dressing room.

The accident had been covered by all the newspapers. From time to time a short news story reported that the Defence Secretary's thirteen-year-old daughter remained in a coma.

At the Ministry and the House of Commons, Andrew was

always asked how things were going. Some friends dropped him a line. Others rang.

One evening when he got back to Cheyne Street and Daisy wasn't there, he found several letters on his ottoman. She'd opened the two addressed to both of them, and he read them first. He sighed.

He opened the one addressed to him. On House of Commons paper, handwritten, it said:

Dear Andrew,
   I am sorrier than I can possibly tell you.
   With all my heart I hope that your daughter will be restored to you.
   Whatever happens, nothing can take away the thirteen years that you and Daisy have had your daughter with you. It may seem a strange thing to say to you at this unthinkable time, but there are people who would envy you those thirteen years, whatever follows them.
                            Yours ever,
                            Rachel Fisher

42

'I wish there was something I could say about Sophie. The trouble is, there's not. I'm sorry, Andrew,' Carl said when he first walked in the room atop the Ministry of Defence.

It was Friday afternoon of the first week in August. The two men were to have half an hour alone before their teams joined them.

'How's Daisy taking it?'

Andrew looked past Carl and out of the window. 'It's a bad business,' he said.

Carl said nothing.

Andrew's lips tightened for a moment.

He brought his attention back to why he was sitting in this room with the American Secretary of Defense. They got down to business.

At its end, when the civil servants had left the room, Carl lingered at the door.

Andrew said: 'I'm going straight from here to my constituency, so I won't see Daisy until Sunday. It's always chancy whether you find her at home. But why don't you give her a ring?'

'I'll certainly try to do that,' Carl said.

*   *   *

'I could come to Cheyne Street,' he said. 'But from what Andrew told me, I should think there was something going for your taking a couple of hours away from the hospital and from home. I gather you've gone back and forth between the two for the last month. I'm staying over a day longer than I'd expected. And you know how thin on the ground Londoners are on a Saturday. I can be free for lunch if you think – as I think – that it would be positively healthy if you came out to lunch. We could have it at Claridge's.'

There was a long silence at the other end of the line.

Carl waited.

'All right.' Her voice was small.

'Do you know yet whether you'll be coming from the hospital or from home? I'll send my car.'

'I don't know where I'll be,' said Daisy. 'I'll come by taxi.'

'Do you want to aim for one o'clock?' he said.

'All right.'

'It doesn't matter in the slightest, Daisy, if you're late. I'll simply go on with work until they let me know you've arrived.'

'All right.'

'The simplest way to deal with the security thing is to go to the front desk and say you have an appointment with me. They'll take it from there.'

'All right.'

The head porter rang upstairs to suite 620–25. Without interest Daisy saw that the clock on the wall behind his desk said 1:25.

'Dr Myer's aide says he is sorry, madam, but Dr Myer is held up on his other telephone. He asks whether you would very kindly let us show you to the sixth floor where an aide will meet you at the lift.'

'All right.'

The head porter held up one hand and snapped his fingers. A bellboy hurried up.

'The lady is to be shown to the sixth floor. She will be met there by an aide to the Secretary of Defense.'

She supposed that must be her in the mirror on the lift's back wall, standing there in a black linen skirt and pink linen double-breasted jacket with large black buttons, a silk T-shirt peeping out. She remembered the jacket as being brighter than it now appeared but perhaps it was the lift's lighting. On the whole she looked remarkably unchanged – strange when you thought about it. She turned away from the doll figure and looked at the back of the bellboy's head. He was not in fact a boy: there was a lot of grey in the neatly trimmed dark hair showing between his cap and his collar. Hairdressers say grey hairs don't exist: they are really white. But his seemed grey.

The lift opened on the sixth floor. Waiting for her was a slim man in his thirties, dressed in a dark blue suit.

'I'm Secretary Myer's aide, Mrs Harwood. Ray Stimson. Let me show you to the Secretary's suite.' He nodded to the bellboy who returned into the lift. The aide was the key person when the Secretary of Defense's private arrangements required discretion.

Outside suite 620–25 stood a security agent with his radio in one hand, the bit of plastic in one ear.

The aide pressed a buzzer beside the door.

It was half a minute before the door opened. Except for the fact he hadn't yet put on his jacket, Carl was conventionally dressed to go out to lunch.

'Hullo Daisy. Forgive me. I'm still on the telephone to Washington in the other room. Come in.'

He said to his aide: 'Thank you, Ray. That's all I'll be needing for now.'

As Carl closed the door behind them, Daisy heard its lock spring shut. He led the way through the hall to the drawing room.

'I'll be as quick as I can. Do make yourself comfortable,' he said. 'When I thought about it, I decided you might prefer not to go through all the kerfuffle of the restaurant. Once you get into this suite and the door is closed, it's completely private. Look inside that china pot and have a taste of the *foie gras*. If you like it, we can start with that. There's a menu so you can brood about what you might eat after that. I'll get this call out of the way.'

He disappeared through one of the doors beyond the sofa.

Under its crisp green cloth, she could see that the table's legs had wheels. Within reach of it was a large console where an extraordinary number of secure telephones stood in solemn array. She could see why Claridge's had for some years declined the honour of having the American Secretary of Defense stay there: the apparatus installed by the US Defense Department was more than considerable.

Indifferently, she looked back to the table on wheels with its dishes set out prettily on the starched green cloth, the wine bottle at an angle in a tub of ice. She didn't take the lid off the *foie gras*: she was sure it would taste very nice.

She hadn't expected to find a table laid for lunch in the suite. Neither was she surprised. On her way to Claridge's in the taxi, she had looked out of the window, unseeing. She had a sense that she was on her way to a play in which she was not terribly interested and where she knew in advance what would happen.

The room was hot. It was one of those heavy August days. She slipped out of her pink linen jacket and laid it over the arm of the sofa.

The person having lunch with Carl seemed rather to enjoy herself. He made her laugh. Once she started to cry, but then that is just another form of extreme display that is often almost disconnected from true feeling. Someone had told her that anyone who looks in the mirror while laughing or crying immediately stops: the reflected image is too crude.

There was so much *foie gras* in the china pot that they wanted only a salad to follow. Carl pressed a buzzer among the battalion on the console; into one of the secure telephones he gave the order for salad to the aide.

'At the same time, could you have them bring some *petits fours* and our coffee?' he said.

'Where *is* all your staff?' Daisy asked.

Carl pulled a face. 'Everywhere, I sometimes think. In fact we have suites along most of this corridor. Occasionally it's a bit frustrating: I cannot go anywhere – any time – without all the security paraphernalia. The British are more relaxed about these things, as you know.'

A buzzer sounded. Carl pressed another button on the console.

Half a minute later a waiter walked in, holding a tray aloft. Beside him was a security agent, his walkie-talkie crackling.

When the waiter had removed the first dishes and set out the rest, Carl got up from the table and followed him into the hall of the suite, the agent one pace behind them.

'That will be all we'll be needing,' Carl said.

'Thank you, sir,' said the waiter, holding his tray on one hand as the other closed over the ten-pound note.

Carl nodded to the agent who followed the waiter out and closed the door.

Daisy heard the lock spring shut.

'Peace and privacy with Daisy at last,' Carl said.

They finished the white burgundy with their salad. She poured out their coffee. He got to his feet.

'Excuse me for a moment,' he said.

She heard his voice in one of the next rooms. She couldn't actually hear what he was saying on a telephone, but she guessed: unless it was from the President, he did not want to accept any calls until further notice.

As he walked back through the door he lifted his chin and loosened his tie, almost simultaneously undoing the top button of his shirt. He approached the table with its crisp green cloth.

Before he reached her, Daisy got up from her chair. She didn't want him to think he had seduced her. She was doing what she was doing because she was doing what she was doing. It hadn't much to do with him. She wanted him to know that.

'All right,' she said.

She was the one who led the way into the bedroom.

He looked back to fasten the bedroom door behind them. When he turned she was unfastening the little buttons on the front of the silk T-shirt. She didn't want him to do it.

He watched her. When she was naked he walked to where she stood and reached out his hand, resting its fingers flat on one of her breasts. She brushed his hand away, not roughly but with a languor that was almost like indifference. She walked silently to the nearest bed and lay down, on her back, watching him as he took off his own clothes.

He knelt beside her. Smiling, he took hold of one of her nipples with the third finger and thumb of one hand, at the same time beginning the same gentle rubbing of her other nipple with the third finger and thumb of his other hand.

She pushed his hands away.

He smiled and reached down and laid one hand flat between her legs. He was skilful at arousing and teasing and arousing again.

'I don't want you to draw it out,' she said.

Afterwards she turned away from him and lay on her side. The room must be facing south: outside the window she saw that the sunlight, dull from the muggy air, touched only the right-hand edges of the roof cornice opposite. Three enormous pigeons had settled themselves at intervals along the cornice.

Carl put one arm over Daisy's shoulder. 'It's better for you, you know. And I observe that we seem to have remembered how to give and receive pleasure.'

She didn't answer. She thought of Waymere: she wondered what Andrew was doing. She thought in an entirely detached way of herself lying naked on this bed. She thought of Sophie in the white gown lying on that white bed. What was the difference between sleep and a coma? Daisy felt within her a deep yearning. Carl had aroused her body to feel sharp desire, culminating in a convulsive physical release and, for a few minutes, a sense of relief. What she felt now was more profound: she wanted to get back to the hospital.

'I must get dressed,' she said.

43

Except at moments of crisis, the minister's private office is not meant to deal with private arrangements that don't affect the ministry; the British civil service is pernickety about taxpayers' money. So it was Andrew's House of Commons secretary, paid for by him, who cancelled the Harwoods' plans to spend three weeks at the Tuscany villa they'd rented for previous family holidays. In the second week of August Parliament finally rose for the summer recess.

Andrew and Daisy agreed he must get out of the Cheyne Street house and go somewhere, with no red boxes – to walk, read novels and biographies, unwind. His parents hoped he would come to Long Green, but he didn't want to be that far away. In the end his secretary booked a room at the Wessex in Winchester, overlooking the cathedral close. In August, most of the tourists were foreigners and wouldn't recognize him. Martin Thrower knew where he would be, but it was not put in the official diary: that way Andrew could avoid having a detective accompany him. He needed a complete break.

It would be the first time Daisy had stayed in Cheyne Street without anyone else in the house. Matty was with his friend's family near Verona. Even Ingrid was away.

Andrew drove to Winchester in his own car – the last of the Scimitar SE6s – which spent most of its time in the garage built onto the Cheyne Street house. He wanted to be able to get back to London at any time of the day or night, and the sixty-five-mile drive was fast on the M3.

His windows looked directly onto the cathedral's north side, only the ancient lime trees and a few tombstones standing on the grass between. When the long summer days drew to their close, spotlights tucked under the hotel's eaves shone onto the tomb-stones, making them an eerie white and casting their sharp black shadows onto the grass – dramatic and sombre.

One morning as Andrew looked out at dozens of rooks perched along the branches of a lime tree, two rooks dropped to the ground and began savagely pecking each other, coal-black wings beating the air until one rook was stretched out on its back, the other standing above, stabbing its beak into the fallen one.

Finding this scene distinctly disagreeable, Andrew was wondering whether if he leaned out of the window and shouted he could break it up. At that instant, the victor flew up into the lime tree and settled itself on the end of a branch, twisting its neck to straighten its disordered feathers. The one stretched on its back hopped to its feet, feathers askew, gave a little shake and flapped up to another branch to begin rearranging itself. A minute later two more rooks dropped to the ground to commence what Andrew now realized was ritual combat. Watching them engrossed him.

Then a totally different image came unbidden into his mind: the larger-than-life clay model in Daisy's studio of two birds folded serenely on each other in an embrace. He remembered when she'd told him in that restaurant – was it the second time that he took her out? – why she loved Epstein's marble doves at the Tate. 'There's this amazing serenity about them, even though they're screwing,' she'd said. Tears began to pour down Andrew's face and onto his shirt front.

He went into the bathroom to wash his face, returning to the window, the towel still in one hand. All the rooks were settled on the branches of the lime tree.

He looked at his watch: he'd make a quick trip to London and

come back to Winchester in the evening. He felt a profound desire
to be at the hospital.

The only holiday activity Ben Franwell enjoyed was sailing. It
made a break from work pressures at the same time as providing
an outlet for his restlessness; he'd have done his nut sitting around
on some godforsaken hilltop in northern Italy, gazing upon an
overrated landscape or contemplating his belly-button. Christ.
What a way to pass your time.

He kept a Nicholson 36 on the Isle of Wight. At the tiller he
had the gratifying sense of being in command, a team working for
him and with him, competing with other yachtsmen, challenging
the sea. The two stockbrokers and a lawyer who made up the
crew shared the pleasure of camaraderie, for it was unthreatened
by fear of Ben: when the sea was rough, all were equals in their
dependence on each other. At the *Rampart*, camaraderie with
Benjamin Franwell was always coloured by everyone's knowledge
that potentially any of them could be for the chop.

Angela detested the cramped discomfort of yachts. 'Unless one
is talking about *Trump Princess* or, at a pinch, old Niarchos and
Atlantis II, the sybaritic image is totally at odds with the reality.
I shall occupy myself ashore,' she said.

It was typical of the international yachtsmen who strutted
around Cowes with their platinum diver's watches that they
thought it amusing that there was not one four-star hotel in the
entire Isle of Wight. Some form of inverted snobbery, she was
sure. Except when they were proving their manhood at Cowes,
they wouldn't have been caught dead in a mere three-star hotel
like the one where she was lounging this very minute.

She lay in a siesta chair on her bedroom balcony, a large straw
hat protecting her face. Though she never ventured into the sun
until late afternoon when it had lost its burning power, she took
no chances with her face. From time to time she opened an eye
and squinted at what the hotel proudly described as a panoramic
view – all those boats whistling over the Solent. Once when she
checked out the panoramic view she saw the QE2 making its
stately passage towards Southampton. Angela wished she was
going to board the QE2 for one of its non-cruise ocean crossings,

beluga caviar on the menu four nights running. She really didn't ask for much when she was on an away-from-it-all holiday: she'd be quite content simply to be comfortable on a luxury liner and mind her own affairs. She reached over for her cigarettes and lighter.

In the evenings the Cowes sailing fraternity continued to enjoy their own company; there was little time for Angela and Ben to be alone together. But after dinner one Sunday they found themselves à *deux* in the bar, and Angela referred to that day's leader in the *Rampart*. The deputy editor was in charge of the paper for three weeks, though Ben must have been on the phone to him four or five times a week.

'I've noticed you haven't put the boot into Andrew Harwood lately. Is that because of his daughter?'

Ben grunted. Some toughies might like to be thought to have hearts of gold. He wasn't one.

'Nobody's interested in politicians in August – unless they're caught with their trousers down,' he said.

Angela very slightly pulled up one corner of her mouth. She said nothing. She knew him well: like many bullies he had a sentimental streak.

Watching her watching him Ben said: 'I suppose you could say that I might have had another go at Harwood in the weeks before Parliament rose. So occasionally I'm a softie. But don't think it will last. When I return to the office in September it will be business as usual.'

Carl and Jocelyn Myer were dividing their August holiday between the Hamptons and the Italian Riviera.

'Jocelyn's family has one of those clapboard palaces that contrive to look modest as they surmount their mile or so of sandy beach on Long Island Sound,' Carl had said when he and Daisy had their second lunch in his suite at Claridge's. 'It takes only an hour to get to Kennedy, and what is Concorde for if not to allow me a short private visit to London?'

This time he had flown from Nice airport. He'd had to telephone from Menton a number of times before he'd caught Daisy at home. Without specifically asking whether Andrew was still away, he had confirmed that to be the case.

'I have to meet the Israeli Defence Minister in London.' He had paused for only a fraction of a moment before going on: 'As Jocelyn cannot abide London in August, I'll be on my own at Claridge's. We could have dinner on Thursday night if you'd like that, Daisy. I'm planning to catch a flight back to Nice late Friday afternoon.'

'I'd rather have lunch on Friday,' Daisy had said.

Her taxi crossed Park Lane into Upper Brook Street. Passing the American Embassy she looked unseeing at the marines flanking the north door. Who was it that she was trying to punish? Andrew? Herself? How was it punishing Andrew when he didn't know? She remembered the answer to that question. It no longer really engaged her interest.

The doorman in his top hat and Parker Ink navy blue overcoat opened the taxi door; she scarcely saw him. Only Americans were in the lobby. No Londoners were arriving for a business lunch because they were abroad or on their boats or playing golf at Gleneagles. No political journalists were together, cheerfully calculating what they could get away with on their separate expense sheets as 'Lunch Cabinet minister for background'.

Had Daisy's eyes met those of any of the various flunkies in their navy blue livery, a small bow would have been made in her direction. But she walked straight to the lift in a manner so preoccupied that no one greeted her. She looked with detachment at the doll in the lift mirror, dressed in the pink linen jacket and black skirt.

Even though she had not gone first to reception, an agent in the foyer had recognized her and rung upstairs to the aides' suite. When she stepped out on the sixth floor, the aide who was waiting was new to her; Ray Stimson must be on his own holiday. The aide introduced himself and escorted her to suite 620–25.

The agent outside the door nodded to her without any indication as to whether he had ever seen her before. Probably he was a new one, she thought.

When Carl opened the door his shirt was already unbuttoned at the throat. He was smiling. The door swung closed behind her, and its lock snapped shut. He followed her through the hall into the drawing room. His smile grew broader.

She looked at the crisp green tablecloth with the bottle of chablis in the tub of ice. An array of covered dishes stood between the two place settings. On a side table spread with another starched green cloth were a gleaming thermos jug and the things that accompany coffee, including a small basket of *petits fours*.

'I thought you'd find it more relaxed not to have a lot of to-ing and fro-ing, so I ordered a variety of dishes for you to choose from,' he said. 'If you don't find anything you like, we'll get the waiter back.'

She took off her jacket and laid it over the arm of the sofa.

Was Carl a distraction or a diversion? Probably a distraction, she thought: his mixture of humour and original ideas and political gossip held her attention and made her laugh. She liked the two deep vertical lines that transected his cheeks, and when the brown eyes twinkled they made her smile.

Yet she had found during these weeks that even though she could be distracted from conscious thought about Sophie, within minutes she forgot whatever had distracted her. It occurred to Daisy that when she seemed to be paying attention to what Carl said and what she said in response, half her brain always was other-occupied and that's why she didn't retain the conversation – or much of anything else which took place between them. Or did she forget it because it lacked any significance compared with the other thing?

This time the china pot held beluga caviar. It was funny: delicacies that she used to adore had lost their taste. They hadn't become unpleasant; they just didn't seem appealing. Some evenings she bought fish and chips on her way home from the hospital. Or she made an egg salad sandwich with lots of mayonnaise. Occasionally she cooked porridge for supper.

'Have you done any work in your studio?' asked Carl.

'I'm not interested in it,' she said.

'Once a piece of clay has entirely dried out, can you work with it again or do you throw it away and start afresh?'

'It's possible to make it workable again. But sometimes I throw it away. I'm not sure why, but it can be curiously satisfying to throw a half-finished head in the dustbin.'

Carl laughed. 'Not a wholly agreeable image – my head in a dustbin. When you are ready to return to your studio – because you will be, Daisy, though I know you find it hard to believe now – shall we have a second go at this famous bust of me?'

Daisy prodded her salad with her fork, rearranging the leaves to clear a neat square in the middle of the plate. She looked up.

'It's funny. I like you. More to the point, here I am in this room with you. Yet I don't want to make the head of you anymore.'

Carl lifted the bottle of chablis from the tub of ice and refilled their glasses. He put one hand over Daisy's where it lay on the starched tablecloth.

Ten minutes later he put the same hand between her legs.

Later as he lay on his back, the bedclothes pushed down to the footboard, he listened to the driving sound of the shower in the bathroom. Turning his head on the pillow to where different-coloured telephones stood on the bedside table, he noticed the message light blinking on one of them. When Daisy had left, he'd buzz the aide and tell him he could let calls start coming through. And he'd better ask the aide what time they were checking out. This was the aide's first time on the job. Even so, when Carl had told him he'd be having lunch in his suite with Mrs Harwood, the aide would have understood the significance of this statement. These things were never spelled out between the Secretary of Defense and an aide.

The sound of the shower had stopped. Daisy must be drying herself. Each afternoon that they had spent together, when she'd left the bed she had gone straight into the bathroom, locked the door, and taken a shower.

As before, when she now re-emerged, the hair near her temples in damp little waves, she seemed entirely occupied in putting on her clothes, almost unaware of Carl lying naked on the bed, watching her.

'Goodbye,' she said.

'When are we going to meet again?'

'Give me a ring some time.'

'Wait a minute, Daisy. Do allow me to see you as far as the hall.'

He swung his legs over the side of the bed and quickly strode into the bathroom to get a towelling robe, pulling it around him with the belt tied loosely as he padded in his bare feet into the drawing room.

'Always the perfect gentleman,' he said.

Daisy smiled. She had already slipped on the pink linen jacket.

Carl went with her only as far as the doorway into the hall so that he would be out of sight when she opened the suite's front door. The agent guarding the door was always discreet. Even so.

Daisy pushed the button releasing the lock, and pulled the door open simultaneously. She looked directly into the eyes of the aide whose hand was outstretched, about to press the buzzer. On one side of him stood the agent, on the other side a bellboy carrying two enormous Harrods shopping bags. Behind them stood Jocelyn Myer.

'Oh,' Daisy said.

Looking directly at Jocelyn, she took a step back into the entrance hall of the suite so she was not blocking the doorway. She thought of a minuet with its prefigured patterns and steps.

'Thank you so much,' Jocelyn said to the aide who stayed where he was.

'I'll take those bags,' she said to the bellboy who handed them to her and gave the slightest bow.

She stepped into the entrance hall, closing the door behind her. The lock sprang shut.

'Well, well, well,' she said, her jacket shoulder brushing against Daisy's as she walked towards Carl who now entered the hall from the drawing-room door, his white towelling robe tied fairly neatly considering his haste.

Daisy remained standing just inside the locked front door. Her face was expressionless. She had a sense of ennui, like someone who has seen the play before. Yet she couldn't remember having ever seen this particular scene. Perhaps it was in a film, long ago.

'I suddenly had a whim last night,' Jocelyn said, ostensibly addressing Carl. 'It would be amusing to catch the early flight from Nice, have a day's shopping in London and join you on the evening flight back. When I got here and came straight upstairs with the bellboy, that new aide was waiting. I thought he seemed surprised at seeing me. He sure looked uneasy when I insisted we come straight to the door and buzz. I told him you would be delighted to see me.'

She smiled. Daisy had forgotten how white the small teeth were. Neither she nor Carl had yet said anything.

'My mother always told me,' Jocelyn said, '"Never surprise anyone. People don't like surprises." I see what she meant.'

She began to remove her jacket.

'Do make up your mind, Daisy,' she said. 'Are you coming back or going away?'

'Away, actually, thank you,' said Daisy. 'Goodbye. Thank you for the lunch, Carl,' she said over her shoulder as she pressed the button and then stepped into the corridor, and the door swung closed behind her, its lock snapping shut. The agent gave no sign of seeing her as she walked past him.

Only then did her cheeks flush, and by the time she had reached the lift, her face had resumed its normal colour. She pressed the foyer button and glanced at herself in the mirror on the wall. The person she saw appeared self-enclosed, indifferent.

As she stepped out of the taxi, she saw the Scimitar parked a little further down Cheyne Street on the left. Daisy tended to avert her eyes from the other side where the pillar-box stood at the corner. She turned her key in the lock.

The house had its now habitual stillness, and the steady tock-tock of the grandfather clock in the hall seemed louder because everything else was so quiet.

She went upstairs. The study door was closed. As she reached out to knock on it, she thought of the aide's hand stopped in mid-action. Without waiting for a response she opened the door.

Andrew was in his armchair, a cup of coffee on the table beside him, the *Spectator* in his lap. He smiled at her, his hazel eyes warm at seeing her.

'You're looking very smart,' he said. 'They told me at the hospital that you'd left there just before I arrived. I thought I'd call in here and say hello before returning to my monastery. Where've you been?'

'Oh. I had a sudden whim to go shopping.' She thought of the shiny dark green bags the bellboy had been holding as he stood outside 620–25. 'I went to Harrods. I'll go downstairs and get myself a cup of coffee. Would you like another?'

'No thanks. Leave the door open. It's nice to know you're back in the house.'

He watched her as she turned and left the room. His unhappiness had been so total that he hadn't quite realized how much he missed her physically.

When she returned she'd taken off her pink jacket. She sat down in her armchair, her cup of coffee on the table beside her.

'What have you been doing in Winchester?' she asked.

He told her about the rooks.

'I hope you're spending a little less time at the hospital,' he said. 'Going shopping sounds like the first positively healthy thing you've done for ages.'

Daisy looked down at her left hand, its thumb and third finger delicately twisting one of the velvet-covered buttons of the armchair.

Andrew watched her hand. He supposed it was being alone with him. He pushed aside his earlier thought that he might stay the night with her, might drive back tomorrow to Winchester, collect his belongings and return to Cheyne Street to move back properly into his own bed with his wife.

He stood up. 'I suppose I should be setting off,' he said.

'All right.'

'Hullo, Andrew. What are you doing here?'

He was dining at the Old Chesil Rectory in Winchester before returning to the Wessex for the night. As he got to his feet, he felt an agreeable thrust of pleasure.

'I could ask the same question,' he said, smiling.

'Are you alone?'

'Yes.'

'May I sit down? I've just quarrelled with my latest admirer.

He's gone back to the Wessex to pack his bag and return to London.'

'I'm staying at the Wessex – on my own. Top floor overlooking the cathedral. Do you suppose our rooms are side by side?'

She gave a pussycat smile.

She had flirted with Andrew to little avail when they had met several times at London parties. She was lighthearted, pretty, blonde, and sexy – in her early thirties, unmarried, and showing no great hankering for domesticity.

'Have you eaten?' he asked.

'Two forkfuls of smoked salmon. Then the heavens fell in.'

He laughed.

'Shall we have a drink while you decide what you want to order for dinner this time round? I'm longing for a second drink.'

He summoned the waiter.

Two hours later as he settled the bill, Andrew said with mock courtliness: 'May I have the honour of escorting you back to our hotel?'

She said pertly: 'Thank you, Minister. Your room or mine?'

'How certain are you that your previous admirer has actually returned to London?'

'I'm not sure of anything in this world. That's why it's so enjoyable.'

Andrew's eyes moved from her mouth to her breasts, then up to her blue eyes which sparkled with anticipation. For the first time in weeks his own eyes had that particular, intent concentration of sexual lust.

'My room, then,' he said.

44

Andrew made his decision.

It had to be put to Cabinet, for it was a highly political decision as well as a departmental one. The Industry Secretary had already circulated a short paper among their Cabinet colleagues, setting out why she thought it imperative that all Satyr's components be made in Britain. But Andrew had more facts at his disposal, and he had argued the thing out rationally with himself. He was sorry Satyr could not be seen as independent from start to finish. But there it was.

Once Carl had guaranteed that the United States would launch the new satellites almost at cost if half of Satyr's components were made in America, the package deal was irresistible.

Given the current political unease about NATO, Andrew had ruled out linkage with America's Sun system. He accepted Carl's assurance that there'd be no risk of American-made components containing a chip which would enable the Pentagon to eavesdrop. He was right to believe Carl.

For on questions of national interest that arose between the two ministers, Carl was entirely trustworthy. That he was having a clandestine affair with Andrew's wife was not relevant: it was in a different compartment.

As the two men faced each other across the hexagonal table, each flanked by his team, their dialogue was largely confined to getting the nuts and bolts in place. Andrew was confident of winning Cabinet's support for his policy decision.

'That's settled then,' he said.

That evening Mrs Benjamin Franwell held a carefully planned dinner party at the St James's Place penthouse. She had intended it for ten people. But half way through the morning Ben had telephoned from the *Rampart*. Jocelyn Myer, he said, had just rung him from Claridge's to say hello. She was here in London for two days with her husband who was doing some sort of official stuff on such short notice that no evening engagement had been arranged. Jocelyn had asked if the Franwells happened to be free for a drink. He had proposed that the Myers come to dinner instead. They were doing so.

Angela was pleased with the addition to her dinner party. Perfectly capable of spending time alone, if she was going to be with other people she liked them to be in power politics – whether in Westminster, the arts, business or bed. She liked watching them interact. She would put the Foreign Secretary on her right, the American Secretary of Defense on her left. Ditto their wives and Ben. On her notepad she drew a second placement, moving the chairman of ICI two seats along from where he'd been sitting at her left a minute before.

When the Myers walked into the penthouse drawing room, Jocelyn looked around at the audacious decoration with open interest. Against walls covered with a white silk fabric, great blobs and flashes of colour shimmered. Over almost the entire parquet floor lay a white Chinese carpet, its restful expanse broken only by two interlooped garlands of mauve and gold woven into big bows which formed the border. A lush nude by Matthew Smith, sweeps of oil paint glowing like a ruby, hung over the white marble mantelpiece. A late Ivor Hitchens in primary and secondary colours was vibrant on the wall at the opposite end of the room. Huge Chinese vases held what must have been at least two hundred scarlet roses bunched with twice again that number of blue cornflowers.

Angela introduced the Myers to those guests who had already arrived. Having smiled at them, Jocelyn walked alone to the wall of windows overlooking Green Park, curious to see the view which Angela always left uncurtained. In September's twilight, the plane trees' stately cascades of foliage gave no intimation that autumn was approaching. Victorian lamps lit a path beneath the trees at this end of the park. Except for two men walking with a terrier on a lead, the path was empty.

'What would you like to drink, Jocelyn?' Ben said.

She turned away from Green Park and faced him. Atop the luxuriant shiny blonde hair heaped on top of her head she wore a chiffon peony of the same violet as her amethyst necklace and ear pendants. Angela had wondered whether they were paste. Ben thought how wonderful they looked against the creamy skin. Jocelyn was wearing a narrow black velvet dress cut low enough for Ben to see the swell of her breasts. She had about her a boldness that he liked. He almost put out a hand and patted her hip, but then he remembered the boldness was that of a rich upper-class New York woman, not a tart. Instead of patting her, he grinned.

Though he had never been at ease with more than a very few women, he found now, as he had when they'd first met at Number Ten, that he could relax with Jocelyn. She was a smashing broad to look at, and at the same time she treated him like a friend. In some mysterious way, she made him feel they were allies, in collusion.

She told him Washington gossip that they both knew would be of use to him. She was skilful, as he would have expected an intelligent political wife to be, in retailing an anecdote that appeared to mock her husband but in fact put him in a good light. Over the pre-dinner drink Ben teased her about this: 'Do you know, Jocelyn, every criticism you make of Carl makes me love him more.' They both laughed, two people from different backgrounds who had met on a pinnacle of success and taken to each other.

At the table they talked with their other partners during the first course. With the arrival of the second, Ben turned from the

Foreign Secretary's wife on his right and resumed conversation with Jocelyn.

'When last I was here on a Sunday, I had the distinct impression from your column that you are not a fan of Carl's opposite number,' she said.

'Andrew Harwood?' Ben shrugged. 'That kind of upper-crust English gent never has appealed to me. You'd hardly believe it Jocelyn: they still don't realize they've become dodos.'

'Have they?'

'You bet they have. When Margaret Thatcher became Prime Minister in 1979, all those fucking Whig nobs thought they'd again be running the show. What did Margaret do? She allowed them to mince about in her Cabinet while she got her footing. Then she began chopping off their heads. Some walked around for years carrying their heads in their hands, unable to believe what had happened to them.'

'How old is Andrew Harwood?'

'Forty-five.' Like politicians, journalists knew the age of anyone in public life.

'He must have started in office under Margaret Thatcher. And he's got one of the plum jobs today.'

'I take your point. But even though he's not one of Margaret's self-made men, neither is he the chinless wonder he might have been with that public-school baronet-father background. He's even had moments of being a fairly competent administrator – but not enough of them. My money is on Rachel Fisher. I'll bet you £5 she'll be Defence Secretary before six months are out. A tough, competent, patriotic woman at Defence could knock people backwards.'

'Would Andrew Harwood get another job? Or would he be out?'

'Probably another job. He certainly wouldn't be promoted to two of the three top posts – Foreign Secretary or Chancellor – and probably Home Secretary would also be out. There've been too many question marks over Harwood in the last few months.'

Ben did not point out that it was he who had engineered those question marks.

'And there's no post that ranks on a par with Defence,' he went on. 'So he would have to be demoted. I don't much care what he ends up with, so long as Rachel Fisher moves ahead of him. An ambitious politician needs always to beat one particular rival: it has more public impact.'

He grinned. He could see the leader page in the *Rampart*: it could almost write itself.

'How well do you know Daisy Harwood?'

'She used to write for me.'

'Did she used to sleep with you as well?'

Ben's naturally ruddy complexion deepened. For a moment a child's petulance showed in the set of his lips.

'No,' he said. 'She wasn't in the market. She's one of those women who goes in for one man at a time. Anyhow, being a ladies' man has never been one of my priorities.'

He didn't give a damn about Daisy Brewster Harwood, yet it still rankled that she hadn't given him a thought. He picked up his glass of claret, sullen.

'She sleeps with my husband.'

Ben checked the movement of the glass to his lips; he replaced it on the table. His mouth slightly opened in astonishment as he turned fully in his chair and fixed his intense blue eyes on Jocelyn's face.

'You must be joking.'

'She was Carl's fancy lady before she met Andrew Harwood. She was his fancy lady at the same time as she was ogling Andrew Harwood when she first came to London. She is my husband's fancy lady at this very time that her daughter is lying in a coma in hospital.'

'Jesus.'

Jocelyn lifted her wineglass and sipped her claret.

'How do you know, Jocelyn?'

'Most men discuss their pasts with their wives,' she said.

'But most of them don't discuss their present extra-marital affairs with their wives, do they?'

Jocelyn looked down at her breasts rising from the black velvet bodice. She was proud of her breasts. Ben followed the direction of her gaze.

Both looked up again.

'He didn't need to tell me. I walked into the Claridge's suite at an inopportune moment.'

Ben pursed his lips in a soundless whistle.

'Why do you tell me this, Jocelyn?' he said. 'I might use it to embarrass your husband.'

'I don't think you would. You and I understand each other. I wouldn't mind, though, if someone sent a shot over Carl's bows – to let him know he'd better look out. If someone could scare him without jeopardizing his job, I think I'd like that.'

She smiled at Ben. 'And I'd certainly enjoy seeing Daisy Harwood get her comeuppance,' she said. 'I don't like these women who present themselves as Goodie Two-Shoes and then jump into your husband's bed the moment your back is turned.'

Ben became aware of Angela surveying him from the other end of the table. He looked down to see the third course had appeared. He hadn't noticed finishing the second course. He turned to the Foreign Secretary's wife.

Angela took pains over these dinners, and Ben met his obligations to her: a deal was a deal. Also, he might get something useful out of the Foreign Secretary's wife. You never knew.

After the last guests had left, Ben said to Angela: 'Why didn't you tell me Carl Myer is screwing your friend Daisy Harwood?'

For a moment her face lost its porcelain inscrutability; he saw she was genuinely surprised by what he'd said. And few things could surprise Angela.

She placed herself languidly on one of the white sofas and stretched out her legs in their red silk trousers, crossing her ankles, one red tasselled satin shoe over the other, her crewcut dark head resting on the back of the sofa. She took a cigarette from the crystal box on the table and flicked an alabaster lighter.

Nonchalantly she asked: 'Who told you that?'

'Jocelyn Myer, that's who.'

Very faintly Angela wrinkled her nose. 'What an udder,' she said.

Ben laughed.

'What makes you think it's true?' she said.

'Because whatever you may think of the size and shape of the lady's boobs, she's straight when she talks with me: I can feel it in my bones. She says that when Daisy first came to London, she was already Myer's floozy. Did you know that?'

Angela exhaled a cloud of smoke. Insouciant as she was, she nonetheless found that occasionally Ben's choice of words grated.

'I'm sure I mentioned to you at the time that Daisy was madly in love with a Jewish professor at Princeton,' she said. 'Her parents took a dim view of the matter. As it happens, and as you know, she then fell in love with Andrew Harwood. At the time I'd never heard of Dr Myer. I daresay you hadn't either and that's why you've forgotten.'

'Since he became American Secretary of Defense has Daisy said anything about him?'

'No. Except that she'd been asked to make a portrait bust of him – for the Pentagon, I think.'

Had Daisy said anything else about Carl Myer? Angela had seen her alone only a couple of times in the months just before the accident. Since then they'd had supper together once at Cheyne Street, and Carl Myer certainly had not been a subject of discussion. Angela couldn't remember much of anything Daisy had said that evening – only her manner: it had been so detached she seemed almost like a robot.

Angela found it improbable that Daisy, in her devastation, had resumed her affair with Myer. Yet when she now thought about it, perhaps it had a certain kind of inevitability, almost a logic in it.

She put out her cigarette and stood up.

'Have you ever noticed how people can be jealous of someone in their husband's or wife's past?' she said. 'Totally irrational when you think about it. If Jocelyn Myer has that kind of crazy jealousy, then she could have embroidered the story. I think it unlikely that Daisy is having an affair with Carl Myer. It doesn't fit.'

'Just because something is unlikely doesn't mean it isn't so,' Ben said. He grinned. 'Jocelyn walked in on them in a bedroom at Claridge's.'

'Speaking of bedrooms, I'm tired,' Angela said.

Unhurriedly she strolled towards the drawing-room door. Better to drop the subject fast. God knows what Ben planned to do with it. Definitely better not to ask.

'Are you coming?' she said.

45

The first subject on Cabinet's agenda was Satyr.

'Defence Secretary,' said the Prime Minister.

Andrew gave a succinct summary of his decision.

When he finished, the Prime Minister said: 'I shall call on one or two ministers who take a particular interest in this matter. Industry Secretary.'

Rachel put her two points effectively.

First, she said, the Defence Secretary should give more weight to the possibility that if some of Satyr's components were produced in California, an element in the Pentagon might manage to penetrate the project's top security.

Second, the Defence Secretary should remember that electronics engineering was precisely the industry at which Britain excelled. 'Surely, the government should reward its best industries. And we should be seen to be creating more jobs,' she said.

Andrew had dealt with each of these points, yet Rachel presented them as if she were adding information he had neglected.

'Foreign Secretary,' said the Prime Minister.

The Foreign Secretary gave a measured contribution to the question of an 'element' in the Pentagon infiltrating a British secret project. He thought this unlikely.

Because both strands of the argument – Anglo-American relations, British jobs – were highly emotive, other members of the Cabinet held strong opinions.

The Prime Minister thought nearly an hour was quite long enough for this debate. 'We have heard pertinent and sufficient views on this subject. There is general agreement with the Defence Secretary's argument that any risk of our American allies attempting a one-way link into Satyr is a risk we can take. He has rightly stressed that Satyr will be part of a military communications system rather than an actual means of defence. I entirely agree with him – and with the Foreign Secretary – that we can trust the word of the American Secretary of Defense.'

The Prime Minister glanced along the faces on the other side of the table before going on:

'There is a sharp division of opinion as to whether British jobs should be given more consideration. The Industry Secretary makes a strong point when she speaks of this government's need to be *seen* to be concerned about the high levels of unemployment.'

The Prime Minister paused to allow the significance of this last statement to register fully around the table.

Then the Prime Minister said: 'I shall ask the Defence Secretary to have his officials look again at the relative costs of production if Satyr were to be made entirely in Britain compared with sharing the production with the United States. I should be glad if the matter could then be brought before Cabinet and concluded next Thursday.'

The Prime Minister moved on briskly to the second subject on the Cabinet's agenda.

Rachel sat straight and proud, her face expressionless.

Andrew tightened his mouth.

Cabinet broke up at a quarter to one.

'These things happen to all of us at one time or another,' the Foreign Secretary said as he walked with Andrew to the front door of Number Ten.

Outside, Ollie waited with other government drivers. Andrew handed him the red box. 'I'll walk.'

When he entered his private office, the secretaries looked up to greet him. He nodded curtly.

'You'd better come in,' he said to Martin Thrower.

Martin closed the door behind him. The Minister had already hung his jacket over the back of his desk chair. He was pacing the floor, hands in trouser pockets, scowling.

Martin stood inside the door, notepad in hand. He waited. In the five minutes it had taken Andrew to walk from Number Ten to the Ministry of Defence, the private secretary to the Secretary of the Cabinet had rung through to Martin Thrower to tell him that his minister had suffered a setback in Cabinet.

Civil servants take a vicarious pride in their ministers' clout. If he is defeated by another, they feel chagrin on their own account. They ask each other if perhaps the minister had not been tough enough.

The minister's private secretary, however, remains in his no man's land of emotions, his loyalty split. Martin Thrower felt for Andrew Harwood. He knew the Minister was extremely angry.

Andrew interrupted his pacing and sat down at his desk. He lit a cigarette. For the first time he looked at Martin. 'You know what happened.'

'Yes, sir.'

Andrew waved a hand towards one of the blue leather chairs on the other side of his desk. 'Sit down, Martin.'

The room was silent except for the occasional 'pfft' as Andrew smoked his cigarette, his eyes looking at nothing in particular beyond the wall of windows.

He put out the cigarette. 'You'll have to get Austin Barthmore in here this afternoon. I want to see him for five minutes alone. Then have the head of F-section join us. We don't seem to be awfully lucky in our heads of F-section. First we have Cartwright, now this one. To be fair, it's not his fault. Perhaps I could have put the argument better than I did.'

Having blamed the new head of F-section and then accepted the blame himself, Andrew felt better.

'If it's the last thing I do,' he said, 'I'm going to get Cabinet to accept the Satyr contract as I think it should be decided, not as it happens to suit the Industry Secretary.'

Having now expressed his resentment of Rachel Fisher, Andrew felt better still. He laughed, albeit ruefully.

'When you've made those arrangements, Martin, I wonder if you could have some soup and sandwiches brought to me here. I'm going to pour myself a drink and then start going through these bloody figures again.'

Martin smiled as he got up to leave the room. He liked the Minister's resilience.

'By the way, Minister,' said Martin, 'did you happen to see an item in the *Telegraph* this morning about Charles Cartwright?'

'No.'

'He drowned. He was on holiday at some jetsetters' resort in the West Indies. He was due back in the office next week. Strange to think of Cartwright at a rich man's playground. I'd never imagined he had that kind of money to throw around.'

There was no particular pattern to Daisy's time at the hospital. She had happened to stay there Thursday night, on the narrow bed alongside Sophie's.

At 9:00 Friday morning Andrew arrived on his way to Richmond Terrace. Daisy was sitting on her neatly-made bed.

He closed the door behind him. He looked at Sophie. He never knew whether she would be lying on one side or on her back: every two hours the nurses changed her position. She was on her back. Had he not known she had been unconscious for eight and a half weeks, he could have pretended to himself that she was sleeping normally. Sometimes he was tempted to deceive himself, but after a moment he always resisted it: that way lay madness.

Her skin under its freckles, though pale, was not without some colour. The nurses kept her hair clean, and it was spread, unironed, on the fresh pillowcase. Sometimes when Daisy and Andrew looked at Sophie's curls, each winced inwardly. Her arms in the short-sleeved white hospital gown had been laid outside the top sheet and white cotton blanket.

'Hullo,' Andrew said.

He could have been addressing either of them.

He watched Daisy as she walked around the end of Sophie's bed and picked up her overnight bag from the windowsill. She turned back and started to pass the end of the bed again, intending to leave Andrew alone with their daughter. She stopped in her tracks.

Lying where it had been put outside the bedclothes, Sophie's right hand moved. It didn't move much: the fingers closed slightly.

Daisy stood transfixed. One part of her brain felt the blood rush through her. Another part of her brain wondered if she was about to faint.

Then she looked at Andrew.

He had already turned and opened the door.

The corridor outside was empty. He ran towards the nurses' station at the apex of the four corridors, nearly knocking down a nurse who happened to step out of a door into his path.

46

It was too soon to make a prognosis, the doctors said. The first thing was for her to return to consciousness. When these things happened, they could happen very fast. The responses on the EEG had never ruled out the possibility of full brain recovery.

'When – I suppose we should not celebrate too soon – *if* your daughter recovers full consciousness, we will then have to think about Stoke Mandeville,' the consultant surgeon said.

Neither Harwood needed to have it explained that the spinal injury might be only partially reversible. Both knew no place was better qualified to deal with this than the spinal unit at Stoke Mandeville Hospital.

Across Andrew's mind flashed a memory of reading about Tito Arias, Margot Fonteyn's husband, paralysed from the waist down after being shot four times by another Panamanian politician. Arias was taken to the hospital near Aylesbury.

Across Daisy's mind flashed the aftermath of the bomb at Brighton during the Conservative party's 1984 conference. She remembered standing on the promenade outside the debris of the Grand Hotel, she and Andrew in their nightclothes, searchlights playing on the crumbled facade, firemen running in and out as they tried to locate the IRA's distinguished victims buried in the wreckage. She remembered how the firemen had found Norman Tebbit and his wife holding hands where they lay, crushed beneath steel and concrete, after the floor fell out of their bedroom and they plummeted four storeys. She could still see the Trade and Industry Secretary's agonized face as he was manoeuvred out of the rubble. Most of all she remembered how Margaret Tebbit had been left paralysed and was taken to Stoke Mandeville. How long a drive was it from Cheyne Street to Aylesbury? An hour?

Matty was upstairs when Daisy returned from the hospital Friday afternoon. When she first told him the news, he smiled. Then his mouth turned down at the corners and he began to cry. It made him look about five years old, not twelve. Daisy put her arms around him. After a minute he pulled away, wiping his nose on the back of one hand, leaving a wet patch on the front of his mother's shirt.

'Can I go and see her tomorrow?' he said.

Daisy smiled as she looked at him. It seemed long long ago – was it really only eight and a half weeks? – since she had smiled and felt any connection between the curve on her face and her insides.

'Maybe I can make her open her eyes,' he said. 'I could tell her how Jason keeps ringing up to ask about her and how he appeared three times on our doorstep looking drippy.'

For the rest of the day and evening whenever Daisy encountered Matty, he was beaming.

She'd just finished doing her face when she heard the Jaguar's engine slowing to a halt, then idling. She looked at the clock on the bathroom wall. 7:10. She had put on a coral silk shirt that Andrew had given her at Christmas. Looking down, she undid another of its buttons.

In the bedroom she slipped on the high-heeled sandals he liked with her narrow white trousers. She took a long string of fake pearls from where they hung with other necklaces like a beaded curtain over her dressing-table mirror. She looped the pearls so they fell in double strands half in, half outside her shirt.

She heard his steps come up the stairs and go into the study.

She'd filled an ice bucket and put it on his drinks table.

When she went in the study he was standing with his back to her. She could hear the ice being put in the glasses. He turned and stood where he was, looking at her.

'Hullo,' she said.

Later that night they slept together in their bedroom, sometimes Andrew's arms around Daisy, sometimes her arms around him.

Matty was the one sitting with Sophie on Saturday when she opened her eyes.

'Hullo,' he said.

Sunday morning Daisy carried the breakfast tray up to the bedroom, the morning newspapers under one arm. When she'd set out Andrew's share on the small table by the window, she climbed back into bed with her coffee, the newspapers piled at the foot of the bed. Andrew got out of bed, put on his dressing gown, settled in the armchair and folded the first section of the *Sunday Times*. He did wish newspapers did not keep getting fatter: it took a good couple of hours to get through them.

Daisy started with the *Rampart*. She'd scarcely glanced at it – or any other newspaper – for two months. She curled her toes under the bedclothes and wriggled her neck into a more comfortable position against the propped up pillows.

Contentedly reading from the front page onwards, she took ten minutes to get to the leader page. Instantly three names jumped out from Ben's column.

She felt herself go cold. Perhaps if she didn't read it, it would be the same as if it weren't there. Her eyes raced over the sentences in the paragraph where her name appeared. It was rubbish, absolute rubbish. Angry, she felt heat rush through her face. She felt hot all over and slightly sick: it wasn't entirely rubbish.

Ben had adopted a tone which was half magisterial and half his usual wide-boy self. She forced herself to start from the beginning, reading slowly, in trepidation as to what was coming next.

What are we to make of a British Defence Secretary who kowtows to a formidable American Secretary of Defense instead of putting this

nation's security first? You may well ask why Mr Andrew Harwood
is planning to hand over half the production of Satyr to the United
States.

Can anyone guarantee US Solar Space will not slip in a chip that
will make it possible for the Pentagon to eavesdrop on Satyr?

Can anyone explain why Mr Harwood should turn his back on the
Prime Minister's efforts to invigorate our own economy?

Before her marriage, Mrs Daisy Harwood was known to have been
bowled over by Dr Myer. Perhaps we will discover if she is just as
bowled over today if ever we're permitted to see the portrait bust of
him that for months has absorbed Mrs Harwood in her sculptress
capacity.

No one can object to our Defence Secretary's wife inviting the
American Secretary of Defense to her Chelsea studio. But if in his
official capacity Mr Harwood has bowed to his wife's interest in Dr
Myer, we as a nation have a right to ask whether Mr Harwood would
be better employed in another job.

And what could be a more imaginative – as well as sound – appointment than for the Prime Minister to give the Defence portfolio to
Rachel Fisher?

The military would know it was dealing with a minister who grasps
the argument and can pilot strategy.

Bureaucrats would know MoD contracts must go to British companies which have proved themselves deserving.

The public would know the person in charge of this nation's defence
understands the profound reasons why we must keep this nation strong.
*Let no one forget that as well as being master of her ministry, Rachel Fisher has
the instincts that only other mothers can fully understand.*

Meanwhile let us hope that the Prime Minister and the more alert
members of the Cabinet will tell the present Defence Secretary that
his intention to hive off half of Satyr will not do.

Ben had been particularly pleased by the way he had suggested
it was Daisy who was importuning Carl Myer; no blame could be
attached to Carl. It was a neat little piece of semantic juggling
which Jocelyn would be the first to appreciate.

Daisy felt panic.

She folded the *Rampart* and put it on the bed beside her, pulling
the bedsheet until it covered half the newspaper. She glanced
across the room at Andrew. He was just turning over the leader

page of the *Sunday Times*. Perhaps he hadn't noticed what she'd been reading. He might forget to read the *Rampart*. Or she could say it hadn't been delivered with the other papers this morning. She pushed it until it was out of sight beneath the bedclothes, then reached for the pile of newspapers at the foot of the bed. She put the second half of the *Sunday Telegraph* on top of the concealed *Rampart*, propping the first half in front of her. She began to read. She couldn't take in a word.

Andrew said: 'Did your erstwhile editor have something cheerful to offer us this morning?'

She'd have to change tack.

'He's become boring,' she said.

Andrew glanced over the top of the *Sunday Times* at his wife. For a moment he studied her face.

Then he said: 'I'm not going to let Ben Franwell spoil our first proper Sunday together. I'll keep the *Rampart* to read tomorrow morning. Whatever he may have to say in his newspaper, Daisy, it pales to insignificance beside what's happened in our lives in the last forty-eight hours. So try not to let your Sunday be spoiled by the bastard.'

When Andrew went to the bathroom to shave, Daisy extracted the *Rampart* from under the sheet. She started to re-read the column from its beginning, but her eyes flicked to where her name was introduced, and she read from there to the end, word for word, trying to imagine how Andrew would respond to each innuendo when he read it tomorrow.

'Oh God,' Frances said. 'Can't Franwell ever let up?'

She and Giles were lounging in two armchairs in their eighth floor drawing room overlooking Tower Bridge. The tall block had been built three years earlier, just behind a Victorian warehouse on the Thames' south bank. One windowsill was cluttered with manuscripts Frances had brought back from her office: most literary agents did a fair amount of work at home.

Her hair was pushed behind her ears, large tinted spectacles perched on her nose. The shortish figure was swathed in a red Chinese silk kimono. A drop of coffee had run down the outside of her mug and onto the kimono. She didn't bother to wash it out before it dried: she liked the sense of being able to slop around on Sunday.

She folded the *Rampart* and slung it along the carpet to Giles.

When he picked it up, Frances moved her spectacles to the top of her head, watching him as he opened the leader page.

Sprawled comfortably in pyjamas and striped dressing gown, he rested his chin on his chest as he read. As his eyes came to where Daisy's name first appeared, the two grooves in his face deepened.

When he had finished Ben's column, Giles tossed the *Rampart* onto the carpet and fished a cigarette from the pack in his dressing gown pocket. Flattening his lips so the smoke trickled slowly from between them, he gazed at the crack which had appeared in the ceiling a month before.

Then he looked across at Frances.

'Two can play that game,' he said.

The telephone rang. It was on the floor within reach of Frances's chair.

'Hullo?' she said. 'He's just here. You okay?' The intelligent, simian face was alight with curiosity. 'Here's Giles.'

She got up and carried the telephone on its long lead to him.

'It's Angela,' she said.

'Good morning, Angela,' said Giles.

At her end of the line, Angela looked at her painted toenails. Her ankles were crossed as she lay atop the bedclothes.

'I'm in Sussex,' she said. 'But I'm coming up to London on Tuesday. Is there any chance you might be free for lunch, Giles? You may not yet have seen Ben's particularly charming column in today's *Rampart*.'

'I just read it two minutes ago.'

'This time he's gone too far. One or two thoughts have occurred to me.'

For a moment both ends of the telephone line were silent.

'Hang on a sec, Angela. I'll get my diary.'

When he had returned to his armchair, he picked up the telephone again. 'I can do Tuesday.'

'Good. What about Langan's? The Brasserie. So far as I know, my delightful husband never goes there. Not that it would worry me if we encountered him.'

'One o'clock?'

'Perfect. I'll book,' said Angela.

In all the years he had known her, Giles had never heard her repeat herself. Just before Angela hung up she said again: 'This time he's gone too far.'

47

Just after one on Tuesday Giles ambled into Langan's, glancing at the bar where Nelly and his bar stool had toppled over in unison. Giles could still hear the horrendous crash. Remembering himself and Frances helping their fallen companion to his feet, he smiled to himself.

The head waiter led him to a table looking out on Stratton Street. Giles leant over to kiss Angela on one cheek before settling himself opposite her.

'They have a new house champagne. I've just ordered a glass. What about you?' she said.

'Do you know what you're going to eat?'

'They have fishcakes today. I was thinking about the spinach soufflé for starters.'

'Good idea.'

'Shall we skip my glass of champagne and ask for a bottle instead and drink it with lunch?'

As the head waiter departed, Angela said: 'When I rang you on Sunday I didn't know the spectacular news about Sophie. Did you?'

'No. Frances rang Daisy yesterday. That's how we learned.

Daisy said the family was in such a state of excitement that she hadn't got round to ringing us yet. She said Sophie's brain is fine. The next step, of course, is Stoke Mandeville: all that is more uncertain.'

'Yeah. I was told much the same when I rang Daisy yesterday. She sounded like a different human being – though when I mentioned that prick's column, for a minute she sounded subdued. I told her I thought there was a way to stop Benjamin Franwell in his tracks – that the cavalry was about to come riding over the hill.'

'Did she ask who the cavalry was?'

'No.'

Angela glanced up at the waiter hesitating to uncork the champagne, uncertain into whose glass he should pour the first gush. Angela's air of self-sufficiency was increased by her appearance: she was wearing one of her parodies of a City gent's striped suit. Watching her, Giles wondered what it was in the delicate mask that today managed unmistakably to convey force. Perhaps it was her anger. He gestured towards her glass. The waiter prodded out the cork.

'Very nice,' Angela said to the waiter. 'I like it better than the last house champagne you had.'

She said to Giles: 'When Ben wrote that column, he assumed Sophie was still in a coma. What I find unacceptable is that he could put the boot in that viciously when, so far as he knew, both Daisy and Andrew were still staggering from the family tragedy.'

She took a cigarette from the pack Giles had placed between them.

'At Cowes, Ben told me that when he returned to the office in September it would be business as usual. I never imagined he would go this far.'

'*Is* Daisy having an affair with Carl Myer?'

Angela's face remained expressionless.

'According to Jocelyn, yes,' she said. 'I genuinely don't know. Jocelyn told Ben some story, and he believes her. Ben is so odd about sex. He's essentially puritanical, you know. He takes a prurient interest in other people's sex lives. At the same time, I think he would feel that if Daisy had stepped from the straight and narrow, she deserved everything she got.'

'No one can touch him for writing innuendo that just manages to stay on the right side of the libel laws,' said Giles.

'And he'll now have the bit between his teeth. Have you had any thoughts, Giles?'

'Yes. Tell me yours first.'

'One line of Ben's new attack has left him open to counter-attack – two counter-attacks, actually.'

'It's just possible that our minds are moving as one,' said Giles. 'I always said it's your mind that attracts me.'

Angela's pretty mouth tipped up winsomely at the corners.

'He went over the top when he wrote all that garbage about Rachel's womanhood being an additional strength for a defence minister,' she said.

'"Let no one forget that as well as being master of her ministry, Rachel Fisher has the instincts that only other mothers can fully understand."' So well did Giles know Ben's prose style that he could reproduce it intact.

'I told Ben I didn't think Rachel's decision to abort her bastard child was everyone's idea of how the instinctive mother behaves.'

'*What!* You've already played the abortion card with Ben?'

With a graceful twist of thumb and index finger, Angela put out her cigarette. Giles glanced down at the ash about to fall off his own dwindled cigarette. From nowhere a waiter appeared and replaced the ashtray with a clean one.

'I tried it out on Sunday afternoon,' she said. 'Ben looked as if he might have a heart attack. One of my analysts told me that people really can forget things they don't want to remember.'

'What did he say?'

'Nothing at first. That great face looked as if it was going to fall apart. Then he seemed to get himself together. He didn't ask me how I knew. He said: "The past is the past. No one can bring it up now."'

Giles watched her take a dainty sip of her champagne.

'I told him there were various people who could bring it up, starting with several of us who knew about it on the *Rampart*: me, Frances, Daisy – plus you. And almost certainly Daisy told Andrew. Shall I tell you what Ben said?'

Giles waited.

'He said Andrew would never exploit that kind of information. "He's trapped by his fucking background."' She mimed Ben's Yorkshire inflections. '"Harwood is too much of a gent to take the gloves off like those of us who've pulled ourselves up by our bootstraps."'

'What about me? I threw off my gentlemanly restraints a long time ago.'

'Exactly.'

She inclined her head towards him as he flicked the purple Dunhill lighter. He laid it on the table between them. Both looked at it as they sat quietly smoking.

Then Giles said: 'Did you mention Rachel's husband being seen in a gay bar?'

'No. I wanted to talk to you first.'

A waiter put down two plates adorned by the spinach soufflé, then offered the hot anchovy sauce.

Giles surveyed the ash growing on his cigarette.

'Funny,' he said. 'I am not averse to applying the old garotte to this and that politician because of their sins and omissions of a political nature. I don't think I've ever written about someone's private peccadillos – except once, and that was not intended for publication. And anyhow I invented that story – to challenge Ben. Do you remember? That's when he sacked me from the *Rampart*.'

'Remind me what you said.'

'There'd been a Dempster item about Nelly being involved in some fracas outside a gay club. Ben wanted me to expand it – to embarrass Andrew. I made up a different version of what Ben wanted: I had the fracas occurring on "mixed night", as they put it – and a woman seen leaving the club with another woman was a Tory parliamentary candidate, i.e., Rachel Fisher. I wrote it for Ben's eyes only. When he read it, he sacked me on the spot.'

'As it turns out, your invented story was inspired foresight, though slightly out of focus,' Angela said.

'If there is such a thing as foresight, usually it's a bit out of kilter,' said Giles.

A waiter reappeared again to exchange the ashtray. Angela and Giles started on their spinach soufflé.

Then Giles said: 'So now I'm about to write a similar gutter story, this time for publication, and I'm doing it in order to stop Benjamin Franwell. Odd world.'

There was silence between them for two or three minutes before Giles said: 'If I try hard enough, I suppose I can persuade myself that a politician's private life *is* relevant if it's in sharp enough contrast to what the politician is preaching to the rest of us. And Rachel certainly has strummed the old Victorian guitar as she extolled family virtues and so forth. The irony is she's not been singing that song much of late; she's been beating out the woman-can-do-a-man's-job tune. It's Ben putting the knife in Daisy that's driven me to respond in kind.'

Angela said: 'Will you allude to both things – Rachel's abortion and her husband's gay pastimes?'

Giles sighed. 'I suppose so. Both will have to be between the lines. But Ben should have no difficulty getting the message that if he pursues his latest line of attack on the Harwoods, I'll pursue the counter-attack. Do I gather you still haven't mentioned the George Bishop number to him?'

'Not yet.'

48

On Wednesday morning Denis and Ollie were in Cheyne Street
by eight o'clock: the Minister wanted a bit more time than usual
at the hospital before going on to Richmond Terrace.

As Denis turned onto the Embankment and headed east,
Andrew looked out of the right-hand window at the far bank
where under a pagoda roof the vast figure of Buddha sat contemplating the ever-rolling stream flowing past his feet. The shim-
mering gold seemed almost aflame in the morning sun. When the
temple had first been erected, Andrew had found it incongruous,
but he'd always thought it handsome and had grown accustomed
to Buddha sitting there cross-legged, presiding over the river
Thames. For a moment Andrew's sense of time was so askew that
he felt lightheaded: he was on his way to spend half an hour with
his daughter; they would talk about one thing and another; this
time last week he had had no idea whether they would ever
converse again.

He looked at his watch. Atop the red box on the back seat were
two morning newspapers he hadn't yet had time even to glance
at. The *Express* shouldn't take long. In fact, it took longer than

usual: when he came to the leader page, he found another piece speculating on his future.

Since Ben Franwell's last column, several newspapers had taken up the idea that when the next ministerial shuffle occurred, there was something to be said for putting Rachel Fisher at Defence. Each newspaper had a different notion of what to do with the present Defence Secretary. The *Telegraph* pointed out how able Mr Harwood had been at Industry. The *Independent* thought perhaps his talents would be better suited to the Home Office. So far no one had suggested the politician's grave, Northern Ireland. Andrew gave a bleak smile as he read the *Express*'s uncritical praise of Rachel. He would be dishonest if he pretended not to mind. This afternoon he would go through the argument about bloody Satyr for the last time before tomorrow's Cabinet.

He noticed his own words: 'the last time'. Odd how often phrases came true but in a way one had not intended. Well, he didn't care: if it was the last thing he did he would get Satyr settled in tomorrow's Cabinet as *he* judged would be best. An image of Rachel sitting across the table, erect, came into his mind's eye. 'Interfering iceberg,' he muttered to himself.

Soon after eleven Daisy was about to set off for the hospital when the telephone rang.

'Are you going to be home any time latish this afternoon? If so, could I call in for an hour?' Angela said.

They took their tea tray to Daisy's studio. Her hair was twisted up on top of her head and held by the green butterfly grip that Sophie had borrowed early in the summer. Daisy had not been able to bring herself to move anything that was in the untenanted bedroom at Cheyne Street – until this week. Now that she knew Sophie would be occupying it again, though no one yet would hazard a guess as to when, Daisy tripped gaily in and out of Sophie's bedroom. On a whim she picked up the green butterfly grip that was lying on the bureau and fastened it as she'd last seen it fastened in Sophie's hair on the day that mother, daughter and Carl had all been in the studio.

Earlier Wednesday afternoon Daisy had gone into the studio

and started salvaging two of the unfinished clay heads. They were now swathed in sopping cheesecloth. One plinth was empty.

'Is Carl around?' Angela asked.

'Only just.' Daisy motioned towards a large squat dustbin across the studio. 'He was only half finished. The clay dried out.'

The corners of Angela's mouth tipped up.

'When's he next due in London?' she said.

'I don't know. Andrew hasn't mentioned it.'

Their heads resting against the sofa's back as they sipped their tea, they gazed up at the windows; though slightly yellowed, the leaves still clung firmly to the tops of the ash trees in the garden.

'What did he say about Ben's delightful column last Sunday?'

'Not much.' Daisy was silent again for a moment. 'Things that seem the end of the world at one time in your life seem much less important at another. "All things are relative." It's true.'

Angela glanced at her.

'That's not to say I don't mind – or that Andrew doesn't mind. It's just that we don't mind as much as if Ben had written it last spring.'

Angela said: 'Prime ministers always claim, naturally, that they take not the slightest notice of the press. Patently that's untrue. But what's not certain is whether they think: "There may be something in it that I should heed." Or whether they react against it. I shouldn't be surprised if this prime minister regards the press as impertinent for offering unsought advice.'

'It gives you a funny feeling, though, when you keep reading that you're not suited to your job. Andrew thinks he is,' Daisy said.

'Most of the press are like a bunch of sheep. If one editor says a Cabinet minister has a question mark over his future, the next day you read it in half a dozen other papers. It always happens, Daisy. You know that. It's as if each political editor thinks he may have missed something and he'd better take no chances. Ridiculous.'

'When I said all things are relative, nonetheless each time this week that I've seen Andrew's name I've had to steel myself lest in the next paragraph I see mine – and Carl's,' Daisy said. 'I dread next Sunday's *Rampart*.'

Angela took another drag on her cigarette, then put it out. 'I don't suppose Carl has telephoned you since last Sunday,' she said.

'No. It was all I could do not to ring him at the Pentagon and say: "How could you possibly have let that story get to Ben Franwell?" Yet that seemed too demeaning – to me, Andrew, and Carl if it comes to that. I just cannot believe that he would have said that to Ben.'

'He didn't. Jocelyn did.'

'I'd wondered about that.'

They sipped their tea.

'Do *you* imagine that I'm – to use Ben's phrase – "bowled over" again by Carl?'

'It doesn't fit,' said Angela. 'Mind you, we live in a strange world.'

Daisy ignored the equivocation offered. 'I don't know why I did it. Before . . .' She hesitated. 'Before the accident, I'd sometimes had flirty-flirty feelings about Carl since he reappeared. Partly it's fun to flirt. But also, I think, the whole situation was so bizarre – Carl turning up as the world's most important defence minister. That must have had a certain appeal to my vanity. And for him to be Andrew's opposite number made it, in a weird way, more intriguing. But I certainly had no intention – or desire – to go to bed with him.'

She turned her head to look at Angela who was gazing at the treetops. 'If it had been you, there'd be nothing reprehensible in it. But we've always thought, you and I, that we were different in that respect, that dear little Daisy was monoerotic and all that stuff.'

'Why did you decide to change course?'

'It's possible that it was because I wanted to punish myself for having caused the accident.'

'You didn't cause the accident, Daisy. The point about an accident is that it is just that.'

'Maybe. But it had – I had – ruined everything for everybody, so I might as well ruin things a little more.'

She was silent for a few moments. 'But I *think* the person I wanted to punish probably was Andrew. The night of the accident he said something that was like stabbing me in the heart. He wanted to take it back – what he'd said – but you can't take back that kind of thing.'

Angela lit another cigarette and resumed her position with her head on the back of the sofa. She wondered whether Daisy would tell her what Andrew had said.

Daisy hesitated. If she said it, would it be exorcized completely? Yet, it already was. She didn't want to think of the words again.

'Last Friday, after Sophie moved her hand, what Andrew had said didn't seem particularly important any more. It seemed like one more thing which is regrettable but which you can't think about for the rest of your life. I decided not to think about it again.'

They sipped their tea.

'Friday night Andrew and I slept in our bed together for the first time in almost two months. We were having breakfast in the bedroom on Sunday when I read the *Rampart*. I went into a panic.'

'Did Andrew say anything about your appearance in Ben's column?'

'No.'

'Did you?'

'No.'

'Do I gather that your little walk-out with Carl was to do with circumstances that are now past?'

'Yes.'

'Do you remember when we had dinner here together in the spring – the night that ended with Nelly bashing his Mini into the ministerial car?'

Despite herself, Daisy smiled at the image.

'Well, before all the alarums began, when you and I were peacefully drinking our coffee in your bedroom, you said that as well as not actually wanting to toddle into someone else's bed, if you did so it would change your feelings for Andrew. Has it, Daisy?'

'It's as if it hadn't happened,' said Daisy. 'Carl used to tell me that "plurality", as he calls it, increases the routine pleasure of sex for a couple who've been married for ages – all that. But my visits to Claridge's don't appear to have had *any* effect on my relationship with Andrew. It's other things that ruptured it – and then healed it. The Carl thing has left no residue at all that I can detect.'

'Will you tell Andrew?'

'I don't know what to do.'

Daisy looked at the empty plinth. Angela glanced at the dustbin.

Then Daisy said: 'I've always told Andrew most things – not at the time they happened, necessarily, but some time. If I felt uneasy about something – I'm not talking just about sex – I could exorcize the unease by telling him about it.'

'That's all very well for you. But in this instance, Andrew might prefer not to know.'

Again they were silent for a minute or two.

'Because of his relationship with me? Or because he has to work with Carl?'

'Possibly both.'

'Are you saying it's almost self-indulgence on my part if I make the great confession to Andrew?'

'Perhaps. I should think he has a fair bit on his mind already. But then you may feel you should clear your mind willy-nilly.'

They sipped their tea.

49

The hands of the mantelpiece clock were at two minutes past ten when the Prime Minister said: 'Defence Secretary.'

Andrew folded his arms loosely on top of the MoD brief that lay before him. Without preamble he said:

'The remaining issue is whether Satyr's components be produced entirely by British companies, whatever the financial cost.

'If we turn down US Solar Space, we can get that part of the work done by a British company for a slightly more competitive figure than I put before the Cabinet a week ago. However, my colleagues will note two factors.

'The British company would take twelve to fifteen months longer to complete Satyr's components.

'We would have to provide our own launchers, which would add a further half billion pounds.'

He paused for a moment, looking at Rachel Fisher, before he went on:

'Like everyone else at this table, I am fully aware of the importance of fuelling British industry and creating jobs wherever we can. This is indeed a primary reason for the existence of the Department of Industry.

'But it would be irresponsible of me to forget my job is Defence.

'If I overspend grossly on Satyr, I must underspend grossly elsewhere in a highly complicated defence programme. Or else the Chancellor must dun the taxpayer for more money.

'And if I allow a priority production to run on for an additional twelve or fifteen months – needlessly – then I ought not to be in my job.'

Andrew stopped speaking.

He picked up the papers to which he had not referred and rattled their bottom edges against the Cabinet table as if they needed to be shaken into place. Then he put them back in the folder and closed it. Placing one elbow on the table, he rested his chin in his hand as he surveyed the Prime Minister and those colleagues who sat across the table, his eyes staying no longer on Rachel's face than on that of any other.

He had not threatened to resign if he failed to win support, but something about the way he had rattled his papers put the thought in everyone's mind.

'I shall now call on the Foreign Secretary,' the Prime Minister said.

The Foreign Secretary was silent for several moments. He seemed preoccupied. Then he said succinctly why he thought his colleagues should accept the Defence Secretary's judgement. When he finished speaking, absently he picked up his own unopened brief and tapped its bottom edges on the Cabinet table, as if he were tidying the brief before putting it away.

Andrew watched him, puzzled by the oddly withdrawn expression on the Foreign Secretary's face.

'Industry Secretary.'

Rachel knew she must shift her ground. Andrew's case was impeccable. If anyone was in doubt, the Foreign Secretary's support would have tipped the balance. She must insinuate that she had always been open to reasonable argument – and that Andrew had been inadequate in making his case last time.

From her seat five places down from the Prime Minister, Rachel leaned slightly forward yet still seemed erect.

'The Defence Secretary has cleared up the doubts that were left when he last presented his Ministry's figures to Cabinet.

'I regret that we cannot seize a golden opportunity to reward our own electronics industry – to show our industrialists and their workers that a bedrock of this government is its determination to offer incentives for higher achievement.

'And I regret that we cannot seize the opportunity to create further jobs in our own nation.

'But in view of the information which the Defence Secretary has now given us, I am prepared to accept his judgement.'

The Prime Minister gave a formal glance around the table before saying briskly: 'We are agreed then that the production of Satyr will go ahead as recommended by the Defence Secretary. Let us move on, please, to the next subject on our agenda.'

The hands of the mantelpiece clock stood at twenty minutes past ten.

Not long after eleven the ambulance drove out of the gates of the hospital. The attendant sat at one end of the stretcher where Sophie lay. Daisy sat at the other end. Matty had positioned himself at a side window. His headmaster had excused him from school for the whole of Thursday.

'From where I am, all I can see is the sky,' said Sophie. 'What are you looking at, Matty?'

'Well, there's the sky. And underneath it is the railing at the side of the bridge we're crossing. And below that is the river flowing. I can see three barges and a white motor launch with people leaning on the rail looking down at the water. Up ahead is Big Ben and that great pile where Dad spends so much of his time.'

Instead of the House of Commons, Daisy thought of Number Ten and inside, at the end of the long corridor, the closed door. Please, please, Somebody, help things go right in there for Andrew this morning. When he'd left home at 9:30, he'd said: 'If things come unstuck with my job, you mustn't worry about me, Daisy. If Sophie can ever walk again, that is what matters. I hope the drive goes well for you. You'll ring me when you can, won't you?'

The ambulance drove three-quarters of the way around Parliament Square, turning into Birdcage Walk. When it slowed to a halt, Sophie said: 'I can hear drums. What time is it?'

'Half past eleven. "They're changing the guard at Buckingham Palace – Christopher Robin went down with Alice. Alice is marrying one of the guard. 'A soldier's life is terrible hard,' says Alice,"' sang Matty.

Daisy smiled.

Sophie's hospital gown had been replaced by a striped shirt of Andrew's, its sleeves rolled up and held in place by safety pins. ('He certainly has long arms,' the nurse had said.) A white cotton blanket was tucked around her as she lay on the stretcher.

She had almost no movement from the hips down. From the waist up, she moved fairly freely, considering her entire spinal cord was braced. It didn't seem to have occurred to her that she would not get well, eventually, all over.

When the last of the Guards was going in through the wrought iron gate, those relieved marching smartly up the Mall, the police waved the traffic on in single file. Reaching the Scotch House, where most of the traffic bore left towards Harrods, the ambulance took the right-hand fork.

'We're passing that big lump of bricks which is Knightsbridge Barracks. Coming up on the left is the Albert Hall. There on the right is that weird statue of Prince Albert. Two big pigeons are perched on his head. I can't see the Round Pond, but it must be off there at the right. On our left is the House of Fraser with those strange metal decorations along the walls. Mama, do you remember when they made buildings like that?'

'It was before I was born, Matty. It's art deco. 1930s.'

'Sort of creepy, but I like it. Did you know, Mama, that the *Daily Mail* moved into the back of the House of Fraser?'

'So I gathered.'

'Did you know that there aren't any more newspapers now left in Fleet Street?'

'Funny that, isn't it?' said Daisy.

'You used to work in Fleet Street, Mama,' Sophie said.

'She knows that, Sophie,' said Matty.

'I know she knows. I was just showing her that I know too.'

At the far end of Kensington High Street the ambulance turned north towards the A40 and, once on it, travelled west for ten miles before turning northwest for another forty miles. Just this side of Aylesbury it came to a halt at the gates of Stoke Mandeville Hospital. Then it was waved through.

When Daisy rang the private office from the hospital, Martin Thrower told her the Minister was at the House of Commons. The Minister had asked him to let her know things were relaxed at his end and he hoped things were going well for her. He'd be at Cheyne Street by 10:30 tonight. He'd ring her hotel then. Daisy had booked a room at an Aylesbury hotel so she'd be able to go in and out of Stoke Mandeville for the first days while Sophie got used to it there.

Late in the afternoon Ollie arrived at the hospital to drive Matty back to Cheyne Street so he could go to school in the morning. Andrew had consulted with Martin Thrower: Martin's view was that the government car on this occasion could be used on what was not official business.

On her way into Aylesbury that evening, Daisy looked out of the taxi window at the moon: it was almost three-quarters full. She couldn't remember how you knew whether the moon was growing or dwindling; you just did. It was growing. She was glad it had not yet reached its fullness. But she mustn't think of the moon as symbolic. That would be stupid, because then what would she feel when it passed its fullness in a few nights' time?

All the same, she was glad.

50

On that same Thursday, Tommy Lowell, the *Rampart*'s news editor, was delayed in leaving for the office. By the time he set off, the weeklies were already on the underground station's news stand. He bought the *Vanguard* to skim on the train.

Giles Alexander's column always occupied an entire page of the *Vanguard*. When the train pulled into Tower Hill station, Tommy had read Giles's main item three times. For as soon as he had reached its end, he'd begun it again, reading word for word.

'Jesus,' he muttered as he and his fellow passengers poured into Trinity Place, 'this Thursday is going to be hairy.'

'Have you seen Giles Alexander's column?' were the news deputy's first words when Tommy reached their back-to-back desks.

'Yeah. Do you know whether the editor has seen it yet?'

'Five minutes ago I went to his office with the Scotland rail story that's just come over the fax. He snatched it from my hand and told me to get out.'

'Count yourself lucky, Joyce, that Ben Franwell makes a distinction between the sexes. If you weren't a woman and soon-to-be mother, he would have been more explicit in expressing himself.'

'For God's sake, Tommy, don't speak of anyone being a mother this morning.'

Ben's jacket hung from the back of his chair. His waistcoat was unbuttoned, his shirt sleeves rolled up, tie loosened. On the mahogany desk the *Vanguard* lay open at Giles's page.

Ben's big-featured fleshy face tautened in concentration as he read the first part again. Ordinarily Giles's style was elegant, his acerbic irony heightening the frisson as he inserted the knife and twisted it. But this week he had chosen to parody Benjamin Franwell's usual style.

> Does it matter that the Industry Secretary, Rachel Fisher, is absorbed in her dreams of higher office? *Yes.*
>
> For you and I – who pay the salary that keeps her in style – expect her shoulder to be put to the wheel of running Industry. Instead, she schemes endlessly to undermine the Defence Secretary, Andrew Harwood – because his job ranks higher than hers.
>
> And what are we to think of Miss Fisher being aided and abetted in her plotting by the editor of the *Rampart*, Benjamin Franwell? Is there a personal relationship that accounts for his unstinting efforts to eliminate Mr Harwood so Miss Fisher can try on his shoes?
>
> Before becoming MP for Bedford Forge, Miss Fisher was already known as Mr Franwell's very good friend – and his 'personal assistant'. Was it then that he first learned she has what he calls 'instincts that only other mothers can fully understand'?
>
> *Would other mothers, nurturing their children, be so sure of the Industry Secretary's maternal instincts?*
>
> And Mr George Bishop? It is Mr Bishop, Miss Fisher's devoted husband, who tends the hearthfire at the family home in Bedfordshire while she pursues her Westminster career. Not every husband would find this lopsided division of parental and domestic responsibility to his taste.
>
> *Let us hope Mr Bishop has his own pastimes to cheer those long nights without a wife.*

With both hands Ben pushed the *Vanguard* away from him. He spun his chair round so he was facing the square sheet of steel on the wall, his eyes fixed on the golden outline of Britain. The sense that his back was to the door made him uneasy: he spun his chair again. His face had darkened to a colour much like beetroot. The solid lips were pressed together so he looked like someone about to cry.

He leaped up and strode around the desk to the wall of windows. Off to the west he could see the Tower of London's turrets glistening in September's watery sunlight.

He recrossed the room and stood beside his desk as he pressed the buttons on his white telephone.

Angela looked down on Green Park as she answered the phone on the windowsill. The morning sunlight dappled the big leaves against the plane trees' flaky bark.

'I hope you don't have a lunch engagement, Angela. If you do, you'd better postpone it. Let's meet at the Savoy at 1:30.'

When he got there, she was already at his table by the window wall. She was looking down through the plane trees of the Embankment to the Thames flowing calmly towards Greenwich and the sea. On the pink starched tablecloth lay the *Vanguard*. She had bought it on her way to the Savoy; better not to pretend ignorance.

'We'll have just one course today,' Ben said to the head waiter. 'And make it fast.'

He fixed his eyes on his wife. 'What did you say to Giles and what did he say to you?'

'When?'

The cropped head tilted for a moment as she lit her cigarette.

'Come off it, Angela.'

She turned slightly to the window as she exhaled so the smoke didn't go in his face.

'What was he getting at, Angela, when he said he hoped George Bishop has his own pastimes? Everything else was clear enough to me. If I thought it was clear to anyone outside your little gang of harpies and your male hangers-on, I'd slap a libel writ on the *Vanguard* and Giles Alexander this afternoon. As it is, I'll wait and see. What the hell did he mean about George Bishop?'

'He meant he's a poof.'

Ben stared at her.

'I don't believe you,' he said.

She shrugged.

Two waiters in their black swallowtails bustled forward and with a flourish put two plates with gleaming domed covers in front of husband and wife, with a further flourish whisking off the covers to reveal the chicken breasts poached in cream with brandy. An image of Charles Cartwright flashed into Ben's mind: that cruddy jerk with his pinstripes and his nancy-boy flower in his buttonhole. They were everywhere, the creeps. Christ how he hated them. Did Rachel know?

'Why did you put Giles up to writing that?'

'There was no need to. When you began stamping your big boots on Daisy, you went too far. She's not in politics. And Sophie's accident has taken a terrific toll.'

Ben's big lips were pressed together. Angela had to make certain her face remained impassive; when Ben wore that expression, despite herself some part of her nature was touched. She could never decide whether he looked like a sulky boy or one about to cry.

After a minute or two he said: 'How do you know George Bishop is one of the creeps?'

'I don't *know* it. But he goes to one of the more discreet gay bars. On one evening his companion was a snake-hipped youth given to sporting gold jewellery. None of that proves anything, of course: George Bishop may have enrolled as a mature student in sociology. There probably weren't sociology courses at Cambridge when he was there.'

'One of these days I hope to meet someone who was at Cambridge who's not a pervert,' Ben said. 'Suppose George Bishop gets AIDS? Everybody knows most queers have AIDS – or should have. Christ, it makes you sick.'

'Speaking of AIDS,' Angela said, 'you do realize that a number of people – including the two sitting at this table – should now make arrangements for an AIDS test? Would you like me to fix up a test for you? Or would you rather let your PA handle it?

He looked at her in total silence.

Angela blew a thin cloud of smoke to one side of him.

'God almighty,' he said.

She said nothing.

'Who saw George Bishop in that den?' he said.

'A friend of Giles.'

'I know who that was. Nelly Harwood.'

Angela always conducted her conversations with care: lie as little as possible; acknowledge what you must; omit what you can. She went on smoking placidly.

'Does Giles intend devoting a series of columns to this dirt?'

'I should imagine it depends on how you proceed.'

Ben's blue eyes were fixed on his wife.

'I've noticed it before,' he said. 'You county ladies and your public-school chums display your exquisite manners up to a point only. Then you take off the gloves. And when you do that, you always go for the short and curlies.'

Angela gave her small smile.

51

When the Jaguar left Cheyne Street on Saturday morning, Denis alongside Ollie in front, Matty was beside his father in the back. Matty always felt important when he rode in the government car.

It was just past eleven when Ollie drove through the gates of Stoke Mandeville Hospital. Daisy was in Sophie's room when Andrew and Matty walked in.

'Hi Dad. Hullo Matty. This is a great place.'

She was propped against the bed pillows, her curls cascading onto the man's striped shirt she was wearing, its sleeves pinned up.

Daisy's suitcase was by the door; she'd brought it with her from the Aylesbury hotel.

Shortly after noon three of the Harwoods climbed into the back of the Jaguar, and Ollie made for the M1. Two and a half hours later he stopped while Matty hopped out to open the wooden gate of the gravel drive. As they drove up to the front door of Stony Farm, Andrew glanced at Daisy. Her face was shining. It was her first return to Waymere since the weekend before the accident.

She cooked Matty's supper early so when Andrew got back from his constituency engagements he could have the rest of the evening with her. After their late dinner, they sat in the small study either side of the stone fireplace where logs crackled cheerfully. September was still mild, but in Shropshire the temperature dropped sharply after dark.

Andrew said: 'As you are kind enough to let me ventilate my political problems, I'll tell you what happened in Thursday's Cabinet. I won the game. Rachel won the match. Satyr will go ahead on the lines I'm certain are the right ones. But it was no great personal victory. Rachel succeeded in casting a cloud of uncertainty over my competence.'

'What happened?'

'I put my case once again. The good old Foreign Secretary supported it. Then the PM called on Rachel. She said she regretted I am less patriotic than she is – less ready to assist my country and all that balls – but nonetheless she would support me now that I'd made a clear case which I had failed to make in the first place.' He smiled wryly.

'She didn't say that, did she?'

'As good as.'

'*Did* you put your case better this time?'

'Not that I'm aware of.' He sipped his highball. 'Both times I put it simply and to the point. I suppose I might have gained something if I'd added a bit of rhetoric, but I am as I am. If I tried to be a different politician, I expect it would be even more disastrous.'

'I like you the way you are,' Daisy said.

'Thank you.'

'Anyhow, it doesn't sound like a disaster.'

'Perhaps it wasn't that bad. But it wasn't brilliant. My difficulty is that I've not dealt with anyone quite like Rachel before. She speaks in that almost majestic way, and at the same time she's constantly scoring points. The only way to combat it is in kind, yet it's not my style. So I end up feeling someone else would have handled it better.'

He got up and put another log on the fire, then resumed his chair.

'How do you know the Prime Minister didn't like the way you handled it?'

'One: the PM is enigmatic. Two: I didn't handle it particularly well. Still, that's enough about that. We'll see what tomorrow's newspapers have to say. Now that I've told you my melancholy feelings, I feel better. Let's talk about something more interesting.'

Sunday morning was leisurely, the newspapers divided among the three Harwoods at the big kitchen table.

From the corner of one eye Andrew watched Daisy's face as she turned to the *Rampart*'s leader page. She looked relieved. He returned his concentration to the *Sunday Times*.

Most of the leader pages endorsed his decision on Satyr, though their personal comments on him were neutral. The *Rampart* said nothing at all about Satyr or the Defence Secretary.

After an early lunch they climbed back into the Jaguar. Two-thirds of the way to London, Ollie turned off the M1 and made for Aylesbury.

Sophie seemed entirely at home in Stoke Mandeville.

'You'd like the swimming pool, Matty. It's really warm, and nobody kicks you. Do you know, Mama, I *think* I moved my legs very slightly when I was floating on the water, though I'm not absolutely sure.'

Near the end of the afternoon, three Harwoods got back into the Jaguar, and Ollie set off for London.

As they crossed South Kensington to Chelsea, Andrew said: 'This is the most peaceful and contented weekend I can remember in a long time.'

'I know,' said Daisy.

'Funny game, politics,' Andrew said. 'Everybody gets so excited about something or other. One's career seems to hang in the balance. Then everybody goes about their affairs as if nothing had happened. I must say, it would be agreeable if our quiet weekend proved a portent of things to come. Too good to be true, I suppose.'

Five minutes after they walked in the door of the house, the scrambler rang. It was Martin Thrower.

'I thought you would want to know, Minister, that it will be announced on the nine o'clock news that the Foreign Secretary has resigned.'

When he put the scrambler back in place, Andrew, stretched out in his armchair, gazed, unseeing, at the ceiling. After five or six minutes, he got up, hitched his trousers and went next door to the bedroom where Daisy was unpacking.

'I knew it was too good to be true,' he said.

She looked at him in terror.

'Everything's all right, darling Daisy. I didn't mean to frighten you. Nothing has happened. That was Martin. He says the Foreign Secretary has resigned. I don't suppose you could stop what you're doing and come in the study for a drink?'

When they were seated in the armchairs that once had stood in the Eaton Place flat he said: 'I hadn't the least idea he was contemplating resigning. I knew his wife hadn't been well, but I didn't know he was planning to leave government so he could spend more time with her. That must be why he seemed so preoccupied – withdrawn – at Cabinet three days ago.'

Both were silent.

Then she asked: 'How will it affect you?'

'I don't know. Perhaps not at all. If the Home Secretary is now made Foreign Secretary, the Prime Minister might decide the time is right to make quite a big reshuffle.'

The regular telephone rang. He picked it up. 'Hullo?'

'Good evening, Minister. It's the *Daily Mail*'s news desk here. Do you expect to be going to Number Ten in the morning?'

'What do you have in mind?' said Andrew, chuckling, on his guard.

'We've heard there may be several changes at the top,' said the reporter. 'There's talk that the Home Secretary will take over the Foreign Secretary's portfolio, and that you and the Industry Secretary may swap jobs.'

'I see. You know more than I do, clearly,' Andrew said amiably.

'How would you feel, Minister, about going back to running Industry? You won a lot of plaudits when you did it before. But you might feel it was demotion – though only a slight demotion, of course. Would you take it or would you resign?'

This time Andrew was not feigning when he laughed outright.

'That's quite a range of separate thoughts you've outlined. Until something is announced tomorrow, there's no comment I can make on any speculation.'

After he'd put down the telephone, he said to Daisy: 'That one thinks I'll be asked to go back to Industry.'

'When will the Prime Minister decide?'

'I expect the PM is at this very minute lining up the players on the chessboard. I wonder who else knows what's happening.' He looked quietly at Daisy. 'It gives one an odd feeling to think some colleagues are being telephoned by Number Ten when no one apart from Martin Thrower has rung here on the scrambler.'

The regular telephone rang. It was *The Times*.

When the call was ended, Andrew said to Daisy: 'These chaps don't know any more than I do. They're simply retailing political gossip. All the same, there does seem to be a general view that Rachel is going to be offered Defence.'

'How *would* you feel about running Industry again?'

'It would be a knock on the head. The pecking order in Cabinet posts shouldn't be important – but it matters to those one works with, not to mention the old vanity. And if Rachel is appointed to Defence, that's a pretty clear statement that I'm not considered good enough at the job. Too bad I didn't handle the last Cabinet better.'

Neither of them said anything for a few minutes.

'If you *are* asked to take over Industry again, would you do it? What's the point of resigning?' she asked.

He was silent for a while. Then he said: 'There isn't any point – unless one has to do so for reasons of some moral issue. If it's a matter of vanity, the history books are strewn with instances of Cabinet ministers resigning, thinking they are indispensable and will be shortly invited to take another grand job, only to discover they are forever out in the cold. I don't *think* I'd resign. But it's hard to take a clear view until I know what I'm being asked to take a view about.'

The regular telephone rang. It was the *Independent*.

When Andrew put down the telephone he said bleakly: 'I thought these newspapers were in competition with one another. They all seem to be in total agreement that the political landscape is not looking rosy for your husband.'

Both were silent again.

Then Daisy said: 'Do you remember what you said to me last weekend – when I was feeling down in the mouth because of Ben Franwell's horrid column? You said: "Whatever he may have to say in his newspaper, it pales to insignificance beside what's happened in our lives in the last forty-eight hours." Whatever the Prime Minister decides, that's how I'll feel. I'll mind for you if you're disappointed. But I won't mind for me. You do know that, don't you?'

Andrew got up and crossed over to her chair. He leaned over and kissed her lightly on the mouth.

'No point in fretting about the thing,' he said. 'We'll discover soon enough.'

He looked at his watch.

52

Every front page on Monday morning assumed Number Ten would make an announcement by early afternoon. With the Foreign Secretary's resignation about to be formalized, there was a desire to have someone else in his place as soon as possible. The consensus view was that it would be the present Home Secretary.

Who then would move into the Home Secretary's shoes? One paper suggested Rachel Fisher. Another thought that as the Northern Ireland Secretary had survived his job with his reputation miraculously intact, perhaps he should be rewarded with the Home Office. Of those who held the three great Offices of State – Foreign Office, Exchequer, Home Office – only the Chancellor of the Exchequer was not the subject of intense speculation: he had not been long at his post, and there was no reason to move him.

Andrew was mentioned only in conjunction with Rachel Fisher. If Rachel went to the Home Office, Andrew would stay at Defence. If Rachel went to Defence, Andrew might be offered Industry again. In every configuration, Rachel Fisher was a feature.

Even though Ben Franwell had been forced to lie low the day before, the *Rampart*'s long-running campaign had had its effect:

everyone seemed taken with the idea of moving a forceful woman
into what had heretofore been regarded as a man's job. Rachel,
having broken across the barrier to Industry, looked set to break
another barrier before the day was out.

Andrew was in the bathroom shaving when the regular telephone rang. Daisy reached across the bed to pick it up.

'Is that Mrs Harwood? It's the BBC here. We're anxious to
speak with your husband.'

'I'll see where he is.'

She left the receiver on the bed and opened the bathroom door.
'It's the BBC.'

'Ask them what they want.' Andrew frowned at himself as he
ran the razor along the edge of his jaw.

She returned to the telephone.

'Could you tell me what you're ringing about? My husband is
shaving.'

'It concerns the rumour about the next Defence Secretary.'

'Hang on.'

Once more she put the receiver on the bed.

This time Andrew came to the telephone. Daisy noticed he
hadn't finished shaving.

'Good morning.'

'Good morning, Minister. It's Percy Jones at the BBC. There's
quite a strong rumour going around that the Prime Minister
intends appointing Rachel Fisher as Defence Secretary.'

Andrew felt his stomach contract.

'Oh yes?' he said.

Watching his face, Daisy felt her stomach contract.

'If that happens, have you thought what your own position
would be?' said Percy Jones.

'No.'

Andrew noticed that Percy Jones had stopped addressing him
as Minister.

'Look, you'll have to wait for a comment until later today. I
must go now. Goodbye.'

He put down the telephone and turned to Daisy. 'He talked as
if he had some basis for thinking Rachel is to be Defence Secretary.'

'But surely you'd be told first by the Prime Minister.'

'Not necessarily.'

He went to the study, lit a cigarette and brought it back to the bedroom. He took a shirt from the chest of drawers and began undoing the buttons.

'Well, well, well,' he said. 'Why didn't you marry another sculptor?'

Daisy smiled wanly.

Lifting his chin to knot his tie, he said: 'I don't see how I can *not* be given another senior job. The trouble is that I've never understood how the PM's mind works.'

Both heard the scrambler ring in the study. He strode next door.

'Hullo,' he said. His voice was curt.

'It's Number Ten Downing Street. Is that Mr Harwood?'

'Yep.'

'Will you please hold the line?'

The Prime Minister's private secretary then came on.

'Hullo Andrew. The Prime Minister would like to see you. Would it be possible for you to be here at eleven o'clock this morning?'

'Certainly.'

Putting down the scrambler he looked at Daisy standing in the doorway, her face pale. Passing her he kissed her on the cheek.

'I wish I could divide any disappointment you may have into two halves,' she said. 'If a bad thing is divided, it's not so bad for either person. I wish we could do that.'

'Even though we can't manage that, the fact of having you with me, Daisy, will *alleviate* any disappointment I may feel.'

As Ollie pulled the Jaguar away from the kerb, Andrew turned and looked out of the rear window. His eyes went up to the first-floor bedroom. Daisy was looking out of one of the windows. She waved.

'Do you know what your future holds, Minister?' shouted one of the reporters as Andrew stepped out of the Jaguar.

He waggled a hand in the air as the front door of Number Ten was opened and he went through.

The Prime Minister's private secretary was waiting in the

entrance hall. As the two men walked together down the corridor, Andrew eyed the Cabinet Room's closed door at the end. As they climbed the stairs past the engravings of prime ministers, he thought of Daisy's interest in Gladstone.

'Could you wait one moment, Andrew?' the private secretary said when they reached the lobby outside the study, and then himself went in, shutting the door after him.

In a moment he came out again, and Andrew went in. The door was closed behind him.

The Prime Minister was seated at the mahogany desk.

'Good morning, Andrew.'

'Good morning, Prime Minister.'

The Prime Minister motioned to an armchair not far from the desk.

'For some time now I've been thinking about making a few changes among senior ministers. With the Foreign Secretary's resignation, this seems the time to do so. You know, of course, that I would never be influenced by the *Rampart*. I'd already given thought to one day putting Rachel Fisher at Defence.'

Andrew wondered whether his face had gone white.

The Prime Minister continued: 'When we won the last general election, the women's campaign for nuclear disarmament was defused. It is tiresome that it should have become an issue again, as you know too well. There would be political attractions in having a woman running Defence.

'And as Rachel has shown she can deal with the industrialists and trade-union leaders, I'm prepared to let her take on the generals and admirals.' The Prime Minister gave a wintry smile. 'I shall be seeing Rachel later this morning to ask her to take over the Defence portfolio.'

'I see.'

'I feel the time has come to give the Environment Secretary new fields to explore. I intend to ask him to take over the Industry portfolio.'

Andrew had a sense of watching the scene from outside himself: he could see his own face – despite his attempts to remain expressionless, he looked strained – as he sat opposite the Prime Minister.

'The Foreign Secretary has certainly earned a respite from his endless travels about the world. I am glad to say, however, that he has agreed to accept a peerage and become Leader in the House of Lords.

'I had considered moving the Home Secretary to the Foreign Office. But as he is in the middle of major legislation which was a key part of our election manifesto, I feel he should see it through to the end.'

The Prime Minister paused.

At the same time as Andrew felt the knot in his stomach, he also felt a detachment as he continued to watch the scene as if from the outside.

The Prime Minister continued: 'All of us have to put up with assaults on our competence and integrity. I have been pleased by the way you've handled the attacks on you and your policies over the last six months. I liked the manner in which you settled the doubts about Satyr. How would you feel about going to the Foreign Office?'

Andrew was now totally inside himself, taut. Demotion to a number two couldn't possibly be on.

'Naturally, I mean as Foreign Secretary,' the Prime Minister said.

For a moment neither spoke.

Then Andrew said: 'I'd be greatly honoured.'

'Good. It occurs to me that after what happened to your family during the summer, you and Daisy might benefit from moving to another house. You know Carlton Gardens is yours if you want it. So far as I know, only one Foreign Secretary hasn't wished to live there.'

'Thank you, Prime Minister. I'll discuss Carlton Gardens with Daisy.'

'I shall see you then at Cabinet, Foreign Secretary.'

The Prime Minister again gave the wintry smile. Not for the first time, Andrew wondered if it was a device to tease or to conceal emotions.

At noon the regular telephone rang at Cheyne Street. Daisy seized it.

'It's Martin Thrower, Mrs Harwood. Your husband has asked me to ring you and tell you that he's coming home for lunch today, if that is convenient to you. He asked me to let you know that he's feeling cheerful.'

When Daisy heard the Jaguar slowing to a stop in front of the house, she looked out of the bedroom window. She couldn't see Andrew's expression.

She listened to his footsteps coming up the stairs. He looked in at the bedroom door.

'Good afternoon,' he said.

He sauntered over to his armchair and took off his shoes.

'I'll have to go back in an hour and a half. Might as well make myself comfortable in the meanwhile.'

Having put on his slippers, he strolled into the study. Daisy followed.

He said he thought he'd pour himself a little drink. 'Would you also like a little drink?'

He poured vodka into a small glass for her.

'What do you think it is?' he said.

'Defence?'

'The Foreign Office.'

They were both still standing up. She put her arms around him. To her astonishment several tears welled from her eyes and ran down onto his shirt.

'Well, honestly, I'm not going to come home with news if all it does is make you weep,' he said.

53

On Tuesday morning the sun glistened on the gilded figure of Victory, wings spread above the marble queen. One of the elaborately wrought iron gates of Buckingham Palace stood open as the Foreign Secretary's black armoured Jaguar approached. Andrew glanced up at the roof of the palace where the royal emblem fluttered brightly in a morning breeze, announcing to all and sundry that Her Majesty was in residence.

This time he didn't have to kneel on successive footstools while advancing to kiss the Queen's hand as he had done when first he became a member of Her Majesty's Most Honourable Privy Council. Today the Queen simply handed him his new seals of office as he gave a small bow.

She asked about Sophie. Andrew told her that Stoke Mandeville was increasingly optimistic. Sophie was already able to move her legs a little more each day. She assumed she would recover completely.

'Why shouldn't Sophie be right?' said the Queen.

When the Jaguar pulled out of the courtyard of Buckingham Palace, Ollie swung around Queen Victoria and headed back down Birdcage Walk the way they had come. At Parliament Square he turned left as usual.

But instead of going up Whitehall until he came to Richmond Terrace, he took the turning before Downing Street. Here in King Charles Street he stopped while barriers were raised.

Then Andrew was driven into the huge courtyard that precedes the nineteenth-century splendour of the Foreign Office.

An hour and a half later Daisy's taxi let her off at the corner of Greek Street. Her high heels clattered gaily as she tripped down the pavement to the picture of the snail. She thought of the first time she had been at L'Escargot, when Ben Franwell was gratuitously rude about Andrew. She thought about the next time she had been there, when first she had met Nelly Harwood.

Upstairs in the back room she spotted Giles at a corner table. He and Nelly got to their feet.

'Hullo, Tulip,' said Giles.

The corners of Nelly's eyes crinkled into a friendly smile. His sandy hair always made Daisy think of Andrew.

'What are you going to drink?' asked Giles.

'If you're having wine with lunch, I'll wait,' she said.

When their orders were taken, Giles said: 'If you look over to your right, Tulip, you'll see a familiar face across the room.'

She turned in her chair.

Seated at a table with a man she didn't know was Ben Franwell.

He and Rachel had won the game but lost the match. At first his face was surly as he and Daisy looked at each other from their separate tables. Then he put one hand to his forehead as if tipping his hat to her.

She would never forget how he had tried to damage Andrew. Yet so great was Daisy's restored happiness that at the moment she didn't greatly care what Benjamin Franwell had done. It was past. On the other hand, in her new confidence there was no need to pretend – as she used to do – that he hadn't hurt her.

She smiled at him coolly. Then she stuck out the tip of her tongue at Ben.

His face deepened to scarlet.

Rather to their surprise, they both burst out laughing.